# Beyond the Truth

*A Hanne Wilhelmsen Novel*

Anne Holt

*Translated from the Norwegian
by Anne Bruce*

SCRIBNER

New York   London   Toronto   Sydney   New Delhi

Scribner
An Imprint of Simon & Schuster, Inc.
1230 Avenue of the Americas
New York, NY 10020

English language translation copyright © 2016 by Anne Bruce
Originally published in Norwegian in 2003 as *Sannheten botenfor*
Published by arrangement with Salomonsson Agency

First Scribner hardcover edition December 2016

For information about special discounts for bulk purchases,
please contact Simon & Schuster Special Sales at 1-866-506-1949
or business@simonandschuster.com.

The Simon & Schuster Speakers Bureau can bring authors to your live event.
For more information or to book an event, contact the Simon & Schuster Speakers Bureau
at 1-866-248-3049 or visit our website at www.simonspeakers.com.

Manufactured in the United States of America

3   5   7   9   10   8   6   4

Library of Congress Cataloging-in-Publication Data is available.

ISBN 978-1-5011-2345-0
ISBN 978-1-5011-2347-4 (ebook)

# Beyond the Truth

# THURSDAY, DECEMBER 19

It was an old dog with stiff joints, damaged by calcification. Illness had caused the animal to resemble a hyena, for his powerful chest and strong neck shrank abruptly into a skinny backside, with the tail curling around his testicles.

The mangy animal came and went. No one could remember when he had first appeared. In a way, he belonged to the district: an unpleasantness impossible to avoid, like the noise of the streetcars, double-parked vehicles, and sidewalks in need of repair. People had to take precautions, keep basement doors closed and locked, haul cats in for the night, and secure lids tightly on garbage cans in backyards. Now and again someone complained to the public health authorities when food scraps and other trash were left scattered beside bicycle racks three mornings in a row. They rarely received any response, and nothing was ever done to catch the beast.

If anyone had stopped to consider how the dog actually lived, it would have been obvious that he moved around the neighborhood according to a pattern, out of step with the calendar, and therefore difficult to spot. If anyone had taken the trouble, they would have realized that the dog was never very far off and that he seldom roamed beyond an area measuring just fifteen or sixteen blocks.

He had lived like that for almost eight years.

He knew his territory and avoided other animals as much as possible, giving a wide berth to lapdogs on gaudy nylon leashes, and had understood long ago that pedigree cats with bells around their necks were a temptation best resisted. He was a stray mongrel in Oslo's upper-class west end and knew how to lie low.

The period of mild weather in early December was over, and now a biting pre-Christmas frost had glazed the asphalt. There was a hint of snow in the air. As the dog's claws scratched the black ice, he dragged his back leg behind him. The glare from the street lamp highlighted a gash on his left haunch, liver-colored on his close-cropped fur and speckled with yellow pus. It had snagged on a spike the previous evening while he was searching for somewhere to sleep.

The apartment building was secluded, set back from the street. A paved walkway divided the front garden in two, and knee-high chain-link fencing, painted black, enclosed the wet, dead grass and a flower bed covered with tarpaulin. A twinkling, decorated Christmas tree flanked either side of the entrance.

This was the dog's second attempt to gain entry in the course of the evening. There was usually a way. Unlocked doors were easiest, of course. A quick leap, a swipe of the paw at the door handle. It was usually immaterial whether the door opened in or out: unlocked doors were a piece of cake. But rare. Normally he had to search for basement windows opened a chink, loose boards around walls due to be repaired, or gaps under rotting cellar stairs. Access points that everyone else, apart from him, had forgotten. They were not to be found everywhere, and sometimes these gaps were repaired, basement shutters shut, and walls replastered. Blocked and impenetrable. He walked on. Sometimes it took several hours to find a place for the night.

There was an opening in this block. He was familiar with it, and though it was easy, it mustn't be abused. He never slept in the same spot for more than one night. On his first attempt that evening, someone had turned up. These things happen. So he made himself scarce, quick as a flash. Trotted on for two or three blocks. Lay down under a bush, behind a bike rack, hidden from anyone who did not look too closely. Then he tried again. A good den was worth a couple of forays.

The frost had worsened during the past hour, and the snow was real now: dry, light flakes that painted the sidewalks white. He shivered: he had not had anything to eat for more than twenty-four hours.

The building was quiet now.

The lights both lured and scared him.

Light brought a chance of being seen. It was threatening. However, light also brought warmth. Blood pulsed painfully through his infected wound. Warily, he stepped over the low chain fence, whimpering as he lifted his back leg. A hole—access into the store where an old sleeping bag lay discarded in a corner—was at the rear of the building, between the basement stairs and two bicycles that were never used.

But the front door was open.

Front doors were dangerous. He could get locked in. A cozy glow enticed him all the same. Stairways were better than basements. At the very top, where people seldom ventured and nobody lived, it was warm.

Keeping his head down, he approached the stone steps and stood perfectly still, front paw raised, before stepping slowly into the beam of light. Nothing stirred anywhere; there were no alarming sounds to be heard, only the distant, reassuring murmur of the city.

He was inside.

There was another open door.

He could smell food, and everything was totally silent.

The scent of meat was strong, and he no longer hesitated. Quickly he limped into the apartment, but came to a sudden stop in the hallway. Emitting a low growl, he bared his teeth at the man on the floor. Nothing happened. The dog drew closer, inquisitive now, and more curious than apprehensive. Gingerly, he thrust his nose nearer the motionless body and tried licking some of the blood around the man's head. His tongue grew more eager, washing the floor, cleaning the congealed clots from the man's cheek, probing into the hole just beside his temple; the starving dog slurped down what he could extract from the skull, before it dawned on him that he did not have to exert himself to obtain food.

There were three more bodies in the apartment.

His tail wagged in delight.

"There's nothing to discuss. Nefis will damn well have to learn how we do things."

Mary slammed the door behind her.

"One, two, three, four," Hanne Wilhelmsen counted, and when she reached the "f" of five, Mary had reappeared in the room again.

"For Christ's sake, if I went to those Muslims at Christmastime, I'd eat whatever they put down in front of me. Pure, sheer good manners, if you ask me. She's not even religious. She's told me that, time after time. On Christmas Eve here in Norway, we eat pork ribs. Enough said, and that's the end of it."

"But, Mary," Hanne made a desperate effort, "can't we have rack of lamb? Then the whole problem is solved. After all, we had your pork ribs last year."

"The problem?"

Mary Samuelsen had once lived under the name "Hairy Mary," the oldest street hooker in Oslo. Hanne had bumped into her three years ago in connection with a homicide case. Mary was near death at that time, high on drugs and freezing in the bitter cold of the big city. Now she kept house for Hanne and Nefis in a seven-room apartment in Kruses gate.

Mary ran her arthritic hands stiffly over her apron.

"The problem, my dear Hanne Wilhelmsen, is that the only rack of lamb I ever put in my toothless mouth before I met you and Nefis was cold, watered down, and arrived on a paper plate, courtesy of the Salvation Army."

"I know that, Mary. We could have both, don't you think? For heaven's sake, we can certainly afford it."

Hanne added the latter as she glanced despairingly around the room. The only furniture that remained from the apartment in Lille Tøyen where she had lived for more than fifteen years was an antique bureau, almost lost in a recess beside the door leading out to a gigantic terrace.

"Christmas is no time for compromise," Mary declared solemnly. "If you'd sat like I had, sucking on a scrap of fatty meat too tough to swallow, year after year, one Christmas Eve after another, out of sight and forgotten in a corner, then you'd realize this has something to do with holding on to your dreams. Christmas Eve with crystal and silver and a decorated tree and a huge fat rib of pork in the center of the table, with crackling so crisp that you could hear it crow. Throughout all those years, that was what I dreamed of. And that's the way it has to be. You could show that much respect for a poor old woman who might not have very much longer to live."

"Come on, Mary. You're remarkably fit. And not so old either."

Without a word, Mary turned on her heel once more and marched out, dragging one leg behind her. Her rhythmic limping disappeared in the direction of the kitchen. Hanne had measured it when they moved in, pacing it out when she thought no one was looking: 52 feet from the sofa to the kitchen door. From the dining room to the largest bathroom was 36 feet. From the bedroom to the front door, 21 feet. The whole apartment was filled with distances.

She poured out more coffee from a stainless-steel pot before switching on the TV.

For the very first time, she had taken the entire festive period off from work. Two whole weeks. Nefis and Mary had invited every Tom, Dick, and Harry to a sumptuous breakfast on Christmas morning, lunches during the following week, and a huge party on New Year's Eve. On Christmas Eve, it would be just the three of them. At least, that was what she thought. You never knew.

Hanne Wilhelmsen was both dreading and looking forward to Christmas.

The television was broadcasting a dramatization of the Christmas gospel story. Oddly enough, the baby Jesus was blue-eyed. The Virgin Mary wore heavy makeup and had blood-red lips. Closing her eyes, Hanne turned down the volume.

She tried not to think about her father. These days, that demanded all her strength.

The letter had reached her too late, three weeks ago now. Hanne suspected her mother of ulterior motives for using the postal service. Everyone knew that snail mail was no longer reliable. The message reporting his death had taken six days to reach her. By then the funeral had already taken place. Actually that was just as well. Hanne would not have attended anyway. She could visualize the scene: the family in the front pew, her brother with his mother's hand in his—a repulsive claw, covered in eczema, sprinkling flakes of skin all over her son's dark suit trousers. Her sister would most likely be wearing some expensive creation and would burst into tears at regular intervals, but not be so distressed that she neglected to look her brilliant best for the assembled congregation; her father's colleagues from home and abroad, a few celebrated academics, elderly women no longer in full control of their morning ablutions and who dispersed an odor of old-fashioned perfume along the rows of pews.

Her phone played an Arabian dance. Mary had tinkered with the list of ringtones and felt that oriental tunes would please Nefis. Hanne grabbed the receiver swiftly, to prevent Mary from reaching it first.

"Billy T. here." The words were spoken before she managed to say anything. "It would be best if you came over here."

"Now? It's past eleven o'clock."

"Now. It's a major case."

"Tomorrow's my last workday before the holidays, Billy T. There's no point in my starting something I won't be able to finish."

"You can damn well forget about that time off, Hanne."

"Cut it out. Bye. Ring someone else. Call the police."

"Very funny. Come on. Four bodies, Hanne. Mother, father, and son. And somebody else whose identity we haven't figured out yet."

"Four . . . four bodies? Four people *murdered*?"

"Yep. In your own neighborhood, by the way. If you want, I'll meet you there."

"Quadruple homicide—"

"What?"

"Do you mean we're faced with homicide times four?"

A demonstrative sigh crackled through the receiver.

"How many times do I have to repeat it?" Billy T. asked her irascibly. "Four dead people! In an apartment in Eckersbergs gate. All of them shot. It looks fucking horrendous. Not only are the bodies punctured, but there . . . There's been . . . someone's been there afterward. An animal. Or something like that—"

"Good God . . ."

On the TV screen, Joseph had begun to knock on doors at nightfall. In a brief close-up of his knuckles rapping on a rustic door in Bethlehem, Hanne noticed that the actor had forgotten to remove his wristwatch.

"Absurd," she mumbled. "An animal?"

"A dog, we think. It has . . . eaten its fill, you might say."

"Eckersbergs gate, was that what you said?"

"Number 5."

"I'll be there in ten minutes."

"I might take longer than that."

"Fine."

They both hung up simultaneously. Hanne gulped down the last of her coffee and stood up.

"Are you thinking of going out?"

Mary stood with her legs astride, her hip leaning on the doorway, and her gaze forced Hanne to sit down again, raising her hands in a defensive gesture.

"This is an extremely serious case," she began.

"I'll give you serious," Mary barked. "Nefis is coming home in half an hour. She's on her way from the airport. She's been gone for a whole week now, and I've been busy in the kitchen since seven. You're not going anywhere."

"I must."

Mary sucked through her teeth. For a moment, she seemed to be thinking of something else.

"Then you'll have to take some food with you. Are you going to meet that slob?"

"Mmm."

Ten minutes later, Hanne was ready. She had two plastic boxes of venison stew in her shoulder bag, half a sliced loaf spread generously with butter, a couple of apples, one and a half liters of cola, a large bar of chocolate, a packet of napkins, two plastic cups, and some silver cutlery in the bargain. She tried to protest.

"It's the middle of the night, Mary. I don't need all this!"

"Yes, you do. We never know when we'll see you again," Mary muttered. "Remember to bring that silver cutlery home with you!"

With that, she shut the door firmly behind Hanne, using all three locks.

Hanne had never grown accustomed to these streets. The wide spaces between the grand apartment blocks and forbidding villas cloaked in darkness created an atmosphere of angst, as if something dreadful were about to happen. Infrequent pedestrians crossed the road diagonally, with their eyes on the ground to avoid being drawn into any kind of intimacy with others. It was natural for Mary to choose to shut herself inside. After almost half a century under the influence of drugs and alcohol, isolation was probably a good idea. It was impossible to understand why all the other residents of this area seemed to make the same choice. Maybe they were perpetually absent. Maybe no one really lived here. *The whole of Frogner is a stage set,* Hanne thought.

She tugged her winter jacket more snugly around her frame.

It was pretty crowded outside the stone villa at Eckersbergs gate 5. Red-and-white police tape constrained a small group of curious spectators, but the interior of the cordoned area was swarming with uniformed colleagues. She recognized several of the journalists making friendly overtures to the youngest and most inexperienced police officers: shocked, immature, on edge, and easy to engage in conversation. The number of journalists swelled unbelievably fast, as if they all lived in the vicinity. At the sight of Hanne Wilhelmsen, they did no more than hoist their shoulders brashly to ward off the cold, conveying a greeting by lifting their heads ever so slightly.

"Hanne! Brilliant!"

Sergeant Silje Sørensen broke free from a group of eagerly gesticulating police personnel.

"My goodness," Hanne said, sizing her up. "Uniform? This must be something to write home about."

"Had an extra shift. But yes, this *is* something to write home about. Come on in!"

"I'll wait for a bit. Billy T. will be here soon."

She was dazzled by the temporary lighting that the police had already managed to rig up, making it difficult to gain a general impression of the apartment block. Hanne stepped back a few paces, using her hand to shield her eyes. It did not help much until she walked all the way to the opposite side of the street.

"What are you looking for?" Silje Sørensen asked, following in her footsteps.

Silje always asked questions. Pestered. *What are you looking for? What are you doing? What are you thinking?* Like a child. A smart but slightly annoying child.

"Nothing. Just looking around."

The apartment block was antique rose in color, with broad cornices. Above each window was a statue of a man battling a hideous fabled creature. The front garden was tiny, but a broad paved path snaking around the western corner of the building might indicate a more impressive backyard concealed at the rear. The building seemed to contain only four apartments. The one on the top left-hand side was in darkness. Frugal lamplight shone from the ground and first floors on the right of the building, leaving little doubt about where the crime had taken place. Through three of the windows down on the left, she could see figures in white overalls and hairnets moving to and fro, precise and apparently purposeful. Someone drew a curtain.

Suddenly Hanne was embraced from behind and lifted off her feet.

"Christ!" Billy T. yelled. "You've put on weight!"

She kicked him in the shin with the heel of her boot.

"Ouch! You could just have said something."

"I have," Hanne told him. "Don't lift me every time you see me. I've said that a thousand times."

"You just say that because you're getting fatter and fatter." He grinned, brushing her shoulders. "You never mentioned it before. Never. You used to like it."

Snow was falling more thickly now, light, bone-dry flakes.

"I don't think you're any fatter," Silje was quick to say, though Hanne was already halfway across the street.

"Let's go inside," she murmured, noticing how dread had made her feel queasy.

The oldest of the four murder victims bore a resemblance to the famous portrait of Albert Einstein. The corpse lay in the hallway with one hand tucked under his head as if he had made himself comfortable on the floor, his hair forming a voluminous garland around his crown, with a bushy mop of hair in the middle. His tongue dangled from his mouth, extended to a bizarre length, and his eyes were wide open.

"That guy looks as if he's had a shock. An electric shock!"

Billy T. leaned inquisitively over the old man.

"If it hadn't been for this here, right?"

He used a pen to point to an entry wound just below his left eye. Not particularly large, it appeared black rather than blood-red.

"And this. And this."

The doctor, obviously responsible for the cadaver's shirt front being carefully folded to one side, waved Billy T. aside. Between the sparse gray chest hairs, Hanne could see two more wounds.

"How many shots are we actually dealing with?" she asked.

"Too early to say," the physician answered tersely. "Quite a number. You ought to have had a pathologist here, if you ask me. It's about time you had a workable rota system sorted out with the Forensics Institute. All I can say is that these people are dead. Pretty grotesque, in my opinion. That man over there's the worst, I believe."

Hanne Wilhelmsen did not want to look at "that man over there." She had to steel herself to step around the old man and take a closer look at the body in the overcoat. An ill-tempered grunt sounded from one of the technicians, who could not bear having police investigators tramping around the crime scene.

Hanne ignored him. When she leaned over the corpse nearest to the front door and noticed how the exit wound in the skull had been licked clean of blood, her nausea increased. Swiftly straightening her back, she swallowed and pointed at the body of the third man, whose age she estimated at about forty.

"Preben," Billy T. introduced him. "The elder son of the father, Hermann, over there. That much we know at least."

His arms were by his sides, as if the son of the family had stiffened into a military pose as he hit the floor. His pale-blue shirt showed two small bullet holes on the breast pocket, and his shoulder was ripped open with dark, fleshy lacerations.

The doctor nodded almost imperceptibly.

"I haven't managed to look at him more closely. The dog has gorged itself on . . . if we are talking about a dog, that is."

"Come here!"

Billy T. waved her toward the kitchen at the end of the spacious, dark hallway. Dressed all in white, he looked odd, with green socks outside his shoes and a paper hairnet stretched tight on his head.

A woman's body stood by the kitchen sink. She had no hair, but a wig lay on the floor beside her. The woman's pale scalp was disfigured by scars. She wore an elegant pink dress and her eyes were wide open, with a piercing, almost reproachful look. A perplexed young police officer was making a feeble attempt to set her hair to rights before Billy T. stopped him.

"Are you crazy or what? Don't touch! Hell and damnation, what are you doing here anyway? This place is overcrowded as it is."

Irritated, he began to sort out those who were necessary from those who were not. Hanne stood calmly by, struggling to make sense of what she could see.

The woman was actually upright.

Her face was singularly sexless. That must be because of the lack of hair. When Hanne approached more closely, she saw that the woman's eyebrows were also fake, painted on, a bit too high, too distinctive. Above her left eye the painted brow formed an arch toward the bridge of her nose that served to reinforce her skeptical expression. Her eyes were open. Pale blue, small, and without lashes. Her mouth was well formed, with full lips, and appeared younger than the rest of her face, as if it had recently been repaired.

"Turid Stahlberg," Billy T. said, having now halved the number of people present in the apartment, and the atmosphere was conspicuously quieter now. "Her name's Turid. Tutta, to the family."

"Stahlberg," Hanne said, slightly confused, as she surveyed the enormous kitchen. "Not *the* Stahlberg family?"

"Yep. Hermann, the father, is the oldest of the three you saw in the hallway. I've also introduced you to Preben. He is forty-two. What is actually keeping this woman on her feet?"

Billy T. leaned forward and tried to peer behind the upright woman. Her ample backside was resting on the kitchen worktop and her feet were planted on the floor, well spaced, as if she had found her sea legs when faced with the killer.

"She's only just supported here," Billy T. mumbled. "By her ass. But her torso . . . why doesn't she topple over?"

A faint tearing sound should have warned him, as he stood halfway crouched over the corpse in an effort to seek an explanation. The woman, who must weigh at least 150 pounds, collapsed on to his back and knocked him off-balance. First he fell to his knees. The floor was slick with tea from a smashed teapot and something that looked like honey or syrup. Fast as lightning, Billy T.'s knee skidded out to one side.

"Hanne! Goddamn it! Help!"

Billy T. was spread-eagled and floundering under a pink-clad female cadaver with a shiny scalp.

"What in all . . ."

The curses of two crime scene technicians reverberated around the room.

"Lie still! Completely still!"

Five minutes later, Billy T. was able to stand up, looking more abject than Hanne had seen him in a very long time.

"Sorry, boys," he muttered, disconsolately struggling to assist them with moving the woman's body onto a stretcher.

"Get away," one of his colleagues snarled. "You've done enough in here!"

Only now did Hanne notice a cake dish, licked clean, on the countertop where the woman's body had rested. The marks left by an animal's tongue could be distinguished in the greasy traces of whipped cream: wiry gray hairs plastered to the porcelain.

"Well, at least Tutta escaped the attentions of the dog," she said crisply. "Saved by cream cake."

"I think they were planning a celebration," Billy T. said. "There's an opened, but full, bottle of champagne in the living room. Four glasses. Yes, okay! I'm leaving. I'm going, I said."

The most senior of the crime scene examiners was literally trying to push Billy T.'s huge bulk out of the kitchen, through the door into the living room.

"I'm going," Billy T. barked. "I'm leaving right now, don't you hear!"

"Four glasses," Hanne repeated, following him into the vast living room crammed with heavy furniture. "And sandwiches. Open sandwiches, that is."

The plate of sandwiches was still on the dining table. Empty, apart from a salad leaf and three slices of cucumber, meticulously licked clean of mayonnaise.

"Did they have a dog?" Hanne asked distractedly.

"No," Silje Sørensen replied, and Hanne noticed for the first time that she had sneaked in. "Pet dogs were forbidden here. Or . . . the owners had agreed that no one should keep pets."

"How do you already know that?"

"The neighbor," Silje said, waving vaguely in the direction of the street. "I spoke to a woman who lives across the street."

"What else did you find out?"

"Not much."

Licking her fingertip, Silje Sørensen leafed through a spiral notebook. A massive diamond ring glittered on her right hand.

"The neighbors directly above . . ."

She pointed at the ceiling.

". . . are away. They have a second home in Spain and traveled south as early as November."

"No one looking after their apartment?"

"The woman outside, Aslaug Kvalheim, says their daughter looks in now and again. She hasn't been there for a few days, though, according to Mrs. Kvalheim. And to be honest . . ."

Silje flashed a smile.

". . . I think Mrs. Kvalheim knows most of what goes on in this street. A real old busybody."

"Just as well for us," Hanne said. "What did she see tonight?"

"Nothing, unfortunately. She was at bingo from seven o'clock, and came back an hour ago. We were already here by then."

Hanne pulled a grimace.

"The other apartments, then?"

"Across the landing . . ."

Silje used her thumb to point, before turning the page.

". . . lives someone called Henrik Backe. A grumpy old man. I spoke to him myself, and he was three sheets to the wind. Bad-tempered about all the commotion. He didn't let me in."

"You didn't go in? Did you just talk to him and leave him be?"

"Of course not, Hanne. Take it easy. Two men are in with him now. For the time being, all I know is that he claims he's been at home all evening and hasn't heard anything."

"That's impossible," Billy T. blurted. "Look around! There must have been all sorts of bangs and explosions in here."

"Whether it's possible or not is something we don't know very much about yet," Silje said, sounding slightly peeved. "The guy could have used a silencer. In any case, the boys will bring Henrik Backe in for an interview tonight, no matter how much he protests. Then we'll see."

"And who reported it?"

"A chance caller. We're checking him out, of course, but it seems he's a young man who was just—"

"Fine. I see."

Hanne caught herself speculating about the size of the apartment. The living room must be more than 760 square feet—at least if you counted the conservatory overlooking the backyard. The furniture was crowded, but each item was beautiful when regarded individually. Pride of place, against the exterior wall, was given to a dark oak sideboard with carved door panels and glass doors on the top cupboards. The dining table was surrounded by twelve chairs with armrests. In addition to the manila-hemp seating in the conservatory, there was sufficient room for at least three more sets of furniture. Only one seemed to be in regular use: the upholstery was obviously worn on the sofa and chairs in front of the TV. The paintings on the walls were probably genuine, all with national romantic or maritime motifs. In particular, Hanne noticed an imminent shipwreck on the wall facing the kitchen. She stepped closer.

"Peder Balke," she said in hushed tones. "My goodness!"

The ice cubes in the champagne cooler had melted long ago. Hanne studied the label without touching the bottle.

"That's the sort of stuff you drink," Billy T. said. "Damned expensive."

"Do we know anything at all of interest?" Hanne asked, without taking her eyes off the bottle. "For instance, what they were celebrating?"

"Maybe they were just enjoying themselves," Silje Sørensen ventured. "After all, it will soon be—"

"Christmas," Hanne broke in. "There are five days left until Christmas. This is a fairly normal Thursday. That bottle there costs 850 kroner at the liquor store. There are limits to enjoying yourself, Silje. They were going to celebrate something. Something pretty major."

"We don't know—"

"Look here, Silje."

Hanne pointed at the TV set, a massive piece of furniture in mahogany or teak.

"The TV set is at least thirty years old. The sofa is so worn that you can see the warp in the weave. The pictures—at least that one there . . ."

She pointed at the Peder Balke.

"It's fairly valuable. The crystal in the cupboard over there is worth a fortune. There are only three kinds of sandwich toppings in the fridge: yellow cheese, liver pâté, and jam. The apartment here must be worth 7 or 8 million, at least. His sweater . . ."

Wheeling around, she nodded to the hallway where Hermann Stahlberg's body was being transferred to a stretcher.

". . . is from some time in the seventies. Nice and clean, but nevertheless so worn that the elbows are darned. What does all this tell you?"

"Tight-fisted folk," Billy T. answered, before Silje had a chance to consider the question. "Miserly. But rich. Come on, let's go."

Hanne made no sign of following him.

"Is there really nobody who knows who that stranger in the hallway is?"

"He's been removed now," Silje murmured.

"Thank God for that," Billy T. exclaimed. "But do we know anything about him?"

"Not a thing."

Silje Sørensen leafed aimlessly through her notes.

"No wallet. No ID. But elegant clothes. Suit. Good overcoat."

"Nothing very elegant about that guy," Billy T. said, shuddering. "The dog has—"

"Overcoat," Hanne Wilhelmsen interrupted. "He was wearing a coat. Had he just arrived, or was he about to leave?"

"Arrived," Silje suggested. "The champagne was untouched. Besides, with all those men out in the hallway—"

"Lobby," Billy T. corrected her. "It's big enough for three dead bodies, for heaven's sake."

"Lobby, then. It looks like a real welcoming committee out there, don't you think? I'll bet the stranger had just arrived."

Hanne scanned the living room one final time, making up her mind to inspect the rest of the apartment later. There were enough people here at present. Photographers balancing on short stepladders. Crime scene technicians moving around quietly with their steel cases, wearing plastic gloves and looking purposeful. The doctor, gray, drawn, and obviously in a foul mood, was on his way out. The silence with which the technicians enveloped themselves was broken only by rapid commands of one syllable, demonstrating both their efficiency and their coordination, but also an ill-concealed displeasure at the continued presence of the police investigators. *Later*, Hanne thought. *I'll look at the rest later.* The thought was accompanied by a grudging sense of relief that the Christmas holiday would come to naught yet again this year.

The idea brought a smile to her face.

"What is it?" Billy T. asked.

"Nothing. Let's go."

In the lobby, Hanne was confronted by her own reflection in the mirror and stopped short for a moment. Billy T. was right. She had put on weight. Her chin was rounded, her face seemed slightly broader, and there was an unfamiliar aspect to the bridge of her nose that made her look away. It must be the mirror, black-speckled with age.

The cadaver of the horribly lacerated and hitherto unidentified male in his sixties had been removed. Marker tape glistened on the parquet.

"Not a single damn trace of blood left," Billy T. said, crouching down. "That dog's had a feast."

"Stop it," Hanne said. "I feel sick."

"I'm hungry," Billy T. said, shadowing her on the way out.

They both noticed the nameplate as they closed the front door behind them: magnificent, almost awe-inspiring, in worn brass with black lettering: "Hermann Stahlberg."

No Tutta. Or Turid. None of the children, even though the nameplate obviously originated from a time long before any of the children had left home.

"Here lived Hermann Stahlberg," Billy T. said. "Cock of the walk."

• • •

They settled on the steps outside Hanne's apartment in Kruses gate. She had brought newspapers from the recycling container to sit on.

"Picnic in the depths of winter," Billy T. said, munching, his mouth full of food. "Can't we go up? Christ, I'm freezing to death!"

Hanne tried to follow the snowflakes, one by one, with her eyes. The temperature had plummeted. As the crystals whirled through the air, she caught them in the palm of her hand. One glimpse of hexagonal symmetry, and then they were gone.

"Don't want to wake the others."

"What do you think?" he asked, tucking into another slice of bread.

"That they'll waken if we go up."

"Idiot! About the case, I mean. Nothing was stolen."

"We don't know that."

"That's how it looks," he said impatiently. "The silverware was still there. The paintings . . . you said yourself that they were valuable. To me, it looked as if nothing had been taken. It wasn't a robbery-related homicide."

"We don't know that, Billy T. Don't jump—"

". . . to conclusions," he completed for her, sounding discouraged, as he got to his feet. "Thanks for the food," he said, brushing snow off his jacket. "Is Mary okay?"

"As you can see," Hanne said, nodding at the leftovers. "Methadone, isolation, and housework are doing wonders. She and Nefis are like this."

She crossed her fingers in the air, and Billy T. hooted with laughter.

"Not so easy sometimes," Hanne said, "for me. There's a lot of two against one in our everyday lives, if I can put it that way."

"Huh. You love it. Haven't seen you looking so happy in years. Not since . . . the old days, you know. It's almost as if everything's the same as before."

They cleaned up in silence. It was past two o'clock, and the weather had turned blustery, with sudden biting gusts. Their footsteps on the courtyard were swept away. There was no longer light from any of the apartments. Only the street lamps beyond the stone wall cast a glimmer of visibility over the snow that now blanketed everything. Hanne squinted into the wind.

"Nothing's like it was before," she said softly. "Never say that. This is now. Everything's different. Cecilie is dead. Nefis has come. You and I are . . . we're older—nothing is like it was before. Never."

He had already started to walk, lurching unsteadily in the drifts, with his hands thrust deep inside his pockets. Her gaze followed his retreating back.

"Don't go!" she shouted. "I only meant . . ."

Billy T. did not want to hear her. As he negotiated his way around the gate and quickly threw a backward glance, his expression scared her. At first she did not understand. Then she did not want to understand. She did not want to catch what he muttered under his breath; she must have been mistaken. The distance was too great. The weather made contours indistinct and sounds unclear.

Grabbing her bag, she fumbled for the keys and let herself in.

"Fuck!" she said through gritted teeth.

She ignored the elevator and slowly took the stairs.

# FRIDAY, DECEMBER 20

As usual, the silence woke her at the crack of dawn. She had always slept lightly in the mornings, and without the familiar friendly clamor of the east end and the soothing sound of heavy traffic through Tøyen, she no longer felt the need for an alarm clock. Not even to be on the safe side. Even though only two hours had elapsed since she had dropped off, she knew how futile it was to turn over and try to prolong the night. An open window would have helped, of course. Fresh air and noise would have kept Hanne asleep for another hour or two. Clammy with perspiration, she pulled the quilt aside and got up. Nefis muttered in her sleep, with half her body visible under her thin blanket. The dark-blue oriental pattern made her skin appear paler than it was. She looked childlike as she lay there, mouth open and arms above her head. A sliver of saliva had left the outline of a stain on the pillow. The room temperature was more than 72 degrees. Hanne felt terribly thirsty.

The copy of *Aftenposten* had already been delivered. The aroma of fresh coffee hit her as she entered the kitchen and closed the door quietly behind her. As usual, Mary had programmed the machine for half past five. The entire kitchen was filled with absurd aids, all with timers and precision controls for every conceivable and inconceivable requirement. Nefis wanted it like that, and Nefis could afford it. Nefis had money for anything and everything. Nefis was building her first real home at the age of forty-one and delighted in filling it with unnecessary gadgets that Mary used with enthusiasm and surprising proficiency, despite the old woman being hardly able to spell her way through an instruction leaflet.

Hanne filled a mug with coffee and poured in some milk before drinking half a liter of juice straight from the carton. She did not feel hungry. To her amazement, her cigarette craving was always acute in the mornings. When she had finally managed to quit about a year ago, she had been most afraid of the evenings. Of alcohol. Of socializing with other people. The stress of her job, perhaps. All the same, it was the mornings that had proved to be the test. She felt the gravitation toward the cabinet above the stove, where Mary's stash of rolling tobacco was kept, bought by Nefis on a monthly basis and painstakingly sealed in plastic containers by their housekeeper, who adhered scrupulously to Nefis's instructions to restrict her smoking to her own small section of the apartment.

The coverage in *Aftenposten* was extravagant. Virtually the entire first page was dedicated to the murders in Eckersbergs gate. A composite image was splashed over six columns: the facade of the apartment block formed the backdrop to three personal photographs of the mother, father, and older son in the Stahlberg family. The photo of Hermann Stahlberg had obviously been snapped on a boat; he stood smartly at the rail, dressed in a blazer with gold buttons and the shipping company emblem on its breast pocket. He gave a faint smile, with his chin thrust forward as he stared past the photographer. His wife's smile was broader, in a photo taken indoors. She was cutting into a cake decorated with more candles than Hanne could be bothered to count; the flash was reflected in her glasses, making the woman look hysterical. The image of Preben was indistinct, though he seemed far younger than his forty-plus years. His hair was midlength and he wore an open-necked shirt. It must have been taken years ago.

*Where did the journalists get them?* Hanne wondered, struggling to drown her cigarette craving with coffee. Only two or three hours after the murders, and they've already acquired some personal photographs. How do they do it? What questions do they ask, when they contact friends and family, before the blood has even congealed at the crime scene? Who hands over such things?

"My dear Hanna," Nefis said softly.

Startled, Hanne whipped her head around. Nefis, stark naked, held out her arms.

"You always jump! What am I to do? Do I have to wear a gong around my neck?"

"Bell," Hanne corrected her. "A gong is huge. Like in an Indian temple and suchlike. You need to get yourself a bell. Hello, by the way."

They kissed tenderly. The scent of night still clung to Nefis, and goosebumps formed on her skin as Hanne caressed her back.

"Don't walk about like that, though. Mary might come in."

"Mary never comes out of her room before eight," Nefis said, but nevertheless plucked an enormous woolen sweater from a chair back and drew it over her head. "Like so? Am I . . . respectable enough now?"

Nefis had grappled with a new language with the same enthusiasm that she embraced most aspects of Norwegian life. Although she still refrained from pork and insisted on an unbearably hot bedroom, she had begun to knit with great fascination, became tolerably good at skiing, and displayed an incomprehensible interest in Oslo streetcars. She wrote angry letters to the editor complaining about the streetcar company's constant cutbacks in public transportation. When Hanne occasionally reminisced about their first meeting, in a piazza in Verona in 1999, it was a completely different woman she pictured, an almost unreal memory. The Nefis of that time was a deep secret, harboring an impenetrable passion. When she encountered Norway, it was as if she were rushing headlong, as if she were desperate to catch up with something she wasn't clear about, something that had never belonged to her at the time when she, despite her impressive academic career, had first and foremost been the beloved daughter in an enormously wealthy Turkish family.

Nefis could use words such as *respectability* and *paradigm shift*. However, she had never learned to pronounce the name of her live-in partner.

"Hanna," she said ecstatically, twirling around in a sweater that reached to her knees. "It scratches! Come on, let's go back to bed."

Shaking her head, Hanne drained her cup and refilled it.

"Is this your case?" Nefis nodded at the newspaper.

"Yes."

"We heard it on the news last night. Mary and I. Hoooorrrible!" She drew out the "o" so much that Hanne simply had to smile.

"Go back to bed. I'm heading straight for work once I've had a shower."

Instead, Nefis pulled a chair over to the table and sat down.

"Tell me," she said. "Some sort of famous family? I got that impression from the radio."

"Famous . . ." Hanne lingered on the word. "Not exactly. But well known to people who read pink newspapers."

"Pink newspapers," Nefis repeated doubtfully, and then understood. "Business papers!"

"Yes. I'm not really up to speed yet. But the family—that is to say, the father, I think . . ."

She pointed at Hermann Stahlberg.

". . . owned a medium-sized shipping company. Not such a huge concern, but pretty lucrative all the same. He'd been smart enough to duck in and out of various tonnages just in advance of cyclical fluctuations. But I don't think he's ever been particularly well known. Not outside the trade, anyway. I hadn't heard of either him or his shipping company until they began to quarrel. The family, that is. That must have been . . ."

She pondered.

". . . two years ago? One year? Difficult to say. I don't know the details. Not at all. I expect I'll know a great deal more before this day is out, though. But if my recollection's not entirely mistaken, then it had something to do with one son being preferred over the other."

"That's an old story, isn't it?"

"Is this where you're sitting, then?"

Mary shuffled over to the coffee machine. Her pink terry-toweling bathrobe was puffed up around her chest and gathered at the waist with a silk cord from an old-fashioned curtain. The pompoms slapped against her skinny thighs with every halting step she took. She looked like a party balloon.

"Mary, for heaven's sake," Nefis said, laughing. "It's far too early for you!"

"Are you aware of all the things I have to do before Christmas Eve?"

Gruffly she began to count on her scrawny fingers.

"One: we're still short of two kinds of Christmas baking, *fattigmann* cookies and *jødekake* cakes. Two: the decorations from last year have

to be vacuumed and maybe even repaired. There was a pretty wild
party here on New Year's Eve, if I remember rightly. Also, I've a lot of
new things to try out. Three: I have to—"

"I'm off anyway," Hanne said, getting to her feet.

"I thought so! And when are you coming back, may I ask Your
Ladyship?"

"I'll phone," Hanne said airily, heading for the living room.

"Hanne," Mary said, grabbing her by the arm. "Does that mean . . ."

She curled her index finger toward the open newspaper.

"Does that mean we can dream on about that Christmas holiday of
yours?"

Hanne smiled feebly, but did not answer.

"Honestly, Hanna."

Nefis rose to stand by Mary's side, forming a wall of familiar complaint and vexatious unanimity.

"I'll phone," Hanne said obstinately, before leaving the room.

When she clambered into her car twenty minutes later, she was still
aware of the vague taste of sleep on her tongue from Nefis's mouth.

What she wanted most of all was to take sick leave. Maybe that was
what she should do. Unequivocally. She would endure this day and all
it offered, and then come to a decision later. In the late afternoon perhaps.

Or over the weekend.


In an apartment in Blindernveien, an old woman sat in floods of tears.
A cleric was seated beside her on the overstuffed sofa, trying to provide consolation.

"Your son will be here soon," said the pastor, a woman who had not
yet reached the age of thirty. "His plane has already landed."

There was not much more to say.

"There, there," she said helplessly, stroking the old woman's hand.
"There, there."

"At least he died happy," the widow said all of a sudden.

The pastor straightened her back, feeling relieved.

"He died in my arms," the old woman said, her grimace changing to
a smile.

The pastor stared into her tear-stained face, partly shocked, but mostly embarrassed, and said, "A cup of coffee, maybe? Your son will be here shortly."

"I can't talk about this with him! That would be far too awkward. For both of us. It's none of my son's business that his father and I still enjoyed the physical side of our marriage. For heaven's sake! What's today's date?"

The pastor quickly racked her brain, but this time did not dare express any sense of relief: "The twentieth. Yes. December the twentieth. Soon it will be Christmas Eve."

She could have bitten off her tongue. The widow burst into tears again.

"My first Christmas without Karl-Oskar. The first one after so many . . ."

The rest disappeared in violent sobs. It crossed the pastor's mind that she would just have to let her cry. And her son had better get here soon!

"We usually go to Duvamåla," the widow eventually said. "Yes, that's our house in the country, you see. Since I'm called Kristina and my husband Karl-Oskar, we thought it would be fun to call it that."

Duvamåla.

Obviously unfamiliar with the Wilhelm Moberg series *The Emigrants*, the pastor did not understand any of it, but she seized on the subject eagerly.

"Our summer cottage is called Fredly," she stammered.

"Why is that?" the old woman asked.

"Well . . ."

"At least he died happy," the widow rashly repeated.

Exuding a scent of light summer perfume, she was remarkably well groomed for someone widowed scarcely twelve hours earlier. The pastor began to notice a whiff of her own stress and clutched her arms to her body to conceal the rings of perspiration.

"Is it too hot in here?" Kristina Wetterland asked. "Perhaps you could open the balcony door? When will my son's plane land?"

"He landed a while ago," the pastor said, feeling quite distraught now. "As I said some time ago, he should have landed—"

"You *are* a pastor, aren't you?"

A slight edge had crept into her voice now. She was more composed.

"Yes. Temporary post."

"You're young. You've a lot to learn."

"Yes," the pastor agreed.

Kristina Wetterland, widow of Supreme Court advocate Karl-Oskar Wetterland, blew her nose energetically into a clean, freshly ironed handkerchief. Then she folded it neatly, pushed it up the sleeve of her sweater, and took a deep breath.

They heard keys rattling somewhere in the distance and someone enter the apartment. A moment or two later, a mature man stood in the living room doorway. Tall and well dressed, he appeared extremely flustered.

"Mom," he exclaimed. "My dear Mom! How are you?"

He ran across the room and knelt down in front of his mother to hug her.

"When did this happen? How . . . I didn't find out until early this morning! Why didn't you phone me?"

"Sweetheart," the woman said, stroking the man's head, though he was double her size. "Your father died yesterday. About seven o'clock. He died in his sleep, darling. Just a little nap. He was going to a meeting at eight. He just needed a little nap, as usual, you know. After dinner. I don't think he suffered at all. We'll have to comfort ourselves with that, my dear. We'll just have to comfort ourselves with that."

Suddenly her eyes caught sight of the pastor.

"You can go now, Pastor. Thank you for your visit."

The young woman slinked out, closing the door quietly behind her. She had not even said hello to the son. She forced back tears all the way out into the street, where it was snowing heavily. It was now four days until Jesus's birthday.

"It's really quite incomprehensible," Hanne Wilhelmsen said in annoyance as she glanced at her watch. "The guy looked Norwegian, well groomed and established. We're not talking about some lost foreigner or poor homeless down-and-out. How can it be so damned difficult to identify a Norwegian in Norway?"

Feeling discouraged, Billy T. shrugged and ran his hand over his shaved head.

"We're working on it. We've a fair amount to get to grips with here, Hanne."

"A fair amount? Yes, you can say that again. But it looks as though the entire police force has forgotten that there's actually a fourth victim here. You'd think the most important thing would be to discover who he is."

Public prosecutor Håkon Sand grimaced before removing his glasses and polishing them with his shirttail. He leaned back in an oversized office chair behind a desk strewn with documents. A phone rang, and he rummaged around in confusion under the folders, struggling to locate the phone. It fell silent before he found it.

"We'll get there," he said wearily. "Relax, Hanne. How many have actually been allocated to this case now?"

"At the moment, fourteen officers, taking everyone into account," Billy T. answered. "We'll have more in the course of the day. The superintendent is canceling vacations and time off in lieu, pulling out all the stops. In other words, the station's in an uproar."

"I see," Håkon Sand said, squinting through his glasses; they did not look any cleaner. "And when do you expect to have identified the fourth man?"

"Pretty soon," Silje Sørensen said, in an attempt to soothe the rattled atmosphere. "Someone must be missing him."

Hanne Wilhelmsen let her eyes rest on her own reflection in the window. Outside, the half light suggested daybreak, even though the hour was already far advanced. The light lacked purchase. A chill blanket of fog pressed heavily on the city, and a gray veil of exhaust fumes and miscellaneous pollution enveloped the streets; even the snowflakes dancing behind her image in the glass seemed grimy.

"Strictly speaking, this unidentified man isn't the most important focus for the investigation either," Billy T. said. "Here's the file on the family. And these are only newspaper clippings. In addition, we're busy gathering all the correspondence and other documentation we can lay our hands on. The lawyers on both sides are putting up a fight, of course. The old story about duty of confidentiality. But we'll win out in the end. This stuff here is all in the public domain anyway."

He tossed a substantial folder onto Håkon Sand's desk. Håkon, yawning loudly, let it lie.

"We're all well aware that this family was engaged in a quarrel," he said finally, still without touching the red ring binder. "It happens in the best of families. People don't kill for that reason."

The room went completely quiet. Fiddling with her ring, Silje Sørensen gazed self-consciously at the floor. Billy T. smirked as he stared at the ceiling. Hanne Wilhelmsen fixed her eyes on Håkon Sand. Håkon spat a gob of snuff into a trash can before straightening up, pulling his chair closer to the desk, and heaving a deep sigh.

"I'm meeting Puntvold, head of CID, later today," he said, raking his fingers through his hair. "This case is so massive. Though the media have given us a hard time previously, I don't think we've seen the likes of this until now, all the same. They're crawling all over us now. The head of CID feels we should have a coordinated plan involving both the public prosecution service and Oslo Police District. From the very outset, I mean."

"If I'm not entirely mistaken, it'll be Jens Puntvold himself who'll take care of that aspect."

A sarcastic smile crossed Hanne's face. Following a career that had started in the Bergen Police Station and subsequently progressed via the Ministry of Justice to the National Police Directorate at its inception in January 2001, Jens Puntvold, Deputy Chief of Police and head of CID, had taken up his post as second in command in Oslo seven months earlier. In his mid-forties, he was brash, blond, and childless. Moreover, he kept house with TV2's most glamorous weatherwoman and was more than willing to turn up for interviews with or without his girlfriend.

Håkon sighed again, almost theatrically. Hanne was not entirely certain whether it was because of her or Puntvold.

"He always succeeds in calling attention to the police force," he said reprovingly. "Always, Hanne. It's true that he appears rather too often, but the police haven't been oversupplied with positive profiles in the past, you know. Single-handedly, Puntvold has managed to—"

"He's competent, I'll give you that," Hanne interrupted. "I just get a bit discouraged about all these campaigns he launches. Many of them are nothing more than pandering to the public."

"It's the public who, at the end of the day, decides how many resources we have at our disposal," Håkon said. "But enough of that. I just wanted to have a chat with the three of you before I talk to him. Annmari Skar will be the prosecutor responsible for the case in your headquarters, anyway. I'm meeting her afterward. I'll probably be working with her more closely than usual, and I'd appreciate you giving me a call if anything crops up. This case . . . Christ!"

He shook his head and tucked another wad of snuff under his lip.

"I wouldn't mind taking a look at that folder," Silje Sørensen said while Håkon fumbled with his top lip: the snuff was too dry and would not grip. "I've picked up a few things here and there, but I—"

"In a nutshell," Billy T. said, "it revolves around a middle-sized shipping company, Norne Norway Shipping. Hermann Stahlberg was the first generation. He built up the whole enterprise from 1961 to the present day. Smart guy. Hard as nails. Cynical—at least if the newspaper commentators are to be believed."

His finger, its nail bitten down to the quick, tapped the red ring binder.

"The man has three children. The eldest, Preben, went to sea in 1981. He had quarreled with his father and wouldn't even sign on with one of his dad's ships. A few years later, he came ashore in Singapore. Started his own ship brokerage firm, which was extremely successful. At home here in Norway, he had been written off completely. The younger son, Carl-Christian, eventually took the place intended for his brother in the shipping company. Obviously he was easier to deal with. Though not as promising as his brother."

"Not as strong," Hanne interjected. "More willing to defer to his father, in other words."

"That may be," Billy T. said impatiently. "In any case, the point is as follows: Carl-Christian works his socks off for Hermann. He does well, without ever distinguishing himself in any way. The father begins to get impatient. He refuses to hand over the shipping company as long as he remains unimpressed by the younger son's abilities."

"But Preben," Håkon asked. "When did he come home?"

"Two years ago."

Billy T. grabbed the folder of newspaper clippings and began to browse through them.

"All of a sudden, he sold the entire business in Asia and came home to the old country, pretty well loaded with cash. His father was still pissed off and dismissive, of course, until the prodigal son coughs up a considerable sum to invest in the family firm and shows himself to be the spitting image of his father. He is given a chance in the shipping company, and after two or three advantageous maneuvers, he's back in his old father's good graces. The younger brother is increasingly side-lined."

"Then the fun begins," Silje said with a sigh.

"Yep. Accusations have been thrown about all over the place. Two court cases are pending at present, and there could be a few more to look forward to."

"We'll be spared them now, of course," Hanne said tartly and yawned.

"But who's the third?" Silje asked.

"The third?"

"You said that Hermann and Tutta Stahlberg had three children. What part has the third sibling played in all this?"

"Oh, her . . . a young woman. An afterthought. Drop-dead gorgeous, as far as I can make out. She's the family's free spirit, loved by all, respected by none. Apparently she made an effort at bridge building, but to no avail. According to what I found out last night, she spends most of her time splurging the unexpectedly generous fortune that her father endowed her with on her twentieth birthday. It doesn't say much about her here."

Once again they heard a piercing ring from somewhere below the chaos on the desk.

"Sand," Håkon said crisply when he finally retrieved the phone.

He listened for three minutes without speaking. A frown appeared behind the heavy frames of his glasses. He fished out a pen and scribbled something on the back of his hand. Hanne thought it looked like a name.

"Knut Sidensvans," he articulated slowly when the phone conversation ended. "The fourth victim. He's called Knut Sidensvans."

"Odd name," Billy T. said. "Who is he?"

"At the moment they know very little. He's sixty-three and works as some kind of publishing consultant. And writer. Originally an electrician."

"Electrician? And involved in publishing?"

"Yes, that's what they said."

Baffled, Håkon shook his head and continued: "It was probably not so strange that he wasn't reported missing. He lives on his own. No children. A quiet, unassuming life, so days could have gone by before anyone began to wonder where he was. But he was to hand in some work to the publishing house this morning—something important— so they sent a messenger around when he hadn't turned up as arranged. Since there was no reply, the messenger thought the man might be seriously ill, and after that it didn't take more than a couple of hours to clarify the situation. Knut Sidensvans was the fourth victim in Eckersbergs gate."

"Clarify?" Billy T. reiterated. "We can hardly claim that the situation has been clarified—"

"No. But it's clearly an advantage to know who's been murdered. Don't you think?"

Hanne stood up abruptly.

"Three well-heeled folk from the salubrious west end and an electrician who works for a publisher. I'm looking forward to finding out what these people had in common. I'm going back to headquarters. If there's nothing further, Håkon?"

"No. Keep me posted. And, Hanne . . . I'm looking forward to Christmas Eve. That's good of you to do the honors like that. The children are over the top with excitement."

"Now you've let the cat out of the bag." Billy T. grinned. "It was all meant to be a surprise party for Hanne. You weren't supposed to breathe a word!"

Håkon Sand looked in confusion from Hanne to Billy T.

"But I . . . Karen didn't say . . . Sorry. I'm really sorry."

"Quite all right," Hanne said, keeping a straight face. "I knew about it. It's okay. Of course I knew about it."

She turned on her heel and left the public prosecutor's office. Before Billy T. had managed to collect his documents, keys, and cell phone, Hanne had disappeared with Silje in tow. When he descended to the street at last, he discovered they had taken the car.

This was the Friday before Christmas, and there wasn't a taxi to be had. When he finally gave up his attempts to flag one down, he was shivering with cold.

"*Bitch!*" he spluttered, and started walking.

The young man who had just left Police Inspector Erik Henriksen's office when Hanne Wilhelmsen arrived on the second floor of police headquarters was chewing gum as if his life depended on it. His pants were three sizes too big. The neck of his sweater was damaged, the rib partly unraveled. His baseball cap was perched back-to-front on tufts of bleached hair. He looked like a teenager going through puberty, but to judge from his face, he was at least twenty-five. His nose was sharp. The bags under his eyes were outlined in dark blue, and his mouth had acquired a fixed ill-tempered grin that must have taken years to cultivate. He shot a cryptic look in Hanne's direction before padding toward the stairs without taking Erik Henriksen's outstretched hand. The Police Inspector rolled his eyes and beckoned Hanne in.

"The neighbor," he said by way of explanation. "The one who lives above the Stahlbergs, diagonally opposite. Directly above Backe—the grumpy old man, that is."

"He surely doesn't live there on his own," Hanne asked doubtfully. "That kid?"

"Yes, he does. A dot.com guy. Lars Gregusson. A lot of money fell into his hands at the age of nineteen and he was sensible enough to invest it in real estate. Why someone like that wants to live in that mausoleum of a place in Eckersbergs gate is anyone's guess, but anyway, he does."

"Is he of interest to us?" Hanne asked, helping herself unbidden to a large bottle of cola.

"Hardly. But I'll pull him in a couple of times to make sure."

Erik Henriksen scratched his carrot-colored hair.

"He insists he wasn't at home. That might well be true. This Mrs. . . ."

Erik's untidy appearance, with spiky hair and flapping shirttail, con-
trasted oddly with the almost feminine sense of order in his surroundings. The numerous ring binders on his desk were arranged by color
and held in place by brushed-steel bookends. On one side of a leather
writing pad, three pens lay straight and parallel in an oblong dish. Even
the curtains seemed freshly ironed, and a faint scent of detergent hung
in the air. Hanne caught herself wondering whether Erik took care of
cleaning the office himself. It was actually peculiar that she did not
know him better. For years on end, he had trailed behind her, often
overlooked, tagging along. Trainee, constable, sergeant, and inspector:
he had climbed through the ranks, all the time secretly and timidly in
love with Hanne Wilhelmsen. It had hindered him in his work, and it
once had looked as if it might turn him into an eternal bachelor. Only
when a terror-stricken Hanne had entered into a civil partnership
with Nefis eighteen months ago had he let go. He became a sergeant,
moved in with a woman in the uniformed section, and began to demonstrate to the entire world that he really was a top-notch detective.

"Mrs. Kvalheim," the name occurred to Erik, without having to
check more closely. "Aslaug Kvalheim, a neighbor across the street.
Silje had her in here at the crack of dawn and, according to her, anyway,
the windows in the Vede apartment were dark—the people were away
on extended holiday—when she went to bingo just before seven.
Another neighbor said the same. In the Gregusson apartment, though,
there was some light in the afternoon and evening, as if he had forgotten that he had left a lamp switched on. The living room light was on
in Henrik Backe's apartment, while the Stahlbergs' windows suggested
that the apartment was 'crammed full of things,' as Mrs. Kvalheim put
it. She also thought that a fire must have been lit. Says she could see the
flicker of flames through the curtains."

"They keep watch," Hanne said. "The neighbors. Keep an eye on
everyone and everything."

"In this case, we ought to be pleased about that."

"Then can we conclude that Henrik Backe was the only one of the
neighbors actually at home when the shots were fired?"

"Not altogether. We don't yet know the exact time of the killings.
An absolutely provisional time frame is fixed between eight and nine

o'clock. As far as our friend Backe is concerned, he was so drunk when he was dragged in here last night that we had to let him sleep it off before we could interview him."

"Here? Here in police headquarters?"

"They had brought him in, yes. Fortunately Silje made the dim duty officer understand that we couldn't haul people out of house and home and put them in a cell when they hadn't done anything wrong. So he was driven home again, to get some sleep. He created merry hell in here. We'll just have to hope that he's more amenable now. He's expected at . . ."

A brief glance at the wall clock took him aback. He double-checked with his watch.

"Now. Any time now. Do you want to be present?"

Hanne considered for a moment. As she opened her mouth to answer, someone knocked angrily on the door, and all of a sudden an elderly man had entered the room.

"Are you Henriksen?"

The voice was gruff and hoarse. The figure stooped aggressively. Hanne recognized the unmistakable odor of alcoholism: poor hygiene and self-deceiving peppermints. Amazingly enough, though, he was on time.

"That's me," Erik said jovially, and got to his feet to shake hands. "Police Inspector Erik Henriksen."

"I'm going to submit a formal complaint," the man replied.

"This is Chief Inspector Hanne Wilhelmsen," Erik said, pointing. "Please take a seat."

"I'd like to know by what authority I was brought in here last night," Backe said, with a racking cough, and neglected to sit down. "And I want it in writing."

"Of course, you'll receive a response to your complaint," Erik said. "But now we'll get that witness statement out of the way. Okay? Then I'll find someone to help you with the formalities afterward. Maybe you'd like some coffee?"

It was possibly the friendliness that surprised the old man. Henrik Backe seemed suddenly unsteady, as if all his energies had been depleted by adopting a threatening pose, the reason for which he no longer quite remembered. With an expression of bewilderment, he ran his fingers over his forehead and sat down in the chair beside Hanne, to all appearances without even noticing that she was there.

"I'd like some water."

"Of course you can have some water," Erik Henriksen said, leaning confidentially across the desk. "I promise this will take as little time as possible. You probably want to return home again as quickly as you can. Here . . ."

He placed an unopened bottle of water and a clean glass in front of the old man before switching on his computer.

"First of all, some personal details," he began. "Full name and date of birth."

"Henrik Heinz Backe, ten-seventeen-twenty-nine."

"Employment? Retired, perhaps?"

"Yes, retired."

"From what?"

"From—what do you mean?"

"What were you before you retired?"

"Oh . . ."

Backe was lost in thought. His face grew passive and expressionless, his mouth half-open. His teeth were brown, and a bottom front tooth was missing. His eyelids hooded his irises so heavily that only the lower part of the pupils was visible.

"I was a consultant," he said abruptly, producing a pack of twenty Prince cigarettes. "In an insurance firm."

"Insurance consultant," Erik said, smiling, and made a note.

Backe's hands were shaking violently as he tried to remove a cigarette from the packet. He dropped three on the floor but made no move to pick them up.

"I'll complain," he said in a loud voice.

"We'll get to that," Erik reassured him. "Let's get these formalities over and done with first. I know your address, of course."

His fingers raced over the keys and he turned again to the old man.

"I understand that you were at home all yesterday afternoon and evening. Is that right?"

"Yes. I was at home."

"What were you doing?"

"I was reading."

"Reading. The whole time?"

"I read all the time."

"Yes, but maybe you did something else as well, in between times. I would like to get it all absolutely precise. Let's begin with the morning. You got up. When?"

"I was reading a book. A trashy novel. Incredible that they publish that sort of thing. One of these newfangled crime novels where—"

He broke off. Hanne unconsciously drew back from him. The stench of dirty clothing and unwashed body had begun to bother her.

"Is that a bathroom?" Backe asked, pointing at a cupboard beside the office door.

Erik looked at him in confusion.

"No, that's a cupboard. Do you want to use the bathroom? I can show you where it is."

"I'd prefer to go to my own," Backe said, his voice reedy now.

The shaking had increased. Hanne Wilhelmsen placed a hand on his back. His shoulder blades almost cut through the flimsy fabric of his shirt. He stared at her, disconcerted, as if she had just arrived.

"I'll show you."

Erik stood beside the door. Backe tried to stand up, but his knees would not let him.

"They're celebrities rather than authors," he slurred. "In this book, in this silly scribbling . . . Where is the liquor cabinet?"

His eyes were wide open now, coated with a dull film of impaired memory. The two investigators exchanged glances.

"I think we'll get you home to your liquor cabinet," Hanne said softly. "I'll find a nice young lady to drive you."

"I'm going to complain," Backe wailed, almost crying. "I want to submit a letter of protest."

"And you'll be able to do that, if you insist. But wouldn't you rather go home?"

Henrik Backe tottered up from his chair and walked over to the cupboard. Hanne stopped him with a friendly suggestion.

"Come," she said quietly. "Come on; we'll go together."

"Do you maybe have a beer somewhere?" the old man muttered, permitting himself to be led hesitantly from the office. "Something to drink would do me good. It certainly would."

He shuffled after the Chief Inspector, along the corridor toward the elevator. Erik stood watching them. Only now did he notice that Backe was wearing one boot and one shoe, below the legs of his baggy trousers.

Hermine Stahlberg dropped her glass on the floor, and the fragile crystal smashed. The dregs of whisky made the glass shards sparkle and acquire an amber-yellow hue. Apathetically she tried to pick up the largest fragments. One of them cut her palm beside the thumb. When she put the gaping wound to her mouth, it brought with it the sweet taste of iron. Iron, alcohol, and hand cream. She retched and threw up.

"My God, Hermine."

Carl-Christian Stahlberg was partly irritated, partly solicitous, as he led his sister out to the bathroom, opened the medicine cabinet, and clumsily applied a bandage. The blood was still flowing freely. He muttered a fierce oath as he made a fresh attempt. In the end, he tore off a wad of toilet paper, folded it to form a thick cushion, and used dental floss to attach it firmly. Hermine stood, impassive, staring at her hand. It reminded her of cotton candy with specks of strawberry and made her giggle.

"You're drunk," her brother said aggressively. "Very smart. What if the police turn up again? Have you thought of that? Have you thought that it's actually *likely* the police will come back?"

"How did you get in?" Hermine slurred.

"The door was open. Come on."

He grabbed her healthy left hand and escorted her into the living room. She accompanied him with reluctance.

"I've spoken to the police," she said. "For hours on end. They were ever so nice. Sympathetic. Really very sympathetic."

Carl-Christian installed her in an Italian designer chair, coffee-brown and uncomfortable. She made an effort to stand up, but her brother held her down, bending over her as he leaned on the brushed-metal armrests. Their faces were only a few inches apart. Her breath was rank from vomit and strong liquor, but he did not flinch.

"Hermine," he said, his voice quavering slightly. "We're in *deep shit.* Do you understand that? We're in terrible, terrible trouble."

Once again she tried to extricate herself. He grabbed her bandaged hand and squeezed tight.

"Ouch," she yelled. "Let go!"

"Then you have to listen to me. Do you promise? Promise to sit still?"

She nodded almost imperceptibly. He let her go and sank to his knees.

"Were you interviewed?" he asked.

Hermine pulled expressive grimaces of pain.

"*Were you interviewed?*"

"What do you mean?" she whined. "I've talked to them. They came here. Last night. With a clergyman—the whole caboodle. Journalists. Outside, though. Crowds of journalists. In the end, I had to disconnect the doorbell. And the phone. But why are you so worked up about that? Mother and Father are dead, and I think you should . . . I . . ."

Now she was genuinely sobbing. Fat tears mixed with makeup and bloodstains to form pale-pink streaks on her face.

"I don't understand anything," she slurred as she wiped snot with her sleeve. "I understand absolutely none of it. Mother and Father and . . . *Preben!*"

Her sobs got the better of her. She was shaking. Blood soaked through the improvised bandage, and she held her hand out helplessly. Her brother put his arms around her and hugged her hard. For some considerable time.

"Hermine," he finally said into her ear. "This is really hellish. Dreadful. But we *must . . .*"

His voice broke into a falsetto, and he swallowed loudly to regain control. Stiffly, he rose to his feet and sat down opposite her on the sofa, resting his arms on his knees and struggling to maintain eye contact, despite her inebriated state.

"We must discuss this," he said, battling to keep calm. "Were you interviewed by the police? Or did they just come here to tell you about the dea . . . about what had happened?"

"I don't really know. They were actually very sweet. Truly. Very . . . empathetic. They didn't stay very long, though. Then they asked me if I wanted to have someone stay with me. If you . . . They said they had talked to you, and asked if I wanted you to come. Or anyone else. If anyone else should come."

"Did they ask you anything in connection with what had happened?"

"I don't know what you mean."

"Okay. We'll keep it very simple. Did they ask you about anything other than whether you wanted to have somebody here?"

"I don't remember! *I don't remember, Carl-Christian!*"

Her brother held his face in his hands and rocked slowly from side to side.

"Good God," he said in muffled tones. "Is it possible? Is it possible!"

He stood up abruptly and snatched the jacket he had slung on the sofa.

"Don't drink," he said. "Cut out the drinking, okay? I'll be back in a couple of hours. Make sure you've sobered up a bit by then."

"I need to go to the emergency room," Hermine complained; her hand had begun to drip again.

"You can't," her brother said firmly. "You can't see a doctor in your condition. Your parents and your brother were murdered last night, and you're wasted. It just doesn't look good."

"'It just doesn't look good,'" she mimicked. "That's the creed in this family. It doesn't look good! Damn it, I need stitches!"

"You stay here. I'll come back."

He stomped toward the front door, and she tottered after him.

"It doesn't look good," she said again in a distorted voice. "This family isn't concerned about anything except what looks good! I'm sick and tired of it all."

"That's all very well for you, then," Carl-Christian said, carefully knotting his scarf. "There's hardly any of it left. Of the family, I mean."

"*Great*," she screamed, so loud that her brother was startled; this was not Hermine, that pleasant, biddable sister of his whom nobody took very seriously. "I *hated* them anyway. I *hated* Father. And Mother, who always simply groveled and smoothed things over and pretended that nothing was wrong. This whole family is a pretty shell around a reality so horrible it would never tolerate the light of day! I'm so . . ."

She was completely overwhelmed by floods of tears. Carl-Christian tried to put his arm, stiff and awkward, around her shoulder.

"It's all too late now anyway."

Forcing herself to breathe more quietly, she straightened her back. They exchanged a long look that neither wanted to be the first to relinquish. Even Hermine, her brain befuddled by pills from a hiding place her brother knew nothing about, realized in a devastating moment that she loved her brother the way her brother loved her—the way it was at all possible for members of the Stahlberg family to bother about one another—but nevertheless, despite this glimmer of something warm and true between them, they were both aware with sudden certainty that they did not trust each other.

They never had, and she closed the door behind him.


Knut Sidensvans's apartment was located right beside Carl Berners plass. Low brick apartment blocks hacked into the greenery of Ola Narr Park, where young children toddled around in snowsuits, pulling their sleds. Their mothers huddled in little groups, with one or two fathers loitering on their own, chain-smoking to keep warm. It was dinnertime. None of the children wanted to go home. A little boy was screaming at the top of his lungs as his mother tried to comfort him. Hanne Wilhelmsen took a deep breath. This was air she recognized: the cold mixed with boiled vegetables, tandoori, and emissions from heavy vehicle traffic on Finnmarksgata. The number 20 bus rolled down toward the Tøyen Center.

"It was lovely to walk," Silje Sørensen said, slightly surprised. "Good suggestion. It's really quite nice here. Even with all the traffic."

"Yes," Hanne said. "It is nice here."

She neglected to turn her face to Lille Tøyen and yet another brick apartment block, where she had once resided in another life, another time.

The fourth murder victim's apartment was situated on the first floor, facing east. The locksmith was sitting on the top stair, looking extremely bored.

"At last," he said grouchily, giving the papers that Hanne held out no more than a cursory glance.

It took him four minutes to open the door.

"The cylinder is still okay," he said. "Will I change it anyway, so that you can have a new key?"

"Wait a minute," Hanne said, stepping inside the hallway.

She found what she was looking for in a bright-red key cupboard and tried the key in the front door.

"Bingo," she said. "We'll use this one instead. Thanks. Bye."

There were no furnishings in the hallway other than the key cupboard and a row of pegs, where a raincoat, a windbreaker, and a knock-off Burberry scarf were hanging.

The living room, on the other hand, was completely disorganized. The room might be around 15 by 20 feet and had three south-facing windows. A huge cork board was suspended between two of them. The other walls were covered in overfilled bookshelves from floor to ceiling. In addition, stacks of newspapers and periodicals, books and magazines were spread out over the floor. On closer inspection, there did appear to be some sort of system in it all. The magazines were arranged in order by date, and when Hanne devoted some time to one of the piles in a corner, she realized there was also some kind of thematic connection among it all.

"Wide-ranging interests," Silje said, holding up a highbrow literary periodical with one hand and something that looked like a textbook on low voltage with the other.

"Mmm," Hanne said absentmindedly as she studied the work area below the window.

A seventeen-inch flat screen towered beside a scanner, two enormous printers, and several stacks of blank sheets of paper. In addition, piles of various documents and something that might be special printouts were strewn across the extensive desk. The cork board between the windows was completely cluttered with notes, newspaper cuttings, memos, and the occasional photograph. At first glance, none of this sparked Hanne's interest. She skimmed an article about the salmon parasite *Gyrodactylus* and a list of email addresses.

"What did they actually say?" Hanne asked. "At the publishing house, I mean."

"That he used to be some sort of textbook consultant. For electricity and electronics. At the high school level, that is, not college. In recent years, they had used him for other things as well, as a matter of fact. At present he was engaged on three different assignments. A few articles. One of them was to be included in a larger work about the history of the police force, by the way."

"History of the police?"

"Yes. I didn't get many details. Should I check that out more closely?"

Hanne was leafing carefully through a book about the outlaw Gjest Baardsen. Old and worn, it was diligently marked with stickies protruding like loose yellow tongues from the pages.

"Sidensvans must really have deserved to be called a nerd," she said, laying aside the book. "Despite his age. This computer system is state-of-the-art as far as I can make out. Impressive that he's taught himself that kind of thing. But he has obviously . . ."

Her gaze swept over the bookshelves and tall towers of knowledge that dominated the floor space.

". . . still a preference for the written word. On paper, so to speak."

Hanne, almost shyly, tugged her hair down over her face.

"When I was little, I used to think that reference books smelled so lovely. We had loads of that sort of thing at home. There was something called *The Family Book*. A strange sort of collection of articles, in several tomes, about all kinds of peculiar things. I loved to browse through it. Mostly because of everything it contained, but maybe just as much because the books felt so good. On my fingers. In my hands. And they smelled—they had a scent, in fact. I liked that. Liked it a lot."

Silje stood stock-still. She didn't notice that her mouth was half open. A certain wariness characterized the situation, as if she was standing in a forest clearing and had caught sight of a timid bird.

"I sometimes think about that," Hanne said into thin air. "That the only thing I ever brought from my childhood was that affinity for thick, oversized books. Nefis laughs at me, actually. I only read huge books. They smell the best. Do you know . . . ?"

She took a deep breath and her lips formed a faint smile.

"It smells like a library in here."

"I'm so sorry about your father, Hanne. I should have mentioned it before, but you're so . . . I couldn't seem to find an opportunity."

"How did you know about it?"

Hanne's voice was crisp and sharp again.

"Billy T. told me. My condolences."

Hanne pulled out her wallet and her deft fingers drew out a newspaper clipping, folded in half. She handed it to Silje.

"Here," she said curtly, as if issuing a command. "Read this."

It was a death announcement: "Our beloved William Wilhelmsen" had passed away, following a lengthy illness. The cross was decorated with the letters R.I.P.

"Rest in peace," Silje said, taken aback. "Are you Catholic, Hanne?"

"Hah! My mother and father converted when I was about fifteen. For the sake of appearances. Neither of them was particularly religious; they were far too snobbish for that. They considered themselves thoroughly intellectual, even though I protested vehemently about such narrow-minded people having the right to call themselves any such thing. It was just far more stylish, you see, to embrace Catholicism rather than steadfast Lutheranism. My mother liked all the finery. All the beautiful buildings. The liturgy. They went to Rome twice a year. Stayed in fancy hotels and went to midnight mass, extremely tipsy after all the good wine they had had. I suspect my mother was quite simply turned on by all the costumes. By the Pope and the red of the cardinals, if you understand what I mean. Father just wanted to be special. He always wanted that. To be special within a dreadfully restricted frame."

She screwed up her eyes and demonstrated a quarter inch of space between her finger and thumb.

"Catholicism was simply something they used to adorn themselves. To hell with that. Read on."

> Now you walk in bliss with the Lord
> And have found eternal rest.
> You have overcome the trials of life
> With prayer's power and devotion's sword . . .

"Spare me," Hanne said quickly. "That's my sister's work. She actually believes she can write. Good Lord."

Her shoulder brushed against Silje's as she leaned forward to point.

"Can you find me there?" she asked rhetorically. "Do you see my name anywhere?"

The list of the bereaved left behind by William Wilhelmsen, Ph.D., was extensive: a wife, son and daughter, daughter-in-law, and grandchildren. Three sisters and two brothers-in-law had been given space, as well as nieces and nephews. Even someone called "Gaute Nesby, devoted friend" was listed among the grieving relatives. The overly sentimental verse and endless list of family and friends seemed pompous. There was something repellently immodest about the text, about the entire format of the announcement.

"You're not mentioned," Silje said softly, without lifting her eyes from the newspaper clipping.

"Not good enough," Hanne said. "I never have been. Do you know . . ."

She gave a forced laugh.

"I sat down and wrote my own special announcement. Something along these lines: 'My father, William Wilhelmsen, who disowned me, finally died after forty-two years of shitty behavior toward his youngest daughter. Please send any flowers to the funeral home, preferably horrible blue carnations. As many as possible.' I had put a stamp on the envelope. Fortunately Nefis stopped me from sending it."

"They wouldn't have printed anything like that anyway!"

"No. But I would have made a fool of myself. So I gave up. Instead I walk around with this."

She returned the announcement to her wallet.

"It's a sort of membership card in reverse," she said. "Proof that the family doesn't want me. I don't want them either."

Her smile never reached her eyes. She patted her pocket lightly and looked around, with a slight air of surprise, as if she didn't quite know why she had ended up talking about her father's death.

"There's something here," she said, carefully starting to pick up one of the many folders on the work table. "It's exactly as if . . ."

There was something. Her movement stiffened.

"Look around," she said, as she replaced the folder again.

"I've done that several times," Silje said. "What should I look for?"

"Sidensvans clearly had a system to his belongings," Hanne said, sotto voce, as if she did not want to disturb her own reasoning. "One pile there by the door is only magazines and periodicals. Over there you'll find medical literature. And there . . ."

A nerve was noticeable at an angle to the bridge of her nose.

"But even though it's all arranged in some kind of order, the overall effect created—this whole room—gives an impression of disorder. Of chaos. Nothing is tidily stacked one on top of the other; there's no symmetry to it all. No neat edges, in a manner of speaking. Agreed?"

"Yes, I suppose—"

Silje tried to look around with a fresh pair of eyes.

"But here," Hanne said, holding her palm peremptorily over the work desk. "Here the documents are placed edge to edge, parallel and linear. Striking."

Silje did not answer. Instead she approached more closely. Now, standing shoulder-to-shoulder with Hanne, she nodded gently.

"You're right, of course, but he may have . . . It's possible he's persnickety about everything he's currently working on, but that it's impossible to maintain that kind of order with everything—sort of thing? So that other things become . . . a bit messy?"

"Exactly," Hanne said tartly. "You can do better than that, Silje. There's a far more obvious explanation: these documents have been moved. And carefully put back again."

"Moved? It's less than twenty-four hours since he was here, Hanne. Of course something's been moved. By Knut Sidensvans himself."

Silje surreptitiously scrutinized Hanne. The Chief Inspector was markedly older now. Her dark hair had taken on a gray sheen at the temples, something to which Hanne had partly resigned herself. It did not suit her, and she really ought to have done something about it. The wrinkle from her nose to the corner of her mouth was deeply etched, despite the recent rounding out of her body—a middle-aged spread that made her pants somewhat too tight to actually sit well. When Hanne suddenly turned to face her, Silje noticed that the only unchanged aspect was her eyes. Deep blue, unusually large, and with a distinct black ring around each iris.

"I'm wondering about the keys," Hanne said.

"Yes, what was that?" Silje said expectantly.

"Sidensvans's body was found with his coat on. He didn't have a wallet. No keys either."

"No keys?"

"I read the report before we came here. No wallet. No keys. Damned odd."

"Not really. He might have put them—"

"What have you got with you at the moment, Silje?"

"With me?"

"Yes. No handbag. Just like men. What do you have in your pockets?"

A jangling of coins was heard as Silje took a look.

"Loose change. Wallet. Cell phone. A small flashlight. And . . . keys. And this here. Do you want some?"

She offered Hanne some chewing gum.

"You see," Hanne said, without taking any. "We always walk about with our keys on our person. Where are the ones belonging to Sidensvans?"

She did not wait for an answer but asked for Silje's flashlight. After examining the documents, books, and loose papers for a few more minutes, she shook her head slowly.

"You're right, of course," she said. "It's impossible to say anything for sure. All the same . . ."

She stiffened, just as she was about to return the flashlight.

"But there is something here," she said abruptly and firmly. "At least it might be something. I'll request a thorough search of the entire place. Prints. Biological traces. Everything."

"We have limited resources, Hanne. Isn't it more important for us to concentrate on the crime scene? And the Stahlberg family?"

"That's exactly what we're going to do," Hanne said, buttoning her jacket before nodding in the direction of the front door. "We're going to expend endless time and personnel on the members of the Stahlberg family. But we need to spend some time on this place as well. There were four victims. Not three."

Locking up carefully, she hooked the key on her own key ring before a sudden idea struck her.

"Would you like to come home with me, Silje? Have some dinner?"

"Yes! I'd love that. I . . . oh, no. I have to go home. Tom's going to a Christmas dinner this evening, and we don't have a babysitter for Simen."

"That's a shame," Hanne said lightly. "You're missing out on something special. Mary's become a real whiz in the kitchen. Another time, maybe."

"Yes, definitely! I'd honestly love to come, but you know how it is with young children, and . . . it's no longer easy to follow your impulses."

A taxi stopped at Silje's signal. She sat inside and waved to Hanne through the rear window, until the vehicle was swallowed up in the afternoon rush. Hanne was left behind, blushing ferociously.

It was the psychologist's fault. And Nefis's. You have to be more direct, Hanne, they nagged at her. Tell other people what you want; that was what they continually dinned into her. It's not dangerous. They'll be pleased. Do it, Hanne.

Now she had tried. She would have liked to eat Mary's Friday meatballs and maybe even drink a pilsner or three with Silje. Nefis would have been delighted about the unexpected guest. Mary would have cursed because Hanne had not phoned first, but would nevertheless set an extra place with the finest porcelain, and maybe even produce some Turkish beer from the refrigerator.

Hanne had done as the psychologist and Nefis had suggested.

The red flush lingered on her cheeks for a long time.


The deceased Karl-Oskar Wetterland had been an old-school advocate. On his death, he owned his spacious apartment in Oslo, his summer cottage that was not winterized in the Hvaler islands, a 1992 Volvo, and a pretty little stock portfolio. It had been conservatively accumulated and carefully administered. Together with the three high-interest accounts declared in the envelope that he had left behind, sealed and with his son's name in elegant handwriting on the outside, they would ensure that his widow would live prosperously during her remaining years.

His son found comfort in that.

His father had taken good care of his family while he lived, and his orderly estate showed how well prepared he had been for his death. Terje Wetterland, the advocate's only child, was not left a single krone. This made him smile as he walked around his father's office, touching the occasional object. Of course his mother should be the sole beneficiary. Terje was forty-seven and well established in France, with a wife, children, and an income far in excess of what his father had ever earned from his small law practice. His mother should be comfortable in her old age. They had agreed about that, he and his father. She should have the opportunity to spend money on help in the house. She should be able to spend long summers in Provence with her grandchildren without having to be subsidized. At least not overtly. They had discussed it one evening about six months ago. Father and son had sat on a rocky outcrop enjoying drinks on Midsummer Eve. The children shrieked from the beach and the night was never-ending. They agreed there and then how everything should be arranged. And that was how it would be.

Terje Wetterland ran his fingers tenderly over a silver-framed photograph of himself and his father, half naked and soaking wet; it was late summer and they were both dark brown. They sat on the edge of a jetty, him a happy kid of four or five with his father's arm around his waist.

He wiped dust from the glass with his shirt sleeve before stuffing the picture into the document folder. There was nothing else here that he coveted. Although his father still had one or two clients, it was impossible to make any arrangements about them at present. He would ask his mother who they were. There could not be many since his father had really wound up his practice three years ago. Only habit and a few grouchy old clients made him step inside his office a couple of times a week. His son would call the clients from France and straighten matters out. If anything were urgent, they would probably call his mother.

He glanced superficially at some documents lying on the desk before

stowing everything into the safe and locking it. Then he switched off
the light, locked his father's office, and returned home to his mother.

A heavy layer of frost covered the ski trails. The forest was silent. The
old man tried to thrust his skis into a snowdrift, but the snow was too
hard and compacted. He put them aside instead, just beyond the track.
Not that anyone would steal them. After all, it was almost midnight.
People were staying indoors. In any case, nobody spent a night just
before Christmas trudging over Nordmarka in the freezing cold. He
pulled a crooked grin at the thought. All the same, it was best to set
the skis under a spruce tree, a few yards beyond the path, well hidden.
You never knew.

These nocturnal trips of his had become a habit. Thirty years ago,
he had returned to the small holding where he had stayed during his
childhood. Now he lived on the landowner's goodwill and odd jobs in
the forest. A walk before turning in for the night ensured a good night's
sleep. In the summer months, he plodded on foot in the evening light
that was reflected in the many lakes dotting the landscape. As soon as
snow took hold in late autumn, he set off on tarred wooden skis. He
knew his forest and the tracks that intersected it.

The cold pinched his cheeks and made his eyes water. It felt reassuring. He took a few tentative steps along a narrow path leading down to
a lake where he often swam in warm weather. Here and there he
tramped his way through, almost losing his balance a couple of times.
After barely 50 yards, he stood beside a rocky ridge jutting beautifully
into the ice-covered lake. All he could hear was the trickling sound of
a little stream. Gingerly, trying not to slip on the slick bare rock, he
stepped over the point to drink some of the cold water. He crouched
down and, using his fist as a cup, plunged it into the water. The ice glittered in the blue moonlight. It would take some time for the lake to
freeze solid; the cold had only really set in over the past few days.

He grew aware of a movement on the opposite side of the water. He
stopped in his tracks, believing it to be an animal and loath to frighten
it off. His hand, halfway to his mouth and covered in water, trembled
slightly from cold and tension. Very slowly he stood up to his full
height, with the dense spruce forest behind him. His clothing was

dark, and he merged completely into the background. The light breeze blew toward him. An animal would scarcely pick up his scent if he did not move.

It was not an animal, though. He saw that now. He stood up straight and caught sight of a man, or at least a person, standing not on the edge but a short distance across the surface of the ice. The being crouched down. Some action was undertaken.

He strained to listen. His hearing was not quite what it had been, and he could make out only his own pulse and a rhythmic rippling of the water in the stream. The person over there finally moved across to the edge of the forest, silently, sometimes staggering, as if creeping back in his own footprints. Soon he had disappeared in an easterly direction.

The old man hesitated, unable to understand why he had not called out. He had felt uneasy, he was taken aback to admit, and had drawn back into the darkness to avoid being seen, without really being able to explain why. Once again he strained his hearing, inclining his head and placing his ice-cold, bare hand behind one ear.

All was silent.

He was alert now. Slightly afraid but also wanting to find out what had happened, what the shadow had been doing here, at a lake in Nordmarka on a December night. An old curiosity was awakened, a long-suppressed feeling, forgotten and packed away, since it was something that had only ever led him into trouble.

It would take just a few minutes to cross the ice, maybe half an hour to walk around it. He cast his mind back to the mild weather that had come and gone since October and set off over the ground.

He gasped for breath when he reached the spot, asthma squeezing his windpipe. Carefully he followed the other person's footprints. They were almost black outlines on the blue-white snowy ground. Since the ice had supported the weight of the other person, it would probably hold him too. Anyway, he did not have to walk out far.

A hole.

Not large, but wide enough to draw up fish. Someone had been ice fishing, in the middle of the night, in the freezing cold.

He chuckled softly, and shook his head at the stupidity of city folk.

## SATURDAY, DECEMBER 21

Hanne Wilhelmsen lay staring at the ceiling. The heat in the room thickened the air with depleted night, and she licked her lips to moisten her dry mouth. Fortunately she had kicked off her quilt during the night. All the same, her skin was coated with sticky perspiration. Stiffly, she sat up in bed and punched her pillow before lying down again.

"You really might have told me about the party on Christmas Eve," she said softly.

Yawning, Nefis turned to face her.

"My dear Hanna, if I'd told you about this party, it would never have come to pass! You would have said no, no, no; and then we'd have been left on our own. You and me and Mary."

"That's the way I would have liked it, though."

Nefis groaned, smacking herself on the forehead. Her black hair was spread out in sweaty clumps, and she smiled broadly.

"Sweetheart. You are odd. Above all, you want it to be just the three of us all the time. All the time! I want to have a real Christmas! When I've been stuck in a wintry country with all these joyful traditions for Christmas Eve, then I want all of it! Lots of decorations and lights, and very, very much people around the table."

"'Much,'" Hanne said, wanting to get up. "It should really be 'many' when you're talking about people. And you could have asked. Anyway, I didn't know that you felt *stuck.*"

"Hanna, honestly."

Nefis tried to grab her, but Hanne was too quick as she set off for the bathroom.

She let the water cascade down her back while she leaned her forehead on the tiled wall. She gradually reduced the temperature of the water. Colder. She felt her skin contract and raised her head.

Nefis was right. Nefis was always right. The odd family in Kruses gate would have lived like hermits if Hanne had had her way.

The thought induced a smile.

"Hanna, you're smiling!"

Nefis sat down on the mahogany toilet seat cover with its inlaid Inca-style pattern: the elaborate wood and metal felt cold and ticklish on her naked thighs.

Hanne struggled to force the smile away.

"Aha, you're laughing," Nefis called out, clapping her hands. "You're happy about this party!"

"No, I'm not," Hanne said, hiding her face in the shower spray.

She *was* looking forward to it. She was not even annoyed that the decision had been taken over her head, the way all decisions of any import were taken by Nefis, and Nefis alone. Nefis who had bought the tickets to the Seychelles and informed her two days in advance; time off work had already been arranged. Nefis who had returned home to the apartment in Lille Tøyen with the prospectus for a sumptuous newly built apartment in Frogner; the purchase had already been made. Nefis organized everything: the moving company and the address change, the moving-in party and partnership agreement, the interior decorating and shopping. Nefis treated Hanne the way a loving wife treats a bull-headed old husband. And Hanne, grudgingly, liked it. She protested loud and often, but never for long.

Nefis came up with solutions that Hanne found it possible to live with. She took Hanne into consideration, but never to such a degree that she had to compromise on her own wishes and needs. The apartment in Kruses gate appeared more like a strange system of communal living rather than a real family—people who seemed to have nothing in common, scraped together hastily and at random. That was how it must look to others, those who didn't know better, who did not know them and therefore had no idea that Nefis and Hanne were married and that Nefis wanted to have children. Hanne knew none of the neighbors, and there were three names on their door. Not two—that dangerous two that made people draw conclusions about who lived there and what they were up to.

Sometimes Hanne felt happy. Not often, but now and again, when reality touched her in brief flashes: Mary padding in her slippers through the dark apartment at night, a glance from Nefis when she thought Hanne would not notice, a hand on her back in sleep. At such moments Hanne felt completely secure. Security was her happiness, and she had never truly known happiness before Nefis arrived on the scene.

Hanne stepped out of the shower.

"Who's actually coming?"

"Everyone! Karen and Håkon, the children, Billy T., Tone-Marit and—"

"Not *all* his children," Hanne said. "*Please!* It will be pure hell."

"No. They're with their mothers this Christmas. Only Jenny will come with them."

"Who else?"

Hanne dried her hair, fearing the worst.

"Well . . ."

Nefis caressed the small of Hanne's naked back.

"Two of Mary's old friends. Just—"

"No!"

Snatching the towel from her head, Hanne flung it on the floor.

"Do you remember how that went last year?"

"But it'll be better this year! They've promised not to bring anything with them and—"

Hanne angrily interrupted her again, slapping the palm of her hand against the wall of the shower.

"Nefis, listen. You can never rely on a drug addict. They can swear as long and as loud as they like, but they will sneak something past you. Besides, it would probably be equal to murder to deny them. They quite simply can't bear twenty-four hours without a fix. It's out of the question, Nefis."

She trotted resolutely through to the bedroom and quickly threw on the clothes she had worn the previous day.

"Anyway, they probably have AIDS. It's far from certain that Håkon and Karen will be particularly happy about their children eating Christmas dinner in the company of sore-infested, ravenous whores with AIDS."

Nefis's hand was only inches from Hanne's cheek when it came to a sudden halt. Hanne stroked her untouched cheek. They stood there like that, Nefis with her hand raised and Hanne drawing back ever so slightly.

"That's a terrible thing to say, Hanna. Terrible. We don't say that sort of thing in our family."

"We don't slap one another in our family either!"

"I didn't slap you," Nefis said, turning on her heel. "But God knows I wanted to."

Hanne Wilhelmsen was in a foul mood when, eleven minutes late, she entered the large conference room where the Superintendent had assembled sixteen investigators, two police prosecutors, and a couple of clerical staff around the table. Hanne gave a brief nod to the Deputy Chief of Police, who sent a wide smile in her direction. She glibly disregarded Silje Sørensen, Erik Henriksen, and Billy T. before taking a seat at the far end of the table, with a trainee officer on either side. Throughout the Superintendent's report, she stared at the table, hiding her eyes behind her heavy bangs. She seemed not to be following what was said at all. Unease spread around her: the others withdrew, as if feeling a physical aversion to her presence.

"There can be no doubt that the ongoing conflict among the family members was brutal enough," Billy T. said, when the meeting was opened for discussion. "There's a great deal of fairly complex case material, but the main quarrel concerned to what degree Hermann Stahlberg had committed himself to leaving the shipping company to Carl-Christian. After Preben's return home, it was increasingly clear that the elder son had a greater capacity for business activities than his brother. The company was functioning better and expanding, including signing contracts for two new small cruise ships that will be completed in a year and a half. A year ago, all the paperwork was drawn up. The shipping company, an unlisted limited company, wholly owned by Hermann and Turid Stahlberg, was to be signed over to Preben.

Admittedly, both Carl-Christian and Hermine were to be provided for
with a smaller block of shares each, but big brother would retain all
the power. When I say that all the paperwork was ready, it's important
to emphasize that it was never signed. Carl-Christian began a suit
against his father and has produced what he claims to be documentation showing that Hermann had promised, with binding effect, to pass
the shipping company to him."

Billy T. wriggled his way up between the wall and the row of chair
backs to an overhead projector and fumbled with the light switch.
Then he placed a transparency upside down on the glass plate. Silje
Sørensen gave him some assistance, and finally they could all see a
chart of the Stahlberg dynasty.

"I think," Billy T. began, "that it may be important for us all to have
some understanding of how this family is composed. So, we have the
mother and father here."

He circled the older generation with a marker pen.

"Tax assessment figures for last year, in themselves, are modest.
Over 4 million in income and something over 25 million in capital.
But of course we all know . . ."

Grinning, he cast a glance at Silje, who twisted her enormous diamond ring around to her palm, a habit she had adopted every time
money became a topic of conversation.

". . . that sums such as these lie. They are forced down as far as possible."

"But anyway, we're not talking about a huge fortune," the
Superintendent commented.

"Well, I think 25 million is a hell of a lot of money," Billy T. said. "But
fair enough. We're not talking about the Rockefellers here."

Again, he circled a name on the transparency.

"Preben Stahlberg, then, is the oldest of three children. His wife—
Jennifer Calvin Stahlberg—is Australian. She's a stay-at-home house-
wife, educated as a dietitian, and doesn't speak Norwegian. They have
three young children. I don't think these surviving relatives have any
major significance for our inquiries. But things get more exciting
here . . ."

He smacked the pen against the younger son's name.

"Carl-Christian Stahlberg. Born in 1967. So he was only in his early teens when his brother ran off to sea. He claims he had definite plans to become a vet, but that he chose business college in order to comply with his father's wishes. One of the letters from father to son at that time, by the way, has been offered to the court as proof to underpin Carl-Christian's assertion that the shipping company was promised to him long ago."

"But . . ."

Erik Henriksen squinted skeptically at the light from the overhead projector.

"Can you really claim rights to something simply because your dad has promised it? Is an ordinary promise actually legally binding?"

"It can be," said Annmari Skar, the Police Prosecutor. "In certain circumstances, a promise can be just as binding as a mutual agreement."

"In any case," Billy T. continued, "he got married five years ago to a strange woman. At that time she was called May Anita Olsen. When she married CC, she wasn't content to change only her surname, but replaced all of it, in fact. Now her name is Mabelle Stahlberg."

A couple of the youngest men grinned boldly as Billy T. took a moment to change the transparency, revealing a shapely blonde with long hair and lips obviously not bestowed at birth. They bulged unnaturally above a sensual chin. Her nose had probably not escaped the surgeon's knife either: it was ultranarrow and straight as a ruler. Hanne Wilhelmsen gave a loud snort, the first sound she had made during the meeting. Billy T. waved his hand apologetically and changed the transparency.

"Doesn't she run a fashion magazine?" Silje asked before he resumed.

"That's right. *F&F. Fashion and Feelings.* A lot of the former, hardly any of the latter. A glossy rag. It isn't doing particularly well, of course— few of that sort of magazine do—but she actually manages okay. No longer losing money, at least. And, of course, Carl-Christian has money. Or put it this way, that was what they *believed*, CC and Mabelle. That they were going to come into money . . ."

He left the last sentence hanging in the air.

"Anyway," he continued after a few seconds' silence, "this Mabelle has something of a checkered past. Nothing criminal, apart from something I'll come back to. What's important in this connection, however, is that she has been despised and opposed by her in-laws from day one. They couldn't stand the woman. She was not good enough for Carl-Christian, and far from good enough for the stodgy drawing rooms of Eckersbergs gate. They got married in Las Vegas, in total secrecy, far from Daddy's fierce protests. Hermann actually made some attempts to have the marriage annulled. That foundered fairly quickly, of course, for he certainly wasn't in a position to do anything of the kind. But it does tell us something. About the atmosphere, I mean. Within the family."

"You said there was something criminal as well," Erik reminded him.

"Yes . . ."

Billy T. scratched his crotch in distraction.

"Six months ago Hermann reported Mabelle for taking a car without consent. She was stopped by the police, and all that stuff. Driving around in an Audi A8 that was actually some sort of company car belonging to the shipping firm, but was normally used by Carl-Christian and Mabelle. Hermann had begun to implement cutbacks and demanded that the vehicle should be handed back. When nothing happened, he reported the car stolen, totally without any further explanation to the police. It led to a fucking Wild West show. The police patrol that spotted the car was infuriated when Mabelle refused to stop, and the trip ended in a ditch in Grefsen. The woman said she had been scared and thought she was going to be robbed. She was handcuffed and left in a holding cell here for six hours until at last CC managed to get things sorted out. The old man stood his ground and wanted to have his daughter-in-law charged, but the case was dropped for lack of evidence. It was quite simply too weird. After all, it *was* her car. For all intents and purposes, I mean."

"Strange family."

The Superintendent yawned and made an effort to shake himself awake.

"Anything more on that, Billy T.?"

"Nothing apart from there being quite an extended family. Aunts and uncles and lots of cousins all over the place. And then there's Hermine, of course. The little sister."

A question mark appeared against Hermine's name on the overhead transparency, tucked away in an insignificant corner of the chart.

"We know a lot less about her. At least for the present. She seems almost . . . stupid. No education. No real job, despite being in apparent good health. She's done a number of odd jobs for her sister-in-law at *F&F*, and from her appearance she would fit in well there. Also, she has done some odds and ends for her father, and for an uncle whom she has a lot to do with. He's an art dealer, I think. The strange thing is that she . . ."

All the focus in the room was directed at Billy T.

"She got a fucking enormous amount of money from her father for her twentieth birthday," he said at length, running his hand over his head, where the short tufts of hair had clearly turned gray. "Ten million plus-*plus*. An apartment, car, and such. This demonstrates, of course, that the family fortune is considerably greater than the taxman gets to know about, but in itself that isn't of any consequence now. What is striking is that the stingy Hermann Stahlberg was so generous. Neither of the boys has received anything like it, from what we know. Even odder is that Hermine seems to be on good terms with everyone in the family. The only one."

"Could the money have been remuneration for precisely that?" Erik speculated. "Nothing less than a reward for being kind and pleasant?"

"Don't know."

"It might just as easily have been a gift to make amends for a guilty conscience," Hanne said slowly. "Even though it would have to be an *extremely* guilty conscience."

It seemed as if the whole room turned to face her, as if the building noticeably flipped over and the center of gravity shifted from the authoritarian end of the table, where Billy T. stood beside the Superintendent and Deputy Chief of Police. They all stared down at the newcomers and at Hanne Wilhelmsen.

"I suppose so," Billy T. said curtly.

"I don't really have any idea, of course," Hanne said, rubbing her neck. "I'm just trying to agree with you here! It's really peculiar that she should receive so much money, taking into consideration the circumstances. Everything about this Hermine character is odd."

"And that's why we'll bring her in for an interview as soon as the funeral is out of the way," the Superintendent said, glancing at the clock.

"I wouldn't have postponed it so long," Hanne murmured.

"Anything further?"

The Superintendent's voice grated as he scanned the room with an expression indicating that any information would have to be of major significance if anyone was going to keep him confined in this stuffy, overheated room for very much longer.

"The guns," Erik said, raising his right hand slightly. "Entirely provisional analysis results."

"So we're dealing with more than one?" Billy T. said.

"Two. Two types of ammunition. A 9mm Luger and a .357 Magnum: one pistol and one revolver. A total of eleven shots were fired with the pistol and five with the revolver. We don't yet have the full type descriptions of the weapons."

"Eleven shots with pistol ammo," Billy T. repeated. "There are quite a few pistols that hold as much as that in one magazine. The murderer wouldn't actually have had to reload."

"Or murderers," Deputy Police Chief Jens Puntvold said, scratching his chin; a rasping sound came from his unshaved skin. "Two weapons may well indicate two killers."

"Not necessarily," Hanne said.

She felt a rising irritation that Puntvold was even present. The Stahlberg case was complex and difficult enough to grasp as it was. In such cases, it was important to find the optimum equilibrium for efficiency: they needed sufficient numbers to ensure that all the work was done, but not so many that it prevented them all from having the opportunity to retain a certain overview. Admittedly Puntvold had made himself increasingly popular, both at police headquarters and with the general public, through his charm, visibility, and tremendous commitment on behalf of the police force, but he should have stayed away from this meeting. The same applied to several others, such as the police trainees and a couple of junior officers. Strictly speaking, they were double the necessary number in this confined room, and Hanne groaned in despair at the thought.

"It might also mean that the murderer is smart," she said, trying not to seem magisterial. "Or careful. That's a good point, about the reloading. With two weapons, it's not necessary."

"I anticipate the technical investigations will be completed as quickly as possible," the Superintendent said, getting to his feet. "I want all the results sent to me as they become available. As far as the tactical operation is concerned, it's obvious that Carl-Christian, his wife, and Hermine are the central focus."

"Especially with those lame alibis of theirs," Billy T. added. "They're so pathetic they could almost be true. Mabelle and Carl-Christian were at home together, with no one to confirm or deny their story. Hermine says she was asleep all evening. At home. With no confirmation either."

"Fine," the Superintendent said, obviously impatient now. "I expect more work to be done on the family members' movements, or lack of such, on the evening of the murder. I'd like to see you, Wilhelmsen, and Billy T. in my office in an hour. And you . . ."

He nodded at Police Prosecutor Annmari Skar.

"We'll have to discuss how to proceed with the interviews and possible arrests. So we'll say that's enough for the moment; we have to—"

"But what about Sidensvans?" Hanne said loudly. "Is he of no interest whatsoever?"

The Superintendent slowly resumed his seat.

"Of course not," he said in a feigned cajoling tone. "Not at all, Hanne Wilhelmsen. I'm simply trying to make slight improvements in efficiency here. Wasting time on meetings is not really my style."

"I'm absolutely in agreement," Hanne began, "that the family certainly seems to be of most interest. After all, it's Hermine and Carl-Christian who have something to gain by the rest of the gang being eliminated. All the same, I think there's something amiss when we just don't know why Knut Sidensvans was there. The Stahlbergs must have been waiting for him. At least it looks that way, since there were cakes and champagne laid out. There were four glasses and four plates set out. They were waiting for a fourth person. But what business did they have with Sidensvans? Shouldn't we discover precisely that, in any case?"

"My dear Chief Inspector," the Superintendent said morosely, "as far as I recall, *you*'re the one who always claims the solution to a murder mystery lies in the simple and straightforward. You're the one who always reminds us that where the motive for the incident is found, that is also where we'll find the perpetrator. And without jumping to any conclusions whatsoever, I would even now point out that the motives in this case are screaming out to us. It seems to me that this Sidensvans was no more than a chance visitor."

"That might well be. But shouldn't we know that for sure? Of course, I totally agree there's every reason to suspect one of those three . . ."

She pointed vaguely at the chart Billy T. had drawn of the family tree.

". . . of the murders. But surely there are not yet grounds for believing that all three of them were behind it? Of course we should find out which of them has the strongest motive. But wouldn't it also be extremely expedient to clarify whether any of the three has any connection to the fourth murder victim?"

The Superintendent bowed his head demonstratively before suddenly straightening up.

"Of course. You're quite right."

Rubbing his eyes, he forced a smile.

"We'll keep all possibilities open, as usual. Since you're the one with responsibility for the tactical investigation here, after all, then you can spend Monday and Tuesday on Sidensvans."

"That's the two days prior to Christmas!" Hanne protested. "Pretty hopeless days to get hold of people to talk to then."

"Two days," her superior officer said dismissively. "That's what you can have. Meantime, if you find anything relevant, then of course we'll follow it up."

A cacophony of scraping chair legs followed. Erik and Billy T. stood in the corridor outside waiting for Hanne, who was last to emerge from the windowless room, breathing heavily.

"It gets so damn stuffy in there," she said casually.

"What do you think about Sidensvans?" Erik asked, frankly curious.

"Don't entirely know," Hanne said, laying her hand on Billy T.'s arm. "You know, I'm incredibly impressed with how much you've uncovered in forty-eight hours. Excellent police work. Honestly, Billy T."

A fleeting smile passed over her face before she marched determinedly in the direction of her own office.

"That's a rare event," Erik said. "Praise from Her Majesty!"

"She was just being ironic," Billy T. said crossly.

"I think you're mistaken. Besides, I thought you were friends again. Aren't you?"

"Ask Hanne. With that woman, it's impossible to know."

When he disappeared in the same direction as the Chief Inspector, Erik was left standing there, watching him leave. It was as if Billy T. had crumpled. The six-foot-seven man had acquired a stoop and his backside had grown broader, heavier. His feet shuffled as he walked, and his sweater stretched unbecomingly over the small of his back.

*I need to get out of here*, Billy T. thought. *At the very least I must start exercising. I really must start to exercise systematically.*

Most of all, Hanne felt like crying.

For the past six months, everything had been so much better. The snazzy apartment in Kruses gate no longer seemed quite so foreign. The weekly appointment with the psychologist was not as degrading and frightening as before. As long as it was only Nefis who knew that Hanne had needed to bow her head and seek professional help, she actually found some kind of relief in the procedure. Hanne had grown dependent on these conversations and had not missed a single appointment in nine months. Even now, she felt terrified at the thought of anyone finding out. She still pulled her jacket across more snugly and wrapped her scarf around half her face as her eyes darted in every direction, before she rang the psychologist's doorbell, as if she were stepping inside a porno store. But she went. She turned up. And it helped.

Billy T. and Hanne had found their way back to something of what they had once shared. The feeling of kinship between them—the nameless trust that had vanished one night in sorrow and sex, while Hanne's former live-in partner was on her deathbed in the hospital and Hanne had sought comfort where that sort of thing could not be found—would never return. She knew that. Billy T. missed it. She saw that on him, in his glances and movements, in the awkward closeness when he, quite mistakenly, thought she would be receptive. She had to reject him then, freeze him out, close herself off. But it didn't happen often. They worked well together, and Hanne had finally begun to understand that she couldn't get along without him. At times, on rare occasions, when he managed to restrain himself from challenging the situation, in his eagerness to turn back the clock, she could feel the closeness between them, the intuitive understanding that she didn't find with anyone else, not even Nefis.

Everything was becoming so much better. Then her father had died.

She did not feel sorrow that he had passed away, even though Nefis insisted that she did. Hanne could not work out why she had reacted so strongly. A sense of loss, the psychologist called it, about what might have been. Anger at something that should have been different. Hanne did not agree. She struggled with an emotion she could not identify, but it did not resemble either anger or sorrow. All the same, it was crushing enough.

"Hi . . ."

Silje Sørensen stuck her head around the door. Hanne forced a smile and busied herself with some documents.

"I just thought—" Silje said, before she broke off. "Would this be an inconvenient time?"

"Not at all. Come in."

Hanne's smile was still stiff, and Silje hesitated.

"I can come back another time, you know."

"Sit down, won't you?"

"You see . . ."

Silje did not take a seat. Instead she placed a well-used, stained, burgundy-red leather wallet on the desk before Hanne.

"What's this?" the Chief Inspector asked.

"A wallet," Silje said, almost apologetically.

"I see that. But who's the owner?"

"Knut Sidensvans."

"I see. Where did it turn up?"

"At Lost Property. Someone had found it. In Thomas Heftyes gate. Not far from the crime scene, in other words. Half buried in the snow. With money in it, Hanne."

Again her voice took on that trace of apology. Even though it wasn't entirely clear to her what Hanne had in mind, with that talk about the missing keys and wallet, Silje more than suspected that any theory would now be almost totally torpedoed.

"With money in it," Hanne repeated. "Presumably he had dropped it, then."

"Probably."

"But you still haven't seen anything of his keys?"

"No."

Neither of them spoke. Snow was falling steadily outside the window. The whirling flakes took on a glimmer of blue as an emergency vehicle screeched its way up Åkebergveien. In the corridor, no footsteps could be heard, no din of shouting voices. No one was laughing out there. No detainees were proving difficult. It seemed as if the entire police headquarters had closed for the night.

"Okay," Hanne said at last. "So he had dropped his wallet. But we don't know if his keys were in the same pocket. Actually . . ."

She got to her feet and checked her own duffel bag, which hung on a peg behind the door.

"Wallet here," she said, patting her left thigh. "And keys here."

She pulled a bulky bunch of keys from her right pocket.

"So there's not too much in each," she explained. "Each has its own pocket."

"Where are you going with this, Hanne? Do you mean that the murderer might have taken the keys? Do you mean that the murders took place *because* of the keys? What use would anyone have for them? We've been there, Hanne. In Sidensvans's apartment. There was nothing there. Nothing of value. Apart from the computer system. No one kills for a computer system. Besides, it hadn't been stolen. We saw that for ourselves, didn't we?"

"But there could have been something *on* the computer," Hanne said, suddenly flashing a broad smile. "And there could have been something lying there, amid all that chaos, something that's been removed now. Enough of that, though. I'll think about it some more. Thanks for the information. You should really go home."

It was five past seven. Silje shrugged and followed her instructions. Hanne remained sitting there, doing little more than thinking, until Mary phoned in a fury and ordered her to come home.

She had lost control.

Hermine Stahlberg was used to stimulants. Even though her family frequently—and mostly behind closed doors—had turned up their noses at her slightly too liberal relationship with alcohol, nobody knew about her use of pills and stronger stuff. Hermine moved in two spheres. She was rich, beautiful, and spoiled. Feckless and yet greatly loved. At the same time, she inhabited another world, on the underside of her own reality. Sometimes in Oslo, but more often abroad. For several years, she had assumed control over her life, and a balance prevailed in her double existence.

Now that was gone.

The room spun, with her as its axis. She tried to lie down but missed the bed. Vomit welled up in her throat. She couldn't breathe. The vomit blocked her gullet. In a daze, she managed to turn over onto her side.

Her brother was towering over her. She thought he was the one who stood there. She couldn't be sure. It could just as easily have been Uncle Alfred.

"For Christ's sake," she slurred, grinning submissively.

She could still speak. She was not dead. Her brother's face was green and distorted. Maybe it was Uncle Alfred after all. It didn't matter. The figure hovered over her. The face changed color; it was yellow now, with red specks that floated out and flew to the ceiling, like bloody soap bubbles. Hermine laughed.

"Alfred," she groaned, yawning.

The man said something. Hermine focused on his mouth, which was moving in strange meaningless shapes, because the sound was missing. She heard nothing. She had gone deaf.

"Deaf," she said, and roared with laughter.

Carl-Christian Stahlberg lifted his sister onto the bed. He lay her on

her side and flexed her left leg to prevent her from rolling over. He
hesitated for a moment before pushing his finger into her mouth. Her
tongue seemed too big, but he managed to straighten it, and cleaned
her mouth of mucus and vomit. He ended up in floods of tears, almost
unable to explain his whereabouts, when he finally contacted the
emergency doctor. When the paramedics arrived, he had succeeded in
pulling himself together and had washed off the stench of his sister's
degeneracy.

He had even tightened the knot on his tie.

The old man in the forest felt indisposed. Since it was Saturday, he had
tried to relax with good coffee and a store-bought cake while he
watched TV. A great stillness had fallen over Nordmarka. He had ventured out for his evening stroll in the light snowfall. The smoldering
logs on the fire now cast a warm glow over the log cabin, and he felt
snug and cozy. Nevertheless, he was troubled.

It was all because of that ice fisherman.

He couldn't have been fishing. The snow around the hole in the ice
showed barely any sign of footprints, and there were no marks left by
any kind of seat. It looked as if the stranger had simply shown up,
bored a hole in the ice, and then left.

The old man had returned earlier that day. The prints were gone;
wind and snow had rendered the stranger's visit invisible. But the old
man had found the hole. He had cleared a small area where he thought
it should be, and the fine, refrozen rings in the ice had been easy to
locate.

He was surprised at his own curiosity. As it now bubbled to the surface again—that blasted tendency of his to stick his nose in other people's business—it dawned on him that this had something to do with
that murder down in the city.

Today he had gone to the village and bought all the newspapers.
The police said they were working on a number of clues. That told him
nothing. But of course he could read between the lines. He understood where it was heading. It was that man, the son of the family.

No weapon had been found, according to the police.

Perhaps he ought to report what he had seen.

On the other hand, that would cause a lot of fuss.

Finally he yawned and threw the coffee grounds on the fire. Having padded off to bed, accompanied by the smell of burned coffee and old bitter tobacco, he fell fast asleep.

# SUNDAY, DECEMBER 22

Mabelle Stahlberg usually spent an hour in the bath every morning. Only a few minutes had now passed since she had risen from bed, and she was already sitting fully dressed at the enormous round glass table in the center of the kitchen. Without makeup, her face looked transparent and her features indistinct.

"My goodness," Carl-Christian said, taking stock of her. "What has become of you?"

Her hand was shaking as she raised her coffee cup to her lips.

"When did *you* get home?"

"A couple of hours ago. I didn't want to wake you. Caught some sleep in the guest bedroom. She'll survive."

Mabelle did not react.

"Did you hear me?" he said, irritated. "She'll survive."

"Good for her. We *do* have other things to worry about, you know."

Carl-Christian sat down opposite her at the kitchen table, holding his face in his hands.

"She was a hairbreadth from destruction, Mabelle. If I hadn't called around, things would have gone badly."

His wife continued to sit expressionless with the cup at her mouth. Steam clung to her pale face. Only now did he see that her eyes were bloodshot and realized that she had not slept. Stretching across the table, he tried to catch hold of her hand.

"What's going to happen?" she whispered. "I'm so scared."

Now he grabbed her cup and put it down with a thump. Brown liquid sloshed over the table. He seized her chin and forced her to make eye contact. The gaze that met his was apathetic, and for a moment he wondered whether Mabelle too had taken something. Then she broke into a sudden joyless smile.

"I'm pleased that Hermine will pull through, CC. Honestly. It was a godsend that you went there in time."

A chill draft gusted through a half-open window, and he stood up to close it. The gray midwinter morning light had begun to creep into the room through the massive panes of east-facing glass, but it seemed not quite able to reach all the way inside. The gloom in the corners made him nervous, and he switched on all the lights.

"When are they coming?" she asked.

"I don't really know. I think they'll wait until after the funeral. After all, I expect we are important witnesses. Since we're the only surviving family members. Hermine and me. And you, too, in a way. Jennifer and the children are there as well, of course, but they . . . They don't exactly benefit from what has happened. The police will very likely give us a hard time. After the funeral."

"They'll have us under surveillance."

"Definitely. That's why I can't go there."

"You must."

"Not yet."

"You must!"

She shouted. Her arms gestured aimlessly, wildly. The coffee cup fell off the glass table and crashed to the floor. Mabelle burst into hysterical tears and refused to be quiet until Carl-Christian had clapped his hand over her mouth and pressed hard. He wrested her arms down to her sides by seizing her forcefully from behind.

"I'll let go once you calm down," he whispered in her ear. "Take it easy, sweetheart. Sh-sh-sh . . . Relax."

In the end, detecting that the convulsive spasms in her body had abated, he loosened his grip with extreme caution. Mabelle was still crying, but more hushed now. Eventually she turned to face him and let him put his arms around her. They sat like that for a long time, she with her face in the crook of her husband's neck.

"The most important thing now is that we both tell the same story," he said softly. "And that each of us knows what the other is saying."

"The most important thing now is that we don't talk at all," she said, with her mouth buried in his sweater.

"We must. It will only seem suspicious if we refuse to give an account of ourselves. But we must take some time over it, darling. We have to sit down and come to an agreement."

"But why can't you go there and check? And put things straight."

"If there's anything we don't need right now, it's for the police to discover that place. Of course they will, sooner or later. But preferably later. For all I know, they're watching us at this very moment. I'll get . . . I'll sort this all out, Mabelle. I promise."

He twined his fingers through her thick hair. Her scent always made him feel giddy. They had been secret lovers for three years, living in fear of his father's reprisals. A crazy, impulsive wedding in Las Vegas, with no witnesses other than a fat woman at a Hammond organ, had been the start of five years of escalating conflict with his family. But Mabelle had never let him down. As far as he knew, she had never cheated on him. Even though she sometimes went through periods of being distant and indifferent to him, it seemed as if she had made a choice, forever and always; after a while she was tender and vivacious again, almost slavishly in love.

Before Mabelle, there had been no one. An occasional chance bed companion, of course; he did, after all, have money, and learned early that that sort of thing could make up for lack of charm. All the same, nothing more ever came of it. In his twenties, he began to appreciate why. He was a coward. He possessed an evasive personality, something physically expressed in an almost nonexistent chin. His eyes were not attractive either: too large, slightly protruding, as if he suffered from a touch of goiter.

His father had caused him to regress. Eventually, as his dependency on the shipping company and everything comprising his father's life and dominion increased, the scraps of independence and strength that Carl-Christian had acquired in his youth, through a career of sorts as a skier, had diminished. He was third in the Norwegian National Junior Skiing Championships, before his father put a stop to that kind of frivolity. Skiing was to be confined to Sundays. For the rest of the week, it was work from eight to seven. Carl-Christian had endured it. Year after year.

Then Mabelle came along: a knockout, a daredevil. She was purposeful where Carl-Christian was ineffectual, courageous where he acquiesced to his father's will.

"It shouldn't happen that way," she whispered through her sobs into his neck.

"It shouldn't happen like that," he agreed.

Mabelle must not break down. If Mabelle were unable to cope with this, then everything would unravel. He was not strong enough; for far too long, his strength had lain in her, and only her.

"What about Hermine?" Mabelle asked in desperation. "It's impossible to rely on that girl. At least now, when everything's screwed up. What will we do?"

Carl-Christian could not bring himself to answer. Hermine was a loose cannon.

"It'll turn out fine," he reassured her, without answering her question. "Everything will turn out fine, Mabelle."

But he didn't believe a word of what he said.


When Hanne Wilhelmsen woke, Christmas had arrived with a bang.

At ten o'clock she was rudely awoken from sleep by a mandarin orange smacking her in the eye. Mary was attempting to hang a stocking filled with goodies on her headboard.

"It's not Christmas Eve yet," Hanne said, drugged with sleep. "What are you up to?"

"I've waited long enough. It's the last Sunday in Advent. The decorations are going up now."

Drawing on her bathrobe, Hanne shuffled out into the living room. The minimalist furnishings were drowned in glitter and trimmings. Red and green snakes crisscrossed the ceiling, with twinkling bulbs inside.

"Photocells," Mary said in delight. "Every time someone walks through here, then—"

"*Dashing through the snow*," a children's choir bellowed.

In the corner beside the balcony door, a sturdy elf sat eating porridge.

"*Ho, ho, ho*," he laughed as he raised his arm in mechanical greeting.

"Good Lord," Hanne whispered.

Plaited red and green baskets festooned the walls, together with spray-painted spruce branches, brass stars, and golden vine tendrils. Like a monument to bad taste, the tree loomed overhead, culminating in the biggest star-topper Hanne had ever seen. Excited, Mary pressed a button on the wall. *"Merry Christmas,"* the star tinkled in two-part harmony, rotating slowly all the while.

Hanne burst out laughing.

"Don't you like it?" Mary yelled. "I've been busy since midnight!"

Nefis was up now. She looked all around her, entranced.

"Brilliant," she whispered in the midst of the melee. "So wonderfully Norwegian!"

"No," Hanne hiccupped. "It's . . . it's—"

Suddenly everything went silent. Mary had pressed some sort of master switch and stood staring in accusation at Hanne.

"What did you say it was?"

"It's—"

Hanne threw out her arms and beamed with pleasure.

"Damn it, they're the most fantastic Christmas decorations I've ever seen! Mary, you're a marvel! I've really never seen anything like it."

"Do you mean that? Nefis gave me permission to order whatever I wanted. Got everything delivered to the door, you know. I've worked my bloody socks off!"

"I can see that," Hanne said, more serious now. "Thanks a million."

"Thank you, too," Mary said with a sniffle. "I'm so happy now, you know."

Pulling a voluminous handkerchief from her sweater sleeve, she dried her eyes, before handing Hanne a yellow note.

"A guy phoned here this morning—at some ungodly hour—though I refused to wake you. I was actually thinking of not telling you, but now I'm so happy, Hanne. Now you've made an old soul happy."

She limped out into the kitchen. Fortunately she had forgotten to flick the switch on the noisy decorations.

"I promise . . ." Hanne said, stealing a march on Nefis while quickly reading the note. "It's my turn to make dinner today, in fact. I'll be back in plenty of time. Promise."

She plucked a halo from the floor and used it to crown the head of a baby angel.

"That's quite sweet, too," she said, still smiling.

The festive season must have put a damper on even the journalists' spirit of self-sacrifice. In any case, there was no sign of any of them in the bitter wind scudding along the walls of the apartment buildings in Eckersbergs gate. Only a cat could be seen ambling along the desolate sidewalk, shaking its paw with every step it took and meowing pathetically.

"I've often wondered," Erik Henriksen said, as they opened the sealed front door, "what these hacks say to their children when they come home and get asked what they've done at work today. Well, maybe they can say: Today I've hounded a guy who's just lost his whole family. Or: Today I've shadowed a crown princess who only wanted to be left in peace while she bought a gift for a friend. Today I've definitely made life really unpleasant for quite a number of people. What a damn job!"

"I don't think they say anything much," Hanne replied. "When they get home, I mean. Good of you to turn out, by the way."

"No problem," he said, wrinkling his nose. "But I don't really understand what good this visit will do."

The Stahlberg family's apartment was far too warm. Hanne still felt she could detect a hint of sweet iron and chemicals: blood and the crime scene investigators' paraphernalia. Maybe it was only a figment of her imagination. She crossed the room and opened a window anyway. The heavy plush curtains stirred slightly in the draft.

"They still think that Sidensvans's body was moved, don't they?"

She hunkered down and studied the taped outline of the publishing representative's cadaver.

"Yes. They think he fell at the threshold."

"Then he must have been standing outside the door, on the stairway. When he was shot, I mean. Is it true he was shot in the back?"

Erik dipped into the slim folder he had tucked under his arm, to produce a drawing of a man's body, stylized and flat, viewed from both front and back, with wounds plotted as red dots on the white paper.

"Yep. Two shots in the back. One on the side of his head."

"Then in point of fact he needn't have spoken a single word to his hosts before he died, isn't that so?"

"No . . . I don't know . . . How's that?"

"He's been moved. That might mean he was lying farther outside the door, on the landing, and that the perpetrator wanted to move the corpse into the apartment in order to shut the door behind him when he left. But the door was left open. Wasn't it?"

"Yes, it was. The dog must have come in somehow. Besides . . . the guy who reported something amiss was on his way to visit Lars Gregusson, the computer guy on the second floor. When he didn't get an answer, he took hold of the entrance door and tugged at it. He was annoyed, he said, because apparently they had made arrangements to have a glass or two here before heading off into the city center. Then it turned out that the front door was open. It had quite simply not been closed properly. So he peeked inside. And saw a pair of shoe soles and an open door on the ground floor. Thank goodness he had the wit not to go inside. He phoned us instead."

"Of course, that means that Sidensvans may not even have rung the doorbell at all," Hanne said, glancing out into the stairwell again. "He might actually have walked straight in."

"Yes . . . How's that?"

"Nothing. By the way, is there an ordinary door telephone here?"

"Yes. You ring the bell outside and introduce yourself, and the resident presses a button to open the door. Standard issue."

"Standard issue," she repeated absentmindedly. "And Hermann lay here."

There could not have been more than five or six inches separating the outline of Hermann Stahlberg's feet from Knut Sidensvans's head.

She squatted again with her hand on her chin.

"Can we surmise that Hermann was about to welcome his guest?"

"We might well surmise that. But we can't know for sure. If . . . if you're right that Sidensvans didn't need to ring the doorbell, then they wouldn't have known he'd arrived."

"I didn't say that was how it was. I said it might be. That's entirely different."

Erik scrutinized his older colleague. He had never understood Hanne. Even now, when he was no longer infected with that idiotic crush and could therefore see her more clearly, he didn't have any understanding of her. No one did. Over a long period of time, Hanne Wilhelmsen had built up a reputation as one of the foremost investigators in the Oslo Police Force, perhaps in the entire country. But no one had any real understanding of her. Not even after all these years. Most of them had also given up. Hanne was moody, impervious, bordering on eccentric. That was how they regarded her, the vast majority of them, even though her renown as an instructor to the younger and more inexperienced investigators had eventually grown quite formidable. There was hardly a single newly qualified police officer who did not make an effort to maneuver his or her career in the direction of Hanne Wilhelmsen. Where the older colleagues saw a stubborn and headstrong detective who could barely be bothered to communicate anything at all, the youngest members of the force found an original, intuitive, and thorough mentor. Her patience, which was almost nonexistent toward everyone further up the system, could be touchingly generous with regard to colleagues from whom she did not expect much.

Erik Henriksen had worked closely with her for ten years.

"It's a wonder I'm not bloody sick of you and your secrets," he said, grinning from ear to ear. "Could you, for example, tell me what you're thinking about while you're sitting there? Or do I have to haul in some trainee or other to ask on my behalf?"

Hanne got up, pulling a grimace at a cramp in her leg after crouching for so long.

"Are you really interested?" she asked distractedly.

With her foot planted in the middle of the white outline of Sidensvans's body, she used the flat of her hand as some kind of sight directed at the living room. She closed one eye, then ran her gaze over the outline of Preben's corpse, nearest the living room door. The three bodies had been stretched out in a row, foot to head: a chain of dead people.

"Hmm," she said, with a slight shake of the head.

"Yes," Erik said. "I am interested. Hanne, we're always interested. You're the one who doesn't want to share."

"Yes, I do," she said, her concentration still focused on how much of the living room you could see from the front door. "I'm happy to share."

"Then do it!"

His voice sounded irritated now: he glanced pointedly at the clock.

"Yes."

Beaming, she put her hand on his shoulder.

"Have you eaten?"

"No—"

"Come home with me then, and I can tell you what I'm thinking. I live just down the street from here. But I have to warn you about . . . about the help. She's a bit peculiar. Just pretend not to notice. And above all, don't criticize our Christmas decorations."

"No, of course not," he said, delighted, jogging after her along the narrow path outside Eckersbergs gate 5.

Hermine Stahlberg's overdose was interpreted as attempted suicide, something Carl-Christian—after spending a couple of hours swallowing the shame attached to such a diagnosis—regarded as an unqualified advantage. The police would not be able to interview his sister. Not for some time. The sense of relief he felt was almost physical and could not be displaced by the growing unease at the discovery that his sister was obviously ingesting stronger substances than were on sale at the liquor store. The splitting headache that had plagued him for more than twenty-four hours was subsiding. Just another dash of good fortune now, and he would be in control.

He felt terribly dizzy when he stood up from the chair by the bed where Hermine had just fallen asleep, and he had to take hold of the bedside table and close his eyes as he took deep breaths.

"Alfred," he said in surprise, when he opened them again.

"Carl-Christian. My dear boy!"

His uncle wanted to embrace him. Carl-Christian stood listlessly, lacking willpower, and accepted the prolonged hug. The odor of cigars and of a man no longer scrupulous about personal hygiene stung his nostrils.

"It's good you're here," his uncle sniveled. "I've tried to phone you, lots of times. We met up on Friday evening—the men in the family and all the aunts. Some of the cousins, too, and as a matter of fact Benedicte popped in and—"

"I haven't been absolutely on top of things, Uncle. I haven't been answering the phone of late."

"I can well understand that," Alfred whispered, glancing over at his sleeping niece. "We've so much to talk about. After all this dreadful business and—"

"I thought you'd come to visit Hermine."

"But she's sleeping—look! I can't wake the poor girl!"

Uncle Alfred seemed aggrieved and had already taken a firm grip of his nephew's arm. He drew him doggedly over to the door.

"Come on now. Let Hermine sleep."

"No!"

Carl-Christian was startled by the sharpness in his own tone as he broke free.

"I don't want to come home with you. I have things to organize. I'm busy, and in any case I don't want anything to drink."

Alfred sized him up. His eyes, small, pale blue, and deeply set, showed a sudden flash of anger and his mouth puckered, showing he had taken offense. Carl-Christian felt disgust at the full lips, always blood-red, moist, almost feminine. He turned away.

"I just want to be left in peace," he mumbled.

"I can appreciate that."

His uncle's voice was cooler now, his tone more businesslike.

"Nonetheless, I should remind you there are a number of things that have to be seen to in connection with the funeral—and, not least, with the administration of the estate. There's a certain disarray prevailing, as far as that's concerned, to put it mildly. Wouldn't you agree?"

Carl-Christian struggled to find something to say. The surprising self-confidence he had felt just a moment ago was gone. He found himself scraping the tip of his toes on the floor and could not bring himself to look his uncle in the eye.

He had actually never understood Alfred's position in the family. He was his father's rather incompetent younger brother. Admittedly, he always had some kind of business project in process—at least it seemed that way, from the perpetual talk of big money always just around the corner. All the same, they never came to anything. Previously, in Carl-Christian's younger days, it sometimes happened that he followed up on his uncle's long-winded talk. He even came up with some more detailed questions, but the answers were seldom specific and mostly went on to depict new enterprises, with broad, colorful brushstrokes. And Alfred had always called himself an art dealer, though Carl-Christian had never heard of him selling a single picture.

It was obvious that Alfred's standard of living was not commensurate with his income. Carl-Christian had some vague idea that his grandparents, long dead when he himself had been born, had left their two sons a tidy sum as a legacy. Their daughters probably had to content themselves with far less. The old couple had been in the clothing trade, and after two or three years of collaboration during the Nazi wartime occupation, they were probably in a position to afford their children a good start in their own careers when they died in 1952. Nevertheless, the money must have been used up long ago.

There was something fishy about Alfred Stahlberg. Even Hermine, the favorite niece who was almost more Alfred's daughter than Hermann's, could sometimes withdraw into conspicuous rejection of everything connected with her uncle. When she was little and Carl-Christian a teenager, he was sometimes taken aback by how she alternated between warm affection and defiant dislike of the charming, garrulous good-for-nothing her uncle was in reality. Later, Carl-Christian stopped bothering. He quite simply couldn't make Alfred out. Neither did he understand his father's indulgence of his younger brother, when it was obvious at the same time that they were far from emotionally close. People laughed at Alfred, but they also laughed with him. They talked about him, but mostly with him, and they all reveled in the stories he could invent: untruthful, almost poetic in their obvious exaggeration of his own excellence, resourcefulness, and flair for business. Alfred was too corpulent and too intense about everything, but until a few months ago, he had nevertheless been quite an elegant man.

Now there was a rank smell about him, and more than anything else, Carl-Christian wanted to leave.

"I have to go home," he murmured almost inaudibly.

As he turned to the door, he saw that Alfred was sitting on Hermine's bed, holding her hand in his. When she managed, only just, to open her eyes, she greeted him with a smile.

Erik Henriksen stood openmouthed at the kitchen in Kruses gate.

"Good God," he said finally. "It's fabulous here, really!"

"So this is your boyfriend, then!"

Mary revealed her new teeth as she poured a generous measure of mulled wine into his glass, adding some nuts and raisins until it looked more like porridge than a beverage.

"Something to heat you up," she said by way of explanation, when she topped it all off with a shot of spirits from a bottle of 60 percent proof.

"Hey," Erik protested, trying to place his hand over the glass. "It's only twelve o'clock!"

"No harm's ever come to anyone from a small nip of the hard stuff on the last Sunday in Advent," Mary concluded, presenting him with a plaited basket crammed with home baking. "Here. Eat. Baked them myself."

"Thanks," Erik muttered, biting dutifully into a gingerbread man while Mary left the kitchen and closed the door behind her.

Putting her index finger to her mouth, Hanne sneaked over to the fridge. Two minutes later, she had buttered a heap of four huge sandwiches.

"I'm starving," she whispered. "But Mary would have launched into a huge meal if I'd told her so. I said we'd just eaten. So . . ."

She pointed at the basket of cakes.

"You're both so kind. For looking after her."

"We're not actually particularly kind," Hanne answered. "She works like a Trojan. Keeps this whole house clean and prepares almost all the food. She refuses to accept any payment other than board and lodging."

"You *are* both kind," Erik insisted. "I would never have taken in an old prostitute and given her a chance like this. Even though she helped you with the case about the chef that time. Wasn't she the one who'd swiped the most vital piece of evidence from the crime scene? Was that how you met her?"

"Yes. She stuck to me like glue afterward. I had to look after her for a while, you see, since we were relying on her testimony. And then she just stayed on."

"I'd never have been allowed to do that, for heaven's sake."

"But then you don't live like this either. Mary is here for my sake."

"What?"

"I . . . I'm a bit allergic to families, Erik. Mary reminds me that this is a . . . chosen arrangement. Not a real family."

"A family is also chosen, you know," Erik said, obviously confused. "You fall in love, have children—"

"We don't need to talk about it any more," Hanne broke in. "It's not really so very interesting."

They continued eating in silence. Erik devoured three of the sandwiches and washed them down with tiny sips of the fortified mulled wine. Mary was right: it gave you a warm glow. Feeling slightly light-headed, he quickly keyed in a text message and sent it off.

"My girlfriend," he explained. "Message that I've been delayed."

Erik wanted to stay there, in Hanne's kitchen, for as long as he could. The liquor hit him all of a sudden. Everything turned warm, and he stripped off his sweater. Only now did he notice that Hanne had not touched her glass, and pushed his own away.

"Have you anything lighter?" he asked weakly.

"Mary no longer drinks alcohol," Hanne explained. "It's as if she makes up for it by pressing alcohol on everyone else. Maybe it's to prove she can manage without it."

"Or that she remembers how good it is. By the way . . . where did all the money come from?"

Hanne brought apple juice from the brushed-steel double fridge. She took her time pouring it into two glasses.

"That's none of your business," she said eventually.

"Fair enough. I'm asking all the same. Where did the money come from?"

Hanne's face was blank. She sat for a while looking at him, as if she expected him to answer his own question.

"Nefis," she said in the end.

"Yes, I realize that. I expect we'd have heard about it if you'd won the lottery. But why is she so rich?"

"Her father. Her father is loaded."

"That doesn't explain very much," Erik said, disheartened. "Why is her father so wealthy? And why has he given so much to his daughter? Is he dead, or what?"

"Jingle Bells" started up again at full volume when Mary and Nefis suddenly entered the kitchen. Erik jumped out of his skin and slammed the glass of apple juice on the table so hard that it cracked.

"Mary," Hanne yelled. "We can't have that on. Turn off that awful song! NOW!"

"I'll turn the volume down," Mary said, looking miffed, and disappeared out the door.

Silence did not descend until Nefis had located the plug and brutally pulled it out of the socket.

"I think I've broken it," she whispered hopefully, saying hello to Erik before adding, "Look who's come, Hanna!"

Billy T. was standing behind her.

"Here's the Christmas party, then! And conspiracies, I see! Why wasn't I invited? Here I am, just popping in with something for the Christmas celebrations, and I find two of my closest colleagues sitting talking shop without me."

"We're not talking . . ."

Erik looked in consternation from Hanne to Billy.

"We only—"

"Don't make excuses!"

Billy T. crashed down on a chair and drew it up to the kitchen table.

"You'd better wipe up that mess," he said, pointing at the puddle of apple juice, before fixing his eyes on Hanne. "Nefis tells me you've decided to share your thoughts on the Stahlberg case with our red-haired friend here."

Nefis stroked his shoulders lightly and asked in a friendly voice, "Can I offer you something, Billy T.? Wine, perhaps?"

Billy T. hesitated, before a faint smile crossed his face and he accepted a glass with thanks.

Erik was relieved. For a moment, everything had seemed spoiled. If Nefis had not intervened, he might just have gone home. So often in recent years he had witnessed how Hanne and Billy T. could reach deadlock in each other's company: turn sour, become withdrawn. Now they both sat smiling reluctantly, with eyes downcast, like reprimanded children.

"Listen up, then!"

"Okay."

Hanne took a deep breath and followed Nefis with her eyes as she left the kitchen.

"I think," she began, "I think the homicide in Eckersbergs gate might have something to do with those fierce family conflicts."

"Incredibly unoriginal," Billy T. muttered.

"I said 'might.' A great deal suggests that Carl-Christian, Hermine, or this Mabelle character has something to do with the murders, either together or individually. It's not difficult to predict that we're going to have increasingly strong grounds to focus in that direction as the investigation advances. There's always a lot of bullshit in those conflicts. And that bullshit suits us very well at present. Everything we find will support our theory."

"Exactly," Billy T. said. "Which is a good theory—"

"But also dangerous. It locks us in, and makes us close our eyes to that important piece we prefer not to see."

"Sidensvans," Erik said, nodding.

"Precisely. Knut Sidensvans. I can't rid myself of the thought that his presence was no mere coincidence."

"We've really nothing to go on," Billy T. said. "It's bloody impossible to find a single connection between Sidensvans and the Stahlberg family."

"We haven't tried very hard, though."

"No, but what could there be? We've already interviewed loads of friends and family of the three victims. No one has ever heard of Sidensvans. There's nothing to suggest the Stahlbergs might have had plans to publish a book or needed any help from a publishing consultant. They probably didn't require a well-dressed electrician without any tools to change a cable late on a Thursday evening. I just can't fathom it. All the same, they must have been expecting the guy. There were four glasses set out on the sideboard, and the champagne was already opened."

"Odd that the champagne was opened," Hanne commented.

"What?"

Erik squinted at her.

"You usually open that sort of thing once all the guests have arrived," she said. "That's half the fun. Hearing the pop. Drinking while it's really fizzing. Isn't that right?"

"You might well know," Billy T. muttered. "I can never afford that sort of thing."

Hanne ignored him and plowed on. "If we go back for a moment to what's most plausible—namely, that the shootings have something to do with the family conflict—then why did the perpetrator choose to act on this particular evening?"

"One evening's probably as good as any other," Erik said.

"No," Hanne said eagerly, leaning forward. "When four people are liquidated in cold blood in this way, we quickly construct a theory that it was all meticulously planned. I see that the newspapers have already begun to quote anonymous sources in the police about precisely that: the homicides were premeditated. But if someone plans to kill three members of his family, would they not ensure they were at least alone on that evening? Wouldn't they, for example, make sure that the neighbors were away and—"

"But they were," Erik interrupted. "All except Backe. He's senile and dead drunk most of the time, and it's pretty certain everyone in the block knows that."

"Backe isn't totally with it," Hanne agreed. "But he has his moments. He does his own shopping and sometimes goes to the theater in fact."

"How do you know that?"

"I drove him home, didn't I? No one else was available, so I did it myself. He's absolutely prepared to give an account of himself as long as he has enough alcohol in his bloodstream and is able to collect his thoughts. My point is that taking the lives of three people called Stahlberg last Thursday, in their own home, seems fairly impulsive. A plan—a real murder plan—would probably have been carried out somewhere else entirely. At their summer cottage, for example. As recently as last weekend, Hermann and Turid were in Hemsedal with Preben and his family. The cottage is situated in quite a remote spot, almost a mile from the nearest neighbor. I would . . ."

She leaned back and intertwined her fingers behind her neck. A smile was just visible at the corners of her mouth as she continued.

"If I intended to take the lives of my parents and my brother, I'd have chosen to do it somewhere I was sure of not being taken by surprise. At a time when most people are fast asleep. Not in the middle of Oslo on a Thursday evening."

Erik and Billy T. exchanged glances.

"And then we're again faced with a whole range of possibilities."

Hanne looked up at the cupboard containing Mary's stash of tobacco, but pulled herself together.

"If one or several members of the family are behind this, then it was an impulsive act. A frenzy of rage. A sudden frenzy, which also cost Sidensvans his life because he, by chance, happened to be present at the time."

Hanne fell silent and closed her eyes. Billy T. tried not to look at her. He felt offended. They were all offended. Not a single soul in the entire police force was unconvinced that the four victims in Eckersbergs gate had been dispatched by one of the Stahlbergs. Even now, the prevailing general opinion was that the killings had been planned in detail, probably over a lengthy period of time. Some even speculated that the ravenous dog had been deliberately planted there. At any rate, the dog had complicated the investigation considerably.

"If the family is *not* behind it," she suddenly went on, "then we have a fucking problem. To put it mildly. Then we might be talking about a homicide with intent to rob that got screwed up. Or a random lunatic. Highly unlikely, but all the same."

She caught Billy T.'s eye.

"We might consider that Sidensvans was actually the target," she said slowly. "The family was simply sacrificed. Either to camouflage Sidensvans's murder—that sort of thing has been done before—or because he had to—"

". . . be killed because he was delivering something to the Stahlberg family," Erik broke in. "Or was telling them something. But then we're probably back to Carl-Christian and Co., are we not? As suspects, I mean?"

Hanne shrugged.

"Possibly. But in any case, you must at least agree with me in my provisional conclusions!"

"Which are what, then?" Billy T. said, genuinely discouraged. "I think you're jumping all over the place! What are you actually driving at?"

"Two things. If it's family members who are behind it, then it was an impulsive affair. Not planned. At least not well, or over a period of time. Moreover, it's not just an obsession of mine to say I believe that we ought to find out far more about this guy Sidensvans. About what on earth he was doing at Hermann and Tutta's house."

"Maybe he had brought something with him," Erik suggested again. "Something that the perpetrator removed when he left?"

"Maybe so," Hanne said, nodding. "Or maybe he *didn't* have something with him. Maybe that's why his keys have never been found. Or maybe he never . . . What if he quite simply didn't . . ."

She became absorbed in thought.

"This theory of yours about it being so impulsive—" Billy T. was more enthusiastic now and gesticulated as he said, "it doesn't wash. You don't get hold of two guns just like that! The perpetrator or perpetrators, whether family or outsider, must have spent some time acquiring them. Do you really mean someone is supposed to have had that sort of thing lying around, just in case the need to execute someone ever arose?"

Hanne did not reply. She sat with her head tilted, deep in concentration, as if listening to something, or not quite sure about what she had actually heard.

"Hello," Billy T. said. "Do you agree?"

"What?"

Hanne looked momentarily mystified, before smiling apologetically. "It just struck me that Sidensvans maybe wasn't . . . It's not certain that he should . . . No. There have to be limits to speculation. Even for me."

"Is anybody staying for dinner?"

Mary's hacking cough was heard in the doorway.

"It's the lady of the house who's taking care of the cooking today, just to let you know. But it might be edible, for all that. You need to make a start, Hanne. We eat at three o'clock on a Sunday. We're not like those dagos that eat at night."

She slapped an enormous bag of lamb cutlets on the kitchen worktop.

"Who's staying?"

"I'd love to," Erik said.

"Okay, then," Billy T. said. "If Mary insists."

"She doesn't, in actual fact," Hanne said, starting to peel potatoes.

A man was trying to pick up his change and eat a hot dog at the same time. The female cashier felt disgusted. The front of the customer's hoodie was spattered with stains beneath an open, tattered pilot jacket. His face, pinched and with several open, weeping sores, bore signs of heavy drug misuse. She placed the money on the counter. Angrily, he swore with his mouth full of food: "For fuck's sake! Put the money in my hand, I said! I'm not a bloody octopus! Can't you see that I'm eating?"

Shuddering, he had to shift his foot to one side to keep his balance. His elbow hit a child held in its mother's arms, and a substantial blob of ketchup dropped on the young woman's coat. The youngster screamed like crazy. Cursing, the man in the hoodie made an effort to pick up the money. The girl behind the counter was obviously afraid now: she drew back and looked around for help.

"You! You over there!"

A hefty man in his thirties poked a finger into the junkie's back.

"Calm down, okay?"

The hot dog eater turned around slowly. It might seem that he was struggling to focus properly. All of a sudden, he thrust what remained of his food into the intruder's jacket front.

"Butt out," he slurred, and made to leave.

The answer he received was a punch in the mouth. Two teeth broke. As he fell, he pulled down three boxes of chocolate and a display stand of *Se og Hør* magazines.

The child's yells were even louder, and his mother sobbed in terror.

The assistant had called the police long before it reached that stage.

• • •

Mabelle Stahlberg was in the process of creating a new version of the truth for herself. She lay on the floor of the apartment in Odins gate listening to music as she fashioned an alternative reality, a story she could make both herself and others believe.

She had practiced meditation earlier, before Carl-Christian, before life with the Stahlberg family, at a time when everything and everyone was against her and nothing was going her way. Admittedly, she was pretty, and that sort of thing could go some distance toward helping in a world that idolized the superficial.

She had been only fourteen when she obtained her first modeling assignment. Not major stuff, a tiny advertising job for a mail-order company, but overwhelming for a young girl who suddenly realized that an attractive appearance could be her ticket away from a dismal apartment, where a disabled mother was slowly smoking herself to death and left May Anita and her three small siblings to fend for themselves.

The girl was barely seventeen when she discovered that she had to lose increasingly more of her clothes to find work. In a sleazy joint in Sagene, with covered windows and a grubby bathtub in the corner, she finally said stop. May Anita was desperate to become Mabelle. She had no idea how. She had nowhere to stay. Her siblings were spread out in three different foster homes by now, but the child welfare service had fortunately not allocated many resources to supporting her, since she would be eighteen in four months. May Anita lacked everything, but she understood for the first time in her young life that she had some kind of intelligence. Intuitive and ignorant it may have been, but despite everything, it had kept her away from intoxicating substances and forced her to draw the line at undisguised pornography. For the next six years she lived from hand to mouth. A casual job here, an assignment there, for an old acquaintance perhaps, who might be pressed into generosity by a poor young girl who, despite it all, had beautiful eyes and a very attractive body.

May Anita never quite succeeded in getting it together. But she learned a great deal.

Then one night she met Carl-Christian. He was plastered; she was sober, as always. There was something weak about the man, something sweet and genuinely helpless. He stood with his head in a garbage can outside the 7-Eleven store in Bogstadveien.

May Anita had taken the stranger home and to bed. She found no need to abandon him when he collapsed into the wide divan with silk sheets. On the contrary, she set to work. Seventy-two hours later, she became Carl-Christian's mistress.

With CC's help, she transformed herself into Mabelle. She had her nose straightened, as so many photographers had encouraged her to do. Her lips increased in size at the same time, and in the end he had proposed.

Mabelle was fond of him in her own way. He worshiped her. His fear, his anxiety that she might leave him, made her feel secure. There was a certain satisfaction in the imbalance between them, this lopsidedness in their relationship. She was dependent on what he owned. He, on the other hand, was dependent on her.

Naturally, her life had to be embellished when she met Carl-Christian. Eventually they became true, the stories she had served up so many times, with ever-increasing precision and richness of detail. It was the same as it was with makeup, she had sometimes thought, like a tiny cosmetic operation: if well executed, then no one could discern its original state.

She did not tell lies. She created reality.

As early as her childhood, Mabelle Stahlberg had appreciated that if you simply entered into the deception, kept firm hold of it, and never let it overpower you, then lies could become utterly true. In actual fact, truth was only for people who could afford it, and Mabelle Stahlberg certainly had no intention of reverting to being May Anita Olsen.

Hermann and Tutta deserved to die. They had asked for it. Hermann was wicked; he was egotistical and wicked through and through. He was vindictive. Obstinate and willful. Hermann was a thief who had intended to steal their life from them. From Carl-Christian— Hermann's own flesh and blood—who had slogged and worked his fingers to the bone for years, entirely at the mercy of his father's moods and whims. Tutta was nothing more than a foolish hanger-on, a spineless puppet. She had to take responsibility for not speaking up about the unfairness, about the raw deal they'd been given. Hermann and Tutta were responsible for their own deaths.

Preben, too.

Mabelle closed her eyes and tried to relax. She was worn out now, almost prostrate. She did not want to think about Preben.

They had not done anything wrong.

It was almost true already.

"My goodness, if it isn't Kluten himself, eh? Thought you'd headed off long ago."

Billy T. slapped the flat of his hand on the prisoner's back.

"Don't you realize, I've had my teeth knocked out," the man in the hoodie lisped, baring his gums. "That wasn't much fun, you know!"

"You didn't have many left anyway, so it doesn't make much difference," Billy T. said, taking a seat opposite him in the interview room. "But it doesn't look as if you're getting much to chew on either. My God, you've grown so skinny."

"Sick," Kluten mumbled, stroking his swollen top lip. "Really bloody sick. I can smell wine off you."

"I'm off duty today," Billy T. said mildly. "I've just had dinner with a nice family. Certainly hadn't intended to come here. But then somebody phoned, you know. And said you insisted on talking to me. And it had better . . ."

His voice was raised to a roar.

"*. . . be important!*"

Kluten jumped so violently that his head cracked off the wall.

"I'm sick, I tell you. And you know fine well, my mouth's bleeding!"

"Keep that filth away from me, I tell you. I hear you kicked up a commotion in a shop up in Vogts gate. Spilled blood on other customers, and that sort of stuff. Little children and nice women. What's all that about, Kluten? Is that the kind of behavior you've turned to?"

"It was ketchup," Kluten complained. "I just wanted my money!"

"And then you didn't have the common sense to get rid of this before our guys turned up."

Billy T. clicked his tongue as he held up a small plastic bag with unmistakable contents.

"Three grams? Three and a half? Kluten, for heaven's sake. You're getting old."

Billy T. squinted and pretended to examine it thoroughly.

"I have something!"

"Had," Billy T. said sternly. "You had four grams of heroin. Now they're mine."

"I have information, Billy T.! I know something!"

Now he was whispering loudly, whistling through the hole in his upper jaw. Billy T. assumed a dismissive air. He knew Kluten well from his years in the drug intervention unit. The guy was totally unable to speak coherently and truthfully for more than three minutes.

"It's true! I swear, Billy T. I know something about that there . . ."

He suddenly stopped speaking and, paranoid, stared all around.

"That there who?" Billy T. asked.

"I want immunity," Kluten said, his eyes still darting around the room, as if expecting someone to emerge out of the walls. "I'm saying nothing until I get immunity."

"Kluten, Kluten, Kluten."

Beaming, Billy T. ran both hands over his head.

"That's not how it works in this country, you know. Where is it you watch TV? At the Blue Cross center? Seen too many American movies, I think. Spit it out, now. What is it you know?"

"Saying nothing."

Kluten clammed up quite literally. He drew his hood over his head, folded his arms, and hunched his shoulders. Then he sank his face down to his chest. He was reminiscent of a fasting monk from the Middle Ages and smelled just as foul.

"Cut that out. Come on, spit it out!"

Kluten sat like a pillar of salt. Billy T. abruptly rose to his feet.

"Fine," he said brusquely. "Sit there then. This stuff here will give you some time behind bars anyway."

He tucked the heroin into his breast pocket as he headed for the door.

"Help me a bit, then!"

Kluten was whimpering now. Billy T. thought for a moment that he had started to cry.

"I just can't go to jail right now. Not right now, Billy T. Give me some help, please!"

Billy T. stopped, but did not turn around.

"Let me hear," he said, facing the door. "If what you have is of any worth whatsoever, then I can see to it that this bag shrinks a bit." He glanced over his shoulder. "Is that okay?"

"Okay then—"

Billy T. looked pointedly at the wall clock as he sat down again.

"But it will have to be something substantial, Kluten. No shit. Okay?"

"Okay, I'm telling you. Listen up now."

Eleven minutes later, Billy T. began to feel hot. Sometimes he interrupted the prisoner with a question. He had produced a notepad and was using it frequently. When Kluten finally slumped in his chair and declared that he was finished, Billy T. fell silent. Kluten bared his toothless gums in some sort of smile. The corners of his mouth were red with dried blood that cracked with his grimace.

"Was that substantial enough, then?"

Billy T. still did not answer. He simply sat there, also with his arms crossed, looking as if he did not believe a word of what Kluten had told him. His mouth was pulled down into a skeptical expression and his eyes were half closed. Kluten rocked impatiently to and fro in his seat, scratching frantically at a cut on his forehead.

"Come on, be nice! Can I go now?"

"Oddvar, isn't it? That's your real name?"

"Yes . . . don't mess me around, now. Can I go?"

"Oddvar."

Billy T. used an intercom to call a police trainee.

"Oddvar," he repeated. "I would have liked to help you. But that's not on. In the first place, it's four grams too much for me to look through my fingers at. Second, you're so exhausted now that I don't really think you'll survive another night in this cold. And third—"

"I can stay at my sister's," Kluten said in desperation. "For fuck's sake, you got the whole lot! Everything I know, Billy T.! I can't face a cell now."

A scrawny young man entered and put his hand on Kluten's shoulder.

"Come on now," the trainee said, struggling to appear mature.

"Fuck you, Billy T.! *Fuck you!*"

He sobbed and whined all the way along the corridor. Billy T. leafed distractedly through his notes.

"That statement of yours," he muttered. "Hanne will have to hear that with her own ears."

Then he stuffed the notepad into his back pocket and went to check if one of the police prosecutors was working overtime. If not, he would have to phone for one of them. Even though it was past seven o'clock in the evening.

The old man in the forest stood in the woodshed, brushing dust and dirt from his old ice drill. It had not been used in years. In fact he was not especially fond of fishing, at least not in winter. A still summer's night beside the water could be very pleasant, with bait and floats and a coffee pot on the campfire; the occasional hiker would sometimes stop for a chat. However, he had never seen the point of freezing like a dog over a hole in the ice.

But he had made up his mind. He would try to discover what the stranger had been doing. Probably it would be futile. Probably he was wrong. Probably he was making a complete fool of himself. In all likelihood, it would be impossible to find anything anyway. All the same, something had stirred within him: a curiosity that made his blood flow a bit faster through his body. It reminded him vaguely of the old days, of wandering around foreign ports, on shore leave or because he had been left behind, as happened to him increasingly often, drunk and broke, but always on the lookout for new possibilities. Life in the forest was static, the way he liked it, the way he had chosen to live. The disturbance of his existence caused by the stranger's behavior—that sudden element of something incomprehensible and stimulating—was nevertheless welcome: a Christmas gift.

Not a soul would see him. He would wait until after nine on the day before Christmas Eve, when good people were at home decorating their Christmas trees. He was going to spend some time doing something that was almost certainly simply ludicrous, and it would be best that no one knew about it.

The old man drilled a trial hole in the air before running his hand thoughtfully over the stubble on his chin.

The ice drill was in good working order.

Two hours prior to midnight, Kluten was found dead in the holding cell. In the agonies of abstinence, he had hit his head off the wall. The doctor thought he must have taken a run at it: his skull was split in two. When Billy T. heard about the incident, he shut himself into his office, on his own.

## MONDAY, DECEMBER 23

Only Hanne Wilhelmsen could have arranged such an interview. Billy T. tried to hide a smile as they were escorted into the private ward. Half an hour earlier, it had seemed totally impossible. The doctor in charge of the unit was so condescending that Hanne flared up. When the man in the white coat eventually agreed to admit them, it was following a combination of coercion and police arrogance, mixed with veiled threats about the extreme unpleasantness of a "seriously legal nature." The doctor, advanced in years, fiddled with the stethoscope around his neck. A decoration, Billy T. thought, the symbol of a craft guild to indicate distance and dignity.

Hermine was awake.

They were greeted with complete indifference. Hanne introduced both herself and Billy T. The patient scarcely blinked, and Billy T. was unsure whether she understood who they were.

"Police," he repeated, smiling encouragingly. "We're from the police."

She sat almost bolt upright in a mechanical bed. Her hair was tousled and uncombed, her complexion as pale as the bedsheets. Some kind of rash surrounded her mouth, small pimples in a butterfly pattern. Billy T. thought of his own daughter, who was allergic to her pacifier. That was how she looked, Hermine, as if she had taken some childish comfort that she could not withstand.

All the same, she was pretty, in a kind of defenseless way. Her hair was tangled, but fell soft and blond around her narrow face. Her eyes were impassive, but big and blue. Even two days after a major overdose, Hermine Stahlberg knew how to use her talents, and now she smiled almost coquettishly at Billy T.

"I heard that," she said. "I expect it's about Mother and Father. And

95

Preben too. I've been expecting you. I'm not having an easy time of it, as you see . . ."

A look of self-pity surveyed the IV stand.

". . . but I appreciate, of course, that you have to talk to me."

Billy T. felt uncomfortable. Like a sticky length of string, Hermine's gaze attached itself to him, even when he moved from the bedside to the windowsill. He reacted by saying nothing and averting his eyes. Hanne was in the process of going through the meaningless introductory remarks. Formalities first, followed by condolences and innocuous questions with worthless responses. Through it all, Hermine watched him, and only him. A pictogram on a door on the gable wall indicated that the room boasted its own bathroom. He excused himself to take a piss. Washed his hands thoroughly. Splashed water on his face. Not until he heard raised voices in the next room did he return.

"Nothing other than that," Hanne said. "I just want to know what you were doing on November 10. Sunday, November 10."

She had caught Hermine's attention now.

"I don't know!"

It did not seem as if she had noticed his return. She sat up even straighter in the bed. Now she was sitting half turned toward Hanne, gesturing angrily.

"I can't be expected to remember what I was doing on one particular day more than a month ago!"

"What about the sixteenth?" Hanne said. "What were you doing on the evening of November 16?"

"I've no idea where you're going with this!"

"That's not necessary either. I just want answers to my questions. But it's obvious . . . we can just as easily drag you along to the courthouse for a judicial examination. If that's what you want. We're only trying to be pleasant here. To make it a bit simpler for you."

"Pleasant, huh!"

Hermine sank back melodramatically in the bed, holding her face in her hands. Muffled sobs could be heard. Hanne sighed as she leaned forward.

"Listen to me, Hermine Stahlberg. The quicker you answer our questions, the quicker we'll disappear. Okay? So I'll ask again: Is there something we can get hold of, to make it easier for you to remember what you were doing on November 10 and 16? A calendar? A diary, perhaps?"

Hermine smacked the quilt with her hands.

"I want a lawyer," she said.

Her voice had changed. It seemed sharper, more alert, as if the overdose and bed rest were simply an act, a staged defense against undesirable questions and uncomfortable inquiries.

"A lawyer . . ."

Hanne lingered on the word, tasting it, before shrugging and giving a slight smile.

"So you mean you *need* a lawyer, then."

Hermine lay with her eyes closed, and Billy T. had to admire her for the way she managed to keep her eyelids still. Only a discreet trembling of her left hand disclosed how tense the young woman actually felt.

"Interesting," Billy T. said. "Hanne Wilhelmsen here and I have more than forty years' experience behind us. In the police, that is. In total. And we know very well that when someone asks for a lawyer, then we've stepped on a tender toe. We like that a lot."

Still Hermine did not react.

"You must realize we know what you were doing on the—"

"I don't think we need to tell the young lady anything of what we know," Hanne interrupted him, sending Billy T. a warning look.

"Hermine doesn't want to talk. Hermine has the right to that. If Hermine would prefer to be hauled in for an interview, then Hermine will be allowed to do that. We'll even get her a lawyer. Isn't that right, Billy T.? She'll have a really good lawyer."

Hermine suddenly grabbed the alarm button at the end of a cord suspended above the headboard. It took only seconds for a nurse to appear inside the room.

"I can't handle it," Hermine murmured, before her tone changed to a falsetto. "I can't cope with these people! Get them out! *Get them out of here!*"

The attack of hysterics almost seemed genuine. The last Billy T.

could discern as he was pushed out of the room by a brusque orderly was the nurse preparing an injection.

"My goodness," Billy T. said once they were well outside. "She could have been an actress, that one. Impressive."

"It's not certain that she's playacting," Hanne said. "In my opinion, she's terrified. She also has good reason to be."

"But now," Billy T. said, slapping her on the back as they sauntered over to an unmarked police car, extremely badly parked halfway across a footpath, "you have to agree that your theory is in tatters."

"What theory?"

"The theory that . . . that it might not be the family who are behind it."

"I've never said that," Hanne retorted. "On the contrary, I've said that theory sounds more likely than anything else I can come up with. But it's far from certain, you know. Not yet."

Billy T. pulled a face at the bad weather. "Not yet! My God, Hanne! Hermine bought a gun, for fuck's sake. She ordered, inspected, made a test firing, and paid for a handgun in a market very few would dare go anywhere near. Why the hell would she do that if the purchase had nothing to do with the murders?"

"You're forgetting so much," Hanne said, narrowly avoiding a slip on a patch of ice.

Billy T. caught her and did not release her arm. Hanne turned to face him.

"For example, you're forgetting that we don't have a shred of anything resembling a motive for Hermine," she said. "She's the beloved child, the one who's pampered. She's everyone's friend. The bridge builder, don't you remember? Of course she can't be excluded. Certainly not. In fact, I . . ."

She tilted her head and ran her tongue over her winter-dry lips.

"I have a stronger feeling there's something about her than I do with her brother and sister-in-law. You and I both know what drugs do to people. From that point of view, her profile fits better with a violent and more or less impulsive killing. Besides, I'm incredibly curious as to why she received that fortune on her twentieth birthday. But for that very reason, Billy T.—for the reason that Hermine is the obscure, the mysterious, and the one of our suspects we have the least information about—we ought to find out more before we draw conclusions. Much more. And in addition . . ."

She squinted into empty space.

"We don't *know* that Hermine has bought a gun. We only have your friend Kluten's word for that. There's a whole heap of loose ends here. You might as well admit it right now: you don't have the best witness in the world as the source for that information. It could be fabrication from start to finish. From what you said yourself, Kluten was pretty desperate at the thought of being locked up. People like that also read newspapers, Billy T. Kluten knew very well what you wanted most of all to hear."

Billy T. had still not relinquished her arm. They stood like that—he with the wind at his back, she sheltered behind his well-built body.

"He was telling the truth, Hanne. I know Kluten. At the very least there's *some* truth in what he told me."

Billy T. used the back of his hand to dry tears—caused by the cold—from his eyes; the wind was starting to blow in fierce gusts.

"But because he told the truth, it doesn't necessarily mean that what he said was correct," Hanne answered, more conciliatory now. "After all, he said himself that it was something he'd heard."

"He had dates, Hanne. Kluten had two dates and the location where it was handed over."

"But no name. No supplier."

"No. No name. But . . ."

He continued slowly toward the car.

"I checked with our undercover officers this morning. It's buzzing down there, in those circles. Every single damn drug addict they've towed in over the weekend has come up with hints of one kind or another about the murders in Eckersbergs gate."

He stopped again, his face to the wind now, his cheeks stinging.

"Kluten was completely convinced, Hanne. I just wish I'd pressed him harder about where he got this story. He avoided answering every time I broached it, and in the end he was so exhausted I thought it best to let him go."

"And now it's too late," Hanne said, opening the door on the driver's side.

"But it is at least a lead," Billy T. said, sounding disheartened.

"A lead," Hanne reiterated, with a burst of laughter. "You can say that again. That's the fattest and ugliest lead we could have dreamed of. What's more, it's about the only one we have. I'll drive."

"Where are we going?" Billy T. asked.

"We're going to the publisher's."

"The publisher's? What are we going to do there?"

"Find out a bit more about Sidensvans."

"Sidensvans?"

Billy T. hit his right arm off the dashboard; he was cramped and uncomfortable in the small police car.

"You don't give up," he muttered, struggling to push the seat back. "Do you still think the key to this case lies with Sidensvans? Good Lord . . ."

Something broke underneath the seat as it jolted back. Billy T. bit his tongue hard in the sudden jerk.

"Ouch! Fuck! I'm bleeding."

"Poor soul," Hanne said, smiling, finding first gear at last.

Alfred Stahlberg had a terrible hangover, even though it was approaching half past ten in the morning. His alcohol intake the previous night had at least made him sleep. Or go out like a light, he thought woozily. He remembered little apart from desperately searching for more vodka.

His brain pulsed rhythmically against the inside of his skull. The pain caused by each beat crept down his neck and made it difficult for him to move his head. He had not showered in four days, and his shirt front was stained. Not until today had he been aware of his own smell: pungent and repulsive. He pulled a face at his reflection. The slight movement caused the pain to radiate toward his eyes. He spilled a few drops as he poured vodka into a kitchen tumbler. It all vanished in a single gulp.

That helped.

A little.

He poured himself another, and his headache slowly retreated. He tried to take deep, calm breaths. He was in sore need of a shower. He had to have clean clothes. He was dead tired, even though it had been ten hours since he last looked at the clock. He must have slept for at least eight of them.

In the shower, he stared down at his body. The water ran over his pale flabby frame slowly, almost like syrup, as if his skin were tacky. Alfred was the ugly one. The useless little brother. The weak one. The one who squandered his father's legacy and never experienced any success.

He was a fool and had expended too much energy on refusing to acknowledge that.

Such a lot had to be organized.

Someone had to take the lead now. Someone must guide the family, steer them through the maze of legalities and gossip they were faced with, without anyone seemingly able to get a grip on it all. It ought to be him. He was the last man of the older generation of Stahlbergs. The thought weighed heavily on him; he sank to his knees, but struck his forehead on the tiles and staggered back into an upright position. The water did not make him clean. He could not even see his own genitalia under his potbelly. Using both hands, he scratched himself, scratching and scraping until his nails were full of dead skin and thin lines of blood trickled over his paunch.

Alfred was a failure and was tired of suppressing that.

The hot water petered out. He shuffled away from the shower, attempting to hide his body in an enormous bath towel. Alfred Stahlberg was a fool; he was unsuccessful and ugly. He could see it for himself, and he sniffed through tears of self-loathing.

On the other hand, it was impossible for him to digest that he was also a criminal.

Åshild Meier of the publishing house was a small woman. She reminded Hanne of a weasel, with her rapid movements and her eyes darting here and there as she tried to clear a space for them both.

"Sorry about the mess," she said, shifting a pile of manuscripts from one chair to an already overfilled work desk. "My grandchild. Say hello to the police, Oskar!"

Oskar, about eighteen months old, sat underneath the desk, looking doubtful. Crouching down, Billy T. snapped his fingers and made noises. The toddler gurgled. Hanne warily said hello and smiled when the youngster peeked out. The child burst into tears. His grandmother took the boy by the arm and they left the small office.

"Me and children," Hanne said, shrugging.

"Get yourself one," Billy T. said. "That helps."

"It's the day before Christmas Eve, after all," Åshild Meier said, when she returned minus the child. "Most people are already on vacation. So it didn't matter so much. About Oskar, I mean. He sometimes comes here because—"

"That's absolutely fine," Billy T. said. "I've five children myself. Know what it's like. Great having grandparents."

"Five? My goodness!"

"And they have a total of no fewer than *twelve* grandparents," Hanne said tartly.

Billy T. blushed slightly and began to pick at a scab on the back of his left hand.

He had grown more submissive in recent years, Hanne thought, wishing she could bite back her words.

At the beginning of their friendship, the first few years—at police college and later at Oslo Police Station—he had been outstanding: a big athletic guy who filled every room he entered. Not only by virtue of being six foot seven in his stocking feet: Billy T. was the perfect police officer. Born and brought up in the inner city, kept in check by a hardworking single mother with old-fashioned values and a heavy-handed approach to child care. She had steered the young boy away from the worst pitfalls in an environment where only half of his friends survived long enough to reach the age of thirty. Billy T.—a streetwise hooligan with invaluable knowledge of Oslo's crooks—knew Oslo better than anyone else in the entire police force. He had been only a hairbreadth away from becoming one himself.

Now the station had been transformed into Oslo Police District, the police college into a university faculty, and the really major criminals no longer came from the east end of Oslo. In a sense, Billy T. had deflated. Even the many children he had acquired, all by different mothers, had turned into some kind of stigma. Earlier, he had paraded them proudly as proof of his enthusiastic libido and excessive virility. Now he was more subdued, and Hanne had twice caught him withholding the fact that they were all half siblings.

"But maybe we could make a start? What was it you actually wanted to know?"

"Knut Sidensvans," Hanne said casually.

"Yes, you said that when you phoned. It was absolutely dreadful, all this about the murder, but I don't really see what I can contribute."

"Did you know him well?"

"Well? No. In fact, I don't think anyone did. He was actually quite a strange person. A bit . . . odd."

"Odd?"

"Yes. Different. Though we're used to that, to some extent, in this line of business."

Åshild Meier gave a burst of shrill laughter.

"In actual fact he was a friendly soul. It was just a bit difficult to see that. Besides, he was a priceless resource for us. As a writer, of course, but first and foremost as a consultant."

"What does that kind of work entail?"

"Here in our department, it can be so many things," the editor explained. "Naturally, we have ordinary language consultants. They edit copy and correct the language. Improve it, plain and simple. But since we publish books that often deal with real events, we also use consultants for the content. Both to assess whether the submitted manuscript or the suggested book is something we want to take a chance on, and later in the process as a sort of assistant, or external examiner, if you like. We also sometimes use legal expertise. To avoid committing libel, for example. So—"

"Sidensvans was a kind of fact checker, then," Hanne broke in.

"Yes."

"In what areas?"

Now Åshild Meier was laughing heartily.

"Yes, you may well ask! The man actually started over in the school textbook department."

She pointed vaguely in midair, as if the school textbook department was situated directly behind Billy T.'s back.

"He is—or was, I suppose I should say now—an electrician. Originally. He taught at Sogn Technical College for years and wrote a textbook himself twenty years ago. It was good, apparently. Then he began as a consultant on school books, until someone discovered that the guy was a veritable fount of all knowledge. Knut Sidensvans was, in truth, one of a kind. And not an easy man to socialize with. But then we didn't socialize."

"What subjects did he deal with?" Hanne asked. "Here at the publishing house, I mean?"

"Quite a number."

Åshild Meier began to search through the crowded wall shelves.

"Cars."

She handed Hanne a coffee-table book about Ferrari.

"Admittedly, it's translated from Italian and therefore fairly safe to publish, but a lot of adjustments were necessary for Norwegian circumstances. Not least, the translator needed help with regard to technical expressions and that sort of thing."

"Sidensvans didn't even have a driving license," Hanne muttered, shaking her head.

Åshild Meier finally sat down.

"He had no formal education," she said. "Apart from his apprenticeship papers, of course. But he knew an incredible amount. Knowledgeable, and a bit stubborn. For instance, he would work only with me. I was granted leave a couple of years ago, and during that period no one here saw anything of him. He appeared again a few weeks after I came back."

"So there's nobody here who can give us any more information," Billy T. said, quite redundantly. "About his family relationships and that kind of thing. About his social circle."

"No, definitely not."

She laughed again, staccato and shrill.

"He was extremely concerned about fairness."

"I see," Hanne said.

"He was thoroughly preoccupied with everything having to follow the correct procedure. By accident, one time we had deducted too little tax from him. He became totally devastated. It was a matter of a very small, insignificant amount, and we corrected it a short time later. But I had the impression that he couldn't sleep for fear of being caught by the tax office."

"Slightly over the top, perhaps. I agree." Hanne smiled easily and added, "What was he working on at present? A colleague of mine mentioned something about—"

"At the moment he was doing some writing, in fact," Åshild Meier interrupted. "A short foreword for a book about classic cars. But much more important: he was to write one of the chapters in a major work about the history of the Norwegian police."

She beamed, as if it had only now dawned on her that she was speaking to two representatives of the force.

"It's really fascinating! We're working with the National Police Directorate and are in the process of getting a number of wonderful writers to contribute. Lawyers and police officers. Several professional historians, of course, as well as journalists. We even have someone convicted of homicide, to write about his experience with the forces of law and order. The wartime chapter will be particularly fascinating, and for that, we've actually got our hands on one of the foremost—"

"But this Sidensvans doesn't exactly sound fascinating," Billy T. objected.

A vaguely disgruntled expression crossed Åshild Meier's face.

"Then I must have expressed myself badly," she said. "Sidensvans was extremely fascinating. A bit odd, as I said, but fascinating people are often strange. Besides, this is a book we knew that he would approach with—"

As she was interrupted by someone knocking at the door, she glanced swiftly at the clock.

"Time flies! I actually have a meeting now . . . Come in! But of course I can—"

Getting to her feet, Hanne shook her head. "No, not at all. We've taken up enough of your time."

A woman, obviously a colleague, popped her head in and said, "The meeting's started, Åshild. Are you coming?"

"Just a minute!"

In some confusion, she gazed from Hanne to Billy T.

"It's fine," Hanne reassured her once more. "I'll phone if there's anything further. Thanks for all your help."

In the end, Mabelle's nagging became unbearable. What's more, Christian realized she was probably right. If the police suspected them—and it would be a miracle if that were not the case—then they would find the apartment sooner or later. It would be better to take a chance now. Empty the place. Quickly remove what was risky. So he had gone, partway by bus, partway on foot, taking absurd detours as he went.

He carefully removed a graphic print from the wall in the bedroom. The safe was locked, in accordance with regulations. He opened it and found the pictures lying where they should be.

He had wanted to burn them at once. When Hermann Stahlberg had triumphantly flung a bundle of semipornographic pictures of Mabelle on the table and threatened to publicize them if CC did not withdraw the legal action he had initiated against his father, what Christian wanted most of all was to destroy them. When he arrived home, without having said a word to the old man apart from a mumbled, "You'll be hearing from me," he had lit the fire. It was Mabelle who had stopped him. When he had reluctantly, and with intense embarrassment, told her about Hermann's last move, she had sobbed bitterly for an hour. Then she dried her tears and became surprisingly rational.

"He has copies," she concluded. "Of course, he has. Besides . . ."

At times like this he admired her more than ever. Mabelle was a born businesswoman, able to be sensible, almost cynical, even under the greatest pressure. If she had chosen to embark on something other than a fashion magazine, she would have made it big. Even within such an unstable and unprofitable line of business, she had built a reputation substantial enough to ensure that she was someone to reckon with. It would have been an exaggeration to call Mabelle a celebrity, but everyone in the trade knew who she was. She was in, and was only just beginning to make money on *F&F*.

"Besides, the damaging effects of these pictures—if they should end up in the wrong hands—are limited, after all."

She had bravely tried to see the positive side of the situation.

"I would hardly be invited to make any comment about the royal family again," she had said, swallowing. "But I'll survive. They're not *so* crude. It would just be unpleasant. Fucking unpleasant."

And she burst into tears again.

He had wanted to burn the pictures, but she had stopped him.

"We need them," she sobbed inconsolably.

"Need them?" he had screamed angrily. "I never want to see them again!"

"Listen . . ."

Her voice was quivering.

"It might come to . . . it might be that at some time we need to prove how your father has behaved. These pictures at least show . . ."

She had been right then, and she was right now. He wanted to burn them, at home.

The pictures lay inside an envelope. He pushed them inside his jacket, tucked well down into the waistband of his trousers. With an unsteady hand, he tried to open the metal container on the bottom shelf of the safe. His fingers would not obey, and his nails scraped against the green metal. Finally the lid opened.

The shock made his stomach contract convulsively. He shut his mouth and tried to force back the sour stuff that wanted to rise and spew out.

The receptacle contained only one gun.

The gun Carl-Christian kept quite legally, a Korth Combat Magnum, was in its place. It had been hugely expensive, one of the most carefully made revolvers in the world. He had purchased it six years earlier in a fit of childish enthusiasm, after enrolling in a gun club. But Carl-Christian had lost interest. On closer acquaintance, he did not like the gun club environment. Anyway, he got a pain in his shoulder from using high-caliber weapons. The revolver had barely been used.

It was still lying in its place.

But the other gun had disappeared.

When Carl-Christian eventually managed to close the safe, he had entirely forgotten to check the ammunition on the top shelf. There was no space left within him for any further problems. He touched his stomach, where he felt the envelope of photos like a shield against his abdomen.

Mabelle was the only one who knew about his safe and the code for the lock.

As well as Hermine, of course.

"So how long do you think this might take?"

Hanne Wilhelmsen looked around without answering. CID Chief Jens Puntvold's office was attractive without seeming cozy and actually quite stylish, despite Hanne being unable to point out anything to distinguish it from other offices in the building. Even though the room itself was far more spacious than others had to make do with, the walls were just as boringly gray, the floor just as marked with wear and tear, and the curtains looked in desperate need of laundering into the bargain. Maybe it was the flowers: fresh lilies in a multicolored vase on the desk and a colorful bouquet of early tulips in the center of the conference table. The pictures must be his own personal property. Two massive oil paintings hung, facing west, both abstracts in shades of blue.

In addition, there was something about the air: a fresh scent of aftershave and a recently showered body.

Jens Puntvold seemed just as exhausted as the rest of Oslo's police force, but was nevertheless strikingly good looking. Hanne caught herself speculating whether he bleached his hair. The blond streaks fell soft and thick over his forehead, with no trace of gray flecks. Although his face showed signs of lack of sleep and long workdays, his eyes were alert. Clasping his hands behind his neck, he waited for a response.

"You're impatient," Hanne said with a smile. "It's only four days since the murders took place, in fact."

"Yes," he said, returning her smile. "But you know why I'm asking. You're the one who knows all this, Wilhelmsen. I'm only looking for a qualified guess."

"Months," she said ambiguously. "Years, perhaps. It's even possible that we don't succeed. In solving the case, I mean. It's happened before."

"We've never had a case like this before."

"No . . ."

She studied the lilies in the multicolored vase.

"But even though the solved rate for homicide is high in this country, both you and I know that these first few days are enormously important. If it really is one of the surviving Stahlbergs behind it all, then this could take ages. But then we'd catch the guilty party, or parties, in the end. I'm convinced of that. A slow churn, you know. Justice, I mean."

She flashed another smile, before adding: "But if it was someone else, a stranger, a failed robbery, or . . . well. Then it may already be too late."

"That just can't happen."

Suddenly he leaned forward and planted his elbows on the desk. His gaze fixed on hers as he continued: "This case *has* to be solved, Wilhelmsen. We can't stand for an unsolved quadruple homicide."

"Who are *we*?" Hanne asked, without breaking eye contact.

"The police. Society. All of us. Our work is an uphill struggle as it is. Increasing criminality, and funding doesn't keep pace in the slightest. The police force has to show its muscle, Hanne. We have to demonstrate our indispensability. Our effectiveness. For far too long, this force has appeared inept and dragging its feet. I would like . . ."

Hanne was taken aback when he used her first name. Surprisingly enough, she felt flattered.

"Of course, first and foremost, my task is to lead the criminal investigation department to attain the best possible efficiency and the greatest possible well-being of staff."

It seemed as if he were using a well-rehearsed platitude. Then his mask cracked as he opened out his arms and cocked his head provocatively.

"But if my modicum of . . . media charm can contribute to increased understanding out there, about the need for greater resources and better working conditions for the police, then I find it highly opportune to make use of that. And what we *don't* need right now is for us to lose our way in this case. I hope you understand what I'm saying."

Hanne did not reply but felt a vague distaste for his gaze, which seemed colder now.

"Do you read the daily newspapers?" he asked.

"No. I don't in fact. I leaf through *Aftenposten* every morning, but I simply can't face the tabloids right now."

She stole a glance at the time, believing herself to be discreet.

"Continue with it," he said, taking a look at his own watch. "I won't detain you any longer. You expect this to take some time then. Some considerable time. But if you . . . if you were to give an off-the-cuff hint, who do you think did it?"

"I never drop hints," Hanne said. "Not in my own cases, anyway."

"Come on," he insisted, almost teasing now. "Just between the two of us."

"Out of the question."

She stood up.

"But we have to hope, in our heart of hearts, that it's one of those three. Because if it's not, I don't quite understand how this case will ever be solved. May I go now?"

He nodded.

"Just one more question," he said when she had almost reached the door. "At the meeting on Friday, it seemed as if you were the only one at all concerned about this guy Sidensvans. I didn't entirely understand why. Can you explain that to me?"

Hanne stopped in her tracks, half turning to face him again, and tugged distractedly at her earlobe.

"Like everyone else in the police here," she said slowly, "I consider it most likely that a member of the family is behind this slaughter. But not necessarily all three. And as in all other homicide cases, it's important to find the actual motive for the incident. If we find that, then we'll find the man who committed the murders."

"Or woman."

"Or woman. Motives positively scream out at us, as far as Carl-Christian is concerned, but I've worked long enough here in the police force to know that there are . . . that all families have hidden secrets. Always. I'm just trying not to be drowned out by the obvious. And I want . . . I *want* to know what Sidensvans was doing in Eckersbergs gate on Thursday evening. Only then will our picture of the crime be complete, and the motive possible to establish."

The head of CID laughed out loud and slowly brought his hands together.

"You're even better than they say," he said, grinning. "Off you go now. Thanks for coming!"

"No trouble," Hanne mumbled in embarrassment as she left.

Silje Sørensen gave a loud, prolonged yawn. Tears rolled down her cheeks and she wiped them away, smiling apologetically, before attempting once again to concentrate on the documents.

"My little boy's sleeping so badly these days," she explained as she read. "Asthma. Last night we needed to use a steam tent and every-thing. It's this layer of cold air pollution, it—"

"Mmm."

Inclining her head, Police Prosecutor Annmari Skar used her fin-gers to comb her gray-streaked hair.

"It's actually curious that no one has seen anything," she said, with-out lifting her eyes. "We've had hundreds of tips in this case, but none of them—not *one* . . ."

She flicked rapidly through the documents and stretched out her arm to hold up a sheet of paper.

"I need to get myself glasses," she murmured. "My arms aren't long enough any more. Not one of the tips says anything about the comings and goings at Eckersbergs gate 5. Extremely conspicuous."

"Not necessarily," Silje said, yawning again. "In a city, we don't notice very much. We don't bother; we don't keep our eyes open. We satisfy our curiosity about other people's lives and misfortunes by reading gossip magazines and the tabloids. It's exactly as if . . . it seems almost as though terrorizing the intimate lives of celebrities has made us less observant about our own surroundings. Of course, it was unfortunate that the street's busybody was at bingo on that particular night. She won five pounds of coffee, by the way, and a gift card for the GlasMagasin store. She's over the moon." She cracked a fleeting smile, adding: "That's the sort of thing you remember. Good Lord!"

"That's exactly what the problem is," Annmari said in frustration. "In a case like this, we're overloaded with facts that are totally irrelevant. It becomes like a jigsaw puzzle with far too many pieces. Impossible to fit together."

"Difficult, anyway."

A candle sputtered in a red wooden candlestick on the narrow window ledge. It was guttering. Darkness had already descended on Oslo. The windowpanes reflected the flickering light. Suddenly the candle decoration caught fire. Paper holly leaves and red cardboard berries burst into flames. Silje grabbed a half-filled cup of tea and tossed the liquid over the little bonfire, which had already left extensive soot marks on the glass.

"It should have burned itself out," Annmari said, alarmed, staring at the damp stain creeping down the wall below the window. "'Police Prosecutor Sets Fire to Police Headquarters in an Attack of Christmas Spirit.' Thanks."

"These candle decorations are dangerous," Silje said, trying to wipe the worst of it off with a napkin.

"I know that. I'll tidy up later. Where did you actually get hold of this?"

She flapped a couple of sheets of paper.

"Preben's widow, Jennifer. She came home from London with the children on Saturday and said that a will had been submitted to Oslo Probate and Bankruptcy Court. She and the children had been Christmas shopping. So they were away at the time of the murders. She's completely shattered. Not strange in the least. It's one thing to be widowed so dramatically and left with three small children. It's another matter . . . Erik Henriksen visited her yesterday. She's quite . . . old-fashioned. That was the expression he used. A 'home-loving' woman—wasn't that what they used to say? In the past?"

"Something like that."

"She has no education, apart from the equivalent of a high school diploma and something Erik understood to be some kind of girls' finishing school for the offspring of upper-class parents. A bit of art history and cooking. The art of setting beautiful tables. On the whole, a lot of art. She's from Australia, as you'll recall, from a middle-class but not especially well-heeled family. I dare say Jennifer is the sort of woman that guys in big business often choose."

"Yes, well, you'd know something about that," Annmari said, smiling. "Like your own mother, I suppose."

Silje ignored her. "Jennifer Calvin Stahlberg could have had 'mother' as her professional status. She forced herself to regain her composure when the eldest boy appeared, Erik said. The ten-year-old was actually supposed to be at a friend's house while his mother was being interviewed, but he had run back home again. Jennifer seemed calm and rational, and showed great concern for the boy until she had managed to phone the friend's mother and hand her boy over again. Then she broke down completely. She doesn't speak Norwegian. She has no real friends in Norway—only acquaintances she's come into contact with through entertaining for her husband and the parents of her children's school friends. She actually has nothing here in this country. At the same time, it's fifteen years since she moved from Australia. She and Preben met in Singapore, you know. Both her parents are dead. No siblings."

"But now, of course, a whole pile of money," Annmari said, studying the handwritten document. "It smells quite scorched in here. Shall we open a window?"

Without waiting for an answer, she opened the window a crack.

"She's not exactly the one who gets the money," Silje corrected her. "But I didn't know this sort of thing was legal!"

"What's that? Disinheriting your children?"

"Yes."

"We ordinary mortals can't do that, either," Annmari said. "According to the law, an obligatory share must go to the lineal heirs. Two-thirds of the total estate."

"Exactly!"

"But only up to a certain limit. One million, if I'm not entirely mistaken. So for you rich folk, we're talking about peanuts. You can quite simply decide that your children get fobbed off with loose change."

The draft from the window was uncomfortable. Silje closed it without asking permission. She carefully laid the copy of the will in front of her.

"It's not actually Jennifer who is the beneficiary. It's her eldest son. Carl-Christian receives the bare minimum he's entitled to. Hermine gets the proceeds of shares redeemed to the value of 5 million. The rest—that is, the entire shipping company, all the properties, cars, and household effects—goes to the eldest grandson, with the exception of a few bits and pieces to his siblings. And our dear Hermann must actually have been farsighted. If Preben was alive at the time of his parents' death, he would get everything. If he was already deceased, then the estate should be transferred into some kind of trust, with an administrator who would look after it all until the boy—"

"What's his name?"

"Hermann. Of course. Preben can't have been entirely lacking in foresight, either. At the time the boy was born, he hadn't spoken to his father in years. All the same, he chose the oldest trick in the book. Naming his son after his father. Well, anyway, the boy will take it all over on his twenty-fifth birthday, under a lot of conditions."

"Such as what?"

"Such as that he must have undertaken an education in economics equivalent to a master's in business and economics, or higher. That he has an unblemished record. And that he hasn't married and doesn't have children."

"Doesn't have children? That can't be legal, at least! Talk about ruling the family from beyond the grave!"

The window snapped open by itself, sending an icy blast into the room.

"It's warped," Annmari said, struggling to close it again. "It's almost impossible to shut it."

Silje pulled her woolen jacket more tightly around herself.

"That man has ruled the family all these years," she said, shuddering. "He obviously didn't intend to give up yet—"

"So, strictly speaking, Carl-Christian doesn't have anything to gain by this homicide," Annmari said slowly. "Not a shred of motive."

They continued to sit there, looking each other in the eye, for some time. Silje noticed that Annmari's eyes were actually green with brown flecks.

"If he was aware of that," she said finally. "It's not certain. The will was signed less than four months ago. The father and younger son have hardly spoken to each other since then."

"But Jennifer knew," Annmari said, without relinquishing eye contact. "Jennifer knew about the will that favored her son."

Silje shook her head energetically.

"No, Annmari. It can't be her. She was away. With three children."

"There are killers for hire. Even here in Norway."

"Heavens above, Annmari!"

Silje slapped her forehead and rolled her eyes.

"She knows nobody! She can't even speak the language, and she has no circle of friends! She—"

"But she's not an idiot," Annmari broke in angrily. "The woman could have obtained help abroad, for all I know!"

"And so she's ordered someone to kill her husband and parents-in-law, the father of her children and their grandparents! There's nothing—absolutely *nothing*—to suggest any conflict, apart from entirely everyday things, between Jennifer and Preben! No infidelity, no quarrel about money, no—"

"We've investigated this case for four days, Silje. Four days. We know just about nada about this family."

"Nada! Do you call *this* 'nada'?"

Silje used the palm of her hand to deliver a hard smack to the three tall stacks of document folders on the desk between them. The last one toppled over, and a ring binder and four voluminous folders fell to the floor.

"Sorry," she spluttered. "But there have to be limits. It just can't be the case that if one of your close relations falls victim to a crime, you immediately get sucked into the vortex of skepticism and suspicion that we whip up."

"The problem is more likely the opposite," Annmari said, unruffled. "I agree with Hanne Wilhelmsen. We're too restrained. We operate with too few suspects. Often, at least. Don't you agree?"

Her voice was steady, without a trace of sarcasm. Nevertheless, Silje felt provoked. She could not understand the sudden rage she felt on behalf of Jennifer Calvin Stahlberg. Silje had not even met her. Admittedly Erik had seemed unusually and powerfully moved following his visit the previous day, and from a purely objective point of view, there was every reason to feel great sympathy for the mother of three now left stranded in a foreign country. All the same, Jennifer was only one of the steadily increasing numbers of people involved in Oslo Police Force's most sensational homicide case in living memory. Maybe it was the vulnerability of the mother's position with which Silje identified. Maybe she felt empathy with being different and alone, just as Jennifer was alone in a situation that hardly any of them could attempt to comprehend.

"This is what you're really angry about, isn't it?"

Annmari held yesterday's copies of *VG* and *Dagbladet* up at face level. The entire front-page splash in Norway's major newspapers was a photograph of Jennifer and her children making their way through customs at Oslo Airport. The woman stared openmouthed, her eyes red and wide in the camera flash. A dark-haired boy smiled meekly at the photographer, while the youngest, a girl clutching her mother's hand, looked as if she was crying bitterly. The middle child was almost completely hidden behind his mother. Only snow-white sneakers with loose laces protruded from a dark-blue pant leg.

"Maybe so," Silje said, sighing almost inaudibly. "It makes me pretty upset. Why do they do that? Why do we allow that sort of thing? I mean, we're talking about three *children*! They've just lost their father, and then . . . I just can't fathom it. How do they manage it?"

"The new surveillance service," Hanne Wilhelmsen said, laughing sardonically from the doorway. "The Surveillance Service became the Security Service, and the Security Service is bound hand and foot, muzzled and monitored. The Fourth Estate has taken over. They shrink from nothing. No rules apply to them. They have illegal archives; they bribe, persuade, force, and badger their sources. They scream, kick, and yell if anyone mentions the word *control* to them. Of course, they're protecting freedom of speech, you know. Every time they make fools of themselves, they run a navel-gazing little debate in their professional journals and call it self-criticism. Then they're at it again."

"Hello," Annmari said.

"Hi. Have you lit a bonfire in here, or what?"

Hanne sniffed the air, her brow furrowed.

"Almost. Just a minor accident."

"Can you make anything of that will?"

Hanne looked with interest at the plastic folder on top of the bundle closest to her, and continued: "I heard old Hermann wrote it himself in pen. Is that right?"

"Looks like it," Annmari confirmed. "Quite strange, really. He has always surrounded himself with a crowd of lawyers at work and in connection with the family squabble. But he writes the will himself. All the formal requirements have been fulfilled, at least as far as I can judge. The witnesses are completely unknown to me, but if they really were present when Hermann and Turid signed this, then everything's in order. But there will certainly be trouble all the same."

"Trouble? Aren't wills like that only a question of formalities, then?"

"Not only. Some peculiar conditions are stipulated. With such enormous sums and controversial contents, this will is bound to be challenged. Just as well to be poor, right!"

Once again Silje felt this unfamiliar annoyance.

In fact she liked Annmari Skar. The Police Prosecutor was honest and trustworthy, and had been in the police force long enough not to score points because she, as a lawyer, was senior to the police officers. Besides, Annmari was one of the few who did not seem particularly preoccupied with Hanne Wilhelmsen. When she heard the young trainees' admiring references to the Chief Inspector, she shrugged indifferently. She refused to listen to gossip from the older ones in the force, but without making a song and dance about it. She simply stood up and walked out. Annmari Skar was competent without being brilliant; she was approachable, open, and had gradually become one of the most experienced lawyers at police headquarters. Vice chair of the civil servants' professional association, she never flinched from essential disputes and was respected by all ranks in the colossal curved headquarters building at Grønlandsleiret 44.

But she seemed obsessed with money.

She seldom let a chance go to drop a hint about Silje's financial position. As a rule, her comments were sarcastic and almost always hurtful. As soon as Hanne Wilhelmsen had moved to the Frogner district, she too had become an object of the ceaseless sarcasm, though she did not seem to take any notice of it. But then Hanne Wilhelmsen hardly ever took any notice of anything.

Silje, on the other hand, had had enough.

"Can you just stop all that!" she roared, and felt the blood rush to her head.

"What?" Annmari seemed dumbfounded. "What on earth do you mean?"

"*Just as well to be poor, right!*" Silje mimicked in a distorted voice, and continued her outburst: "I'm so tired of this eternal mudslinging of yours to do with my money. In the first place, we're talking about absolutely honest money. What's more, I don't spend especially much of it. I live well, that's true, but *I can't help it if my father is rich and generous!* He's a lovely, decent, and loving father, and I'm certainly not going to feel ashamed of him. At least not because *you want it that way!*"

She smacked herself on the thigh—too hard, in fact, for it smarted badly.

"Ouch," she said automatically.

Hanne chortled, wide-eyed.

"There's more of a temper in you than I thought!"

"And as for you," Silje snarled in her direction. "You can just keep your mouth shut. You go about pretending you don't have a penny to your name. I've seen the tax return for that professor woman of yours. You're an inverted snob, Hanne. Take a look at yourself!"

Two eyes bored into Hanne. She glanced down at her own body. The college sweater with NYU emblazoned on the chest was unwashed. A white bleach stain was obvious on the pale blue of her left shoulder. Her jeans were too tight and were worn white at the knees.

"Okay," she said, nonplussed. "But look at these!"

She lifted one leg. Her boots were dark-brown embossed leather, the toes and heels reinforced with metal.

"Real silver," she announced, tapping the floor. "Not cheap."

Annmari burst out laughing. Silje tried to resist, but her mouth twisted into a diffident smile.

"I'm really sorry," Annmari said sincerely. "I'd no idea I carried on like that. I didn't mean it. I'll get a grip on myself. I promise."

The sparkle had gone out of Silje. She knew that wicked tongues called her "Little Hanne" as soon as she was out of earshot. Until now, she had taken it as a compliment, but it struck her all at once that the nickname might not have so much to do with her competence. Sulky diatribes over insignificant casual remarks would probably be grist for the mill only if Annmari were one of the bigmouths. Silje consoled herself that she most likely was not.

"I'm the one who should apologize," she said sullenly. "But sometimes I get my back up."

"How many times do I have to tell you not to bother with what people say," Hanne said, patting her head in a motherly fashion.

Silje wriggled out of reach, slightly too abruptly. Hanne shrugged.

"Besides, no one should envy you your money. Your father, on the other hand . . ."

She caught Silje's eye, and held eye contact.

"Your father sounds enviable. Lucky you."

Then she turned on her heel and disappeared. Annmari and Silje were left sitting there in silence, as the click-clack of Hanne's heels faded along the corridor. In the distance they heard a Christmas carol, piercingly off-key. Someone shouted out, and the response was raucous laughter.

"You really are lucky," Annmari said softly. "Hanne's genuinely fond of you."

Outside, snow continued to fall. It looked as though there might well be an old-fashioned white Christmas despite the fluctuating temperature.

Billy T. had not visited Ronny Berntsen for several years. Now he stood outside Ronny's apartment in Urtegata, wondering why. Ronny was not an informer. Admittedly he had helped Billy T. in a handful of cases with valuable information and smart suggestions. All the same, never for his own personal advantage. Ronny kept his mouth shut about himself and his family and never uttered a word about things he thought none of his business either. Not even when he would obviously have gained by it.

Ronny had his own moral code. It might not be totally in agreement with the Ten Commandments, since he had made his living from breaking the fifth and the seventh, had great fun contravening the sixth, and for the most part couldn't care less about the rest. Nevertheless, Ronny had his rules for life. One of them was never to slander anyone who didn't deserve it. He eventually took a pragmatic view of the people who were protected by this attitude.

The apartment block was one that had avoided all attempts at improvement of the inner city. The facade was peeling. It was impossible to see what color the building had originally been: the daubs here and there on the outer walls gave a drab gray impression. The cornices had collapsed long ago. The windows, crooked and wind battered, must be from the thirties. Billy T. smiled to himself as he walked through the entranceway that stank of garbage and cat piss. While eleven of the apartments in the two-story-high block were rundown storage boxes for drug addicts and other birds of passage, Ronny's apartment was an oasis of pastel colors and expensive designer furniture.

"Hello," Ronny said, opening the door slightly.

Almost as tall as Billy T., he had paradoxically enough taken far better care of himself. His complexion was suntanned; the contrast made his teeth look sparkling white when he grinned at the policeman.

"Work or pleasure?" he asked, opening the door slightly wider.

"A little of each," Billy T. said. "Both, in fact."

"No house search?"

"Nope. Just want to chat."

The door opened wide. The light from inside flooded out into the pitch-dark stairwell, where the bulb on a single lamp was broken. Billy T. squinted as he followed Ronny into a spacious living room. A colossal bowl on the coffee table was overflowing with tropical fruit. As he sank into a huge five-seat sofa, Billy T. flipped off his shoes and hoisted his feet. The top of a pineapple tickled him through his socks.

"Very nice in here," he said.

"You look fucking awful now, Billy T. Have you stopped exercising or what?"

Without waiting for a reply, Ronny headed for the kitchen. Billy T. heard the sound of something being poured into a glass and closed his eyes. The sofa cushions were soft. Jenny, as usual, was sick and had kept them awake half the night. He had still not bought any presents. His bank account was almost empty. His mother had phoned him twice in a row on his cell phone about the very same things. She was going to spend Christmas at her daughter's, but it sounded as if she thought they would all be gathered there. The early signs of senility were too obvious to overlook now, but he didn't have the energy to deal with it. His sister was cross because he avoided the subject. Tone-Marit, Jenny's mother, was cross because they had no money. Everybody was cross. Hanne was cross and odd. Billy T. was indescribably sleepy. His arms felt so heavy that he couldn't even bring himself to check his watch. He was short of time. Always short of time, and all these women stood around him, scolding. Hanne had blue angel wings and flew to the ceiling in an enormous cathedral. The light from the glass cupola was dazzling, and Hanne was transformed into a bird with a human head, carrying his mother in a pink cloth. Suddenly she let go. Billy T. tried to run and catch her, break her fall, but he was rooted to the spot in a field of flesh-eating plants that curled around his legs. Sucking, they held him fast and threatened to drag him under a bog full of children's corpses.

"Hey!"

Startled, Billy T. sat up abruptly and took the pineapple with him as his feet suddenly thumped on the floor.

"For Christ's sake, you were fast asleep! Are you ill, Billy T.?"

"Just tired."

"Here, drink this."

Ronny put a tall glass of reddish liquid before him on the glass table. Billy T. studied it, partly confused, partly skeptical, without making any sign of willingness to drink it.

"I've cut it out. No alcohol. No other kind of shit, either. Just fruit. Things that'll do you good, my friend. Drink up."

Slowly, Billy T. raised the glass to his mouth. He drank all of it in one swallow and forced a smile of gratitude.

"Sorry," he said. "I'm just so fucking tired these days. A lot to do at work and with the kids and—"

"And then it's Christmas Eve tomorrow, and no money," Ronny said with a grin. "I get it. Is it that big murder in Frogner you're working on?"

"Among other things."

"It must be pretty straightforward, though."

"It's anything but straightforward."

Ronny interlaced his fingers at the back of his neck.

"There're loads of fucking rumors going around the place."

"I know that."

"Is that why you came?"

"I suppose so. One reason."

"Can't offer you much help. It's all just rumor. Except . . . But I expect you already know about that."

"What's that?"

Billy T. actually felt far more wide awake now. His skin tingled slightly, and he raised his right hand to examine it. The veins on the back of his hand were pronounced, and he could actually see the blood running faster. He felt light-headed.

"Was there something in that drink?" he asked, without lifting his eyes.

"Juice, Billy T. The juice from fruits and one vegetable. It's just your blood sugar that's elevated."

"What is it you think we know?" Billy T. repeated.

"About that woman Hermine."

"Yes, Ronny. We know there's someone called Hermine Stahlberg."

"Not all good. But you probably know about it."

"Mmm."

The Stahlberg inquiry had developed into a monster. There were twenty-three investigators allocated now, working just on the tactical aspects. In addition, there were the technical experts, from those with weapons expertise to the forensics team and crime scene examiners. The case documents already filled several yards of shelving. More than eighty people had been interviewed, the apartment in Eckersbergs gate had been combed, an effort had been made to build the victims' life histories into comprehensive pictures that were still hopelessly incomplete, with gaping holes. The Stahlberg case was a conglomeration of information and profiles, theories and facts. Billy T. could not manage to keep abreast of everything that flowed in, documents and interviews, anonymous tips and more or less realistic hypotheses. At the numerous meetings held in an attempt to ensure that as many people as possible were kept up to speed, he had to admit grudgingly that he grew less and less loquacious. He continually lagged behind, but at the very least he knew who Hermine was.

Ronny raised an eyebrow and broke into a crooked smile.

"She's been around the block a bit, you know. So now everyone's going about, boasting that they know her and that they . . . Nobody's talking about anything apart from this case of yours."

"We've noticed that, yes. Do you think there's anything in all this talk?"

"Well, hardly. You know the territory, Billy T. Almost as well as I do."

That was no longer true, but Billy T. nodded in agreement.

"People like to make out they're damned important," Ronny said. "Lots of muttering about selling guns and that sort of shit. And there might well be something in that. Guns are easier to get hold of than drugs at the moment. These Yugo-boys, for example, they've easier access to hardware than the police have."

"That wouldn't take much, you know—"

"That's where the police are outmaneuvered. You do whatever the hell you can to stop the flood of narcotics, with dogs and customs officers and surveillance and intelligence and international cooperation. Not that it fucking helps such a lot, but there's obviously no shortage of resources. The boys who cruise north from the Balkans with vehicles full of weapons, and women and children in the backseat as camouflage, you never catch sight of them, though. It would have taken me half an hour, Billy T. Half an hour! Tell me what kind of gun you want, and I'll get it for you in thirty minutes flat. This city will soon be overflowing with shooters. Look here!"

He bent over and pulled out a newspaper from the shelf below the table. It was open at an article about the impounding of weapons in Oslo. The picture showed a perplexed head of CID, Jens Puntvold himself, his hand open and inviting, above an enormous collection of guns.

"That's your haul in the course of just twenty-four months," Ronny said. "If you want a gun in this city, it's simply a matter of helping yourself from whatever your lot have impounded."

"You should have been a policeman, Ronny. Then we'd have got things moving, you know."

Ronny did not pick up on the irony. Instead he smiled, in a new and different way.

"People like us actually should be, Billy T. You and me. Do you remember that?"

Billy T. rested his eyes on the coverage in Friday's *Aftenposten*, presented opportunely as a framed article in the middle of the four-page spread about the murders in Eckersbergs gate.

Of course he remembered.

The open area called Kuba in springtime. The Aker River with water discharging far across all its banks. Two boys with cropped summer haircuts and tin revolvers in their cowboy belts, slanted over skinny hips. The sheriff stars with peeling gold paint. Ronny wore a cowboy hat with short fringes around the brim; his father was a sailor and had come home at last. Billy T. had eczema on his back; it itched and was exacerbated by the effluent from the soap factory. He was not allowed to swim—his mother boxed his ears if he ventured into the river—but they went in for a dip all the same. They swam in the strong currents and slid down the waterfall at Nedre Foss, getting beaten black and blue on the stones, laughing all the while. Billy T. hit a duck with his bow and arrow. They cooked it, still covered in feathers, on an illegal bonfire and fed it to the cats: semiwild scrawny animals that gobbled down the burned duck meat and followed them.

"We were going to be cops," Ronny said. "Both of us. But that's not how things turned out."

"No . . ."

Billy T. let his gaze slide around the apartment. There was barely an object in the room that he could afford to buy. Even the fruit in the sumptuous bowl was foreign, far beyond the reach of a policeman's salary with deductions for four love children. Ronny had spent nine years in jail, in total, since he was nineteen. Now they were both middle-aged. Billy T. held his face in his hands and struggled to breathe evenly.

"You didn't really come here to ask about these things," Ronny said.

*Yes, I did,* Billy T. wanted to say. *I came to hear what you know about a case that, for us, has come to a standstill.*

*It was not true, though,* he thought silently. *I came to remind myself that you're an* outsider *with no true values, Ronny. I came to assure myself that I don't want what you have, because you've never done any-thing important, anything useful, or anything true and honest. You could have been like me,* he thought. *You could be struggling from one payday to the next; you could bounce like a rubber ball between work and children and mother-in-law and hopeless colleagues and a system on the brink of collapse due to people like Ronny—people like you, Ronny, who have checked out of everything and just pay with the occasional trip into a prison system that offers education and entertainment, hot food, and medical assistance whenever you need it.*

"I need to go," Billy T. said, without moving a muscle.

"Here," Ronny said. Billy T. noticed something being placed on the table in front of him.

"What is it?"

"Look. A present."

Slowly Billy T. removed his hands. A little scrap of paper. A betting slip.

"It's unregistered," Ronny said. "I always bet on unregistered betting slips. This is completely legit, Billy T. Seven winners, paying out big money: 153,432 kroner. Legal money."

"A present," Billy T. murmured. "What the hell do you mean by that?"

"Take it. It's yours."

It was an absolutely ordinary betting slip from the racetrack. Worth over 150,000 kroner. Presents for the children. Maybe a vacation that would not have to be spent at his parents-in-law's cottage in Kragerø, with a big family and beds that were too short. Breathing space. His head above water. Entirely legal.

"Money laundering," Billy T. said, refusing to touch the slip of paper. "The easiest way to launder dirty money. You buy a ticket for more than the winnings."

"No. We do that at Bjerke. Not with official ones from Hamar. That gets too complicated. How would we get in touch with the winners? This is just a hobby of mine, Billy T. I'm the one who handed it in. I guarantee you it's a legal prize. Take it as a thank-you."

"Thank you?"

Ronny responded with a smile.

Billy T. knew what he meant. On two occasions, he had looked the other way. It was a long time ago now. Neither time had been particularly serious. He had closed his eyes and let Ronny get away, the last time eight years ago. He had helped Ronny because he remembered that Ronny had once been scared of the dark, and what's more, had wet his bed until he was quite a big boy. Ronny was a wimp as a kid, and he had been Billy T.'s best pal until he had robbed a kiosk for 100 kroner when they were both fifteen. Ronny was sent to a school for young delinquents and Billy T. shaped up. His mother grounded him for two months just for speaking to Ronny before he was bundled into a local police car and driven off. Billy T. had to keep away from scum like that, and his mother tightened her grip on her son until he completed high school. It was Ronny with the bad acne and the pitiful cock that Billy T. had thought of when he let him escape. Not the suntanned Ronny with a luxury apartment and an Audi TT.

"You know I can't accept that," Billy T. said. The blood was ringing in his ears, and he could not take his eyes off the magical note. "That's sheer corruption."

"Not at all," Ronny said firmly. "I don't expect anything in return. This is just a childhood friend stretching out a hand, Billy T. You redeem it, and nobody is going to be any the wiser. Tax free and legal. And fucking brilliant!"

Billy T. felt dizzy. He was light-headed, and his eyes tingled as he stood up and staggered toward the hallway.

"If you were going to buy a gun," he said, aware he was slurring his words a little, "if you were a totally ordinary person and you wanted to get hold of an illegal gun, what would you do?"

"A totally ordinary person?"

Ronny leaned against the door frame and handed him his shoes.

"You forgot these," he said. "I've no idea what totally ordinary people do. But that Hermine Stahlberg character isn't totally ordinary either."

Billy T. fumbled with his shoes and kept losing his balance.

"As I said," Ronny went on, "this city is overflowing with guns. But if you don't have the right contacts to get connected to the big boys, it might be you'd have to make do with . . ."

He considered it.

"Per in the Shack. Do you remember him? He ran an absolutely legit gun store over at Vålerenga, until the police put an end to the business. Now he sticks mainly to small stuff. Or Bjørnar Tofte. I think he's still in the game. He's quite a major player, of course. Or Sølvi. Sølvi Jotun. She's probably the easiest one to get hold of. But she's so unstable that long periods can go by between times when she can actually get her hands on anything."

Billy T. stood up stiffly and ran his hand over the top of his head. He still felt oddly light-headed.

"Sølvi . . . but she's an out-and-out junkie!"

"Off and on. She's a smart cookie. Doesn't look like it, but she hangs in there. Earns money wherever she can."

Billy T. felt cold. Then warmth flooded along his arms and he had to study his hands again to check that the blood was still contained within his skin.

Sølvi Jotun was Kluten's girlfriend. At least she had been, for years.

"Okay."

He had to get out. He had to get air. He could not bear to be here any longer. Ronny smelled of fruit and cologne, and Billy T. had to get out.

"Was there anything in that drink you gave me?" he groaned as he fumbled with the door handle. "Fuck, Ronny, have you slipped me something?"

"Nothing dangerous—only a pick-me-up. But keep away from your colleagues for a few hours. That'd be best."

His voice was steady: soft and with an undercurrent of laughter. Finally the door opened.

Billy T. crashed down the stairs. When the rank odor in the backyard hit him, it seemed fresh and homely and, gasping, he opened his face to the world.

The betting slip was tucked inside his breast pocket, neatly folded. Ronny had placed it there as Billy T. pulled on his leather jacket.

*Sølvi Jotun*, he thought sluggishly.

He needed to find Sølvi Jotun.

•  •  •

Carl-Christian bitterly regretted going along with the decision to hold the family meeting at home. Mabelle walked silently among the soft-spoken relatives, pouring coffee. They numbered nineteen now, and heaven only knew whether more would turn up.

Mabelle looked fantastic. Mourning suited her. Normally she never wore black, which made her look pale, colorless; her light complexion and blond hair could not take the contrast with total darkness. Now she was beautiful. Her complexion was almost chalk-white against her sweater and she wore her hair loose, newly washed, and it fell like a veil over her face every time she leaned forward to offer one of the guests a refill. Even the faint, almost invisible blue circles below her eyes, with only a judicious attempt to use makeup as camouflage, seemed appropriate at a time like this. Carl-Christian was strangely proud as he scrutinized her and accidentally overheard a cousin whispering to her sister: "She seems completely devastated, poor thing. But, my goodness, just gorgeous!"

Nonetheless, he regretted it. Here at home he had no control. He could not get up and leave his own home if it all became too difficult. He was required to wait until the last distant relation condescended to depart. He had certainly not been keen to have the meeting in his home, but Alfred had insisted. The apartment in Eckersbergs gate was out of the question. The police had sealed it, and, besides, it would be entirely unseemly, Alfred declared, before calling the whole family to remind them of Carl-Christian's address.

Mabelle disappeared into the kitchen to switch on the coffee machine again. A woman, of whose identity Carl-Christian was not entirely sure, followed her. He saw her place her hand, light and comforting, on Mabelle's shoulder. It disgusted him. He was sick of all these people, this family, this hastily assembled group of people who, for no reason other than tradition and genetic kinship, had made an appointment with one another every Christmas Day, stiff in their best clothes, tucking greedily into Hermann and Tutta's generous festive table.

"Well, it looks as if everyone's here," Alfred announced. He was newly showered, and the smell of his aftershave had overwhelmed Carl-Christian, who had refused to sit down at his uncle's command

and stood propped up against the wall beside the bathroom. "Apart from dear Hermine, of course, who as we all know is in the hospital and unable to attend. Welcome to you all, anyway."

Carl-Christian ran his eye over the gathering. Some seemed genuinely sad, while others had attended out of pure inquisitiveness and found it difficult to hide that. The cousin who stood in a relaxed pose beside Carl-Christian, trying to smother a yawn, had obviously come out of a sense of duty. Jennifer Calvin Stahlberg and her three children had been given pride of place to some extent, on three chairs ranged beside one another at one end of the living room. The widow held the youngest child on her lap. The little girl was about to fall asleep with her thumb in her mouth. The two boys sat on either side of their mother, looking serious but not crying. Jennifer's eyes were swollen and tear-stained, but she was now sitting erect in the chair, whispering sweet nothings into the little girl's ear.

Alfred suggested a minute's silence in memory of the dead. No one protested: it had been quiet enough already.

"The reasons I wished to call this meeting," Alfred announced, after more than two minutes, "are, of course, first and foremost because it felt right to come together after such a brutal experience as the one we are all now going through. Admittedly, some of us gathered last Friday, but at that time, everything was probably sufficiently recent and we were all so shocked that . . ."

He cleared his throat.

"Not everyone could come. But now . . ."

He thrust out his hand as if blessing them all.

". . . we are here. Does anyone wish to say anything?"

No one answered. Alfred's sisters, one slender and ailing, the other plump and round like Alfred, sobbed into their embroidered handkerchiefs.

"No? I see," Alfred said, unable to hide his displeasure at the passivity of the assembled company.

He slurped some coffee.

"There's not so much to say about this tragedy," he said. "What has happened is absolutely terrible and completely beyond comprehension. At least mine."

He gave a little burst of laughter, intended to be self-mocking, but had misjudged his audience. They all looked down.

"We simply must stick together," he added quickly. "We have to support one another. For example, we must choose someone to speak to the press. Some of you have already been sought out by these journalists, and that has almost certainly been unpleasant—"

"I think the right thing has to be not to give any statements at all," a man in his thirties interrupted him. "At least not before the funeral."

Carl-Christian had always liked his cousin Andreas. He had something of Hermine about him, something warmly dependable: he never took sides. So it was quite surprising to see him oppose his uncle.

"The press has been at us all," Andreas went on. "And we know what they're after. What theories they're using."

Carl-Christian's cheeks were on fire. No one looked in his direction. On the contrary, their interest in the interior decor and view from the window was immediately obvious.

"I just want to say one thing straightaway," Andreas continued. Having stood up now, he had his back to Alfred. "I don't believe a word of what they're hinting. We know CC well. None of us here . . ."

He fixed his eyes on Carl-Christian.

". . . none of us believe for a minute that any member of the family is behind this dreadful act. But journalists are journalists. They put words into people's mouths, especially people like us who have no experience of that sort of thing. We ought to ask them to respect our decision not to comment until our family members have been laid to rest. Then we can take it from there."

A murmur of assent spread around the room. Alfred appeared offended.

"As I was going to say myself," he interjected. "Then we are all agreed on that. But there are other items on the agenda. Things that have to be arranged. As you may already know, there is a will in existence."

Carl-Christian closed his eyes. Since Jennifer had phoned him the previous evening, after the police had collected the document from the Oslo Probate and Bankruptcy Court, he had felt hurled into a tumult of conflicting emotions. He still had not seen the will, not on paper as such, but in the course of the conversation with his

sister-in-law, he had already understood enough to know that he was
in serious economic difficulties. He had been fobbed off with nothing.

But the will might also be his salvation.

He gained nothing from his parents' death. He must maintain that
he had long known of his father's last wishes. Mabelle had realized
that; she had hassled him about it all night long. In fact they knew
about this document, of course they did, she had whispered insistently
while they lay unable to sleep. Anyway, they had known something
was brewing, and it was far from surprising that his father had taken
such a dramatic step as to disinherit him, considering the circumstances. And since it had actually dawned on them that something of
the kind had become unavoidable, it could hardly be such a major
falsehood to claim that they had specific knowledge of it. Mabelle was
persuasive, and CC quite simply had no choice.

"And I don't have any knowledge of the contents," Alfred said.
"Jennifer here . . ."

He turned elegantly in the widow's direction.

". . . for the time being has been unwilling to share that with me. But
I understand that there will be a meeting . . . I expect all the same that
we—"

"Honestly!"

It was Andreas again. Frowning indignantly, he opened out his
arms.

"It's totally inappropriate to discuss the inheritance before the
funeral has taken place! Don't you agree, folks?"

He looked around. The others nodded, some quite eagerly. Alfred
blushed deeply and grew short of breath.

"Of course it's not," he said. "Of course it's not. But despite everything, it's about a *going concern*, and it's not in the interest of any of us
if that's not taken care of—"

"The shipping company will manage," Andreas concluded quickly.
"In any case, it won't be a matter of more than a week or so. Do you
know anything further about when we can expect the release of the
bod . . . of your parents and your brother?"

He looked benevolently across at Carl-Christian, who shook his
head without a word.

"I see," Andreas said. "But it can't take all that long, can it?"

"I have a suggestion."

Andreas's sister Benedicte got to her feet. No more than twenty-five, she had the same blond wavy hair as her brother. She looked embarrassed but raised her voice all the same.

"I suggest we choose Andreas as the family spokesman," she said, clearing her throat.

Flabbergasted, Alfred stared all around the room. His mouth was open, as if he intended to say something, though not a sound passed his lips. A tentative clap was heard from the kitchen doorway. The ripple of applause spread, with even Jennifer freeing herself from her little girl, who had dropped off by now, and warily putting her hands together.

"Then we'll agree on that," a blushing Benedicte concluded with satisfaction.

"And the first decision I make," her brother took over, "is that this will only be a get-together, not a formal meeting. CC and Mabelle have welcomed us hospitably. There are cakes and sandwiches in the kitchen for those who'd like them. Let us thank them for that and make an effort to enjoy ourselves as best we can. Under the circumstances. Jennifer, if you'd like to go home right away, then of course I'll drive you. *I'll drive you home if you wish. Okay?*"

Before Jennifer had managed to reply, Carl-Christian's cell phone rang. Mumbling an apology, he withdrew to the bedroom.

It was Hermine.

"Have you discussed the will?" she slurred at the other end.

"Only just," he whispered in return, since he was unsure whether he had closed the door properly. "But Jennifer and us are the only ones who know what it contains. How . . . how do you know about it, by the way?"

"I have another one," she said in a monotone. "I have a newer one. A completely new one."

Carl-Christian pressed the wrong key and a piercing beep made him drop the phone.

"Hello," he spluttered when he finally raised it to his ear again. "Hermine, are you there?"

"I have an entirely new will. I got Daddy to write another one, one that—"

"When? When did you do that?"

"Three weeks ago, CC."

Carl-Christian did not possess a comprehensive knowledge of the law, but he was aware that a more recent will superseded an older one. His throat thickened. His pulse hammered in his ears.

"How—?"

"Come here, CC. I'm back home again."

"At home? You shouldn't be."

"I'm at home. Come."

The connection was broken. Carl-Christian sank slowly onto the bed, staring at his cell phone as if it was a totally new invention and he did not quite know what use it might be.

"Who was that?"

Mabelle had entered without a sound.

"Hermine," he murmured. "It was Hermine."

"What did she want?"

He was still staring in astonishment at the cell phone.

"She has a new will," he whispered, finally looking up. "I've no idea how she's arranged something like that."

His expression was a mixture of surprise, hope, and pure fear.

"Is that more advantageous for you? For us?"

"My God, what sort of thing is that to think about now! I haven't the foggiest. She asked me to come. She's at home."

"We must go," Mabelle said firmly. "You know we can't stand for anything like that now. We can wait, we can hide it until . . ."

As they exchanged glances again, they were unsure which of them was more afraid. Carl-Christian clutched the bedclothes, his nails digging into his palms.

"We must go to Hermine," he said eventually, his voice rising at least an octave.

Of course he didn't find anything. Around an hour's work in the cold and snow flurries had been to no avail. He was certain he had found the right place, since the marks from the previous hole were still evident on the ice. When the drill finally broke through, he heard water lapping darkly on the lid of ice. His skin tingled as he lowered his arm into the hole.

He felt ashamed. The entire idea had been idiotic from start to finish. In the first place, he had developed a suspicion, an anxiety, about a person who, admittedly, had behaved oddly; but there were plenty of odd people about; the old man was well aware of that, for he was one of them. Second, he had had no idea in advance of the depth of the water. He had not brought anything with him that he could use to dredge. Fortunately luck was with him. When he lay flat on the ice with his whole arm stretched down into the cavity, he could just feel the slick, uneven stony bed with his fingertips. He examined perhaps half a square yard of the lake bed, until he could not manage any more and had to give up.

The old man was annoyed with himself. The excitement he had felt had now dissipated and, besides, he felt ill. A damp weight pressed down on his chest, and he sneezed repeatedly. Fortunately it was the day before Christmas Eve, and there were plenty of entertaining programs on television. He brewed himself a big cup of tea with honey and sat down in comfort to try to forget the entire business.

His fever increased, and, outside, it was freezing cold.

He stood up on stiff legs to put more wood on the stove.


Hermine Stahlberg was at the point of coming down. In vain she attempted to cling to the remains of that afternoon's high, but it was no use. The toxins were soon depleted, leaving her feeling completely confused about what she ought to do.

She staggered along Bogstadveien, struggling to understand what had happened.

At first, frankly, she had not noticed anything.

They had reluctantly allowed her to sign herself out of the hospital. The doctor had made a halfhearted effort to persuade her to stay. He seemed more concerned about the imminent holiday. Only an hour after she had risen from bed, she was visiting her regular supplier in Majorstua. The transaction was quick. She had gone straight home and been more precise about the dose this time.

The high steadied her hands. She was able to pull out the drawers in one of the kitchen cupboards and remove the loose board screwed there, in front of the hiding place in the wall behind. The photographs were there, as well as the will. She returned the pictures and pushed the will between two deluxe editions about Egypt on the lowest book-shelf. After that, she phoned Carl-Christian.

But he never came. It took such a long time. Unable to settle, she trotted around the room, continually checking the time.

She noticed the rug in the living room first of all, lying the wrong way. She knew that because a red-wine stain, always kept concealed underneath the sofa, was now exposed and obvious. Her fear increased as she stood rigidly to attention and tried to absorb other changes. The books in the bookcase had been moved. She was sure of that. The spines were uneven, with several of them jutting beyond the edge of the shelf.

Carl-Christian, of course. She tried to force her pulse into a normal rhythm. Carl-Christian had been here, hadn't he, and had helped her last Saturday. Got her to the hospital. It must have been him. She had no idea why he would upend rugs and pull out books, but Carl-Christian was her brother and was fond of her and did not pose any danger.

The bedroom was a shambles, with bedclothes and vomit every-where.

Two pictures were hanging crooked on the wall.

She had not touched the pictures. However, she remembered noth-ing. She might have fallen, arms flailing against the wall, furious at Carl-Christian, who wanted to take her to the hospital. What did she know, since she remembered none of it?

Why would she have moved the pictures?

They were not even hanging anywhere near the bed. Carl-Christian had not said anything about her putting up a fight.

The door had not been forced, but someone had rummaged through her apartment.

That was when she decided not to wait for her brother. She pulled on her coat and shoved her feet into a random pair of sneakers, before staggering from the building. Five minutes later, she found herself in the normally most crowded shopping street in the west end of Oslo.

Christmas decorations bathed Bogstadveien in garish light. Suddenly she stopped beneath a star fashioned from spruce branches and laden with snow, hanging from an old-fashioned lamppost. She was alone. It was the night before Christmas Eve and there was not a single person to be seen. She had no idea which way to turn.

Actually she never had known, not since as a little girl she had been brutally forced to realize that no one was able to protect her.

Later she had headed for where it was worthwhile going, where someone was willing to pay with money, attention, or a momentary feeling of belonging. None of that was true or real, apart perhaps from the glimmers of love she had found with her brothers, especially Carl-Christian. Among other people, attention was subject to barter and Hermine paid in submissiveness, a little-girlish irresponsibility in which great secrets were overshadowed and hidden behind a sweet, artificial personality.

That was why it had been so difficult to take control. These past few months, when for the very first time Hermine had acted according to what she thought right and proper, had completely drained her of vitality.

All she wanted was for someone to take care of her, comfort her, and ensure that everything would be okay again. She wanted to be told she was loved, that she was needed by someone—anyone.

Eventually she decided where she would go.

A smell of tobacco in the kitchen greeted Hanne when she arrived home from police headquarters just before midnight.

"Hello," she said, screwing up her nose. "Has Mary been allowed to smoke in here?"

"A tiny exception," Nefis said, smiling. "She's done an incredible amount of work today. Have you seen the table?"

Hanne nodded. A spectacular Christmas table had been set in the living room, with red tablecloth, crystal, and green branches on display, as well as a gold-plated candelabra and a dinner service emblazoned with a pattern of Christmas elves. Above it all, suspended from some sort of latticework attached to the ceiling, was a closely packed array of transparent glass balls in all sizes, with painted designs.

"Beautiful," she said, with a smile. "You must have helped her. A bit over the top, perhaps. The children will love it."

"Come on," Nefis said, patting the chair beside her. "Sit down. Have you had a hard day?"

Hanne kissed her lightly on the forehead and sank into the chair.

"Guess. I'm so tired I probably won't be able to sleep. You look amazing."

Nefis's hair was hanging loose above a bright-red V-neck sweater. Her makeup looked recently applied, and a fresh fragrance wafted from her.

"I stink like a horse," Hanne said, sniffing.

"Just a sweet little pony," Nefis replied, pouring wine from a dusty bottle. "Are you looking forward to it?"

"To this?"

Hesitantly, Hanne looked around.

"Maybe. A little. Not much."

It was a lie, and they both knew that. Insofar as Hanne Wilhelmsen was at all able to look forward to anything, she was looking forward to Christmas Eve. She liked the fact that it was not about family. She was happy about Nefis's hospitality and that there would be a variety of guests around the table. She realized she had not thought about her father for several hours. That dull, empty feeling of something being too late was about to be laid to rest. She and Nefis had chosen each other. Together they had chosen Mary. Nefis had shaped an existence so full of excess and enveloped in generosity that Hanne on occasion considered following her suggestion about leaving the police. Hanne could set up a small private detective agency; Nefis pestered her time and again. She would have just the right amount to do. An exclusive little office with three investigators, perhaps, who would not bother about unfaithful spouses and missing tourists in Mediterranean countries, but would concentrate instead on industry and security. She had the start-up capital, and she had a name.

Hanne would no longer exist outside the police force, and she was well aware of that.

"I think maybe I'm about to fall out with all the others," she said, yawning. "In this case of ours. I've been wrong before. It's exactly as if—"

"As if you must always think along different lines from everyone else," Nefis completed her sentence. "It's an excellent quality, as a rule. The world is propelled forward by people who think differently."

"That's a bit of an overstatement," Hanne muttered into her glass. "I'm not exactly a pioneer like Semmelweis, you know."

"To some degree you are," Nefis said. "But sometimes you're wrong, of course."

"This time too perhaps. Anyway, everything points to Carl-Christian Stahlberg or his sister. Or someone working on their behalf. The family, in other words. I must say that . . ."

Eagerly, she began to rattle off the links in the chain of circumstantial evidence.

"Stop," Nefis said, putting a finger to Hanne's lips. "This is your time off, Hanna. Think about something else."

"It's difficult."

"I want to have a child, Hanna."

All of a sudden, Hanne noticed that the parsley intended to represent grass in Mary's enormous nativity scene on the kitchen worktop had been replaced by chopped-up scraps of crepe paper. She got to her feet and began to rearrange it more neatly around the open stable. When she picked up a sheep, she broke one of its legs.

"It's better with paper," she said. "The parsley was getting shriveled."

"Hanna—"

"I don't want that. Not children, and not any talk about it. When are our visitors arriving tomorrow?"

Hanne felt tears sting her eyes. Swallowing, she took a deep breath. No children. That was what Cecilie had fussed about. Continually. Hanne had been right. They should not have had children, because Cecilie had gone and died, hadn't she?

"If I only understood why," Nefis said. "You never want to explain why. You just walk off. *Don't!*"

Hanne had picked up the statuette of the Virgin Mary and was about to tear off her halo. Startled by Nefis's eruption, she put the figure carefully back in place.

"I'm tired," she said, heading for the door.

Nefis blocked her path.

"No. You're not leaving. We're going to talk about this. I want to have children—you don't. We need to find out which one of us has the stronger motorating."

"Motivation," Hanne corrected her. "You shouldn't use words you're not sure of. Motivation. Mine's the stronger."

"Well, I don't know about that."

Hanne was afraid of children. She needed to know them well before she could even speak to them. Children were frightening, boisterous, demanding creatures who required commitment. She had been a child herself. She had spent her entire adult life forgetting what that had been like, and in her encounters with children, she grew terrified of all the things she did not want to remember. Then she remembered them all the same.

She remembered the grand villa where they had lived. Her mother, father, sister, and brother. Hanne the afterthought. Hanne who was scared of her room. Scared of the whole house, apart from the attic, where the belongings her grandparents left aided her escape into dreams, creating her own little home in the dust among the things no one needed or thought about anymore, the same way no one needed or thought about her.

Hanne stared at the baby Jesus and recalled those nights. One night. She had gone up to the second floor early, but not to her own room. As usual, she sneaked up into the attic, where she opened an old chest and took out the things stored inside. Hung them around the place, from hooks in the ceiling, from crooked nails banged into beams and joists. The attic was transformed into a theater, and she dressed up. She might have been ten. Possibly older. She play-acted, taking on leading dramatic roles until she fell asleep. The moon was only just visible through the attic window. When she woke, she was stiff with frost, and it was daylight. No one had come looking for her. No one had wakened her or carried her back to bed, to her quilt, to the warmth, and maybe even sat down beside her so that she wouldn't be so afraid, always so terribly afraid.

Her father's eyes across the breakfast table, uninterested, indifferent, and Hanne had to go to school in the same clothes that she had worn the previous day, the ones she had been wearing when she had slept in the attic between African face masks and old photograph albums, holding a stuffed weasel in her arms.

As an adult, she appreciated they had quite simply been under the impression that she had slept in her room. Probably they would have been alarmed had they known the truth.

But no one had checked.

No one had investigated whether she was okay before heading for bed. Hanne did not go to school that day. She had gone to the carpenter who lived next door, who cooked her a breakfast of porridge and taught her how to use an angle iron. When she began to cry because she had to go home, it was the carpenter who had taken her on his knee and rocked her, a big girl, until she had calmed down, and who helped her write a fake absence note for the teacher.

"I can't have children," Hanne said quietly as she sat down.

"Can't you? Are you . . . do you know that?"

"Not in that way. I've no idea whether I'm . . . fertile. Doubtful, at my age."

She gave a listless smile.

"But I just can't take responsibility for children. I don't know what a childhood should be like. Only what it shouldn't be like."

"That might well be more than good enough. You're kind, Hanna; you're—"

"I'm a damaged individual," Hanne broke in smoothly. "I've probably managed fine, considering the circumstances. But I've so much crap inside me that cleaning up will take . . ."

She glanced warily at the door—always that worry that someone might get to know, other than Nefis, that anyone might find out about her seeing a psychologist.

". . . a whole lifetime," she concluded.

"A child is a blessing," Nefis said. "Always."

"Maybe for the parents," Hanne said. "But a child would absolutely not have a good upbringing with me. Not even with you here. You understand that, Nefis. You know me so well. You actually agree. If you think about it, you'll agree that I'm right."

Nefis remained silent. The contents of her glass were untouched.

She merely held the stem and let the glass rotate slowly as she studied the light splitting into nuances of red on the tabletop.

"I'm going to bed, then," Hanne said. "If that's okay with you. I'm cross-eyed."

Nefis did not reply but remained in her seat. She had still not touched any of the wine.

When Hanne rose from bed on the morning of Christmas Eve, Nefis was asleep in the guest bedroom, and the bottle was still full.

# TUESDAY, DECEMBER 24

Oslo was covered in an absolutely extraordinary amount of snow. The banks of snow were several feet high in a number of places. Everything outdoors sounded muffled. The window in Hanne Wilhelmsen's office was opened slightly, but not even the rumble of trucks in Schweigaards gate reached all the way to the heights where police headquarters curved between a house of God and an ancient prison.

Hanne stood at the window feeling the cold draft on her face. There was a raw smell of winter, and on the extensive snow-covered lawn in front of Oslo Prison, three immigrant children were playing with a sled. It would hardly budge. A young boy, maybe ten years old, tried to push it forward to get the runners to grip properly, as if steering a wheelbarrow. At last the youngest child—a girl, to judge from her pink snowsuit—realized that they needed to venture out into the street below the prison. Hanne closed her eyes as the children rushed at top speed toward Grønlandsleiret. A truck braked abruptly and skidded into a parked Volvo. The youngsters were unharmed, but a police patrol car drew to a halt and the uniformed officers had their hands full trying to restrain the angry driver. The children, laughing and shrieking, took off as soon as the police turned their backs. The sled, lying upside-down in the middle of the road, was abandoned.

Hanne shut the window.

She produced her father's death announcement from her wallet. That old grudge, the involuntary anger mixed with sorrow, seized her again. The scrap of paper was becoming grubby and looked about to tear. She ought to have it laminated, before it was too late. Hanne's inverted membership card had turned into something that made her remember, after all these years of persistent, resolute forgetting.

Best of all, she remembered the Christmas when she was twelve years old. Both of her siblings were at school outside the city. In a way, Hanne had been looking forward to their returning home. It made her mother happier. Her mother was almost invisible in Hanne's memories of that time: she worked late and was always tired.

All Hanne wanted was a toolbox with tools in it. Her wish list was on the wall above her bed. A couple of times she had wondered whether to pin it up in the kitchen to make sure her parents saw it. Something held her back: a vague feeling that they would be annoyed by her audacity. She wanted a hammer and plane, screwdrivers, and an awl. Hanne so desperately wanted her own tools, for the third year in a row, and as Christmas approached, she began to believe that her wish would be granted this time.

She received instead a leather-bound deluxe edition of the works of Snorri Sturluson, a new nightgown, and a bottle of perfume that dropped and smashed on the floor when she opened the package. No one registered that she slept in the attic again, and no one noticed that she crept over to the carpenter's house at first light the next morning. There, she had hot chocolate and thick slices of bread, and was presented with the carpenter's old plane tied with a pink bow.

The Christmas she was twelve stank of 4711, and in the years that followed, she no longer wasted her energies on expecting anything whatsoever of the festivities.

"Hanne!"

Quick as a flash, she put the obituary back and turned around.

"Erik," she declared.

"Do you have a minute?"

"Of course. Come in."

Only now did she notice that she had been crying, and she wiped her eyes swiftly with the back of her hand.

"The draft," she said, pointing at the window. "I had to close it. What's it about?"

"Look at this!"

Erik's hair was sticking out in all directions, in boyish contrast to his elegant suit and pale blue, crisply ironed shirt. The knot on his tie was tight, and he unconsciously put a finger under his collar.

"I'm going through all the documents we've got relating to these disputes between the Stahlbergs, father and son. And it is . . . what a family! That people can . . . Anyway, look at this."

After searching for a document, he handed it over. Hanne sat down slowly as she read.

"A typed sheet of paper," she described, somewhat puzzled. "From Hermann to Carl-Christian, as far as I can see. And it has to do with—"

"With telling CC just to take it easy. You see that the letter is dated March 3, 2001, not very long after Preben had begun to maneuver himself into the family business. His dad assures his youngest son that he will naturally receive what he's entitled to. He has been as clever as anything, the boy, worked hard for a long time, and there will be no change to what they have agreed on for so long about the future of the shipping company."

"I see."

"Signed by Hermann, though not using his name, but as 'Your Father.' And as you see at the foot of the page—"

Hanne beat him to it: "'Acceded to. Mother.' An old-fashioned turn of phrase, I must say!"

"Yes, yes. What is more important is that Hermann claimed for a long time that he had absolutely no knowledge of this document. That it is forged!"

"Forged?"

"Yes. Hermann demanded at one point that a handwriting expert should examine the letter. But then Tutta put her oar in."

"What?"

"Tutta. Turid. The mother!"

"Yes, I know who she is, but what do you mean by her 'putting her oar in'?"

Erik laughed aloud and ruffled his hair with both hands. His cheeks were flushed with pleasure.

"She claimed it was genuine! She said she remembered the letter being written and that she was present when Hermann signed it. And so the whole application for examination of the handwriting was withdrawn. It may well be that it's pretty unclear what significance the document has for the case anyway, since it's nothing other than some kind of letter of reassurance, of course, but according to Annmari, it might—"

"We should get someone to go through the entire collection," Hanne interrupted.

"That's what we're doing right now!"

"I see, yes. But this ought to be investigated by an expert in inheritance matters, family law, contract law . . . I don't know what's required, but anyway it's essential to get a proper, independent assessment of where the parties actually stood."

"Who had the best chance of winning, you mean?"

"That, too."

"You're almost certainly right. But you haven't heard all of it! A few weeks ago, something must have made Hermann change his mind. He wanted to have a handwriting test all the same. And the result . . ."

Erik patted his chest and fished out a little note from his inside pocket.

". . . I received today. Not only is Hermann's signature forged. But Turid's as well!"

The frown between Hanne's eyes grew even deeper.

"Did she lie?"

"Obviously! She insisted that the document was genuine and that both she and her husband had signed it. So it's all a forgery. Carl-Christian's up to here in shit!"

He ran his finger along his hairline.

"We don't know that he's the one responsible," Hanne countered.

"But think about it," Erik said, leaning toward her. "Who would have any interest in falsifying a letter such as this? No one except CC. And now he was a hairbreadth away from being exposed! If you stack up everything we have now, it's looking bad for good old Carl-Christian, Hanne. He has motive, he has—"

"The gun," Silje said in a flurry of excitement as she virtually stormed into the office. "He has a permit for a revolver!"

"Now you're running away from yourselves," Hanne said, running her finger along her nose. "Relax, both of you. Sit down, Silje."

Hanne's cell phone rang. She glanced at the display and chose to ignore it.

"Carl-Christian is a member of a pistol club," a breathless Silje said. "Not active at all; it looks as if he derived some sort of childish kick from it years ago. Then he grew bored. But he has a gun. A German Magnum."

"Not caliber .357?" Erik asked with undisguised hope in his voice.

"Yes, it is."

"Good grief!"

"We really must charge the guy. If for no other reason than to be able to conduct a search—"

"Have you spoken to Annmari or—"

"There are three lawyers in the Chief's office right now and they—"

"For Christ's sake, Silje! This is completely—"

The two younger officers were both speaking at the same time. As Hanne leaned back, she heard the joints of the chair creak. She massaged her neck, still amazed at how much enthusiasm her colleagues could muster. How they seemed to have such personal engagement; how they regarded a new lead in an already fixed direction as a brilliant triumph.

To Hanne Wilhelmsen, police work was actually quite sad. She liked her job, found it meaningful and sometimes satisfying, but many years had passed since she had felt anything resembling enthusiasm or happiness in her work. Being a police officer fundamentally concerned reaching the truth in an increasingly complex reality, where possibly nothing was any longer entirely true or entirely false.

"Wait a minute," she said slowly in a loud voice. "Surely neither of you believes that Carl-Christian Stahlberg would be such a monumental idiot as to shoot his family with his own gun? His own, officially registered revolver?"

"No," Erik admitted. "But it does mean that he knows something about guns. That he knows how to get hold of that kind of thing. That he knows people in shooting circles."

"Shooting circles in Norway," Hanne said, trying not to seem patronizing, "as far as I know, are a collection of extremely stable people with decent, age-old Norwegian interests: hunting and often fishing as well.

Shooting circles in Norway take good care of their guns, meet at conventions, and maybe drink a bit too much moonshine in their camper vans."

"Now you're being narrow-minded," Silje said. "Now you're talking about the sort of people who go to national shooting competitions. That's mainly people from rural areas. Here in the city it's different, as you well know. Lots of immig . . . completely different people."

"And who's being narrow-minded now?" Hanne flashed a smile, before adding: "Of course, this is of interest. Especially the stuff about the forgery. I agree that Carl-Christian's motives are mounting. It wouldn't surprise me if Annmari and Co. are soon writing out a charge sheet."

She shrugged.

"Even if I'd prefer it if we waited."

"Wait?" Erik said angrily. "Why should we wait? The more time that passes, the more opportunity he has to cover his tracks."

"But I've—" Silje ventured, before being interrupted by Hanne.

"It's not certain he has any opportunity to cover his tracks. If he gets rid of the gun, for instance, then he knows he's in a damned tight corner. You know just as well as I do that pulling someone in before we have a watertight case can be far more damaging than letting them hang loose out there. The best approach is to bring them in for an interview. Press them, drop them. Haul them in, then let them go. They know we have them in our sights. They get worried. They don't sleep, and they get tired. Scared, exhausted people make mistakes. Arrest them, and they mobilize energy and resistance. I would wait. At least until after Christmas. After the funeral. I really think . . ."

"I've found—" Silje ventured again, but was unable to continue this time, either.

". . . the best thing would be to wait," Hanne concluded, before smiling at Silje. "What was it you wanted to say?"

"I've found an apartment," she answered, sounding miffed. "It's all a bit strange."

Something gleamed in Hanne's eyes.

"An apartment? What kind of apartment?"

"I'm going through the estate. Actually I was supposed to

concentrate on the old folks. The . . . deceased, I mean. But then I was sitting there with this search engine, and it struck me that it might be useful to get an overview of what the others in the family owned also."

Hanne nodded in approval.

"And then, when I was finished . . ."

Silje gave a quick smile.

". . . I remembered that Mabelle was originally called May Anita Olsen. So I did a search on that name too. She owns an apartment in Kampen."

"What!"

Erik tugged so energetically at his collar that his top button fell off.

"What is that used for?" He balanced the button on his right index finger. "Can either of you sew?"

"I don't know what the apartment is used for," Silje said, irritated. "You can surely sew a button on yourself! Anyway, it's Mabelle's apartment. It's the right personal ID number. Why it's registered in her old name and why they've kept it is anybody's guess. No one lives there, in any case. Not according to the Population Register."

"An empty apartment in Kampen," Hanne said slowly into midair, as if thinking aloud and trying to ascertain what purpose something like that might have. "An office? A guest apartment? An investment?"

"A guest apartment in Kampen, when you live on the other side of the city?" Silje pulled a disapproving face and added: "Neither of them needs a private office. Not as far as I can see, anyway. And if the apartment was intended as an investment, then they would have rented it out."

"I'm going straight to my mother-in-law's," Erik complained. "Can it really be true that neither of you can sew a button on for me?"

Hanne drew on her jacket, pulled a hat down over her ears, and stood in readiness to leave, before either of the others had gotten as far as standing up.

"Your mother-in-law probably won't notice your button, Erik."

"Where are you going?" Silje asked.

"Me? I'm going out to buy presents."

"Now? In the middle of Christmas Eve?"

"Never too late," Hanne said, heading for the door. "By the way . . ."

She wheeled around to face Silje again.

"That stuff about the apartment's bloody fascinating. Write a special report, and make sure that Annmari knows about it. Now. Before you leave for the day."

Then, her face shining, she addressed herself to Silje's forehead.

"Merry Christmas! Enjoy yourselves."

She turned on her heel and disappeared.

"Is she just going to . . . leave? Now we're approaching an arrest and everything?" Silje was whispering.

"No one's going to arrest anybody in this case yet," Erik said, struggling to attach the top button to his shirt with a stapler. "No one's going to be arrested without Hanne being informed. Believe me. I'd like to see the prosecutor here in headquarters who would dare to do anything of the sort. Bye, then!"

He tossed the button into a corner of the room.

"Merry Christmas!"

Silje was left sitting alone in Hanne's office. It was so curiously quiet everywhere. The vast building was about to empty out for a couple of days' holiday. She sank back into the chair and breathed deeply through her nose. Over and over again, in an effort to capture Hanne's perfume, which she refused to acknowledge.

Sølvi Jotun was not difficult to locate. She was quite simply at home. At least in a purely physical sense. Billy T. had obtained her address late the previous night. He had postponed his visit, since he was in no fit state to do anything other than sleep. He had hardly said goodnight before collapsing into bed. After being in an almost comatose condition for eight hours, at least he did not feel so tired.

When, without the duty sergeant's permission, he had picked open the lock on the door in Mor Go'hjertas vei in Sagene, he found Sølvi Jotun lying in a corner like a discarded bundle of clothes. Otherwise the apartment was remarkably tidy. The bathroom, where he fetched some water in a toothbrush glass because the kitchen door was locked for some reason, had recently been cleaned. In the poky little living room, everything was in place. A well-worn sofa covered with a throw and two mismatched chairs. A coffee table that reminded him of the sixties. A blue glass bird perched on the TV set. To top it all, there was even some sort of bookcase in the room: old brewery cases stacked one on top of the other, crammed with crime novels and a series of Dostoevsky's collected works.

On a good day, the apartment might well be termed cozy. Now it was icy cold. Billy T. was worried about the price of electricity himself, but there had to be limits to saving power. He squinted at a thermometer on the living room wall: 52 degrees.

"Hi," he said in a friendly tone, hunkering beside the curled figure and tentatively nudging her shoulder. "Sølvi! Hi there!"

She groaned and clicked her dry tongue.

"Water," Billy T. said, lifting her head carefully to allow her to swallow.

Sølvi Jotun tried to take a drink. Half the water ran outside her mouth, but in the end she managed to open her eyes.

"Oh, hell," she moaned. "Is it you?"

"Take it easy," he said calmly. "Nothing to worry about this time, Sølvi. Just want to talk to you."

The woman slumped back, and he got his arm trapped between her head and a switched-off radiator. It was difficult to break free because his leather jacket was caught on a pipe. Eventually he succeeded in settling the woman into a stable position on her side. The little welcome scene had obviously used up her strength. He forced her eyes open with two fingers. Her pupils had contracted but were not terrifyingly tiny. Though her breathing was shallow, it was regular enough that there was no real need for him to feel afraid. People had ended up in holding cells despite their health being in a worse state than this. All the same, this time Billy T. did not want to take any chances.

"I'll get you to the hospital," he said softly, hoisting her up. "Then we can talk tomorrow."

Sølvi Jotun's face took on a surprised, almost incredulous look, before she passed out again.

It took him an hour and a half to get her admitted to Ullevål Hospital. He had to berate a doctor in the most disparaging terms, charm two nurses, and knock over an IV stand in the bargain. Fortunately it was not in use at the time. In the end he had threatened them with the Court of Human Rights in Strasbourg. The doctor began to laugh, discouraged and stressed after hours of overtime, and they finally promised to care for Sølvi at public expense for twenty-four hours. Not a minute longer, Billy T. was told. And the doctor could not guarantee what would happen if, in the meantime, the patient took it into her head to leave.

Billy T. felt weak once he was able to sit in his car at last.

He took a note of the time. Quarter to twelve. He would have to collect Sølvi Jotun before ten the next day, to be on the safe side. Christmas Day, he thought despondently, and could not bring himself to work out how he would effect his escape from breakfast with his sister's family.

The betting slip was still in his breast pocket. He hadn't even taken it out to examine it.

The police trainee was only twenty-two and everything was still exciting. Even sitting by a telephone receiving tips from the public. As a rule, they were cloaked in excessively long stories and seldom had any real value. Nevertheless the young man felt important. He had not yet completed his studies, but despite that, he was participating in the investigation of Oslo's most brutal homicide inquiry in ages, perhaps of all time.

As soon as the murders in Eckersbergs gate became public knowledge, the tips had started to flood in. The department had to conscript extra staff, two officers on two daily shifts. The young trainee took meticulous notes and sorted the incoming calls exactly as he had been told to do. Normally he contented himself with scribbling down three or four lines about what the caller had to say, together with the name and telephone number. He had made a habit of checking whether the number given matched what appeared on the display. After that he placed the sheets of paper in three different piles. One for drunken drivel and nonsense, one for what was of little apparent interest, and one for tips that ought to be checked.

The last pile was depressingly scant in comparison with the other two.

"Police," he said automatically, accepting another call.

"Good day," a gruff voice spoke at the other end.

"Good day, who am I speaking to?"

"Err . . . hmmm. I wonder if that matters."

"We'd prefer to have a name."

The police trainee glanced up at the display and jotted down the number on a sticky note.

"I'd rather not say," the voice mumbled into the receiver; it sounded tense and hesitant. "Prefer not."

"What do you want to report, then?"

"It's to do with this murder."

"Yes. The Stahlberg case."

"Yes. I was just thinking that . . . this gun—"

"Yes?"

"I just wanted to say that on that day—or that night, really; the day after the murders—somebody drilled a hole in the ice up here. Strange business. Don't know if it was a man or a woman, but it was pitch dark, and there's no fish there."

"Wait a minute now. Where was this, did you say?"

"I was just out for a . . . well, I was going out for a breath of air, you see. On skis. And the conditions were so lousy that I started walking instead. Went down to the lake, and that was when I saw him. The hole was there when I checked later. But there were no other signs of ice fishing, exactly. And it was the middle of the night, you see. I've never heard of people ice fishing in the middle of the night."

"Now I'll need to ask you to wait for a moment. Let us take this from the beginning."

Tingling with excitement, the police trainee stole a glance at the computer screen to assure himself that the tape was running. Then he took out a fresh sheet of paper and began over again.

"Where are you calling from?"

"Well, I just wanted to let you know, you see."

"And we're very pleased about that. But we need to take this right from the beginning, okay?"

"That's fine," the voice said, sounding less tense now.

Seven minutes later, the trainee disconnected the call and sat idly lost in thought, even though the phone kept ringing incessantly.

•  •  •

The worst aspect was that he was no longer sure he could rely on Mabelle. He tried to convince himself that his suspicion was a result of lack of sleep. Since Thursday, he had hardly slept a wink. That impaired his judgment and filled him with doubt and fear, and he knew that. Hostile to everyone, he thought disconsolately, as he stared at himself in the mirror above the bathroom basin. He was thinner already. His eyes seemed even more prominent, and a greasy film of stress had spread over his face.

"Mabelle," he said hoarsely as he tried to push out a nonexistent chin.

Hermine, of course, could not be relied on. She had always been the sweet little bunny rabbit of the family, hopping now here, now there. There was something predictable about her unpredictability. Mabelle, on the other hand, was the anchor in his life. She could be depended on. She had always been someone who could be depended on.

The farcical family gathering of the previous evening had turned into the Christmas party from hell. No one wanted to speak to the flabbergasted and deeply offended Alfred. The more distant relatives could barely control their curiosity; they overtly studied the apartment and everything in it as they chatted quietly in tones of voice characterized by scandal and malicious pleasure. Getting rid of Andreas had almost been worst of all. He had strutted about with unaccustomed pomposity and was slightly too eager to assure Carl-Christian of his belief in his innocence. When all the others were finally out of the apartment, Andreas had wanted to have a strategic discussion, as he called it. Carl-Christian had pretended to faint and smiled wanly from the floor with a rather nasty cut above his eye, pleading to be left in peace.

When they arrived at Hermine's apartment, it had been more than two hours since her phone call.

She was no longer in the apartment. At least she never opened the door. She did not answer any of her phones. Hermine had simply disappeared, and Carl-Christian had no idea what he should do.

Mabelle wanted to alert the police.

Mabelle no longer understood. Hermine was sitting on a new will. Hermine was the only one who knew about the unregistered gun in the safe in Kampen. They had to talk to Hermine before the police had reason to interview her again. Carl-Christian had to know what she intended to say; he had to track down the missing pistol and secure the new will, the contents of which he did not even know.

Hermine might have thrown the pistol away.

Of course she hadn't thrown the pistol away.

Where do you dispose of a pistol?

Carl-Christian's laughter was forced, and he bit his lip to prevent himself from losing his composure. Slowly he began to smear shaving cream over his jaw, using his fingers to outline little pathways in all the whiteness, drawing the cream up over his nose and around his eyes: he covered his face in cream.

"What are you doing?"

Mabelle was totally transformed. He knew, of course, that the fragile, sorrowing figure of the previous evening was a fabulous concoction, though it seemed as if most of them had been taken in by it. Despite all of them knowing about the destructive conflict between the family members, it was as if Mabelle's convincing performance had reinforced the family in their belief that there were limits to what a member of the Stahlberg dynasty would permit himself to be forced into.

Mabelle had mastery of her own face. Now her eyebrows were well defined, her lips a deep red. A touch of rouge on her cheeks signaled energy and resolve.

"What on earth are you doing?" she repeated.

"Nothing."

"Nothing? You look absolutely crazy!"

Without answering, he washed all the cream away.

"You need to shave," she said harshly. "Those little stubbly whiskers of yours aren't very becoming."

"That's what I was in the midst of doing," he said, lifting the shaving cream canister.

"You're in the midst of falling apart, CC. We can't afford that."

Indolently he began to soap his face again. Mabelle continued to stand there.

"Hermine's a problem," she said in a monotone. "You're right, of course. But we'll have an unbelievably worse problem if the girl has really disappeared and we haven't reported it."

"We don't need to have known anything about it," Carl-Christian said.

Mabelle took a step forward into the bathroom and leaned toward him.

"Now you'll really need to pull yourself together!" she roared. "We're being watched! When are you going to understand that? The police probably already know that we were outside Hermine's apartment last night. They're most likely taking continuous printouts of all our phone conversations. They know we've tried to reach her. And they know . . . *they know . . .*"

Her voice assailed his eardrums.

"*. . . that it's Christmas Eve!* Have you ever not known where your sister was on Christmas Eve? What? *Have you?*"

Carl-Christian began to cry. He wept like a small boy no longer bothered that his friends could see him; he sobbed noisily and dipped his head. The cream became too wet and ran in tiny rivulets down his scrawny chest.

"I'm so . . ."

He couldn't speak. Mabelle put an arm around his shoulders, turning him toward her, and wiped the shaving cream with the back of her hand as she murmured reassuring insignificant words. In the end, she held him close, hugging him to her body, caressing his head, and rocking him slowly from side to side.

"I'm so scared that something's happened to Hermine as well," Carl-Christian sobbed into her shoulder.

"I know that," Mabelle said, stroking his wet hair. "We're both scared. But now you have to listen to me. Then everything will be okay. The two of us, we only have each other, you know."

"And Hermine," he gasped.

Mabelle did not respond. She embraced Carl-Christian as hard as she could and met her own gaze in the mirror over his shoulder. She did not look away. By keeping a tight grip on herself, she could steer Carl-Christian. She must assume control. There was no one to turn to; no one would help any of them.

She would hold him for as long as necessary.

• • •

The prostitutes never turned up. Mary had delayed dinner by an hour and a half and phoned four different cell phone numbers without obtaining any answer anywhere. In the end she had heaved a deep sigh and kept up a litany of complaint, as if it had been her own children who had let her down. Her mood improved when all the others were seated at the table, wide-eyed, and the food was praised resoundingly.

By around nine o'clock, the spacious living room was an absolute riot of Christmas wrapping paper and snacks, half-filled glasses and soft drink bottles, games, clothes, and books. Mary had unwillingly agreed to turn off all the power-operated decorations before they ate. Now the children were pestering to have them switched on again, but Mary had succumbed to a bribe of a carton of cigarettes and insisted that Father Christmas in the corner had gone to sleep for the night. He was tired out, you see, and they ought to allow him a little break from all the commotion. Billy T. crawled around the floor with Jenny on his back. The four-year-old, dressed in a far-too-large pair of bright red pajamas, was waving a Barbie doll about.

"Present from Daddy," she yelled in delight, kissing the Muslim Barbie's burka.

Billy T. bumped past Hanne's chair while trying to make camel noises. The look he gave her was brimming with gratitude. Hanne merely smiled and shrugged slightly. She had checked the contents of the bag he had brought last Sunday. As she thought, it had contained no gifts from Billy T. to his wife and daughter. Probably he had shelled out all his money on presents for his sons. Hanne had bought an Afghani Barbie and a miniature doll's house for the little girl and a deep-red cashmere sweater for Tone-Marit. To crown it all, she had cornered Billy T. in the bathroom during the commotion before dinner and made him write gift cards in his own handwriting, to avoid being exposed.

Håkon and Karen's children were busy assembling a racetrack. Håkon, slightly tipsy, was sitting rosy-cheeked on the sofa with his son's Game Boy, while Karen, Tone-Marit, and Mary played Scrabble at the newly cleared dining table.

"You can't write that," Karen said, laughing. "'Gooday' . . . it should be 'good day'. Two words, and not written like that."

"Do you say 'good day'?" Mary asked peevishly, creating a dramatic pause between the words, with an emphasis on the "d" in *good*. "Does anybody say it like that?"

"No, but—"

"Let her write 'gooday,'" Tone-Marit said. "We can surely have slightly different rules for Mary."

"Different rules, no!"

Furious, Mary threw the letters away.

"I don't need different rules, you know! I don't want special treatment, no I don't!"

"Scrabble might not be quite the best game for you," Hanne said. "Shall we go and do the dishes, you and me?"

The doorbell rang.

At first no one really paid any attention. Then Tone-Marit looked in surprise at Nefis. Karen inclined her head.

"Are you expecting someone? Now?"

She glanced at the clock.

"No," Nefis said, taken aback.

"I'm not working at the moment," Mary said.

She had mixed herself a drink of cola, mineral water, Fanta, apple juice, and black currant cordial and had decorated the glass with a red-and-yellow paper parasol and a little Christmas elf impaled on a straw. The children were jumping around her demanding ones exactly the same.

"Somebody else will have to open the door."

Nefis went. Thirty seconds later, she returned wearing a puzzled expression.

"It's for you, Hanna."

"Me? Who is it?"

"A . . . a boy. A young man. Come on."

Hanne ran her fingers through her hair as she headed for the hallway.

The boy was about sixteen years old, lightly dressed, with no cap or scarf. His jeans were painfully tight, and underneath his denim jacket, he was wearing only a white T-shirt. He looked up ever so slightly when Hanne tentatively held out her hand and said, "Hi. Who are you?"

He was good looking, with an oval face and straight nose. His eyes were blue, Hanne could see, and she suddenly felt dizzy: they were dark blue with a distinctive black circle around the iris. His hair was brown, shining, and recently cut.

"You're Hanne," the boy said without taking her hand, and a fleeting smile made his mouth curl inconspicuously, a crooked smile, and Hanne stared in disbelief at this mirror image of herself when she was young. "Hi."

"Come in," she said, stepping back.

The boy did not move. Only now did Hanne notice that he had a brown canvas duffel bag with him; the sleeve of a sweater was bulging limply between the laces. A cardboard box sat beside the bag.

"I don't know whether . . ." the boy ventured, and gulped. "I—"

"You must be . . . is it you, Alexander?"

His eyes filled with tears. His Adam's apple bobbed up and down, and once again he lowered his gaze. His lashes were dark, with an odd curl that made them seem longer than they really were. Hanne's lashes were like that. Hanne had the same mouth as this boy. Even the way he tried to feign indifference, one foot placed lightly in front of the other, as if he hadn't quite made up his mind whether to come or go, was Hanne's gesture, Hanne's movement.

The boy barely nodded.

"They've thrown me out," he whispered. "They've fucking thrown me out. On Christmas Eve, of all days. I didn't know where to go. You're not in the phone book, but I remembered the name of your lady friend."

He gave a half glance at Nefis, who was struggling to keep curious children out of the hallway.

"From the announcement. When you got married. I cut it out."

Strangely enough, she understood all of it, all of a sudden and with the greatest clarity. This had happened before. Not in the same way, not by the same people, but for the same reason and with exactly the same result.

"Come in, Alexander," she said, making an effort to keep her voice steady before turning abruptly to Nefis, who stood surrounded by children in the living room doorway. "Can you leave us by ourselves for a while, do you think?"

The boy still stood outside on the landing. Hanne put her hand on his arm, feeling how narrow it was, how thin the boy was, and he let himself be led into the apartment. She picked up his luggage and placed it in a corner, before closing the door behind him. He leaned his shoulder against the door frame, turning away slightly, as if he still had plans to leave. Now he was crying soundlessly, still struggling to appear nonchalant, with his chin pressed on his chest and his hands deep inside his pockets.

"Look at me," Hanne said, lifting his face carefully.

He was so unfinished: his nose a bit too large and his neck too narrow. His forehead was smooth and bare. He tried to pull his hair forward to hide his eyes.

"Now you're going to come in with me, okay? It's a slightly weird gathering of people." She beamed and continued: "But we'd really, really like to have you here with us."

The same smile appeared, obscure and crooked, and he was no longer crying. He took a deep breath and dried his eyes with the back of his hand, in a pseudo-manly gesture that ended with him getting snot on his fingers and wiping it on his pant leg.

"I'm not exactly dressed for a Christmas visit," he mumbled, but followed her in to meet the others.

"This is Alexander," Hanne said in a loud voice. "My brother's youngest son. He's had quite a serious . . . argument with his parents. So now he's going to stay here with us."

The boy looked doubtful. His eyes scanned the assembled company and stopped at the power-operated Father Christmas. Mary muttered curses into the glass filled with her newly concocted drink, which the children were also slurping from huge, half-liter mugs.

"That's lovely," Nefis said blithely. "Great to have a man about the house!"

"I want to move here, too," complained nine-year-old Hans Wilhelm. "Why can't I get to stay here?"

"No, you're bloody not," Håkon slurred, quite drunk now. "I'd die of sorrow if you left me. You're going to live with your mom and me until you're forty at least."

"Alexander is . . . How old are you?"

"Sixteen," he said softly. "I'll be sixteen in a month."

"Sixteen in four weeks," Hanne repeated loudly.

"He looks amazingly like you," little Liv said skeptically, prodding Alexander's thigh with a stubby finger, as if she wanted to check that he was real.

"Incredible," Karen whispered to Tone-Marit. "Well, I never!"

Billy T. slapped Alexander between the shoulder blades.

"Want to help me in the kitchen? It's the boys' turn. My pal over there's pissed and totally out of the game."

The boy nodded, smiling now more broadly, exposing his teeth, and Nefis burst out laughing when she saw that one of his front teeth was slightly in front of the other, just like Hanne—the same tooth, the same peculiar angle.

"I'll phone your parents," Hanne whispered in the boy's ear as he made to follow Billy T. out into the kitchen.

He stiffened.

"Take it easy," she said quietly. "I just don't want to have any trouble with the child welfare service, okay? I'll deal with it all myself."

Jenny had fallen asleep on her mother's lap, in her red pajamas and with Mickey Mouse ears on her head. Hans Wilhelm was playing with the racetrack. Liv was standing in the kitchen mixing fresh drinks with Mary. This time they were experimenting with a mixture of milk, apple juice, and tonic water in tall glasses with peanuts at the bottom. Håkon had vanished into the bathroom, where he had apparently fallen asleep. The others were sitting in the living room chatting, with voices lowered to avoid waking the sleeping four-year-old.

Hanne felt an astonishing sense of well-being. It felt liberating, from a purely physical point of view, as if she had gone for a long, strenuous walk and could at last completely relax.

"What has actually happened?" Karen asked cautiously.

"Happened?"

Hanne found a more comfortable position on the sofa and put her feet under Nefis's thigh.

"What has happened is that I've had the most brilliant Christmas Eve of my whole life. And in a way, of course, I've received an extraspecial gift. A sort of child. That's what you wanted, after all, Nefis. A child."

For some reason, Nefis was no longer smiling. She raised her glass to her mouth, something Liv had put down there, tomato juice and apple crush, and took a long drink, as if to hide her face.

"And now I'll call my brother and tell him he's a homophobic idiot," Hanne said, so pleased with herself that she did not think to speculate why Nefis had almost entirely stopped touching alcohol.

Christmas Eve was over, and the guests had headed home long ago. Alexander had gone to sleep early. He had said very little. It could wait. His parents knew where he was, anyway. Everything else could stay on hold; it was school vacation, and Hanne felt happy that the boy could stay for a week or so in any case, perhaps longer. She had studied him all evening, discreetly, following his hand when he lifted his glass to his mouth, watching his fingers curl the way hers did, with the index finger curved into the palm.

She could not sleep, even though it was almost half past one.

Through the west-facing window, partly hidden behind the blinds, she stood watching as light after light was switched off in living rooms and bedrooms in the neighboring houses. She was surprised to feel a contented excitement, a restless sense of belonging. Shuddering, she drew her bathrobe more snugly around her frame. Her breath formed transitory clouds on the cold surface of the glass.

She couldn't sleep, and she didn't want to work.

Once again, the skin on her lower arm contracted. Nevertheless, she continued to stand in the almost indiscernible draft.

It crossed her mind that she didn't want to go to work, and that was something she had never felt before.

There was so much that she had never wanted: situations and people she had withdrawn from. But never her job. Police headquarters in Grønlandsleiret had always been Hanne's place of refuge. Only when Cecilie had died, and it proved no longer possible for her to hide, had she fled, to a convent in Italy and six months of being alone.

Now she had so much. Life was tolerable and sometimes even pleasant. Now and again she felt these glimmers of happiness and might even take an extra day off work.

Or just a few hours.

The Stahlberg murders scared her, and she really did not want anything to do with them. She wanted to take time off. To be with Alexander, which would be like spending time by herself. Alexander is my past with some kind of future, she thought, and I don't want to know anything about the Stahlberg case.

When the thought first struck her, she really began to shiver. Slowly she grabbed a blanket from the back of a chair behind her and draped it around her shoulders. Something made her stay by the window all the same, staring out into the subdued light from the street lamps. The shadows of the trees were stark against the wet asphalt, and the wind made the street appear autumnal. The temperature was fluctuating too much at present. Yesterday, snow had lain white on the ground. Tonight, dead rotting leaves were floating in what was left of the dirty slush, and melted ice was streaming along the sidewalk.

"Four people," she whispered to herself, a pale image in the glass. "Who kills four people at one time?"

No one. Not in Norway. Not in Oslo, in Hanne's police district. Not here in a country where nearly all homicides were the tragic consequences of drunkenness and fatal quarrels.

Nonetheless, someone had done it.

Her cell phone was in her pocket, and she dialed the number without hesitation. It rang five times, and she was just about to press the Off button to avoid voice mail and try again, when she heard a slurred voice at the other end: "Hello?"

"Billy T.," Hanne said. She realized she was speaking in a whisper, even though there was no chance of waking the others with a conversation conducted in the living room. "It's me."

Penetrating noises told her that his phone had been dropped on the floor.

"It's ten to two," he finally groaned.

"I know. Thanks for a lovely evening."

"I'm the one who should really say that. Thank you. For everything, you know."

"Sorry to—"

"*Sorry* is your middle name, Hanne. It doesn't help much to keep saying *sorry* all the time. Tell me instead why you're phoning."

It sounded as though he was sitting on the edge of the bed.

"Shouldn't you go into another room?" Hanne asked him.

"I'm sleeping in the boys' bedroom. On my own. Tone-Marit complains about me snoring when I've had a drop or two to drink. Why are you phoning?"

"I just want to try out a line of thinking."

"Okay, then. It's two o'clock on Christmas morning. Fire away."

"Why do we commit murder, Billy T.?"

"What?"

Her eyes had caught a movement below in the street. Something dark had disappeared under one of the trees, beside the trunk. For a moment she had been concentrating on the conversation and had not quite taken in what it was.

"Are you there?" Billy T. asked.

"Yes. Who commits murder here in this country, and why?"

"My God, Hanne—"

"Just answer me, Billy T."

"We both know," he said impatiently. "Christ, what *is* this?"

"Please. Stay with me for a moment or two."

He sighed so loudly that the line crackled.

"Murder is committed mainly in anger," he began, sounding magisterial. "By perpetrators who neither previously nor subsequently commit the same crime. The act is usually performed under the influence of alcohol or other intoxicating substances, and the perpetrator and victim are often related or acquainted in some other way."

"Exactly," Hanne said, squinting at the point where she thought she had spotted something, underneath the largest oak tree. "Far from exciting stuff, in other words. Sad but not exciting. You said it's often like that. Otherwise, then?"

"Sexual crimes," Billy T. continued. "Where the murder takes place either as part of a sexual act or, more often, is committed almost by accident or to conceal an attack."

"Thanks. But what about premeditated killings, then?"

"Hate, revenge, or money. But there aren't as many of—"

"Hate, revenge, money or . . . one more thing."

"What's that?"

"Honor," Hanne said, drawing out the word. "Honor is lost and can only be reinstated by the act of killing, something that strictly speaking applies to only a tiny number of our new countrymen. Isn't that so?"

Billy T. muttered something that sounded like agreement.

"But it can also be because honor *may* be lost," Hanne said. "The murder is committed because the victim is sitting on something, usually knowledge, that is threatening to the perpetrator."

"Do you mean," Billy T. started to say, ill tempered, "that Carl-Christian and company are supposed to have slaughtered the entire family to preserve their *honor*?"

"Well, the forgery of that letter from Hermann might well suggest something of that nature," Hanne said. "It would undeniably be an unwelcome exposure for a man such as CC to be caught cheating with documents in a case against his own parents. But that's not actually where I'm going with this. I want—"

"The motive for CC," Billy T. was almost shouting now, "and Mabelle and Hermine is a *sum total*, Hanne! Of years of strife, subjugation, browbeating, court cases, danger of a fucking inheritance rip-off, and exposure for forging documents—and, what's more, knowledge of guns! When you add all this to a lousy alibi for all three concerned, it gives better grounds for suspicion than I can damn well ever remember having had!"

"Take it easy, won't you?"

It was a person. It looked like a man. Hanne was not sure. The sharp shadows and dim light distorted the perspective. The figure was wearing dark clothes and a big cap. It moved slowly along the fence on the other side of the road. Underneath the next tree, hidden behind a parked delivery van, it came to a halt.

"Take it easy," she repeated mechanically. "Of course I agree with what you say. But can't you return the favor by going along with me and playing with the thought that the motive is not money and inheritance, not hate and revenge. Just for the sake of my hypothesis. Just hold the thought for a moment, Billy T."

"I am holding the thought," he said in a tired voice at the other end. "I'm holding the thought as tight as I damn well can."

"Honor," she reiterated slowly, and blinked: something was moving beside the delivery van. "And then we must be talking about a real loss of honor. An absolutely horrendous humiliation. Which has to be avoided. By killing four people."

Billy T. gave a noisy, long-drawn-out yawn down the receiver.

"Can we talk about this tomorrow?" he pleaded feebly. "I'm completely zonked."

"Okay. Sorry."

"Don't keep saying *sorry* all the time. I get so—"

She clicked him off, before withdrawing slowly from the window. There was no sign of life underneath the trees now. The delivery van remained just as still, and only now did she notice that it had a puncture and rust marks on the left rear fender. Damp snowflakes had started to fall again, vanishing into nothingness as soon as they touched the ground. She peeped out from behind the curtain with one eye, as if she were taking aim at something she could not quite identify.

People killed wives, children, and then themselves for the sake of honor. Because someone wanted to leave. There were men who countered a divorce petition with mass murder. Tragically, it was increasingly common. They did it for the sake of honor, it was said. Subsequently, by others.

For the sake of shame, she thought.

Honor and shame. The same concept, the right side and the wrong side. Short stubs of words that actually dealt with the great fear of falling, of losing something that might be greater than life itself: the frames around that and all the fragments that held existence in place and defined a person's position in relation to others.

No one could bear to fall, if the fall was great. Some chose to take their own lives: captains of industry and other celebrities, for seemingly trivial things, circumstances that after a number of years would be relegated to mere parentheses in their lives. They did it to escape from the shame. To avoid losing honor. Some took their children's lives as well.

"Some take the lives of their children," she whispered. "When the fall becomes too great."

A figure came into sight down below, a person. A man. He stepped out from the shadows behind the rusty vehicle. For a second or two, he stood facing her, his face nevertheless hidden by the cap. Then he dipped his head and began to walk on slowly.

In a flash she was struck by a totally unfamiliar anxiety. She gripped her throat and stumbled back into the room. Her pulse hammered on her eardrums. Gulping, she sat down, gulped again, and noticed all of a sudden that her bare toes were bleeding. The pain made her breathe more freely, filling her lungs with air and then forcing it back out again.

At first she could not understand what had frightened her so. She was safe in her own apartment. It was at least four stories down to the stranger walking in the street, and there was nothing to indicate that he had a gun. When she closed her eyes and tried to reconstruct the incident, she was not even certain that he had looked up at her. Maybe he had just taken a leak behind the van. He was out for a walk. With his dog, even though she had not seen any animal. Dogs had to be walked, even on Christmas Eve.

It took an hour for it finally to sink in that she was merely overtired.

# WEDNESDAY, DECEMBER 25

Henrik Backe woke early. He was confused between day and night at midwinter. There was no morning light to tell him what time it was. He fumbled for his glasses on the bedside table, where the alarm clock showed eleven minutes to six. Too early to get up, but at the same time he knew there was no point in sleeping on. Wearing only his pajama bottoms, he headed for the bathroom to press piss past his swollen, bothersome prostate gland. Then he brought a bottle of cognac and a sizable glass, before sinking heavily back into bed.

It was Christmas Day, but that made no difference. This was no real Christmas. Unn had died six weeks ago. Without her, Christmas was nothing. They had never had children. Without Unn, there was no meaning in anything. Christmas should be allowed to drift by, like every other day, just as hollow as the empty bottles that filled the kitchen.

He filled the glass almost to the brim.

The book he was reading was no use.

His sight sometimes failed him. It was just a matter of closing his eyes for a few seconds, and then it passed. His memory was not what it used to be either. That scared him more. In the beginning, a year or so ago, it was only small practical things that slipped his mind. Sometimes he might find himself in the kitchen with no idea what he had intended to do there. Just ordinary distraction, but it eventually grew worse. Now he sometimes had problems remembering the content of a book he had just read. After a while, he began to mark them: a red cross on the last page meant he had finished reading it. It made him nervous about opening books. The fear of finding the red cross in a book he thought he had not read made him look for different

169

strategies. He divided literature into bundles, constantly arranging them in different ways that slipped his mind immediately afterward. The coffee table had become a kind of archive, and the effort involved in keeping order and oversight made him edgy and frustrated.

The house was quiet. The oaf in the apartment above, a young man who held parties until far into the wee hours and didn't even open the door when someone came to complain, was away. Backe had seen him load his luggage into his car the day before Christmas Eve. Or yesterday. He wasn't sure, and it didn't matter.

The neighbors across the landing were dead.

He drank, and coughed.

Anyway, they had been disagreeable and arrogant. Maybe not Mrs. Stahlberg. She had actually seemed quite browbeaten. Henrik Backe had always felt a kind of vague contempt for the woman, she was so servile. Her servility irritated him; it reminded him of his own burden, his own submissiveness, and the treachery that could never be forgotten. Not even through alcohol, that damn liquor.

Turid Stahlberg was servile, and he did not like her. That little smile of hers, for example, when she drew into the wall if anyone passed her on the stairs: detestable.

Anyway, Hermann Stahlberg was far from obsequious.

Henrik Backe sniggered in contempt and took another drink.

Unn was dead, and life was over. It was merely a matter of waiting. The drinking that he had fought with such determination—a useless battle over far too many years—could curtail the waiting time. So he drank.

Now there was no one left for him to take care of. All of a sudden, he burst into shrill laughter.

Unn was gone and there was no longer anyone who needed to be protected. From him and his treachery.

But now there was no one who wanted to hear about it.

Mystified, Henrik Backe stared at the book he was holding in his hands. It was a novel by Sigrid Undset. He must have read it before, then. With stiff fingers, he leafed through to the last page. No red cross. That could not be. He must have read it before, when the system of red crosses had not yet been devised, before everything had become mixed up and he could not remember what *Kristin Lavransdatter* was all about.

The clock on the bedside table soon showed ten past six. It was dark outside.

He did not quite understand why he was wearing his pajamas; after all, it was well past dinnertime. He would open a can of asparagus soup. That's what he would like most of all.

It was so strangely silent everywhere, but of course the neighbors were dead.

Sølvi Jotun shuffled her too-big winter boots through the snow, cursing that they had not taken the car.

"Some fresh air will do you good," Billy T. said. "It'll be good for both of us."

She pulled the fake-fur coat more tightly around her and blew on her hands. Billy T. took off his mittens.

"Here. You can borrow mine."

"They're a bit big for me, you know."

She studied them skeptically, but put them on when he insisted.

"Good of you to let me go home," she mumbled, instead of thanking him. "I couldn't have put up with an hour in a holding cell today. It was bad enough in that damn hospital."

"Of course you can go home," Billy T. said, slapping her lightly on the back. "You haven't done anything wrong, after all. And as soon as you've answered my questions, I'll leave you in peace as well. That's a lovely apartment you've got, by the way."

"Public housing," she said tersely. "It's good that tax money goes for something sensible."

My tax money, Billy T. thought, suddenly remembering the betting slip still untouched in his breast pocket. Last night he had speculated about how long a winning betting slip like that was actually valid.

"Agreed," he said to push the thought away. "But why do you keep the kitchen locked?"

"That's none of your business."

They crossed the Nordre Gravlund cemetery. The snow lay deep between the graves, with here and there nothing but a nameless stone

sickle jutting out from the snowdrifts. Some of the graves were beautifully decorated, with candles in little lanterns and spruce branches
with red bows. Sølvi Jotun obviously felt uncomfortable. She pulled
her cap down over her forehead, grumbling indistinctly and bitterly.
They walked in silence until they emerged into Uelands gate and began
to intersect Sagene, between brick apartment buildings from the 1930s
and snowed-in vehicles.

"For fuck's sake. Couldn't we have come by car?"

Sølvi was obviously exhausted now. The distance from Ullevål
Hospital and Mor Go'hjertas vei was barely more than a couple of
miles, and they were no farther than halfway. All the same, she was
breathing heavily, and she had a hacking, unhealthy cough, so bad that
she suddenly had to stop entirely.

"Come on," Billy T. said, without slackening his pace. "You live just
right up here, you know!"

"Get lost," she snapped. "I'm not going home."

"Listen to me . . ."

He stopped and retraced his steps. Sølvi Jotun really was in lamen-
table shape. Billy T. began to wonder what they had actually done for
her at the hospital. Probably nothing more than offering a clean bed.
The whistling from her lungs might indicate an infection or maybe
severe asthma. In any case, she ought to have been given help.

"There isn't a fucking pub in the whole of Oslo open now," he said
despairingly. "Not even Sagene Lunsjbar. It's Christmas Day, Sølvi.
And it's only half past nine in the morning. You have to go home now.
I switched on the heating yesterday. It's probably fine there now."

"The heating!"

She stamped on the ground.

"Do you know how much heating costs these days?"

Billy T. grasped her arm and tried to take her with him.

"Come on now."

"You're *not* coming home with me!"

Her feet were firmly planted on the sidewalk, and she showed amazing strength when he took a better grip and began to pull. It was like
bringing Jenny with him, when she refused to budge at the nursery.

The difference was simply that the screaming child could be carried off. That was not so easy with Sølvi Jotun.

"Okay, then," he said, letting go. "But then you'll have to answer whatever I ask you. Now."

Something flashed in her eyes. Sølvi Jotun had turned thirty in an environment most people would not have been able to withstand for a month. She was not stupid and tolerated drug-induced intoxication better than most. Yesterday's collapse must have been accidental. Or bad dope. Now she tilted her head and looked up at Billy T., who towered almost a foot and a half above her.

"Why on earth should I answer anything at all?" she said. "I don't want to, and I can't see any reason to take part in a police interrogation in the middle of the street, in the middle of Christmas, without even having been hauled in. I haven't done anything wrong; you said so yourself."

Billy T. scrutinized her. It struck him that perhaps he might be able to carry her after all, since she couldn't weigh more than 90 pounds.

"Sølvi," he began to say, before clearing his throat. "You and I are going to make a little deal. An exchange, you might say. What do I get from you? Well, I get to know whether you have anything to do with Hermine Stahlberg . . ."

He let the words hang in the air, but could not decipher anything from her expressionless face. She did not even blink when he mentioned Hermine's name.

". . . and in particular whether you saw her at two specific points in November. What you get in return is that I don't arrest you on the spot."

"*Arrest me?*"

She started screaming and grabbed at her cheek histrionically, as if he had slapped her. An elderly man on the opposite side of the street looked ready to cross the narrow road to come to her rescue. However, when he took a closer look at Billy T., he marched on, studying the terrain in front of him.

"You can't haul me in now! You promised! Besides . . . what the fuck have I done?"

"Shh," Billy T. said, looking around swiftly. "Of course I can just break down your kitchen door. There are definitely piles of reasons to let you stew in a cell for a while. But . . ."

He raised his voice to drown out her protests.

"There's a completely simple solution to this. That you quite simply tell me what happened on November 10 and 16."

He had her now. Her hard, provocative expression wavered, only just, and he knew she would let herself be bought off. Looking anxious, she clapped the enormous bright red mittens together.

"Do I get to keep these?" she asked obstinately. "As well?"

"Okay," Billy T. said. "The mitts are yours. But then we'll go home to your place to have a chat in peace and quiet."

"You swear to leave my kitchen door alone?" she asked menacingly.

"Promise," Billy T. said, crossing his heart.


Once again Hermine had forgotten to lock the apartment. Carl-Christian was deeply worried at the thought that he had not heard from her since she had phoned and asked him to drop by nearly forty-eight hours ago. Nevertheless, he felt the familiar irritation rise when he put his hand gingerly on the doorknob. They should of course have checked that the door was locked on the day before Christmas Eve. They had contented themselves with ringing the doorbell. He tried to cast his mind back: Had they not also tried to get in? Concentrating hard, with his eyes squeezed tightly shut, he made an effort to reconstruct their last attempt to find his sister. He remembered clearly that Mabelle had stood one step below him, restless, as if totally unconvinced that there was anyone at home and she had already decided to head off again. But he could not re-create anything more of the situation.

Of course, Hermine might have been home since then.

It was so typical of her to leave the door unlocked. She was so afraid of everything: of the dark, of flying, of dogs. Hermine was scared to death of dogs, a coquettish fear with which she adorned herself to make herself seem childlike and helpless. It annoyed him on occasion that she was so appealing, and it had long stood in the way of a deeper sibling relationship between them. Sometimes he had simply had enough of her and pushed her away.

Most of all she was scared of burglars. The door was equipped with three locks. All the same, he had arrived several times to find an open door and an empty apartment. She could not manage to take responsibility for anything, not even for her own residence. Her thoughts took flight and never landed where she actually found herself.

He walked slowly into the apartment. The air was heavy and sweet: he wrinkled his nose at a bunch of dark-brown bananas in a bowl on the coffee table. He had an uncomfortable sense of doing something illegal. Slowly he crept from room to room. Hermine was nowhere to be seen, and Carl-Christian's concern was gradually superseded by anxiety.

When Public Prosecutor Håkon Sand arrived at Oslo Police Headquarters at quarter to twelve in the morning, he was suffering from a dreadful hangover. Three painkillers for breakfast had not helped his severe headache. He could not bear even to think about food. His clothes were sticking to his body with sweat, even though he had showered for twenty minutes.

Fortunately Karen had stopped him when, out of habit, he had sat behind the wheel to turn up on time for the extraordinary meeting. It had been a slow business getting hold of a taxi, and he came panting into the conference room all of fifteen minutes late. Silje Sørensen, sitting right beside the door, had held her nose when he leaned over her to pick up the documents Annmari Skar had laid out.

"Hope you didn't drive your car to get down here."

He muttered something unintelligible and dropped yet another mint into his mouth, before squeezing behind the backs of four of the ten people assembled in the room, holding his breath all the while. He smiled sheepishly at the Chief of Police and sat down at the far end of the table. Håkon was the only public prosecutor in the room. However, two police prosecutors had broken off their Christmas celebrations, in addition to Annmari. The Superintendent sat beside the head of CID and two chief inspectors, while Hanne as usual had taken a seat right down at the far end. She patted Håkon's thigh under the table.

"Thanks for yesterday," he whispered. "Sorry that I—"

Hanne hushed him in a friendly tone.

"I can of course give a summary of what we've gone through up to this point," Annmari said deliberately. "Since we couldn't all be equally punctual."

"I'm really sorry," Håkon said, louder this time. "The children were totally impossible and wouldn't let me leave."

Someone sniggered, and Håkon busied himself polishing his glasses.

"So, we believe there are reasonable grounds to suspect Carl-Christian of the murder of Hermann, Turid, and Preben Stahlberg," Annmari said. "Throughout the night I've tried to—"

"The night," Silje interrupted her. "Have you been here all night?"

"Somebody has to get the job done," Annmari said brusquely, without a trace of self-pity. "Christmas or not. We've collected a colossal amount of material, as you all know. We have more than 120 witness interviews now. The vast majority of them are worthless. We have a number of items of technical evidence, though most of them have not yet been organized systematically. The DNA analyses are not ready yet. There are also a number of investigations still to be conducted in the actual apartment. It is enormous, full of objects—and after all we're dealing with four victims here. That dog . . . it's now been clarified that we *are* talking about a dog. Very likely a mongrel. It makes the work somewhat more complicated, to put it mildly. All the same, I think . . ."

She smiled fleetingly, almost shyly, and drank some water from a plastic tumbler.

". . . we've achieved a remarkable amount in less than a week. Credit to you all. I appreciate that it isn't especially popular to call you in from family parties and Christmas fun on a day like this, but in consultation with the Chief of Police . . ."

She nodded in his direction.

". . . I've come to the conclusion that we can't wait very much longer. At least, if Public Prosecutor Sand agrees."

Håkon was startled by the sound of his own name, as if he had only now realized this was something that concerned him. The coffee he had gulped down to alleviate his hangover symptoms now sat like a pillar of acid in his gut. He swallowed noisily but said nothing.

"I might be preempting you a little here," Puntvold, head of CID, ventured, running his hand over his damp hair, "but after the discussion I had with Annmari Skar last night, I would even now assert that we have come further in this inquiry than we could have dreamed of last Thursday. I endorse her admiration of you all. We're moving toward arrests as early as this afternoon, and that makes me—"

"I don't mean to be impolite," Annmari broke in. "But would it not be an idea to take this in some kind of order?"

Puntvold beamed, reclining in his chair.

"Of course," he said. "As I said, I'm jumping the gun. On you go."

"Then I'd suggest the following course of action," Annmari said. "I'll give a report on the main points we ought to emphasize in a possible request for imprisonment. After that, we can throw it open for discussion. Our aim must be to come to a decision before . . ."

She drew back the sleeve on her left arm but had left her watch in her office.

". . . four," she said, letting her gaze travel around the assembled company. "Okay?"

A murmur of approval encouraged her to continue.

"First and foremost, we have an unusually good motive," Annmari said, writing *MOTIVE* in slanting, childish handwriting on the flip chart behind her. "I have prepared a special report that you've all hopefully received by now . . ."

Another murmur of approval, and all except Hanne and Håkon began to leaf through pages.

". . . in which I attempt to summarize all the conflicts between Hermann and Turid Stahlberg on one side and Carl-Christian on the other. I might as well immediately . . ."

Hesitating, she spun the marker pen with her right hand.

"I might as well anticipate the course of events a little and give you advance warning that I'd like a discussion about whether we should also attempt to have Mabelle imprisoned too. The evidence against her is weaker, but the two of them are very closely attuned. I'll come back to this. As far as the legal conflicts are concerned, then, there's one thing that indicates a sort of . . ."

Again she stood in silence, as if she could not quite find the words.

". . . escalating war between the parties," she suddenly concluded in a firm tone of voice. "It all began with minor issues, such as a discussion of Carl-Christian's salary, conditions of service, and that kind of thing. That took place directly after Preben's return to Norway. Thereafter the pendulum has swung to and fro, with increasingly serious results, I would contend. The first citation, in which Carl-Christian consequently wanted to take his parents to court, had to do with a relatively banal dispute about a summer cottage in Arendal. The family has owned it for three generations. Everyone has had an informal right to use it. Until Hermann decided to refuse access to Carl-Christian and Mabelle. A trivial matter, to some extent, since the couple have their own cottage by the sea and didn't use the family place very often. It seems to me that one thing led to another and . . ."

Once again she paused to have a drink. Hanne noticed that Annmari was swaying slightly and had to take a little step to one side with her left foot.

"Have you really been awake all night?" she asked.

Hanne had never seen Annmari so tenaciously involved in a case. It seemed like an obsession, a mania with a predetermined goal. Even Hanne would never have spent Christmas night at work. It was as though Annmari had staked her personal prestige on imprisoning the surviving members of the Stahlberg family as soon as possible. Hanne again felt that inexplicable unease, bordering on anxiety; she realized that a close alliance had developed between CID Chief Puntvold and Annmari Skar. For them, the case was already solved. The remaining investigation could be regarded as little more than a formality. A necessary but irritating process. Hanne let her eye flit from Puntvold to Annmari. In one short, cold second, she understood that they had all the others with them.

"Have you been awake," she asked again, "all night long?"

"Yes," Annmari said. "But it's fine."

"Sit down, at least."

As if she had not heard, or perhaps did not dare to sit for fear of collapsing, Annmari remained on her feet and continued: "In total, three lawsuits have moved back and forth between the parties, but two of them were merged, since they both had to do with access to and use of the property. The quarrel about the car that sent Mabelle into a cell here for a few hours is included in that group. Which clearly is the least interesting. The main lawsuit is concerned, quite simply, with settling the ownership arrangements in the shipping company."

"But . . ."

Erik Henriksen looked like a set of traffic lights when he stood up to fetch a soft drink: red hair, yellow sweater, and bright green track-suit pants. He poured some soda into a glass as he continued: "I thought there was no doubt that Norne Norway was Hermann's property?"

"That's correct. But when, a year ago, Daddy Stahlberg prepared a transfer of shares that would give all the power to Preben, Carl-Christian took action. He quite simply disputes that this is possible, bearing in mind the agreements he claims were previously decided between him and his father."

"Doesn't exactly sound like a strong case," Silje said doubtfully.

"No. And maybe that's why Carl-Christian tried to help things along with documents that aren't genuine."

"We don't know that he was the one who forged it," Hanne said.

Annmari puffed out her cheeks, discouraged.

"No, Hanne, that's true. Of course we don't *know* that for sure. But it's exceedingly improbable that anyone else would have had the remotest interest in such a document. Agreed?"

Her voice was loud, almost falsetto, and Hanne lifted her palms as a sign that she conceded.

"We've requested handwriting analysis of some of the other documents as well, but it will take some time to obtain the results. To sum up, and as emerges from the missives before you, there are strong motives for Carl-Christian to want to take his parents' lives and, for that matter, his brother's too, in this ongoing dispute. The young married couple were actually in danger of losing everything they owned. Their apartment and cottages, car, and other possessions are heavily mortgaged. Obviously in anticipation of wealth and affluence in the future too. But then we have this will, you see."

Some of them began to browse through the papers.

"It's not in there. But we all know the contents. It was drawn up three months ago and leaves Carl-Christian as good as disinherited."

"Not especially smart to do away with the instigators, then," Erik said, making a rustling noise as he opened his lunch pack.

"No. It's a weakness in our reasoning that can only be countered by asserting that this was something Carl-Christian was not aware of. Which is actually likely. Father and son have not spoken to each other, except through their lawyers, for more than nine months. There are no copies of the will, at least as far as we know. Jennifer, Preben's widow, only knew there was a will deposited at Oslo Probate and Bankruptcy Court—nothing about what it contained or when it was written."

"That's what she claims," Hanne said.

Annmari fixed her gaze somewhere on the wall.

"Naturally, we won't exonerate Jennifer Calvin here and now, Hanne. Under the present circumstances, it looks as if her oldest son is the only one who really benefits greatly from this crime. On the other hand, the boy has lost his father, and in a brutal way. Which involves a not inconsiderable loss. Anyway, most of us would consider it to be so. Agreed?"

She shifted her gaze to Hanne and refused to drop eye contact. Hanne did not reply, did not nod, and did not blink.

"Besides," Annmari continued, "besides, there's nothing so far to indicate that Jennifer would want her husband dead. Silje and I have done a pretty thorough examination of the woman, and we agree that a woman in her position, with her sparse and very selective network, would hardly be able to plan or perform such an act. Okay? So far at least?"

Hanne shrugged nonchalantly.

"Then of course we have this matter of Carl-Christian's familiarity with guns. He has a license for a high-caliber revolver, of course, and a dormant membership for a shooting club. In other words we can, with a fair degree of certainty, conclude that he knows how handguns are used."

Annmari noticed the small signs now. One by one, her listeners leaned back in their chairs. No one any longer found it necessary to take notes; hardly anyone thought it worth the effort of browsing through the document summary she had drafted in the early-morning hours.

They agreed with her. There were far more than reasonable grounds for suspicion.

"And their alibis are quite simply ridiculous," she rounded off. "Carl-Christian and Mabelle, as you all know, say they were at home. Alone. With no one to confirm that. When all is said and done . . ."

She struggled to smother a yawn. With tears in her eyes, she shook her head energetically in an effort to stay awake.

"I believe we have enough for an imprisonment on remand. So that we can also make further inroads in the investigation, among other things by being able to conduct a search. The question is whether we should try for both spouses or only for Carl-Christian."

"Both," Silje and Erik said in chorus, and this was followed by nodding and affirmative comments around the table.

Only Hanne sat quite still, her eyes half closed, her face expressionless. Not even when the discussion ran on, informal and somewhat boisterous, did she make any comment. No one seemed to pay any attention to that, before Annmari suddenly blurted: "Do you know, Hanne, sometimes you're a pain in the neck. What is it you're sitting there ruminating about? *Must* you be so secretive? Do you think the rest of us are idiots, or do you have some other reason to look as if you're sitting down there, perfectly aware of what happened in Eckersbergs gate last Thursday, but can't be bothered sharing it with us?"

Hanne smiled feebly and shrugged yet again.

"No, of course not," she said indifferently. "I don't know what happened. None of us knows what happened there that night."

"*But what is it then?*"

Annmari smacked the palms of her hands on the table. The Police Chief turned around abruptly to face her.

"Now then, let's calm down," he said. "I appreciate you're exhausted, Prosecutor Skar. But that's no reason to take that tone with your colleagues. We get enough of that when these folks . . ."

He tapped the documents with his forefinger.

". . . get their lawyers involved. Then there'll be real chaos. We should save our energy for arguing with them, don't you think?"

"No," Annmari said harshly. "Now, for once, I want to speak up. Hanne Wilhelmsen—look at me. Look at me, I said!"

Hanne raised her head lethargically.

"Share it with us," Annmari said. "Share your thoughts with us, Hanne!"

Her voice was no longer aggressive. Instead something desperate, almost sad, came over her entire being: she stood with her shoulders hunched and her head inclined.

"If Hanne Wilhelmsen doesn't wish to participate in the discussion, I don't see any reason to force her," Jens Puntvold said. "Strictly speaking, we're more concerned with following up this line of inquiry that you have presented, Skar."

"I absolutely insist on hearing what Hanne thinks," Annmari said. "Nothing other than that."

Now almost whispering, she sat down unceremoniously.

Hanne scratched her cheek with her thumb for some time. It seemed as though she still had no intention of saying anything whatsoever. She sat leaning back in her seat, looking nonchalant, and began to move her head vigorously from side to side, as if more preoccupied with her stiff neck than with Annmari's unexpected fit of temper.

"Hanne," Håkon Sand said, sotto voce. "Maybe you ought to—"

He pressed his knee against hers, and she tensed all of a sudden.

"I'm sorry if I seem reserved," she said, staring at Annmari. "I don't mean to be, really. I'm . . . concentrating in fact. And I'd have liked to share my thoughts with you, but they're . . . more of a general character, and this is probably neither the time nor the place—"

"I think we should take your word for that," Puntvold broke in. "Continue, Skar!"

"We'll take our time," the Chief of Police said. "If Skar wants to take your comments into consideration for the actions she is now contemplating, then she should hear them. Make a start, Wilhelmsen."

Shrugging, Hanne snaked her way forward to the flip chart, where she took a fresh sheet and drew the letters from A to E.

"This is how we all think," she said, pointing under the B with the marker pen. "That if B follows after A, C after B, and D after C, then we take it for granted that E is the next letter in the sequence. That's elementary, banal logic, quite simply because, when presented with the letters A, B, C, and D, we assume that we're looking at the beginning of the alphabet. It's so probable that we could almost swear that E is what follows. Our entire system of justice is built up around such a mind-set. And that's all to the good."

She replaced the lid on the marker pen and turned to face her audience. Erik sat with his mouth open and his eyes nailed firmly to the alphabet. Jens Puntvold doodled in annoyance on a paper cup and appeared demonstratively uninterested. The two youngest investigators sat taking notes, as if they were at a lecture on a topic they were going to be tested on. Silje twisted her ring repeatedly.

"Every single day, people are sentenced to imprisonment on the basis of such conclusions. Since specific, precise, and incontrovertible proof is unfortunately in short supply in our business, then as a rule, courts have to come to a decision about guilt and innocence on the basis of circumstantial evidence. And I . . ."

She raised her voice to forestall Håkon's interruption.

". . . I'm not really criticizing that. That's simply how it is, and we all have to live with it. Our system would come crashing down otherwise. That A and B and C and D come one after the other, by sheer chance, is totally unlikely. But I can't help thinking a great deal about the fact that our prejudiced attitude toward the sequence, consequence, and connection of things can sometimes be abused. At the very least it's *conceivable*."

Again she turned to the flip chart, and wrote "ELL" in capital letters on a new sheet of paper.

"There's a letter missing here," she said, pointing. "An initial letter. Which one?"

"*C*," they answered in unison.

"Sure?" Hanne asked. She sensed a certain enthusiasm in the others now. "Are you quite sure?"

"*C* for *cell*," Erik said. "It's obvious."

"*C*," several of them repeated.

"Are you all *absolutely* sure?"

Impatience spread as a slightly irked ripple through the room.

"Okay then," Hanne said, and completed the word. "It becomes 'CELL.' But if I tell you that you have chosen *C* because you are all in the police force, what would you say then?"

"Where are you going with this, Hanne?"

Puntvold frowned and looked at his watch.

"I'm illustrating how mistaken we can be," Hanne said tartly. "I'm trying, since you insisted we had time for this, to demonstrate how we interpret a set of given but incomplete information according to who we are and where we believe we are heading with the information. The missing letter doesn't have to be *C*. It could be *B*, *H*, or *S*, for instance."

"'BELL,' 'HELL,' 'SELL,'" she wrote, underlining each three times. "If we had a teacher in the room, then it's more likely he would have gone for *B*. A clergyman would most likely choose *H*. And a shopkeeper would almost certainly come up with *S*," Hanne said. "For the simple reason that they would not relate to the word *cell*, but make daily use of *bell*, *hell*, or *sell*, depending on their line of work."

Hanne tore the sheet off the flip chart. "The point I'm trying to make is . . ."

"That's what I'm honestly wondering!"

Now it was the Superintendent's turn to show irritation. "What on earth has this to do with the Stahlberg case? With all due respect to both you and the Chief, I'd like to remind you that we're sitting here on double overtime on Christmas Day and surely have more important things to do than learn new guessing games!"

"It's all the same to me," Hanne said. "By all means. I really wasn't the one who insisted on this. Really, I'd prefer to be eating Christmas breakfast at home right now, so . . ."

She put down the marker pen and tried to make her way past Silje, who had tipped her chair against the wall behind her.

"No," Annmari said so loudly that Hanne stopped in her tracks. "I'm the one, at the end of the day, who's going into court to petition for imprisonment on remand. I find Hanne's explanations interesting. I want to hear more. You can just leave if you think this is a waste of time. Go on, Hanne. Please."

The Superintendent seemed caught completely off guard and distractedly lifted his coffee cup to his mouth without drinking, before returning it to the table.

"She's pulling rank," Erik whispered in Silje's ear. "My God!"

The situation was practically unheard of. Even though Annmari was a police lawyer and, therefore, from a prosecution point of view, senior to the superintendent, it had been years since any of the lawyers at police headquarters had taken such a tone with experienced and highly placed officers. The silence in the room became unbearable. Even Puntvold, the self-confident head of CID, seemed bewildered: he opened his mouth a couple of times without finding anything to say.

"I'm merely attempting," Hanne began at last, trying not to look in the direction of the Superintendent, "to show how our interpretations are guided by our expectations and experiences. The more comprehensive and complete a picture, situation, or case is, the easier it becomes to draw definite conclusions about what is missing. Here . . ."

She retrieved the torn-off sheet of paper from the floor and held it up.

". . . the word fragment I gave you was as good as complete. No one here was in any doubt about what was missing. But you were nevertheless wrong. Or more correctly: you *could* have been wrong. No one can know for certain whether I was thinking of CELL, BELL, HELL, or SELL."

Even Håkon seemed alert now: he had put on his glasses at last, and his eyes appeared clearer, more focused.

"No matter how long the chain of circumstantial evidence in a case may be," Hanne went on. "Not to mention the motives being ever so convincing, ever so solid, so . . ."

The Superintendent sat like a pillar of salt. Hectic red blotches were obvious on his cheeks. He was at a loss as to what he should do with his hands. In the end, he clasped them firmly. Hanne could see that his knuckles were white.

"If the three deceased Stahlbergs are $A$, $B$, and $C$, then Knut Sidensvans is an alien $X$," she continued. "He doesn't fit in. My worry is that we are pushing him aside like a stray letter of the alphabet instead of asking ourselves: What was the man doing there? Is there an explanation for his presence? Might it be the other three who are accidentally on the scene, and it's the $X$ that gives this case meaning? It seems illogical, of course. It's so much easier to search for cause, connection, and meaning where they hit us between the eyes—namely, in a family so dysfunctional that it resembles the one I . . . My point is that . . ."

Hanne was speaking to Annmari now, and to her alone. The Police Prosecutor sat with her arms crossed, and nothing could be read from the blank expression beneath her graying bangs. But she was following Hanne's argument. At the end of the day, it was Annmari who would decide which direction this investigation would take. Not Hanne herself, not the Superintendent, not the Head of CID, or the Chief of Police. Not even the Public Prosecutor. Annmari Skar was the lawyer with responsibility for the case, and from the very first moment, she had taken unusually forceful control. It seemed that she had hardly gone home for the past week, and no one was in any doubt that Annmari was the only person at headquarters with anything like a comprehensive overview of the entire, enormous set of case documents that the Stahlberg inquiry now comprised.

"Where are you actually heading with this, Hanne?"

Annmari's voice was neither hostile nor skeptical. A furrow appeared on her brow, that was all, and she shook her head gently as she went on to ask: "Should we just let the Carl-Christian lead lie?"

"No, of course not. It might even be that you are right that we ought to arrest him—and his wife. I just think it's important that we have . . ."

Hanne held back. She felt hot and reluctant to continue.

"The motive doesn't *have* to be what we see. And then . . . then it might just as well be Hermine who killed all four of them. Or someone else entirely."

This last sentence was said almost in a whisper. Silje glanced up at her in surprise.

The door crashed open and hit Hanne on the back of the head.

"Sorry," Billy T. said. "Are you okay?"

Hanne mumbled and nodded as she rubbed a nascent lump.

"Hermine Stahlberg bought a gun in November," he said in a loud, triumphant voice.

His jacket lapels were caught above his shoulders and the buttons were uneven, as if his clothes had been thrown on in a hurry. Red-cheeked and breathless, he continued: "I've been talking to one of my old stoolies. On November 10, Hermine met a gun dealer in a café in Trondheimsveien. She needed an unregistered handgun, preferably a pistol. She was—"

"Sit yourself down," Annmari said calmly. "Take it easy now."

"There's not enough room here," he said. "The deal was that the weapon should be obtained and delivered on November 16 and—"

"You're behaving like a trainee," Hanne said. "Sit down and relax."

"Where, then?"

There were no spare seats. Hanne held out her own chair and moved to sit on the sideboard. A soft drink bottle toppled over, but she ignored the spreading brown stain.

"Naturally I'll write a special report," Billy T. said. "But—"

"A special report," Annmari interrupted him. "Why not a witness interview report? I take it you've interviewed this gun dealer of yours?"

"Forget all that now!"

He waved her away impatiently. Without removing his jacket and scarf, he sat down abruptly.

"Anyway, my source says that the arrangement was to obtain a handgun. 'Suitable for shooting big game.'"

His fingers curled into quote marks.

"Hermine had actually said that. 'Big game.' My source was lucky, got hold of a Glock, and handed it over to Hermine in the restroom at the same café on November 16."

"Your source got hold of a Glock," Annmari reiterated slowly. "Does that mean that you've spoken to the actual supplier? That you have firsthand knowledge?"

"Yep! As you know, I'd heard the story before, from Kluten, that junkie who died on Sunday. Since he tells more lies than a bishop, I had to . . . now I've—"

"I hope, for your sake, that this gun dealer is now sitting in a cell waiting for an in-depth interview," Puntvold said, noticeably, almost palpably, eager.

It was as if the air suddenly went out of Billy T. He sagged somehow, sliding forward in his seat, letting his shoulders slump, and bowing his head. Then he took two deep, demonstrative breaths before looking up again and saying: "This is what I have to offer—a special report making reference to a conversation I've had today with a source, a gun dealer on a petty scale, who informed me that on November 10 this year, Hermine Stahlberg was in contact with h— with the person in question. Hermine was looking for a handgun of a specific caliber, 'suitable for shooting big game.' The transaction was conducted six days later. The report can be written, signed by me, and placed on Annmari's desk in three-quarters of an hour. That's it. I don't intend to reveal my source. Not yet, anyway. I don't intend to take any guff from anyone, either. And I don't intend to stay here any longer. If you accept my offer . . ."

A big, dirty index finger, its nail bitten down to the quick, quivered at Annmari.

". . . then you can always send me a text. Bye."

He got to his feet and left. The door slammed behind him with just as much noise as when he had entered ten minutes earlier.

"Tired," Hanne said, smiling faintly at the Chief of Police. "Just terribly tired."

After a moment's silence, an infernal uproar erupted. They were all speaking over one another, their voices ricocheting off the walls as they grew increasingly loud in an effort to be heard. Only Hanne sat pensively quiet, using her finger to lead the spilled cola to the edge of the table in tiny rivers that dripped on to the floor.

"All I understand is that we must go for an arrest," Annmari screeched, waving her hands to induce silence. "And maybe we'd be as well to operate on a fairly broad front. We'll haul in all three, what do you think? Hermine, Carl-Christian, and Mabelle?"

Some of them began to clap, and the applause eventually became deafening. Annmari smiled happily. Hanne could have sworn that the Police Prosecutor was on the verge of tears.

"That's fine," Puntvold said in her ear; she had not noticed that he was standing beside her now. "This might move faster than you anticipated. Excellent outcome."

Hanne smiled politely without meeting his eyes.

"It wasn't so important to solve the mystery of Sidensvans after all," he continued. "It must be acknowledged that Billy T. has quite a network of contacts. But you, too, of course! You've been looking at Hermine the whole time, haven't you?"

Hanne turned around to answer, but by then Puntvold was already engaged in conversation with the Superintendent. Hanne scanned the room, looking from one face to another.

They all seemed so happy.

As for herself, she felt only disquiet, and left to track down Billy T.

Hanne had searched everywhere. No one had seen anything of him, apart from Erik Henriksen, who claimed to have caught a whiff of Billy T. in the men's bathroom fifteen minutes earlier. Liquor and sweat, he maintained, wondering aloud what kind of Christmas Eves they were in the habit of celebrating.

Finally she gave up and headed back to her own office.

She hovered on the threshold for a few seconds. The office was in semidarkness, but nevertheless something gave her a feeling that all was not as it should be. Once again she felt that glimmer of anxiety, of an obscure reluctance to be there in police headquarters and at work. Slowly she raised her hand and flicked the light switch.

"Hi," she heard someone behind her speak and almost jumped out of her skin.

"Heavens above! Billy T.! You scared me."

He crossed over to the window. "It's as if we never get any proper sunlight these days," he said softly.

"It's winter, Billy T. But it's turning now. Every day will be lighter from now on."

"I notice I'm not able to put up with it so well these days."

"Winter?"

"The darkness. The fact that it's never completely bright. Just a gray, halfhearted sort of daylight. Then evening comes, far too early. I get so fucking tired of it."

He took a seat. Hanne approached him and slowly stroked his bald head. The stubble tickled the palm of her hand. At the nape, a roll of fat divided into two thin sausages. He relaxed, she noticed, leaning back and closing his eyes. She pressed his head warily against her own body and massaged his forehead.

"We're getting on in years, Billy T. It's nothing serious, really."

Outside the windows, all the colors had disappeared. The temperature had climbed above 32 degrees, and the trees stood black and bare of snow, just visible in the fog that drifted slowly in from the fjord. The wind had died down. In half an hour or so, it would be pitch dark.

"I've allowed myself to be corrupted," he said.

"You have . . ."

A squad car raced down toward Grønlandsleiret. Blue lights sliced fleetingly through the fog, before the sirens dwindled as the vehicle vanished toward the city center.

"Look at this."

He sat erect and withdrew a note from his breast pocket. Hanne accepted it hesitantly and unfolded it.

"A betting slip," she said quizzically.

"Yes. Horses. Seven winners. Worth over 150,000 kroner."

"That's . . . that's lovely, then! Congratulations!"

He stood up and headed over to the window. "Tear it to pieces. I can't bring myself to do it."

"Billy T.—"

"Tear it to pieces!" His breath formed damp, pulsating patches on the glass.

"You'll have to explain this to me," she said.

"For fuck's sake, Hanne! Tear it to pieces, I'm telling you!"

"Turn around."

He stood with shoulders hunched and his head slumped between them. Now he leaned against the window with the top of his head on the pane. Hanne closed the door carefully.

"Billy T., I want to know what this is."

"A betting slip."

"I understand that. But where did you get it? Why do I have to tear it to pieces?"

"Because . . ."

At last he turned around. His complexion was pale, and deep furrows were etched from the sides of his nose past the corners of his mouth, all the way down to his chin. He was unshaven. His eyes were sunk deep into his skull, and it was almost impossible to tell what color they were.

"Because I got it from a prize slob. Ronny Berntsen, Hanne. He gave it to me. And I desperately need the money."

He hid his face in his hands and turned away again, facing the wall now. He banged his head against the wall panel over and over again.

"Bloody hell, Hanne. I need that money. Tear the damn ticket to pieces!"

"Billy T. . . ."

She threw her arms around his waist, resting her head on his broad back. The heat from his body radiated through his jacket.

"You have to do it yourself," she said. "So far, you haven't done anything wrong. You haven't drawn the money."

He did not react.

"Billy T.? You haven't drawn the money?"

"If I had, then I wouldn't still have the ticket," he said dully.

"Then everything's okay. But you have to destroy it yourself. It will be really important to you. Afterward. Later. That you were able to draw the line. To resist."

"Resist the devil's temptation, you mean? Have you gone all religious, or what?"

Hanne smiled and hugged him even more tightly. "Me? Are you nuts? Turn around now."

He was breathing more easily now and wheeled around. She started to undo the buttons on his jacket and tried to take off his scarf. He stopped her.

"I have to go," he muttered. "There was a hell of an argument when I had to skip Christmas lunch at my sister's. If I leave now, I might at least be in time for dessert."

"You can have some money from me."

They were standing so close to each other. Hanne patted his chest, tugged his jacket lapels into place, and adjusted his scarf.

"I can't accept money from you, Hanne."

"Of course you can. It's my money. I spend hardly anything these days; my bank account just sits there, growing fatter and fatter. Nefis pays for everything, or so it seems. Admittedly I don't have 150,000 yet, but I can help you part of the way."

"You know well and good that's just not going to happen. I can't accept money from you. Not from anyone."

"You're my family, Billy T."

"No."

"Yes, in a way you're the only family I have. You knew Cecilie. You

knew me for a long time before the others, before . . . You can have
100,000. As a loan."

Suddenly she pulled back.

"But of course you'll have to decide for yourself."

"Do you have a headache?"

"What?"

"I walloped the door on the back of your head."

"Oh, that. It's fine. A tiny lump, that's all."

Billy T. fished out a cap from his pocket and pulled it on.

"You ought to sort through your mail soon," he said, pointing at her
in-box, a towering stack of unopened letters and internal mail.

"Sure. What are you going to do with the ticket?"

She held it out to him and, after a moment's hesitation, he grabbed
it and pushed it back into his breast pocket.

"I'll sort it out myself," he said tersely.

"I know you will," Hanne said. "You must remember to write that
special report of yours before you go."

"The level of interest in my information was not exactly resound-
ing," he said abruptly, glancing casually at the list of arrests over the
past twenty-four hours at the top of her pile of mail.

"Don't be an idiot," Hanne said. "You just walked out. Annmari
hadn't finished speaking. There was a round of applause in there."

"She hasn't been in touch."

"Is your cell phone switched on, though?"

In confusion, he extracted his phone from his pocket.

"Oh," he said. "It's off."

"Go and write your report. And prepare to disclose your source. My
God, Billy T.! He's the most central witness we have!"

"She," he muttered. "It's a woman. And I'm not letting the cat out of
the bag until I'm forced to do so."

Hanne hurried downhill from police headquarters. The paving stones
were slippery, and a couple of times she almost lost her balance. She
had hardly progressed halfway when she heard the shouts:
"Wilhelmsen! Hanne Wilhelmsen! Hey, Chief Inspector!"

She stopped and turned around. The man running after her appeared too young for his uniform. The epaulettes on his shoulders revealed him to be a second-year police trainee. His head was wreathed in tight curls, and his face was as round as a ball, with narrow, crooked eyes and a broad, flat nose. If the boy had not been blond and pale, he might have been mistaken for Afro Asian. He was also short, unusual for a police officer. Hanne caught herself wondering whether he was tall enough to pass the entry qualifications for the police force.

"Hi," he said breathlessly, holding out his hand. "I'm Audun Natholmen."

Nodding indifferently, Hanne glanced at her watch.

"You see, I'm taking the tips called in. So . . . I receive the tips from members of the public in the Stahlberg case, you know. And then . . ."

He looked back and dropped his voice, as if keen to share a secret with her.

"There's a lot of crazy stuff, you know."

"Yes."

"Yes, of course you do!"

He laughed shyly and ran his fingers over the sleeve of his uniform jacket.

"But then there was this guy who phoned in. Anonymous. He refused to say who he was, you see. But I noted down the number on the display and checked it afterward. It was from a public phone booth in Maridalen, you know, just where the road—"

"That's not so important," Hanne broke in.

The boy gulped and took a deep breath, before starting over: "The man had seen something suspicious. Someone had bored a hole in the ice on a lake in Nordmarka. This caller explained that he was quite strange. This person who bored the hole, I mean. The day after the murders. The person had spent hardly any time there. Drilled a hole in the ice and then left again. The caller thought the hole was big enough to drop something into. That is . . . a gun, for example."

"You'll have to take this up with someone else," Hanne said, starting to walk on slowly. "I don't exactly remember who has responsibility for sorting out the tips. Guldbrandsen, I think. In any case, it's certainly not me."

"Wait!"

He would not desist and followed close behind her as she walked downhill, gesticulating all the while.

"I've actually spoken to Prosecutor Skar!"

"Annmari? Have you bothered her with this?"

"She was a bit grumpy, I must admit. But you see . . . first of all I spoke to . . . then . . . Can't you stop for a minute?"

Hanne stopped and looked the boy up and down in surprise, feeling almost impressed.

"I just don't understand what you want from me," she said, sounding friendlier now. "As I'm sure you know, or at least understand, the Stahlberg case is quite a comprehensive affair. As far as personnel, tactics, and technical aspects are concerned. We have to hope that some people sit in the midst of it all with some sort of overview. Annmari Skar is probably one of them. If you have a hunch that a tip should be followed up, then you really ought to take it up with your immediate superior all the same. Who is that?"

"*Just listen to me, won't you?*"

The young man was almost screaming now. An elderly woman on her way uphill came to a sudden halt and studied the two of them in alarm. On spotting the boy's uniform, she shuffled off with a stiff gait, obviously afraid of falling.

"I've spoken to three people higher up in the system," Audun Natholmen continued eagerly. "Nobody is interested."

Hanne gave a broad smile as she answered: "You know very well that the vast majority of tips we receive are totally worthless. You really can't expect the system to leap into action just because an anonymous guy has phoned in to say that he's seen a strange ice fisherman!"

He nodded grudgingly. The irises were ice blue in the narrow slits of his eyes, and his mouth resembled that of a child. Hanne could swear that it quivered, a minute movement of his lower lip, as if he was moved by the situation of being able to stand there in the drizzle with Hanne Wilhelmsen and discuss the Oslo Police Force's most important case.

"You understand that, don't you?"

She slapped him on the shoulder, before pushing her hands into her pockets.

"Now, I'm freezing to death out here and I'm going to get buckets of abuse when I get home so late. So if it's okay with you, I'm off now. I simply can't help you. Other than that, I'll look more closely at this tip of yours tomorrow if you put it in my pigeonhole. Then I'll see what I can do."

"But there was something else I meant to . . ."

Hanne had started walking again, with more determination now.

"But I just wanted to ask whether . . ."

Irritated, Hanne wheeled around for the third time. This guy was absolutely wearisome.

"You see—I'm a diver. It's my hobby, in fact. Would it be really crazy of me if I took a couple of buddies and conducted a little search up there? In my own free time, so to speak? Since nobody is the least bit interested in this tip anyway?"

Hanne considered it. A couple of colleagues passed them by quickly, nodding briefly in Hanne's direction.

"Yes," she said at last. "It would be absolutely crazy."

Then she smiled ever so slightly.

"But that doesn't mean that I wouldn't have done it if I were you. Only I would have kept my mouth shut about it. If I hadn't found anything, I mean. But you'd best give it a miss."

The boy stood gaping and looked as if he wanted to say something. Then he snapped his jaws together instead and rushed off up the slope. Partway uphill, he half turned in his mad dash and raised his hand.

"Thanks!" he called out, overjoyed, and sprinted on.

Annmari Skar had problems with her sight. Her vision was flickering, and she had no idea how she was going to survive the press conference that Puntvold had insisted on holding.

The arrests of Carl-Christian and Mabelle had gone smoothly. The intention was to bring them in for questioning and then make them aware of the charges. However, when they flatly refused to come, making reference to the holiday and the imminent funeral, they were arrested at home. According to Erik and Silje, both showed signs of shocked apathy rather than anger. They had not even asked for a lawyer, until someone reminded them that it might be an idea to arrange something of that nature before they allowed themselves to be interviewed.

Annmari was ill through lack of sleep and felt downright nauseous at the thought of what faced her. She leafed through the arrest reports over and over again and simply waited for the final one. Hermine Stahlberg was obviously more difficult to find than her brother or sister-in-law. It was now almost six o'clock in the evening. The press conference was to begin at half past six, which meant a live broadcast at the top of the TV2 news and, in the worst-case scenario, ten confused, undigested minutes half an hour later on the NRK channel.

"She's vanished into thin air," Erik Henriksen said, slamming his fist on the door frame.

"Vanished?"

Annmari stacked the documents tidily one on top of the other, edge to edge, and ran her hand over her hair in an attempt to appear composed and prepared, before looking up at the new arrival once again and repeating: "Vanished, did you say? Who?"

"Hermine. Gone. Not at home. She doesn't have a job, actually . . ."

He shrugged and plumped down on the spare seat.

". . . and what would she be doing there anyway on Christmas Day? We were—"

"We were quite simply too ill prepared," Annmari interrupted him, sounding desperate. "That's what I call a real beginner's error. My God, Erik, can't any of you find her?"

Erik shook his head reluctantly. "Sorry."

"Sorry? It's too late for that. I can't fathom . . . It's impossible for me to have control of everything, Erik. I have to rely on the rest of you to get your jobs done as well!"

"You were the one who wanted to make the arrest," he retorted angrily. "I've done exactly what you asked me to do. *We*. We have done as you said. But we can't find Hermine."

Annmari closed her eyes. Her saliva production increased to a dangerous degree. She swallowed vigorously and drank some water. Finally she was able to look him in the eye again.

"When I give instructions about an arrest, then—"

"Three," Erik corrected her. "Three arrests."

"When I give instructions about three arrests," Annmari began over again, "then naturally I expect you police officers to make the necessary preparations in order to be able to carry out these arrests as painlessly as possible and at least . . ."

Her voice rose, almost shrill.

". . . at a level acceptable for professional police officers!"

"*You police officers*," Erik mimicked. "Is that how it is now? That you're not one of us?"

He measured her with critical eyes. His gaze ran over the uniform she was wearing, because she was already dressed for the press conference, glancing off the insignia on her shoulders, and resting on her left breast pocket: POLICE, in golden letters on a dark background.

"Bloody lawyers," he spluttered, and Annmari began to laugh.

He bit his lip. Stonily, he struggled to concentrate his attention on the rain that had at last begun to fall.

"Not us," Annmari said, smiling. "The two of us don't quarrel, Erik. Not you and me."

"No. But I still think you're the one who has responsibility for us not keeping a good enough eye on these folk. In my opinion, it's risky to arrest anyone right now anyway. In the middle of Christmas, and all that stuff. They'll get every sympathy, you mark my words. From outsiders. From good people who are gorging themselves on Christmas and family and presents and churchgoing. And who can't imagine anyone killing off half their family. Not now, Annmari. Not now at this damned, holy, Norwegian Christmas season."

"But when it turns out to be right, Erik. When everything we've done and everything we know and every possible sign indicates that we *must* pull in the suspects, what are we to do then? Sit on the fence and wait for Christmas to be over? Wait for the suspicion to fade, to disappear? For everything to be more palatable? For us, or for them?"

"Well . . ."

Erik rumpled his hair, which was growing too long. He clumsily rose to his feet. On his way out of the office he turned around, hesitating for a moment, before continuing in a soft voice, with an intensity at odds with his unkempt appearance: "I feel for you, Annmari. I'm keeping my fingers crossed that you succeed with this case. Go full throttle, to hell with the press. They're after you, regardless of what you come up with. And we'll find Hermine for you. Give us twenty-four hours, and you'll have her head on a silver platter."

"Do you promise?"

"I guarantee it. Alive or dead."

Then, with a protracted yawn, he left her.

Hanne chose to walk, even though it took almost an hour to cross Oslo from the Old Town to Frogner. What's more, she took a detour. Billy T. was right. When she looked at herself in the mirror these mornings, she noticed that the fat was no longer sitting where it had been in earlier slack times. Also, it was far more difficult to get rid of it.

She headed from the area surrounding police headquarters that had become so popular with immigrants, down through the Medieval Park. What had previously been a disagreeable, enclosed no-man's-land was being transformed into a beautiful reminder of how the city had once sprung up. The surface of the water was frozen and gray now, and the excavated ruins almost merged into the fog and dirty slush. Her feet were sodden, and she broke into a run to keep warm. The traffic in Bjørvika, where the Opera House that had been planned for so long looked as if it would never be built, was quiet. She approached the square outside the railway station. Bars and pubs were closed and locked, with shutters pulled down in front of their windows. Only at Plata, a litter-strewn spot southwest of Central Station, was trade proceeding as normal. The dismal traffic island was the main business center for Oslo's street trade in narcotics. Junkies and skinny young girls wearing too much makeup exchanged goods, money, and agreed services, while the occasional train passenger shrugged at the sight and gave them a body swerve. Recognizing a couple of the miserable wretches in Plata, Hanne swiftly cut a diagonal detour toward Karl Johans gate. From the open space at Egertorget, she could only just make out the outline of the Palace. The lights on the linden trees lining the city's main thoroughfare took on halos of dampness; an avenue of indistinct, dwindling light. Hanne stopped at the Tanum bookstore to view the window display. She had never experienced such a silent Oslo. She crossed the Palace Park without encountering a single soul.

Soon she was home. The streets broadened out. The towering buildings were statelier and set back from the sidewalks. Christmas was more subdued in this part of the city. The lights were not garish and multicolored as they were in Grønland, and the spruce sprigs in the door garlands were the genuine article.

She fumbled to look at her watch between her gloves and the slightly-too-tight edge of her sleeve.

Ten past five. It was probably all over. Hermine, Mabelle, and Carl-Christian Stahlberg would all have been arrested and each installed in an interview room at police headquarters. It was unnecessary for Hanne to be present. If it all progressed as everyone seemed to believe, then they would spend a long time in custody. Weeks, probably, maybe the entire time until the main proceedings commenced, and the first interview was therefore nothing but window dressing anyway. They would be subjected to the anxiety of being exposed, hauled in, and locked up.

Then it would be her turn. It had been decided that she would interview Carl-Christian at nine o'clock the following morning. She crossed her fingers that there would not be a single lawyer in the city willing to spend ten hours at police headquarters in the middle of the Christmas holidays. Although, as things had developed among Oslo's criminal law advocates, they might even be waiting in line. They seemed prepared to do almost anything for their fifteen seconds on TV. In this case, there might well be considerably more. The Stahlberg case could easily be their ticket to fame, if not exactly glory. Hanne found herself making a mental wish list: an overview of lawyers with integrity and willingness to cooperate in their client's best interests. It was uncomfortably short.

Kruses gate was deserted.

Not one of the curtains stirred. No faces suddenly retreated. Hanne ought to enjoy this; she ought to feel at home among people who took care of their own business and were almost inaccessible to one another. To Hanne, Frogner was a district where people were reduced to names on door plates and a tentative nod on the stairs was all you could expect of your neighbor. She ought to be predisposed to living in such a place.

Instead she was disturbed by the lack of curiosity. It robbed her of the possibility of assuming what others might think. They were to be found, of course, behind closed doors and drawn curtains; there were people here too—many in fact—but it would be impossible for her to serve them up half truths about themselves. It made her uneasy and tense when she traveled home, escalating as she neared her apartment and not diminishing until she could shut herself in behind the anonymous door with three meaningless surnames engraved on a brass plate below the doorbell.

She rounded the corner of her own apartment block. She was on the point of passing through the gate when she started so violently that she dropped the ring binder she had carried all the way home.

A dog brushed against her leg. It emerged from behind the low wall where a garbage shed of stained timber had been built only a few weeks earlier.

The dog was gray and ugly, its neck too large in comparison with its narrow, squat hindquarters. One ear had been practically torn off. The street lamp highlighted a gash along its left flank. The animal was limping badly, but maintained a remarkable pace as it traversed the street and disappeared into a backyard a hundred yards farther along the street.

Hanne's breathing was labored. Her body had received such a powerful rush of adrenaline that she felt warmth creep back into her frozen toes. She crouched down to retrieve her ring binder, taken aback by how afraid she had actually been. It was the silence of course; besides, she had been completely lost in her own thoughts when the horrible beast had suddenly appeared. Her pulse was still pounding when a thought struck her: she straightened up slowly and neglected to pick up the ring binder.

She had heard about this dog. Nefis had attended the residents' meeting some time in the autumn when a decision had been taken to build a special shed for the garbage bins to keep rats and other animals out. Hanne remembered it now, clearly; she had laughed out loud at the belief of people in the west end that a simple shed could keep rats at bay. But Nefis had also mentioned a dog.

In truth it was a frightening creature, and Hanne lingered for a long time, deep in contemplation, without noticing how cold she had become.

She scared so easily these days, and that worried her.

Alexander slept the way teenagers do, almost spreadeagled across the bed, on his stomach, with his face resting on his right hand and his left arm dangling over the edge. The quilt covered only the middle of his body. In the dim light that sneaked into the room from the hallway, Hanne could just discern a single buttock. The boy was sleeping naked with his socks on. At one time they might have been white. Now the soles of his feet were finely outlined with dirt and dust, and the elastic was loose around his legs.

A cardboard box sat beside the bed, along with a duffel bag stuffed full of clothes. They had still not been opened.

"He doesn't really believe all this," Nefis whispered. "He's doing nothing to settle in."

"What did you expect?" Hanne said. "He's only been here for twenty-four hours."

"What was it like?" Nefis asked, still whispering, even though the boy was fast asleep.

"What do you mean?"

"To be thrown out."

"I was never thrown out. I was frozen out. That's even worse. Or . . ."

She would have to resist the urge to tuck the boy in more snugly. Actually they shouldn't be here at all. He had closed the door when he went to bed. It crossed Hanne's mind that Alexander was a big boy, entitled to privacy and being left to sleep in peace, undisturbed by two lopsided aunts he didn't even know.

Slowly she approached the bed. She lifted the quilt carefully and replaced it the right way around, covering him and tucking the edges lightly under his feet. The dangling bare arm she left well alone.

"Like that," she said quietly, nudging Nefis gently aside, before closing the door. "I must go to bed," she said. "Tomorrow will be a long day."

Nefis crept along after her to their own bedroom.

"Are you ever going to be able to take a proper holiday?" she asked, before answering her own question: "Never, of course."

"I took a week off last summer."

Hanne padded into the bathroom and began to brush her teeth.

"Five days," Nefis corrected her.

"Are we going to argue now?"

"No. What was it like?"

"Wonderful. Unaccustomed. Strange." Hanne smiled with her mouth full of toothpaste.

"I didn't mean your days off," Nefis said, stretching out on the unmade bed without taking off her clothes. "I meant being frozen out."

"It's too late, Nefis. I can't go into that now. I survived."

Nefis pulled a smile as she picked up the remote control from the bedside table. Hanne finished in the bathroom and, standing stark naked, opened out her arms.

"Aren't you getting ready for bed?"

"Yes, of course. But first you can tell me something about what it was like."

"No. I can't face that just now."

"Then I want a story."

The video on the massive LCD screen on the wall a couple of feet from the foot of the bed flickered convulsively as Madonna cavorted mutely. Nefis took Hanne's hand and drew her close.

"A story before we go to sleep!"

Sometimes Hanne had the idea that Nefis thought she was less talented. For a long time Hanne had realized that the short stories Nefis demanded in exchange for acceptance of Hanne's silence about the real things in life were fragments she pieced together to form a complete picture of Hanne's childhood.

"It won't be a long one," Hanne said.

"Not too short either."

Pulling her down onto the bed, Nefis rolled Hanne onto her back.

"No," Hanne said with a smile; on the big screen, Madonna was dancing a Spanish flamenco to deaf ears.

"Yes!"

"I have to ask you something first."

Nefis was almost on top of her now, a pleasant weight on her abdomen and mound of Venus.

"Wait," Hanne said. "That dog . . ."

Nefis's mouth tasted of olives and parsley.

"Wait," Hanne said, trying to wriggle free, giggling and slapping the hands that stroked her thighs. "That mongrel you were talking about during autumn—when you decided to build that ridiculous garbage shed out there—what sort of animal was that?"

Nefis was right on top of her now, with all her clothes on, and entwined Hanne's arms with her own. The buttons on her blouse scraped Hanne's stomach. Nefis's tongue was toying with her earlobes.

"Listen to me, Nefis! That dog . . . I just want to know if it's been here long. Does anyone own it?"

Nefis hauled herself up abruptly. Her hair hung like a dark curtain over her face. In the backlight from the TV screen, Hanne could scarcely distinguish her features.

"A dog, Hanne. A stray dog. Someone said it had been here for a long time, for years. It's frightening, especially for children. Besides, it makes a mess of the garbage. Somebody said they were going to phone the health authors."

"Health authorities," Hanne said, laughing. "Fine. Are you going to get undressed?"

"I thought you could do that," Nefis said, kissing her again.

Hanne unbuttoned her blouse.

She had escaped yet again. She had escaped telling about the time when she was five years old and wanted to sleep with the light switched on.

In her mind, the closet was full of blood-sucking bats, and the only way to keep them shut inside was to leave the light shining all night long. When she woke to a dark house and clear, terrifying, rustling noises from the closet in the corner, she had hardly dared to lift her hand to switch on her bedside lamp. The bulb had been unscrewed and removed. The ceiling light had also been disabled. Her father got into the habit of casting her room in darkness at nighttime. A year later Hanne had declared at suppertime that bats lived in caves, churches, attics, and other dark, roomy places and naturally could not survive in a little closet full of clothes and shoes. Anyway, she now knew that vampire bats did not exist in Norway at all. Her father had nodded in satisfaction and stopped coming into her room at night.

Hanne had now stripped Nefis naked, her whole body, soft and firm and voluptuous.

# THURSDAY, DECEMBER 26

The old lady in Blindernvei was alone again. Her son had left her early that morning to catch a flight. He would return on Monday for the funeral, but in the meantime he had to return home. It was only fair. After all, he had a wife and child and a demanding job. His own life. Just as she would also have to carve one out for herself now that Karl-Oskar was dead. *One of us had to go first*, as her husband always used to say. They had both sent up a silent prayer that it would be them. In the end it turned out that he was the one.

Terje had cleared things out for her. It would be more correct to say *with* her: they had slowly gone through drawers and cupboards. It had been so good, almost beautiful, to clear Karl-Oskar out of the house without him ever being truly gone.

Terje had left only the bedroom in peace. No one apart from her would go through Karl-Oskar's most personal possessions.

His pajamas were still tucked, neatly folded, under the pillow. She sat gingerly on the edge of the bed and touched her cheek with the worn, soft fabric.

His clothes would go to the Salvation Army. They had decided on that together, several years ago, on one of those evenings when they had sat out on the terrace, each with a drink, watching the sunset over Tåsen. Material things should not be romanticized, Karl-Oskar felt, insisting that they should send all of it to people who needed it more than they did. Clothing and everything else that had no special significance for the surviving spouse should go. He had been almost brusque when he said that, as if he suddenly found it tasteless to discuss departure and death.

She was the surviving spouse.

Setting the pajamas down on the blanket, she stood up stiffly and walked over to the wardrobe. Halfway across the room, she stumbled across something.

Seeing that it was a folder, she picked it up.

The paramedics had been in here of course. They had genuinely tried to revive Karl-Oskar that Thursday only a week ago. It felt longer. It was so difficult to remember. The folder must have been lying on the bedside table and must have fallen on the floor in the midst of all the commotion caused by their resuscitation efforts. She hadn't been over on that side of the room since Friday morning, when that odd little clergywoman was due to arrive and Kristina had made her husband's bed for the last time. She hadn't noticed anything then. Perhaps that was not so strange, since she had hardly any recollection of tidying up.

The house was overflowing with flowers. Even now, in the midst of the Christmas festivities, friends and acquaintants, business connections and distant relatives had gone to the trouble of sending condolences. No one had left behind a folder. It was probably nothing important.

Kristina tried to remember which meeting Karl-Oskar had actually intended to attend on that fatal evening just prior to Christmas. She rubbed her hands together, rocking from side to side.

He might simply have omitted to mention it to her.

She would have remembered, of that she was certain.

She had been married to a lawyer for nearly fifty years and had never once touched her husband's papers.

Kristina placed the unopened folder on her husband's bedside table. Terje could skim through the contents when he came back. She took a deep breath as she crossed to the wardrobe. Sooner or later, she would have to clear things out, and she might as well get it over and done with now.

Carl-Christian Stahlberg did not dare to raise the glass of water to his mouth. Instead he sat on his own hands. Thirst made his tongue grow large inside his mouth, and he smacked his lips to stimulate his saliva secretions. Someone had forgotten to provide him with water for the night, perhaps deliberately. He did not know for certain, but rumors flew around. Torture was of course not something that Norwegian police engaged in, but letting someone sit in an overheated cell for ten hours with neither food nor drink was not very friendly either. Now that he had finally been given something to drink, he was more consumed by fear of revealing how scared he was. The glass of water could just sit there.

"Thirsty?"

The woman who was about to question him might be in her early forties. Carl-Christian tried to memorize her, to focus his attention on her oval face with the first signs of wrinkles around her big blue eyes. They weren't entirely blue, though: it was as if someone had placed a washer over the iris, a coal-black border around the light. Carl-Christian reluctantly called to mind a science-fiction film in which invaders from another galaxy sneaked around in human guise among fortunately unwitting earth dwellers, who had not yet discovered that the strangers could be unmasked by their eyes, which were black and blue at the same time.

He had to stare at this woman, intently. Last night, through all the absurd hours in a room stinking of urine where there was barely space to walk three steps in any single direction, he had felt his grasp on reality slip away. He visualized glimpses of his mother in summer wearing an unbecoming dress that his father had claimed to like: it had a floral pattern, and little Carl-Christian had thought the yellow sunflowers looked like smiling lions. A contented cat's head had grown in his thoughts until he hit his fist against the cell wall to force the pain in his knuckles to bring him back to his present surroundings.

For a moment he had thought he was asleep; that must have been about three o'clock. They had taken his watch away, so it was difficult to know for sure. He felt cold. The snow blinded him; he squinted at a pale spring sun, wearing skis that were far too large and which he struggled to lift off the ground, when he discovered he was standing in the cell pissing into the bricked-up hole in the corner. At daybreak he had realized the only way to anchor reality was to fix his eyes and keep his focus on one specific object.

In fact the woman was attractive, even though Mabelle would have advised her to lose some weight. Her hair was uneven at the edges and probably hadn't been cut in a long time. But it was shiny and brown and fell beautifully over her shoulders. Her clothes were another story. Carl-Christian tried to think about clothes. About fashions. About Mabelle's magazine, about *F&F*, which now appeared to generate a tidy little profit. If only this hadn't happened. Only the fates now knew how things would turn out. He didn't even dare to consider how the press would be treating them as they sat in prison.

"You should know that we are doing what we can to emphasize that this case remains unsolved," the policewoman said. "To the media, I mean. If that's what you're thinking about."

Carl-Christian tried to remember what the movie was called, that film in which the invaders with blue-black eyes could read human thoughts and in the end our entire civilization gets dumped into a gigantic space shuttle.

"Are you actually willing to say anything at all?"

He could not remember her name. He no longer remembered anything, no matter how much he concentrated on something other than his thirst—that dreadful thirst that he lacked the courage to do anything about. He kept forgetting her name, but she seemed friendly enough, with an inexplicable mild manner that confused him and made it impossible to recall who she was and what he was supposed to say.

"Hanne Wilhelmsen," she repeated for the third time. "My name is Hanne Wilhelmsen."

Carl-Christian Stahlberg was no stranger to lies. He had once read that the average person lied five times every day. He thought that seemed an underestimate. As for himself, he could easily nod approvingly at something he found idiotic. He thought nothing of nattering enthusiastically with his neighbors about things he found totally uninteresting. Lies were tools to maintain an expedient harmony with your environment.

All the same, the lie he must now tell was too enormous. It had no beginning and most certainly no end. This was a real lie, so fictional and contrived that he quite simply had no idea how to make a start on it. Each time the policewoman posed a question, he opened his mouth to answer. He wanted to say something. He wanted to be reliable and trustworthy. He wanted to satisfy this dark-haired woman in her slightly-too-tight suit jacket and flamboyant footwear, with her dangerous eyes. He wanted to get her on his side. But the lie was too far-reaching. Carl-Christian was not adult enough for his own story, and so he closed his mouth after uttering a few incoherent words.

"Of course you have the right to refuse to provide a statement," Hanne Wilhelmsen said. "But it would be beneficial really if you could say so. That way, we avoid wasting time."

All of a sudden he realized that she smelled nice. Something struck him. A soft stroke on his face, almost physical: he shut his eyes and grew aware of a heavy scent that reminded him of something that was almost over. He smiled and breathed deeply for the first time in fifteen hours.

"It's Turkish," Hanne Wilhelmsen said, returning his smile; now at last he remembered her name. "I have a . . . friend from Turkey who makes this perfume herself. I've no idea what she puts into it, but I do like it."

Then she laughed, slightly self-conscious, as if they were two strangers reluctantly seated together at a dinner party who had finally found something to talk about.

"I do, too," Carl-Christian said. "It smells of autumn."

"Autumn?"

Now she laughed again, inclining her head and sizing him up.

"I have to ask you again," she said gently. "Are you sure you don't want a lawyer?"

He nodded hesitantly. He did not know definitely. Most of all he wanted this to be over. That it was all a jest, a rude practical joke that had gone much too far and would soon be uncovered when someone popped up with a clown nose and a bunch of balloons. A deception that would be broadcast on TV, so that people could laugh at how stupid he looked and how easily he had allowed himself to be duped. He could have put up with that. He would have laughed at himself, slapped his thighs perhaps, sworn a little, and entered into a play-fight with the presenter, because it was all over and of course Carl-Christian could go along with a genuine prank.

A lawyer would only make it all bigger. Truer.

"You really should have a lawyer."

Now she was leaning toward him. The tape recorder was switched off. There were only the two of them in the room and, from the corridor outside, no sound could any longer be heard. Carl-Christian tried to think, tried to return to where he should be.

He had a terrible thirst and would give anything to know how Mabelle was getting on.

Mabelle was actually looking good. Erik Henriksen thought she could have been really attractive if it hadn't been for her hair being lightened a touch too much and her face having a tad too much makeup. Her eyes lingered slightly too long on his, as if she felt the key to credibility was a steady and unflinching gaze. Instead, it all seemed inappropriately flirtatious. Erik did not quite understand where and when she had managed to fix herself up like this. It appeared as if she had come directly from a beauty salon, and not from a night's uncomfortable stay in a holding cell.

Mabelle had an enormous range. That much, at least, was clear. Even her lawyer seemed tired of her fluctuations between pleading and rage, tears and disbelief, desperate laughter and affected indifference to what must now take place: her life was in ruins anyway, thanks to the terrible mistake made by the police.

Of course Mabelle had accepted a lawyer. However, she had contented herself with her usual shyster, an elderly business lawyer, partner in one of the middle-sized firms in Oslo. He sat erect in his chair, immaculately dressed in a charcoal-gray suit, and had immediately shown himself to be an approachable man. Erik was relieved and somewhat surprised. Gunnar Huse, the lawyer, had shown up a mere half hour after Erik's phone call to explain the situation. He was polite, borderline friendly, and had no objections to the actual arrest. Admittedly, he was alert and watchful when Mabelle was on the point of saying too much, but he did not seem excessively eager to spoil the interview situation. That made Erik more vigilant, preparing himself for a long day. After this, other lawyers would come. The guy with the alert eyes behind discreet glasses would hardly last the next twenty-four hours. The next one would be worse. Gunnar Huse had said as much himself when he arrived, in a confidential tone, bending to speak in Erik's ear: "I'm the young Stahlbergs' regular lawyer. My domain is business affairs. I see no reason to object to my client being interviewed today, but I'd like to draw your attention to the fact that my office is already working on finding a replacement. A lawyer with better qualifications to handle a case of . . . these dimensions and character."

Then he had given Erik an apologetic look, as if washing his hands of having to contribute to the noise and fuss to follow, and the roughly handled preliminary procedure that a case like this would be subject to, the moment a high-profile criminal lawyer got his claws into it.

"Our relationship was absolutely fine, I'm telling you!"

Now Mabelle was playing discouraged. She smacked her forehead and rolled her eyes dramatically before suddenly switching to logical argument.

"I mean, we all have our family quarrels, don't we? Our disputes and disagreements. With our parents and our parents-in-law. That doesn't mean that we want them dead, does it?"

All of a sudden she burst into tears, and once again fixed her eyes on Erik's: Mabelle turned into a hurt child, unfairly treated.

"I don't understand any of it," she sobbed. "I just don't understand how this could happen."

Impatient, Erik threw his pen down on the desk.

"Listen to me," he said, trying to appear relaxed. "This is going nowhere. You haven't answered anything I've asked you. All you say is just disconnected . . ."

Drivel, he thought, but checked himself just in time.

". . . fragments of something that bears no resemblance to an explanation. I suggest that we—"

"We'll start over again," Mabelle's lawyer said firmly.

He leaned toward his client and laid a reassuring hand on hers.

"Mabelle, this is something you have to go through. The police officer is entirely correct. You don't have a duty to say anything. However, it's my firm conviction that it will benefit your case if you give a statement, and be a little more . . . attentive and focused, you might say. Now you and I will have a little chat without . . ."

He nodded benevolently toward Erik.

". . . Inspector Henriksen here. Could I have a few minutes alone with my client, do you think?"

Again that smile—almost sympathetic—to Erik, who had already stood up.

"Of course," he replied as he left the room.

Not a word about Mabelle going to wait for a new lawyer, it crossed his mind as he closed the door behind him. She wanted an audience, now as always. Erik had already understood that much. Mabelle had no intention of returning to a foul, deaf cell. If only she could weep, threaten, and beg long enough, everyone would understand that it was hair-raisingly unreasonable to keep her locked up. Mabelle Stahlberg seemed far from stupid. Probably she had planned to stay silent. It was her self-absorption that ruined this for her, the selfsame egocentricity that had helped her earlier, in situations in which it had been advantageous to be quick-witted, always to the fore, first in line. Reserve was quite simply a strategy she had not mastered.

Mabelle wants to go home, Erik thought, and so she was going to make a statement at an early stage in the proceedings.

"Is everything going well?"

Annmari placed a hand on his shoulder, and he gave a start.

"Yes," Erik said. "I think in fact we're having a bit of luck here. Her lawyer actually seems to be going after . . ."

He searched for a word, but couldn't find the right one.

"The truth?" Annmari suggested.

"Exactly," Erik said in surprise. "But he'll be replaced shortly."

"You'll have to strike while the iron's hot, then."

She gave him another encouraging pat on the back and went off to find a sofa to sleep on. Even if only to snatch forty winks.

They had already taken three breaks. Carl-Christian had at least begun to take something to drink. It had loosened his tongue a little. The account he gave was disjointed, brief, and so obviously fallacious that Hanne felt an increasingly intense unease at the man's refusal to permit the assistance of a lawyer.

"This document," she said dispiritedly, placing a copy of the disputed letter in front of him for the third time, "has been demonstrably falsified, then. Do you have no opinion about who might have done this?"

"No."

"Did you receive it in the mail?"

"Probably."

"Have you kept the envelope?"

"No. People don't usually do that."

"But you have received it then, since you were the one who presented it to the court?"

"Of course."

"And you didn't write it yourself?"

"No. Mother confirmed that it is genuine. She remembered signing it."

"Carl-Christian Stahlberg," Hanne said, emphasizing each and every syllable, "you see, we have the word of two handwriting experts that neither of your parents signed this letter."

"Mother confirmed that it's genuine."

"But then she can't have been telling the truth. I think she was trying to protect you."

"Me? I had taken her to court."

"Yes, on paper. But really this conflict was between you and your father. I honestly think she felt a great degree of discomfort about it all. Sorrow, maybe. For sure. That the people she loved most could not get along. I think that . . ."

She paused. She had to concentrate intently in order not to disclose her growing irritation.

"No one will ever know why your mother chose to lie about this matter. But it's pretty obvious to imagine that she—when she hadn't been able to stop the escalating conflict between you and Hermann— at the very least wanted to save you from being charged with a crime."

"A crime?"

At last he looked up. His complexion was pale, but tiny patches of red had formed over his cheekbones.

"It's a crime to falsify documents, Stahlberg."

"But it's not an official document! After all, it's only a letter! A lousy little letter!"

"The minute you present such a letter to a judge and claim that it is genuine, in bad faith, you commit a crime. A man in your position and with your education should both know and appreciate that."

"I've no idea who did it. Mother said it was genuine. I believed her."

Hanne tried to recall whether she had ever questioned a detainee who lied more openly than this. Carl-Christian Stahlberg looked down, to the side, stuttered, mumbled, flushed, and rubbed his feet against the chair leg. He looked like a stubborn, willful ten-year-old, caught red-handed stealing apples, who subsequently claimed that a doppelgänger must have raided the neighbor's garden.

"I know you're lying," Hanne Wilhelmsen said gently. "And I've never ever said that to anyone in an interview before. Just so you know that. Interesting, actually."

She stood up, stretching her arms and legs. Slowly she walked around the interview room and flexed her fingers. The clicking sound was nerve-racking, so she took another tour of the room. Finally she resumed her seat and kicked off her boots.

"I never usually do that, either," she said, placing them neatly side-by-side. "In fact, they're so difficult to pull on and off. But I realize we're going to sit here for a long time. A very long time. And there's something you should know before we go any further."

All of a sudden she switched off the tape recorder and leaned forward. Carl-Christian Stahlberg seemed more afraid now and drew back to the wall, reacting strongly when Hanne pushed the desk after him, so that he was sitting trapped between the desk and the wall.

"That's uncomfortable," he muttered, trying to push it away.

"In this entire building," Hanne whispered, finding it impossible to catch his eye, "there's only one person who can in any way envisage the possibility that you haven't done what you're charged with. One person, Stahlberg. Me! All the others—and I really mean *all the others*—are convinced that you're the villain of this piece. I, on the other hand . . ."

Suddenly she pulled the desk back toward her again. Nevertheless, he remained sitting close to the wall, stiff and motionless, his gaze resting on her navel, as she continued.

"I think that other answers are feasible. In fact, I have a certain . . . experience that there can be a considerable distance between planning evil deeds and going through with them. I actually know, just as you do . . ."

His gaze was wandering now. He raised his head slowly, and when his eyes met hers for the first time, it was sheer terror that she saw in his large pupils. The man was scared out of his wits.

"Just like you," Hanne said, "I know what it's like to want your father in hell. That doesn't necessarily mean that you speed him on his way."

A small tear spilled from his left eye. The teardrop trickled by fits and starts down his cheek, before gathering momentum and turning into a little damp trail at the corner of his mouth.

"If I were you, I'd make use of the opportunity," Hanne said. "The one you have here and now. You're telling such fucking lies that a young girl at elementary school would have exposed you. The rest of the gang out here . . ."

Her hand swept toward the door.

"They subscribe to the strange belief that whoever lies about one thing is lying about everything. I, on the other hand, know that not to be the case. Now I'm going to switch on the tape recorder again, and then we'll start all over. It's up to you how that goes."

Then she started the tape again.

"How long is it since you heard from Hermine?" she began.


"It simply can't be true! My God, that girl gets up to a lot of strange things, but this! What in heaven's name has she done?"

Erik Henriksen let Mabelle roar and rage without interruption. He had to focus to avoid finding the whole situation downright entertaining. It crossed his mind that it was like being at the theater: a cabaret in which Mabelle played all the roles. She was quite good at it too. Truly splendid in the more feminine parts, when she appealed to his protective male instinct and played on her appearance, which, despite all the lies she was dishing out, he found increasingly attractive. They had been sitting in the cramped, stuffy room for more than four hours now. He was beginning to feel weary, and Huse the lawyer had eventually been forced to take off his suit jacket and loosen his tie a notch. Mabelle, however, seemed unaffected. Her hair was still light and luxuriant, newly washed. Her makeup looked as if it were a permanent part of her face. On a couple of occasions, she had applied fresh lip-stick, turning away discreetly, with no mirror, precise and perfect each time.

Erik opened his mouth to interrupt the vociferous outburst.

"Wait," she said, on the brink of tears. "Hear me out! Hermine's hopeless! She must be the one who told you this. It's not true! And how did you get hold of her? Has she been hauled in?"

Only her speech slipped here and there, divulging an upbringing far from shipping companies and filthy rich in-laws.

Erik did not answer.

"So, you have absolutely no knowledge of Hermine buying a hand-gun on the illegal market in November?" he asked instead.

"No, I'm telling you! My God, a handgun? What on earth would she want with a handgun? And if that were the case, how would I have anything to do with it? I don't even know what a handgun is! Is it a pis-tol or something like that? What is Hermine saying?"

"I just want to have this crystal clear: you have never heard or seen, or in any way known about, anything to indicate that your sister-in-law Hermine Stahlberg has obtained an illegal gun?"

"No!"

"But Carl-Christian knows about guns."

"Carl-Christian?"

"Yes."

"No—well, I suppose so, if you mean all that stuff about the shoot-ing club. That's such a long time ago. Word of honor! He didn't think that was fun any longer. He wasn't any good, either. Who is it that's mixed us up in this dreadful story?"

Mabelle began to cry. Quiet, extravagant weeping; weeping for dead children and irreparable catastrophes. Erik was impressed. For a second or two he felt grudging sympathy for this little creature. His hand rose to stroke her hair.

Abruptly, he pulled it back as Huse got to his feet and said: "I think we'll draw a line now. My client needs another lawyer. I can't allow any further questioning until this situation is regularized."

"Okay," Erik Henriksen said, rattled. "You're probably right."

Mabelle finally looked up. She gave a couple of sobs, wiped her tears, and mumbled something incomprehensible as she blew her nose into a handkerchief handed her by her lawyer.

"Hermine tells lies all the time," Erik heard her yell as she was escorted back to the custody room.

Hanne could not shake off the dull feeling of melancholy, a dull pressure in her diaphragm that robbed her of her appetite and threatened to make her burst into tears for no reason. Anyway, there was no cause that she could recognize. Once again, her father's death impinged on her thoughts. That could not be what was niggling her. Not in that way. These past few days, she had mostly felt a resigned sense of satisfaction that William Wilhelmsen no longer existed. Hours could pass between each occasion she thought of him. It was as if Alexander's intrusion into her life was a final end to what remnants there must have been of sorrow over relationships that could never be repaired. Alexander and Hanne had hardly spoken to each other since he had appeared on Christmas Eve, thinly clad and disowned. All the same, she knew that she was the one he had come to, and it was to be with her that he had settled down in Kruses gate. He would not go to bed until she was safely home each night. No matter how early she got up to go to work, he came padding through to the kitchen wearing an old sweater and tracksuit pants; they drank coffee in silence, and all he asked was when she would be home again. They secretly watched each other, as if they did not entirely know whether their kinship was something good, or maybe instead something that would destroy everything.

Hanne touched her stomach, unable to understand her own state of mind.

"Not feeling too good?" Silje asked, knocking unnecessarily on the door frame. "How did the interview go?"

"Come in. Fine. Or . . . badly, in fact. It depends on what point of view you adopt. The guy's lying. That much is clear. Of course he knows nothing about the gun. Hermine has been on a bender, he says. That's probably true, as far as it goes, but he got himself completely mixed up and lost the thread when I asked where he thought Hermine might be now. First of all, he hadn't spoken to her since he visited her in the hospital. When I hinted that, naturally, we would check his phone calls over the past few days, he suddenly remembered that he had spoken to her the day before Christmas Eve. I said I found it remarkable that he didn't know where his sister was on Christmas Eve, since they had just lost their parents and suchlike, and then he just went silent on me. So if the aim of this interview was . . ." She rubbed her face with both hands before finishing: ". . . to get the man to talk himself into a remand order, it was successful. But—"

"That's never Hanne Wilhelmsen's aim," Silje said. "She just wants to discover the truth, doesn't she?"

She sat down and took a cigarette from a pack of ten.

"Just for the moment with all this stress," she whispered. "Do you mind?"

"By all means. Just before I succumb myself. By the way, have you been in here since the crack of dawn?"

"Here? No. Why do you ask?"

"Nothing," Hanne mumbled. "It's just . . . every morning when I arrive, it seems as if someone's been here."

"Well, Hanne. That happens all the time! People collect documents and leave messages and . . . your door is never locked, is it? Something, as far as I remember, that you got called out for from the Superintendent just last week."

"Forget it. Any news of Hermine?"

"No. We've been in her apartment, but there's nothing there to give any indication to where she might be. Admittedly we haven't managed to search it properly as yet; we'll do that tomorrow. But anyway there are signs that suggest she hasn't gone away anywhere. Her passport is lying in a drawer, and all her toiletries are on the bathroom shelf."

"I'm worried," Hanne said.

"You're always worried."

"This case really bothers me. I sort of haven't . . . it's as if I'm getting—really sick. Queasy."

"Well, it's not particularly pleasant to think of four people being liquidated like that. Enough to make you queasy, I'm sure."

"You say four. But really we're only talking about three."

Suddenly she leaned forward to the cigarettes. She pulled one out and sat fiddling with it.

"It's exactly as if everyone has forgotten poor old Sidensvans," she said, momentarily holding the cigarette right underneath her nose. "It's as if he was of no consequence. As if his death is less shocking than the Stahlbergs'. Just because he was a peculiar guy who had neither money nor power. I find it provocative, in fact. In addition to that, I really *believe . . .*"

She resolutely grabbed Silje's lighter and lit the cigarette.

". . . that it's a serious slipup in this investigation not to clarify what he was doing there. In Eckersbergs gate. They were expecting him, that seems clear. Four glasses on the table. Cakes and champagne at the ready. They may have been about to celebrate something."

She reclined in her chair and blew three perfect smoke rings at the ceiling.

"A smoke is always good," she said, smiling. "Always. Don't you feel curious, Silje?"

"About Sidensvans?"

"Yes."

"Of course. We all are. And I'll bet we find out in the course of the investigation. We've only been working on it for a week! And it is Christmas, after all. This is going to take months, Hanne, but we will get to the bottom it. By spring we'll have Sidensvans's life in a huge folder. Every tiny detail."

"But in the meantime," Hanne said, "in the meantime, we're destroying the lives of three people. Even though they may have done nothing."

"Honestly . . ."

Silje angrily stubbed out her cigarette in a dirty coffee cup.

"You don't still think that Carl-Christian and Co. are innocent?"

"No. But we can't know whether they've all been in on it. Firstly, we have to find the motive. To find the motive for the act, we have to know why Sidensvans was there. It's as simple as that. And all the same . . ."

Now it was Hanne who sounded hot-tempered.

". . . there hasn't been *damn shit* done in that apartment of his! I asked for a full search of that bloody place four days ago. I want to know what's on his computer, to find his appointments book, if such a thing exists. I want to have fingerprints, I want—

"That'll come, Hanne. It's Christmas, for heaven's sake!"

"Christmas . . ."

Hanne twisted the word, drew it out with a grimace, as if it tasted foul.

"Why did you come, actually?"

"Have another cigarette, Hanne. Relax. It actually looks as if you should take some time off. I'm being honest. Why don't you take some time off? This case is so smoothly on track now that nobody will mind if you're gone for a week or so."

"Why did you come?"

Silje shrugged and lit yet another cigarette.

"The keys to Sidensvans's apartment. They hadn't disappeared after all."

"What?"

"They had just fallen down into the lining."

"What are you saying?"

"I'm saying," Silje said, taking a deep drag, "that there's nothing mysterious about Sidensvans's keys. He had them all along. They had just fallen down into the lining of his coat."

"But . . ."

Hanne seemed completely thunderstruck.

"I examined it myself! I personally examined his coat in minute detail, looking for his wallet and keys. He had dropped his wallet, of course, but—"

"The keys were in the lining. Why are you so agitated about it? It's just a detail, Hanne! The only reason I came here to tell you this is because you were so hung up about the business of the keys that I thought it would be a good idea to get it straightened out."

Hanne made no reply. She sat stiff and silent, with her eyes fixed on the window. The ash on her cigarette grew slowly into a gray pillar that broke soundlessly and dropped to the floor.

"Okay," Silje said.

"Okay," Hanne muttered.

"Then I'm off," Silje said, almost as a question, asking for permission.

"Okay," Hanne repeated without changing position.

"Bye."

The door slammed behind Silje.

Hanne could not fathom how the keys could have been lying in the lining. She had felt inside the pockets several times. She did not remember a hole. She thought she had shaken the coat, as she did with her own garments when looking for keys.

Had she really forgotten to shake the coat?

A young man stood in ice-cold water up to his waist. Darkness had already descended. The wind had abated, but the temperature had dropped to below freezing. Cloud cover brushed the edge of the hills to the east; it looked as though the weather was going to deteriorate. The young man yanked his mouthpiece from his mouth and shouted a string of spirited oaths.

"It's really shallow here, you know. Damn! It's impossible to dive!"

They had taken their time excavating a hole in the ice. Since none of the three youths had experience diving under ice, they had struggled with the equipment as well. When the hole was finished at last and the youngest of the three stood at the ready, in the only dry suit they had managed to procure, they had totally forgotten to check the depth of the water.

"Maybe you're standing on a stone," Audun Natholmen suggested; he was wearing a quilted jacket and ski pants outside his wet suit, hoping to escape having to jump out into the water. "Walk forward a little."

"Walk! I've got flippers on my feet, for fuck's sake! You walk yourself!"

The third one intervened: "If it's so fucking shallow, then you can just stick your hand down, can't you?"

"I'm freezing."

Audun slapped himself on the forehead. He was already regretting this. First of all, he had tried to get one of the experienced club members to take part in the mission. The guy had laughed hysterically and wondered if Audun had a screw loose. He would certainly not work for the cops free of charge in the middle of black winter. No one should.

"You've got ten to fifteen divers of your own! Not a single one of them under that ice. Get lost!"

Audun had muttered something about maybe just dropping the idea, before phoning his pals on the course for new beginners. They had neither experience nor satisfactory equipment, but had a spirit of adventure in spades. One of them even had an uncle who was a professional diver and was away over Christmas: the boy knew where his key was hidden. Just a little loan, and no one would notice anything.

"Do it, then," Audun said. "Stick your arm down!"

"Whereabouts?"

The fellow in the open channel roared and nearly fell over when he tried to pull off his mask.

"I just can't manage it."

With clumsy movements, he tried to haul himself up on to the edge of the ice. His friend slapped him on the shoulder.

"Fucking wimp. You're the one with the dry suit! Use your arm to rummage around down there for a bit, won't you! It's not dangerous since it's so shallow, anyway."

Audun tried to calm them both down.

"He can do as he wants," he said loudly. "I'll give it a try myself."

The threat of being degraded had the desired effect. The young man in the water slid down again from the ice and made an effort to find his footing.

"Christ!" he snarled between clenched teeth. "I think I'll take off these flippers. Wait a minute."

He tried to lift his foot up on to the ice. Audun held him by the arm, and the third friend shook his head and flailed his arms. Suddenly the diver slipped back. Audun lost his grip, and the eighteen-year-old fell on his back, disappearing underwater with a splash.

"Look," the diver gulped. "Look here, guys!"

His voice rose an octave and he was on the brink of falling yet again, when with a huge effort he managed to tip his backside up on to the ice. His right arm was held up in the air and he gave a high-pitched laugh.

"I found it! Hell and damnation, I found the bastard!"

He was holding a revolver in his hand. The two other boys stared mesmerized at the find. Audun gave a prolonged whistle.

"Let me see," he finally said, producing an official-looking evidence bag.

"It's mine," the boy yelled. "There has to be a fat finder's fee, or something of the sort!"

"Cut it out," Audun shouted. "Give me that revolver now. At once!"

The third man stepped in: "Don't mess around. Give it to Audun. It's a murder weapon, you know!"

The sudden thought that the revolver could have been used to take the lives of four people deflated the diver. Slowly he lowered his arm and handed the weapon to Audun. He seemed almost apprehensive as he let go of it.

"Is it loaded, do you think?"

Audun placed the gun in the bag as carefully as he could. When it was safely wrapped in plastic, he ran the beam of light from a pocket flashlight over the barrel.

"MR 73 Cal 357 MAGNUM," he read out slowly. "With a silencer attached. Damn it all, guys. This might well be the murder weapon!"

"But is it loaded?"

"Don't know. You need to search further."

"Further? But I found it! I want out of this fucking refrigerator!"

"Listen to me, though."

Audun was more enthusiastic now, more assured: he had acquired a new hold over his rowdy friends now that they had actually found a gun. He was the oldest of the three, and a police officer to boot. Almost, anyway.

"Two guns were used," he said. "There should be another one down there."

"Then you can find it yourself," the diver said, crawling all the way back onto the ice. "I'm freezing my balls off!"

A hundred yards away, sheltered by the spruce tree trunks, an old man stood watching the noisy boys working. He had been at the lake several times since he had made up his mind at last and alerted the police. That same morning, he had cleared some of the undergrowth in the immediate vicinity. After a break for food, he decided to move a pile of wood that he had stored close to the road, just beside the path leading down to the small lake. On the couple of occasions that anyone had approached, he had slipped behind the woodpile. The first time, it was only a couple on skis. The next time was half an hour later, with loads of equipment. It must have been them, and he had sneaked down to the lake by a different route. Fortunately he had been specific with his directions. They headed directly for the stake that was frozen fast in the ice.

They made a terrific amount of noise. They didn't seem particularly skilled either, and they swore like troopers. They were young too, but then it was usually the youngest ones who were assigned the dirty jobs, in the police, as well as everywhere else.

When one of them made an amazing leap and came out of the water with a gun—he heard them screaming the word *revolver*—he breathed a sigh of relief. He had done the right thing. His instincts had been correct. He felt a certain pleasure in that, a quiet satisfaction that made him long for home and its warmth.

They didn't seem entirely satisfied. Their voices blasted over the ice: it was odd that they were quarreling now that they had made the find. The man in the water scrambled up again, while the smallest of them tore off his jacket and pants and jumped out.

The old man did not understand it. They had found what they were looking for now. They should pack up their belongings and go back to the city. It would soon be late afternoon, and it was getting steadily colder. He tried to curl his toes inside his shoes to bring them back to life: they felt numb and his nail roots were tingling.

He suddenly flinched. This guy had found something as well. He was floundering in the water, holding something aloft, the same way the other one had done with the revolver. The darkness had thickened now, and even though the flashlight over there swept frequently over the ice, it was difficult to see what it was.

A puff of wind coming directly toward him made it possible to hear their shouts.

A pistol. Yet another gun.

The old man put the lid on his ancient thermos flask and screwed the plastic cup back on. It was unnecessary to stand here any longer. He had done his duty to society. Extremely satisfied, he silently withdrew between the trees.

Tonight he would make a point of watching the evening news.

•  •  •

Hanne Wilhelmsen stood leaning against the railings on the second floor, peering out into the enormous open space that stretched from the ground to the sixth story. She noticed it clearly now, a distinct vibration, as if the gigantic pocket of wasted space was a lung, a slowly pulsating, life-giving mechanism. An unusual number of people were at work in the massive police headquarters building, with no specific duties or reason. They did not hurry. They waited. A dark-skinned man leaned on his mop out on the barren expanse in front of the desks at reception on the ground floor. The water in his bucket was no longer steaming. Two police trainees stood chatting at the automatic passport machine, one of them dangling a soft drink bottle indolently between two fingers. Behind the closed information counter, a woman sat with a weekly magazine, nonchalantly leafing through the pages, as if she couldn't really be bothered with anything.

Hanne had experienced this before but not often. The clerical staff who moved purposelessly from waiting room to waiting room, carrying papers that were moved back an hour later; the young police officers who suddenly wanted to use the gym facilities in the middle of the Christmas holidays; the woman from the dog patrol who had taken it into her head to walk her dog for an hour or two; the young, insecure police lawyers who intended to use the holiday to make inroads into the stacks of traffic violations: they were all really going around waiting.

"Strange atmosphere," Annmari commented.

"Yes," Hanne said, and smiled. She had not noticed her colleague arrive.

"It's quite . . . lovely, in a way."

"Mmm."

"We'll give them the good news now—that we have more than enough to remand both of them in custody. We'll present the petition to the court tomorrow. Don't really think anyone will make a fuss about them sitting for another twenty-four hours without a court order now, in the middle of the Christmas festivities. Just spoke to Håkon Sand on the phone, and he agreed we should spread the news here at headquarters first. Then they can feel that their waiting has been worthwhile. It's fine, now. Kind of a community spirit, you know."

"Crisis with Hermine," Hanne said.

"Crisis?"

"That we can't find her, I mean."

"We're turning the city upside-down. She has to turn up sooner or later."

Hanne nodded wordlessly and let her gaze follow Head of CID Puntvold and the Chief of Police, who came in through the main entrance. The Police Chief was in plainclothes, jeans and a bright-red sweater with a huge red-nosed Rudolph on his chest. He must have an evil-minded sister in America.

"Strange outfit to wear for a press conference," Hanne said.

"He'll probably change. He has an hour to spare. Just read the provisional printout of your interview. Thanks for handing in the tapes for typing up, one by one. It didn't occur to Erik to do that, so I won't get a sniff of his interview until tomorrow morning."

"But it'll be okay, I think. I read the report writer's notes. He can both think and write."

Standing up straight, Hanne used both hands to rub the small of her back.

"It's actually Billy T. you should thank."

"To be honest, I'm a bit worried," Annmari said, "about Billy T's methods. He really can't believe he can shield a gun dealer who is a principal witness in a case like this?"

Hanne gave a hearty laugh.

"Don't concern yourself about Billy T. He's a pro. Of course he understands that. He just wants to do things at his own pace."

Once again she leaned on the banister. Annmari studied her from the side. The Chief Inspector seemed different now. Less reserved. This case could be a kind of breakthrough for the two of them as well. Annmari had no expectations that Hanne could ever become a friend, but if something of her ill-tempered tone could disappear, that unnerving indifference and eternal distance, it would be more than sufficient.

"It's almost impressive how they lie," Hanne said, a faint smile on her lips.

"Yes. Have you ever come across anything like it before?"

"Well, sometimes, I suppose. But on this scale, and from people with such a background? No. In fact, it's quite fascinating. For instance, they must know that we'll check phone records. It's just so stupid to tell lies about when you spoke to people, so incredibly pointless!"

"Obviously."

"The whole thing's so absurd that I begin to wonder—"

"No, Hanne. Not that. Don't say that you think they might be innocent *because* they're lying so openly. That won't do. It just won't do. I like your frown. I've told you that once before. It's healthy to be skeptical. But we know too much now. Far too much to have the remotest belief in the direction of the Stahlbergs' innocence."

"We should always hold that belief. Regardless."

"Don't split hairs, Hanne."

"I'm not doing that. I'm pointing out a duty we have."

Hanne turned to face her. Her smile was different. Resigned or friendly, Annmari could not really interpret it.

"You've had an unbelievably lucky hand in this case, Annmari. A week has gone by since the murders, and you're going to court tomorrow with a rock-solid petition for remand in custody. You're smart, I must say."

Annmari searched for a hint of irony, a sarcastic undertone. It was not to be found.

"Thanks," she said, discomfited.

"If only we can find Hermine. Do we know anything more?"

"No. She's quite simply gone. We've initiated a full missing-persons report. In the course of that, it has emerged that the woman has, to put it mildly, a . . . complicated circle of friends. But no one has seen her, and no one has heard anything. She's vanished into thin air."

"'A complicated circle of friends,'" Hanne reiterated. "They must have, of course."

"What do you mean?"

"You know," Hanne began, "to the extent that people from the top drawer have dealings with us, then it has to do with—"

She stopped midsentence and peered at Annmari with an eyebrow raised, as encouragement to complete the sentence.

"Well," Annmari said, "financial crimes, traffic violations, some domestic violence."

"Not much of the last," Hanne said. "They hide themselves very securely behind their plush curtains. But otherwise, you're right. If we for a second . . ."

She smiled, almost teasingly.

". . . assume that Carl-Christian, Mabelle, or Hermine—one or several of them—is guilty of these killings and at the same time assume that it is a premeditated crime, then it pretty automatically tells us something about what sort of background you have, what sort of circles you frequent."

Annmari's expression was incredulous and she blurted: "That sounds absolutely fascinating, Hanne! Do you mean that criminal tendencies are something we're born with? Heavens, Hanne! It's—"

"Not born with. Bred into."

Hanne was curt now, as if she had already grown tired of her own argument. After a brief pause, she continued all the same.

"In the first place, you have to obtain a gun. An unregistered, illegal, and untraceable gun. Would you know who to contact?"

"No . . . I, of course I do know—"

"You're in the police, Annmari. You know how, but you would never have succeeded. You've no idea how to maneuver in that environment. But Mabelle obviously does, from what I've picked up about her background. Hermine has been mixed up in all kinds of shit through her dependency on drugs. Those two women there . . ."

She suddenly fell silent, and shook her head.

"Premeditated homicide is rare, Annmari. You know that just as well as I do. At least the obviously premeditated, the ones planned over a long period of time. They're virtually absent from our statistics. And we both know why."

"Why?" Annmari asked.

"Because we humans step back from murder when we mull it over. We can do it in the heat of the moment. Good Lord, people kill in the heat of the moment every five days in this country of ours now. Every five days! Some people commit murder to cover up another crime, of course—miserable pedophiles who stand with a withered cock in their hands and it dawns on them that the little girl they have defiled might tell her mommy what has happened."

"Now you're really a bit—"

"Vulgar? Disgusting? Absolutely. My point is not that an upper-class family with a sprinkling of drug-dependent members and doubtful in-laws necessarily perpetrates terrible crimes. I'm just saying that gruesome, premeditated crimes are difficult to perpetrate *without* that kind of family structure."

"Do you mean that, Hanne? Do you really believe that?"

"Not entirely."

Grinning broadly, Hanne looked at her watch.

"But I do mean it just a little, you know. I have to dash."

"Wait—"

"We'll talk tomorrow, Annmari. Go home. Get some sleep. You look bloody awful. You can't go into court as exhausted as that."

"I have to take part in the press conference," Annmari said. "Thanks for the compliment. Beside that drop-dead-gorgeous head of CID, I'm going to look like a toilet."

"No, you won't. He looks fairly wrecked as well. We all do. Bye!"

The heels of her boots clicked on the steps as Hanne rushed down the stairs. She left her scarf behind, like a sad little trail on the blue flooring. She paid no attention to Annmari's shout, and merely waved as she launched herself at the massive steel exit doors. They closed heavily behind her.


"How . . . how did you get in here?"

Billy T. was surprised rather than angry, in fact. In recent years, the security systems in police headquarters had been considerably reinforced. It was inconceivable that Sølvi Jotun, with her appearance, could manage to reach as far as his office without challenge or escort. She stood in the doorway, small, slight, and ravaged. First of all came her cough; Billy T. thought he had heard her before she came into sight. She seemed sicker than before. Her face was distinctly tear-stained, and she gasped for breath as she used the door frame for support. Her hair, thin and tangled, was glued to her skull. A herpes sore bloomed angrily on her top lip. Her fake fur was grimy.

"You shit! You bloody prick."

There was no force in the abuse, other than in the words

themselves. She was almost whispering, and Billy T. was scared she was about to kick the bucket. He approached her and tried to help her down into a chair.

"Don't touch me. Don't touch me, for fuck's sake!"

With astonishing strength, she tore herself free from his grip. Then she tottered over to the chair under her own steam and collapsed like a sack. Every breath, both inhaling and exhaling, wheezed nastily. Billy T. shut the door.

"That's what I think. And I think you don't want anybody else to know how big a shit you really are."

She was really sobbing. Enormous tears ran down her cheeks.

"What . . . what is it, Sølvi?"

Billy T. remained on his feet a couple of yards away from her, totally thrown.

"You said nothing about Oddvar. You said nothing about Oddvar."

Finally she looked up directly at Billy T. It startled him.

"I haven't been so unhappy in my whole life," Sølvi said. "And so damned angry with anybody. Why did you say nothing?"

Billy T. suddenly understood what she meant. He breathed more easily now but couldn't quite bear to look in her direction. Instead he sat in his chair and began to sort the bundles of papers scattered chaotically across the entire surface of his desk.

"You think you don't need to give a fuck about people like me," Sølvi said.

"No," Billy T. replied.

"Yes, you do. You and all these folk in here. You think that people like us don't have feelings. And then you, Billy T. You, who're actually okay. As I thought, anyway. Now I know better."

He didn't know what to say. Naturally it had struck him, when he had picked her up from the hospital. He should have told her that Kluten was dead. But he was after something. Something important. For him, and for the case he was working on. He didn't know, either, whether they were still a couple. It wasn't his business to tell her. She wasn't really his concern. Sølvi Jotun was not his responsibility, and he had milked her for all she was worth without telling her anything about Kluten.

"I didn't know," Billy T. ventured.

He did not get any further.

There was not much to fix your gaze on. Billy T.'s office was gray and lacked curtains. There had been many changes of office since he had had an almost homey room, with potted plants that Hanne had given him. The children's drawings that had once hung all over the walls had been stowed away long ago.

"You didn't know . . . ?"

Sølvi spat out the words through her sobs.

"You knew very well, Billy T. You knew that Oddvar and I have always been together. You should have said something. Instead I get . . . Here I am, trailing around the city, and all of a sudden I hear . . . by chance, from some down-and-out or other."

Her sobs became increasingly bitter.

"And I can't even work, either. I can't go whining to my customers, can I?"

Billy T. had had an inkling. Sølvi must have some way of adding to her income from dealing in guns. She was too small scale. Besides, she had crashed down to the lowest rung of a junkie's existence. She supplemented her earnings with blow jobs and spread her skinny thighs to get a meal.

"I loved Oddvar, you know that! Loved!"

The word seemed strange coming from her mouth. Billy T. did not want to laugh. At any rate, he did not want to cry. He clutched his breast pocket, an impulse, sudden and unthinking.

"Here," he said, handing her the betting slip. "Take this."

"Eh?"

"Take this."

"What is it?"

"Money," Billy T. said.

"Money?"

"Yes, take it. A betting slip, Sølvi. You've seen ones like it before."

"Horses . . ."

Her sobs changed to short gasps. Eventually she leaned forward slightly and squinted at the note.

"And what did you say it was?"

"This is a betting slip," Billy T. said, losing his temper. "Take it!"

He stood up, skirted around the desk, crouched down beside her, and took hold of her hand. At last he managed to look her in the eye.

"I'm sorry, really sorry. It was fucking stupid of me not to tell you about Klu . . . about Oddvar. And I can well understand that you can't work, the way things are just now. With the social security offices closed over Christmas and suchlike, then it really must be fucking awful. Take this. It's more than 150,000 kroner, Sølvi. It should keep you from walking the streets for a while. A bit of a holiday—what do you say?"

She glanced around. Her body shrank back into her seat. She pulled her hand away from his.

"Is this some kind of conspiracy or what? Hidden camera?"

"Who would be interested in tricking you on TV?"

"I've been fucked up all my life," Sølvi said. "Nothing surprises me any more. I just want to make that clear. And this here . . ."

She obviously did not dare to touch the paper. She still cast her eyes around the bare room, glowering. There were no curtains behind which to hide a camera. No two-way mirrors. The cupboard door in the corner was locked.

"And why are you giving me this?"

Now her tears were held in check. She used the back of her hand to knead her eyes.

"Don't ask. I assure you it's entirely legal."

"But where can somebody like me cash a ticket like this, then? My God, Billy T. Look at me! There's not a bank employee in this city who won't blow the whistle and bring that whole gang of yours to the counter to haul me in if I pull a stunt like that."

"You can ask them to phone me," he said, without thinking. "I'll give you my cell phone number. If that's too much trouble, I'll come and vouch for you."

Getting to his feet, he grabbed a sheet of paper from the desk, tore off a corner, and scribbled down the numbers.

"I don't understand any of this," Sølvi said.

"You don't need to. Don't entirely understand it myself."

A slender hand was extended to Billy T., closing around the betting slip and the phone number.

"Thanks," she mumbled, before coughing violently. "Maybe I'll check into a hotel. A real, proper hotel. With a bathtub and everything."

"Don't use it all up at once."

"No, of course not. But you, Billy T. . . ."

She stood at the door now, about to leave.

"I'm still really angry," she said softly, racked by another cough. "Not saying anything about Oddvar, that was—that was . . . totally mean."

"I know that. I know."

"So these here . . ."

She pulled Billy T.'s red thermal mitts from her pockets.

"I don't fucking want them anymore. You're still a shit. Bye."

She flung them on the floor and disappeared. Billy T. stared at them, two bright-red specks on the worn blue linoleum floor. He picked them up and stuffed them into the wastepaper basket.

Jenny had given them to him for Christmas.

Hanne shivered in the chilly weather, happy that her taxi ride was over. There was a light in the living room on the fourth floor, a cozy warmth that made her smile. She wanted to have a bath and soak for a long time in the tub. With a glass of red wine. Music. She jogged beside the low stone dividing wall.

"Hanne."

A tall man stepped from the shadows beneath the trees by the street lamp on the opposite side of the road.

"Do you have a minute?"

Hanne slowed down, feeling her anxiety change into an almost uncontrollable anger so sudden it took her breath away. Quick as a flash, she tried to remember when she had seen him last. It had been many years ago. Certainly six. Possibly more. She did not recall. Did not want to recall.

"Kåre," she said dully, and regretted it at once.

To speak his name was to give him acknowledgment. Recognition;

it was to admit that he was someone to her. He never had been, even though he had had the chance for so many years.

"Hanne," he said again, stiff and awkward.

His hand was only just extracted from his coat pocket and quickly thrust back down again, as if on closer reflection he did not find it entirely natural to hold out his hand to his own sister.

"What do you want?"

Her voice was sharp, loud. She began to walk.

"As a matter of fact—"

Abruptly, she turned to face him.

"I'm not interested. In talking to you. In whatever you want. Bye."

"I must really insist."

"You can, if you like. It makes no difference."

Once again she tried to leave. She wanted to run but didn't; she forced herself to step away quickly, but she simply walked, and now, at last, she found herself in front of her gate.

He grabbed her arm.

"You must talk to me, Hanne. Alexander can't live with you. He has to come home, and you need to talk to me about this. You understand that very well."

His grip on her upper arm was hard, almost painful.

"Let go of me," she spluttered.

"Yes, if you promise to stand still. You must appreciate that you can't just take a sixteen-year-old into your house without discussing it with the child's parents. For God's sake, Hanne, you're—"

"I discussed it with you on Christmas Eve. That's enough for me."

He laughed despondently.

"Discussed it? Are you telling me that phone call was a conversation?"

"You were told where he was. Let me go."

He did not let go, but loosened his grip a little, as if he finally understood that he had no right to force her. She tore herself free.

"You both threw him out," she said, rubbing her elbow. "You threw out your own son on Christmas Eve!"

"Indeed we did not. Of course we didn't throw him out."

He suddenly looked diminished. His shoulders slumped in his

expensive coat, and his facial features grew sharp in the overhead light from the street lamp. His eyes disappeared below his heavy forehead.

"We didn't throw him out, Hanne. We just had a . . . we quarreled."

"About what?"

"That's not really anything to do with you."

"You wanted to send your boy to see a psychologist because he's in love with another boy."

"That's not why, Hanne. Because he's so . . . Alexander is a confused soul. He's so . . . stubborn. Rebellious. I think he's unhappy. He keeps to himself too much, and he's no longer doing so well at school. So we . . . Hege and I think he could benefit from talking to a professional person. And this homosexuality business . . ."

"*Homosexuality business!*"

Hanne had to pull herself together to stop herself from hitting him. Instead she threw her arms up and to the side and took a step back.

"There you have it! Where have I heard those words before?"

She placed her forefinger on her cheek in an exaggeratedly thoughtful pose.

"Hmm . . . well, then—yes, that's it. Now it's come to me. It was Dad, of course, I do believe. That was exactly what he said to me. Or mostly *about* me, actually. I can barely remember him ever saying anything *to* me. Homosexual business. *What the hell is 'homosexual business,' Kåre?*"

Her brother ran his fingers over his eyes. There was something helpless about the gesture, something childish and discouraged; her father had never done anything like that, but Kåre was so like him otherwise, as all three of them were: Hanne, her brother, and Alexander, all carriers of the most dominant genes in the universe, as her mother had once said, and for a moment Hanne thought that Kåre was weeping.

"Don't you understand that the boy has to be allowed to choose?" she said, to put an end to the unbearable silence. Her brother just stood there, opening and closing his mouth, running his fingers over his eyes, shrinking into his coat. "Alexander has to find his own way. He's in good health, but he's a teenager. Being a teenager's a bit distressing."

"And you know that," he said, pulling himself up to his full height.

"You, who have almost never spoken to him. As far as I understand, you've hardly been home since he turned up. It's quite typical of you, I have to say. Expressing yourself with the greatest authority about a boy you've only just met. Hege and I can just be discarded, of course. We've only known the boy, looked after him, and loved him for sixteen years. I appreciate that you haven't exactly changed."

"Changed? Have you ever known me?"

"I was twelve when you were born, Hanne. A twelve-year-old boy. You can hardly hold it against me that I didn't find a snotty little child much fun. And besides . . . Have you ever considered that it might not have been *only* our fault, everything that's happened? That it wasn't *exclusively* Mom and Dad who bear the responsibility for you being an outsider?"

"I can't be bothered listening to this."

"You're difficult, Hanne. Difficult and moody. You've been like that since the day you were born. I remember when you turned three . . ."

His laughter, rasping, desperate, nasty, made her listen, yet again.

"Mom had baked a lovely cake. Bought you a new dress. It was red, as I recall. A red dress was what she had bought, and I was forced to stay at home. I was fifteen and had to stay at home because of a snotty brat's birthday. Mom had invited some children from the neighborhood. You spoiled it all."

The words seared into her back. This was a story she did not remember, that was not hers. Kåre knew things about Hanne that she had no knowledge of herself. He owned a piece of her, of her life and her story, and she did not want to know any of it.

"You cut the dress to ribbons," he continued. "I can still remember the thin strips of red fabric. Mom was in tears. You just sat sulking in a corner, staring at her with those eyes of yours, those eyes—"

"I was only three," Hanne said slowly, without turning around. "You're holding something against me that took place when I was three years old. Incredible."

Again that laughter of his, hoarse, almost desperate.

"I could easily mention other birthdays," he said. "Your eleventh, twelfth, thirteenth. Just give me a number. I could continue all night long with stories about how you never wanted to be part of us. How you always resisted. You wanted to be different, at any cost. If you didn't get your own way, you just upped and left. You're the one who runs away, Hanne. Which was demonstrated most forcefully when Cecilie died."

Hanne closed her eyes. Something tightened in her chest. Her lungs would not do their task.

"Don't put that name on your lips." She squeezed the words out. "You've no right to talk about Cecilie."

It was not certain that he heard it. It was really impossible to breathe. She had to use the wall for support. He came closer, his steps were distinct, and she wanted to go but could not breathe.

"At least *I* was at her funeral," he said. "That's more than can be said for *you*. You had gone off, as you always do when things are tough."

His voice was right behind her now, low, close to her ear, she could feel his breath on her cheek.

"Yes, I was there. I wanted to talk to you. Wanted to show you that I was sorry on your behalf. But you weren't there. Exactly as you weren't there when it was Mom's fiftieth birthday. You were nine years old, Hanne, and quite clear about how much you hurt her. You're never there when anyone needs you. So don't come here and say that I'm not there for my son. I love Alexander, I want to help him, and I want him to come home."

Breathe, she thought. Breathe out. Breathe in.

"You didn't fit into our family, Hanne."

His voice was gentler now, less strained. His hand settled on her shoulder, burning through the fabric of her jacket, through her woolen sweater; she felt his fingers on her skin and wanted to brush them away. All her strength went into breathing, to forcing her lungs in and out, and Kåre's hand remained where it was.

"Of course it's mainly Mom and Dad's responsibility. They were adults. But it became so much, Hanne. Of you. Of your bloody-mindedness, your oddness. You just absolutely didn't want to. You always wanted to think, do, and say something different from all the others. *Always*. Exactly like . . ."

A heavy downpour began. They both peered up, unconsciously, as if they did not believe it possible for the weather to turn so suddenly from light drizzle and silence to torrential rain in a matter of seconds. Hanne felt her breathing ease.

"Alexander," she called out in the racket made by the rain drumming on the ground, the rooftops, on the shoulders of Kåre's coat in tiny muffled beats. "Exactly like Alexander. He's like me. You're going to destroy him."

She began to cry. She did not register it at first, did not realize that she was crying until the raindrops tasted salty on her tongue.

"We won't destroy him," Kåre said. "We'll help him. These homo . . . This homosexuality he uses as an excuse—"

"He uses as an excuse?"

She was whispering now. Gasping out the words, again.

"Uses as an excuse. So that's what you think. That he has fallen in love with a boy in order to be difficult and moody."

"It's not just like that. I didn't mean to say . . . 'uses as an excuse.' Apologies. That was expressed stupidly. But Alexander's too young to make such decisions yet. We have to help him on to the right path, to . . . He'll find it so difficult if he takes the wrong steps as far as this is concerned. You know that yourself, Hanne. You know that. Really. Everything will be so much easier if he understands that this is just an episode. A phase in his life."

Hanne managed to turn away from him, managed to walk backward. She was in floods of tears, and the full force of the rain was hitting her in the face. Her clothes were sodden now, water running everywhere, ice-cold winter rain down her back, underneath her clothes, her shoes gurgling with every leaden step she took, away from her brother.

"And what if it's not a phase?" she sobbed. "What happens if Alexander really is gay, and what have you already done to him? With his differentness? With his bloody-mindedness, his stubbornness—all of what you feel is so god-awful? With everything that's like me? What?"

"Hanne . . . *Hanne!*"

Her feet slapped against the rainwater as she sprinted across the courtyard. Her pocket was pasted to her jacket with the moisture, the keys icy cold. She fumbled, sobbing, and finally managed to pull them out. The right key slid into the lock.

"Hanne! But you must—"

Her brother's shout was abruptly truncated as the door slammed shut. It took her a quarter of an hour to stop crying. Then she mounted the stairs, home at last.

# FRIDAY, DECEMBER 27

"**W**ell done, Annmari."

Erik Henriksen gave her an encouraging prod in the side and began to pack up the ring binders and loose documents, without turning it all into too much of a mess. The judge had already left the court following a meeting that had been shorter than anyone could have anticipated. The ruling had been that Carl-Christian and Mabelle Stahlberg should be remanded in custody for four weeks, two of these including a ban on letters and visits. The decision was in accordance with Annmari's plea. They had all prepared themselves for an extremely lengthy court session. The couple's newly appointed defense lawyers, two heavyweights from the top rung of Oslo's celebrity circuit, had obviously hit on a different strategy. They had given a brief account of their clients' viewpoint: neither wanted to appear in court, but both accepted imprisonment in order to provide the police with an opportunity to clear up this obvious, hair-raising misunderstanding. Of course, neither was guilty, and the defense counsel emphasized several times that four weeks was the limit of what the accused would tolerate.

"The cat-and-dog fight postponed until the next round," Erik whispered. "They must have tortured CC and Mabelle to get them to go along with this. At least Mabelle!"

"If only we could find Hermine now," Annmari murmured in return as she helped him fill the flight bags. "We *must* find her soon."

The journalists swarmed around the courtroom. Their initial targets were the defense lawyers, but four or five of them were already waiting impatiently for Annmari, held in check only by one of the court officers, who wanted to afford her the chance to get her documents packed away. She gave a loud sigh and glanced at her phone for text messages.

"I have to call Silje," she said, sotto voce, turning her back on the reporters. "It's urgent, it says. You take care of them over there, please."

"Me? I can't very well—"

"Yes, you can," she said, tapping in the number, before putting the phone to her ear and taking a few steps across to the judge's desk.

"Did it go well?" Silje asked at the other end.

"Yes. Four weeks. What do you want?"

"You have to come here. To Hermine's apartment."

"Have you found her?"

Annmari was whispering now, with her hand over her mouth to hide the sound.

"No. But you must come."

"What is it?"

"Don't want to say over the phone. Come, please."

"Okay. It might take some time."

"I'll wait. Come as fast as you can."

Annmari clicked the connection off and tucked the phone into her handbag.

"You can all speak to Inspector Henriksen here," she said, clearing a path for herself through the photographers and journalists. "But really there's nothing more to add."

When she finally reached the door leading to the hall, she heard Erik's voice: "You heard what Police Prosecutor Skar said. There's nothing more to add. Nothing. Can't you hear? There's nothing to add."

Smiling faintly, she hurried on. In C. J. Hambros plass she tried to hail one of the taxis continually cruising by. It crossed her mind that she should have helped him with the cases. Eventually a silver Mercedes stopped. As she sat inside, she spotted Erik rushing down the courthouse steps with one case under each arm and one in each hand, like a porter with a group of dissatisfied hotel guests trailing after him. He looked wildly in every direction. A patrol car rolled up beside him.

So he'll have some help after all, Annmari thought, with a prick of guilty conscience.

•  •  •

Hermine Stahlberg's apartment appeared to be a peculiar mixture of good taste and sloppiness. The furniture was modern and boxy. The walls, floor, and furnishings were light, almost washed out. Color was only to be found in rugs, paintings, and cushions. The pictures were well spaced on the walls, without ostentation, without clashing with one another. The stuffy atmosphere made Annmari Skar screw up her nose. The place couldn't have been cleaned for a long time. The floors were dirty and the table in the living room dull with dust, and covered in rings left by glasses. Four bananas, almost black, lay in a bowl.

"It looks like something set up for an interior design magazine and then forgotten about," Annmari remarked.

Silje nodded absentmindedly.

"And something tells me that someone's been searching for something here," she said. "When we arrived, a few of the paintings were hanging crookedly. Lots of the drawers weren't properly closed. Inside was nothing but mess. It could be that the woman's a notorious scatterbrain. There's a great deal here to suggest that."

She ran her finger over the TV set, lifted it to her eyes, and pulled a grimace.

"But women like Hermine Stahlberg usually manage at the very least to keep their own toiletries in order. The cabinets in the bathroom were fairly chaotic as well. I mean, there was no system that I could make out, anyway. The mascara was lying at the very back, for example. But you use that all the time, don't you?"

Annmari cracked a smile.

"I don't know much about that."

"But, you see, *this* is really why I asked you to come. It was stuck between two books about mummies and hieroglyphs. In all honesty, a strange woman, this Hermine. Loads of books here, but they're almost all brand new. They creak when you open them! It looks as if they're just for show, to be honest with you. Look here."

Annmari took the document Silje handed her. She had already pulled on plastic gloves and tried to be as careful as possible with the paper.

"Yet another will," she said in a monotone, leafing through to the last of the three numbered pages. "Dated December 3, 2002."

"Dated and signed by Hermann and Turid Stahlberg, and, what's more . . ."

Silje pointed at the final paragraph in the document.

"'*This sets aside all earlier wills*,'" Annmari read. "But . . ."

She browsed through the document, from the first page to the last.

"This hasn't been witnessed."

"What?"

"Look! No witnesses. Therefore it's invalid."

Silje took the will and leafed through it again. She studied each page thoroughly, held it up to her face, and turned the paper to one side to catch the light from the windows, as if the witnesses might have signed using microscopic handwriting.

"Now I don't understand any of it," she said, flabbergasted. "But the contents are pretty sensational, though."

"What does it tell us?" Annmari asked, ready to take a closer look.

Silje was reluctant to relinquish the document. Instead she took a seat on the window ledge and beckoned her colleague. They both leaned toward the window, where the fading daylight was intensified by a lamp directly outside on the terrace.

"Look here," Silje said, pointing. "It decrees that the shipping company should be divided in three. Or . . . if I understand this correctly, Hermine, Preben, and Carl-Christian are to have 30 percent of the shares each. Then there would be 10 percent left over, isn't that right?"

"I can manage to calculate that, yes."

"That is to go to Preben's oldest son."

"That means, then, that Preben actually gets 40 percent," Annmari said. "Not a particularly favorable share arrangement, really. No one holds a majority. But whichever two of the siblings can come to an agreement can overrule the third. What on earth . . ."

Both of them fell silent. Annmari raised her head to study the dust motes dancing in the light from outside: minuscule particles whirling about in an invisible draft.

"Hermann Stahlberg was well aware of how a will should be formulated," she said slowly, as if thinking aloud. "After all, he had written the previous one by hand. All the formal requirements were attended to there. With witnesses and all that. Why would he hand over—"

"Hand over?"

"Yes!"

Annmari gestured with her hand.

"He must have handed it over, mustn't he? He doesn't live here, after all. And why would he hand over a will—the contents of which are totally different from the last one, which must mean that he had changed his mind about Carl-Christian only three weeks ago—and then not make sure that it's legally binding? I mean . . . it does look fancy, of course, on personal notepaper and all that . . ."

She bent over the will, on thick creamy-yellow paper.

"And then he forgets something as essential as witnesses—"

"It might be that it wasn't finished yet," Silje suggested.

"But it's signed! That's supposed to happen in the presence of witnesses!"

"Maybe he changed his mind."

"In this family, there's no longer anything that surprises me, but if he changed his mind, then he wouldn't have signed it. No." Suddenly Annmari walked across the floor. She scanned the room. Her gaze settled on the profusion of bookshelves and, without turning to face Silje, she added: "You found this on a bookshelf, was that it?"

"Yes."

"I want this place turned upside down. I mean really turned on its head. All the books out and checked. All cupboards emptied. The pictures will have to be taken down. Look for a safe. Pull out drawers, rummage through clothes, make—"

"I understand, Annmari. What do you think we'll find?"

Annmari, sucking on a strand of hair, did not answer. She stood motionless in the middle of the room. Her phone rang, but she did not answer.

"I don't know," she said in the end. "But I can't think of anything other than that Hermann was threatened or forced to write this will. If it's genuine, that is. We must have it checked. But let us say that these really are Turid and Hermann's signatures . . . then he made sure that it wasn't valid. He could only do that to a person who isn't well acquainted with the legal world. And then I'm talking about someone who really doesn't keep up with much, Silje. There's only one person in the Stahlberg family who might not know that a will requires witnesses."

"Hermine," Silje said softly. "She seems pretty well all at sea."

"Exactly. And we're here now, aren't we? At Hermine's. But what has become of her?"

They looked around and let their eyes linger on the same picture. A color photograph in a simple frame of polished wood was displayed on a sideboard. Hermann and Tutta Stahlberg were surrounded by their three offspring. Hermine could be about five years old, a pretty girl with blond hair and tiny, pearl-white teeth. Her brothers stood solemnly on either side of their parents, while Turid Stahlberg looked out from behind her husband's right shoulder. She was smiling too, more warily than her daughter, a nervous, almost apologetic smile.

Hermann sat enthroned in the center of the picture, with only little Hermine allowed to stand in front of him when the photo was taken. He was the only one who stared directly at the camera. The little girl looked obliquely up at him, admiringly, laughingly.

"They were once a family," Annmari said.

"Well, an interior decor magazine certainly wouldn't come here," Silje said, peering into the bathroom, where Billy T. was ransacking shelves and a little cabinet above the sink.

"What?" he mumbled as he squinted into a jar of pills.

"Hermine's apartment was really beautiful, you see. Filthy but stylish. In here looks more like a hostel for junkies."

"That's where these pills belong as well," Billy T. said, pouring several different types of tablets out into his hand. "It says vitamin C on the label, but these don't look particularly damned healthy."

The apartment Mabelle Stahlberg owned in Kampen in the name of May Anita Olsen was soberly furnished. A couple of chairs from IKEA sat beside a veneer coffee table. It had started to split at both ends. The sofa was lopsided, and a big stain was outlined, dark and distinct, in the middle of one of the seating pads. The walls were bare, apart from a lurid painting in the living room and an old dresser beside the kitchen door. It was empty. Mabelle had herself, rather reluctantly, explained that she had lived there earlier, before she met Carl-Christian. They had never found any reason to sell it. She persistently claimed that the apartment was hardly ever used. Admittedly Hermine had stayed there on a couple of occasions, she had confessed, but apart from that, the apartment was empty. The fact that it was registered in Mabelle's former name was quite simply down to their never having bothered to change the deeds. She could not understand why the place would be of any interest to the police.

"It almost looks as if the woman's right," Billy T. said. "There's nothing here. Unless we're going to make a fuss about these pills. We probably won't bother. Four Rohypnol, some Valium, and some stuff I can't quite identify. They were probably left behind by Hermine."

He entered the small bedroom. A pine double bed took up most of the space. A narrow closet in the corner was empty. The curtains were closed. Billy T. drew them apart carefully. The windows could not have been washed in years, and the ledge was sticky with asphalt dust.

"I don't understand what Hermine used this place for," Silje said. "Why would she sit in such an unsavory place when she has a sumptuous apartment on the other side of the city?"

"There could be many reasons for that," Billy T. muttered as he began to knock on the walls. "She might have acquaintances she doesn't particularly want to drag along to where the rich people live, for example. Hey, listen to this!"

His clenched fist suddenly created a different, heavier sound on the wall. He struck a number of blows from the floor in an upward direction one more time.

"There's something here."

He took down a graphic poster showing a woman bathing with a dark blue night sky in the background.

"Bingo!"

Billy T. had a wide grin on his face.

"Do you know anyone who can open this kind of thing, Silje?"

The safe was badly mounted. There were gaps between the metal and the plaster on the wall on both sides, and the contraption was obviously off level.

"This could probably just be ripped out," Billy T. said, touching the simple lock tentatively with his finger. "But it would be a fucking nuisance to have to haul it with us. Fucking heavy, for sure."

"It's a code lock," Silje said, sounding discouraged. "We'll have to bring someone here who can pick it open."

"That's probably not necessary," Billy T. said. "When was CC born?"

"Don't mess around. He must have a better code than that!"

Billy T. rapped hard on the safe with his knuckles.

"A man who sets up a safe like this is stupid enough to choose his date of birth as a code—his or his wife's or their children's. Everybody warns against it; most people do it. Quite simply because we have so many numbers we have to carry in our heads that we choose the simple option when we can. Fish out your notebook, then! Now at last we can make use of those clever-girl facts of yours."

Silje pulled a pink notebook out of her handbag.

"August 17, 1967. But that can't be the code. You only need four digits. Not six."

Billy T. fiddled with the combination lock.

"One seven zero eight," he said aloud.

The handle did not budge.

"What did I say?" Silje muttered.

"One nine six seven," Billy T. ventured.

This time the metal handle slid down with a mechanical click and the door opened easily.

"Look at this," Billy T. said. "What have we here, then?"

Silje leaned toward the container. A shelf divided the little safe into two spaces. The lower part held a green metal canister. In the upper part were three cardboard boxes, one of them with an open lid.

"Billy T.," she whispered. "It's ammunition."

"Of course. What had you expected? That he stored his aftershave here?"

"But—"

"Not very professional to keep something like this in a place where we'll obviously find it. That depends, then, on what kind of ammunition this is. If I'm not entirely mistaken, then . . ."

He pulled the green canister from the safe and placed it on the unmade bed. The lid was not lockable. He opened it.

"Look at this then!"

Excited, he lifted the revolver from the container, holding it up to the harsh light from the ceiling lamp.

"This, Silje, is one of the most exquisite handguns ever made. Korth Combat Magnum. I've never seen the like."

He looked tempted to take off his rubber gloves, feel the metal, run his fingers over the stock, and feel the heavy tactility of a handcrafted revolver.

"It weighs close to two pounds," he said as he felt it, moving his hand up and down as he smiled broadly. "It takes four months to construct one. Do you see this screw here?"

He pointed with his little finger.

"This is where you make fine adjustments to the pressure on the trigger. Look how solid everything is! Compact and heavy. And feel that stock!"

He seemed unwilling to hand over the revolver.

"Walnut," he mumbled. "This is the Rolls-Royce of revolvers, Silje. Costs just under five thousand dollars in the United States. Haven't a clue what the price is in this country. Have you seen . . ."

Billy T. turned the gun over, weighing it in his hand yet again, turning it toward the light; the steel gleamed harshly blue.

"But what about this?" Silje said; she had lifted out one of the boxes and took hold of something farther back in the safe. "This doesn't belong to a revolver, does it?"

At last Billy T. looked up. He squinted at the object Silje was presenting to him, using a pincer grip between thumb and forefinger.

"This belongs to a pistol, don't you think?"

Billy T. put down the revolver, reluctantly and carefully, wrapping it in a soft cloth and replacing the lid of the green container.

"A cartridge clip," he said. "That's a cartridge clip. And this . . ."

He opened one of the cardboard boxes.

". . . is 9mm subsonic ammunition. For use with a silencer. And it can't be used with this baby here at all."

His fingers tapped on the green metal as he shook his head slowly.

"But it suits a Glock excellently. And I don't see such a gun anywhere. If that cartridge clip there slides into a pistol of the same type . . ."

He smacked his lips and shook his head.

". . . then Carl-Christian and Co. are up shit creek, I must say."

"They have been for some time now," Silje replied.

It was already past three o'clock in the afternoon when Hanne Wilhelmsen walked along the corridor to her own office with a large hat pulled down over her forehead.

"Wilhelmsen," Audun Natholmen said, obviously relieved. "You're here at last."

He leaped up from a chair he had dragged over to the wall.

"Lots of people have been looking for you," he said, his smooth forehead wrinkling as he took in her swollen, bleary eyes. "Is something wrong? Are you ill?"

"Yes," Hanne lied. "An eye infection. It's kept me at home. Have you been waiting long?"

"I've been searching for you all day long," he said. Only now did she notice that he kept looking around, as if afraid of something or someone. "I must . . ."

His voice cracked. He swallowed noisily.

"Chief Inspector, I'm really in hot water now."

"Come in," she said, unsure whether it was curiosity or annoyance she felt. "You could just have let yourself in and waited in my office. Sitting here in the corridor, like any other visitor . . ."

He followed so closely behind her that she could feel his breath on her neck. The moment they were inside, he closed the door behind him, emphatically, as if he really wanted to lock it.

"I've found the guns," he said.

Hanne was about to sit down. She stood for a moment with her knees bent, tensed, before sitting down.

"You've what, did you say?"

"The guns," he said in a loud whisper. "I found a Glock and a .357 Magnum. In the lake I told you about, you know. The place where I—"

"What . . . what is it . . . ?" She tore off her hat and tossed it on the floor. Her mouth opened, but her thoughts would not form into words.

"Well, you said that *you* would have done it," he complained.

"I said it would be really crazy!"

"But that you would have done it and kept your mouth shut."

"I was joking! I was joking, for God's sake!"

She desperately struggled to gather her thoughts. *Rational*, she thought, *be rational*. All she heard was the scraping sound of her own teeth as she ground them together. Audun Natholmen just sat there, like a lanky schoolboy with a guilty conscience—too small for his uniform, with a blank face, a childish face, a puppyish parody of a policeman.

"You're a police officer, Audun."

"Trainee," he muttered.

"Where are they now?"

"At home," he said.

"At your house?"

"Yes. I've been so scared, and then I didn't quite know . . . My pal said he was going to phone the *VG* newspaper, because there's lots of money in—"

"Let's go."

Most of all, she wanted to give him a thrashing.

He tagged along after her, subdued and with head bowed, but nevertheless with a childish, irrepressible delight that he might have solved the biggest homicide case in the history of the Oslo Police Force.

Annmari had to compose herself, to avoid turning away in disgust. As a police prosecutor, she had seen enough pornography to feel pretty inured. She had fast-forwarded through endless amounts of evidence from inner-city dives, searching for molestation of children. As far as sexual congress between adults was concerned, there was hardly anything that had the ability to shock her. However, this was something else. The young woman and the far older man were pictured in sexual activity that to some extent was not unfamiliar to Annmari, but all the same it knocked her sideways. She felt physically sick.

"It's just because you know them," Erik Henriksen said quietly. He stood leaning over her as she flicked through the photographs.

"I don't know them."

"You know who they are. That makes it worse. More embarrassing. All that shit we have to watch after those useless raids Chief Puntvold insists on conducting from time to time, they only have to do with strangers. Nameless, almost faceless people. This is far worse. Don't you think?"

Annmari nodded imperceptibly.

"But it doesn't help that they're so bad," she said. "From a purely technical point of view, I mean. If I screw up my eyes a bit, I can barely identify the two of them."

"The images must have been taken with a hidden camera," Erik said, straightening up. "Now things are really getting serious."

He pulled a grimace as he rubbed the small of his back.

"When did you last get some sleep?" he asked.

"Don't remember. Do you think Hermine's the one who's ensured that these photos are found?"

"Difficult to say. They were in her possession, of course. Brilliant that you ordered a more thorough ransacking of her apartment, by the way. She had some sort of hidden cupboard. Behind a set of drawers in the kitchen she had mounted a sheet of plywood. The pictures were inside there, together with an empty bag with traces of what we provisionally believe to be heroin. From experience, I'd say it's most likely that he's the one who'd want to preserve them. You know, to relive and enjoy later. Anyway, it's too early to say where the photographs were taken. We're investigating that, of course, and since they were found at Hermine's . . . No, I don't know."

"Damn and blast," Annmari said in disgust, turning the pictures over. "It's nothing to do with me, what people do behind closed doors, and maybe I'm being judgmental. But there must be forty years between them. And then they're uncle and niece. Good Lord, what a family! Killing and fucking each other . . . yuck!"

"Is it illegal, what they're doing?"

"No. She's an adult, after all. But . . . yuck!"

Erik laughed and patted her on the shoulder.

"Now you're being just a tiny bit childish, Prosecutor Skar."

"Maybe so. In any case . . ."

She glanced fleetingly at the clock. It was twenty minutes to five.

"Where's Hanne?"

"I've no idea. Everybody's asking for her. Her phone's switched off. Even Billy T. doesn't know what's become of her. But what are we going to do with this, in actual fact?"

Again he pointed at the photographs. They were now stacked, picture side down, at the far edge of Annmari's desk, as if she had no wish to defile her workplace any more than was strictly necessary.

"We'll go straight to Alfred Stahlberg's house, of course. He obviously has a closer relationship to Hermine than we thought." Once again she made a tart grimace and added in slight irritation: "Has the guy been interviewed at all in connection with Hermine's disappearance?"

"Oh yes. Over the phone."

"Over the phone," Annmari fumed. "I can make sure it's not over the phone this time. Send a patrol car. Uniforms. I want the man here. Now. And if he won't come willingly, then I'll write a summons."

"For what, though? What would you charge the man with, then?"

"No idea. Something or other. *Obstruction of justice*. But try the straightforward way first. I'd really prefer you to go in person, Erik. But what on earth's happened to Hanne?"

"I was wondering that too," Billy T. said, having crashed into the room without knocking on the door. "Someone had seen her around three o'clock, but she left just after that."

"Hello," Annmari said. "I see you're the same polite boy as usual."

"Cut it out. We're all shattered, Annmari. No need to be sharp for that reason. Look at this little gizmo here. I'm sure that'll put you in a better humor."

He placed a transparent bag in front of her.

"A . . . a cartridge clip?"

Annmari poked at the bag with her pen.

"It's not dangerous, you know! Not for us. But I'll bet CC won't find it very easy to explain. It's a Glock cartridge, Annmari. Which was lying in a badly mounted safe in Mabelle's apartment in Kampen. I've just had it confirmed that it does in fact belong to a Glock. The problem for Carl-Christian is, of course, that he doesn't have such a gun registered in his name, and there was nothing resembling a pistol in the apartment either. A revolver, yes, a legal one, I've checked that out, too. But no pistol; just this, plus a whole box of 9mm parabellum. Subsonic ammunition. For use with a silencer."

It seemed as though Annmari could not quite absorb the information she was given. When four bodies had been found in Eckersbergs gate eight days earlier, they had all prepared themselves for an investigation that would take months and, in the worst-case scenario, even years. Homicide cases normally took time. A quadruple murder was something she had never faced before, but she had reckoned that the investigation would have to be comprehensive: a slow and painstaking inquiry, building toward something that might result in an indictment only in the distant future. She had lain in bed last Thursday night, tossing and turning with dread: she had anticipated a procedural nightmare, with lengthy periods of stagnation and actual setbacks of various kinds. Instead they were heading for a solution in record-quick time.

She sat vacantly staring at the cartridge clip. Billy T. scratched his crotch, swearing loudly.

"Say something, then! This is an honest-to-goodness breakthrough, isn't it? There's a fair amount for our ballistics team and gun technicians to work their way through for a while yet, but I'll bet you a cup of coffee that this is starting to get interesting for them!"

The phone rang.

Annmari picked up the receiver and barked a greeting. Then she fell silent. Her expression changed from irritation to interest, before she said with a look of incredulity: "Then come straight up to my office. We'll take it from there. Thanks."

She slowly put the receiver back in place.

"A witness," she said, "has come forward. A man who distinctly believes he saw a woman running along Eckersbergs gate in the direction of Gyldenløves gate last Thursday night."

"Eh?"

Billy T. squinted at her in disbelief.

"And he's only now phoning in? Eight days later?"

"It was the sergeant at the duty desk who called. The man's

downstairs. He tried to phone us last Friday, but got annoyed when he couldn't get through on the phone. Only to the central switchboard, he said, and then it went quiet once he was being transferred through."

"Well, it was like the Wild West here last Friday," Billy T. commented.

"Exactly. This guy then went to Italy with his wife for Christmas and gave up on the entire business. Came home today. After reading the past week's newspapers, he was so shocked that he's now downstairs at the front desk."

"Shocked?"

"Yes," Annmari said, slowly stroking her cheeks. "He's seen the pictures in the papers. He says it was Hermine he saw. In a real fucking hurry away from Eckersbergs gate 5. 'Running like a madwoman' was apparently the expression he used. 'Running like a madwoman'..."

Then she slapped her hand on the desk.

"But what in hell has become of Hanne Wilhelmsen?"

Hermine Stahlberg was not dead. Her lower arm was uncovered, and a vein was only just pulsating under her skin. Signs of life were also visible in the hollow of her neck. Silje felt it, to be on the safe side. She did not dare move the woman, who was stretched out, half naked, on the floor in a storeroom. A bottle of detergent had fallen from a shelf just above her. The synthetic fragrance combined with a whiff of urine and feces. Silje spread a tartan blanket over her. Hermine was clutching a toy rabbit, a grubby pink creature with a torn ear and staring, over-large plastic eyes. Silje cautiously tried to loosen her grip. It was as if her fingers were frozen stiff to the dirty nylon fur. She let Hermine keep the soft toy.

Erik Henriksen struggled to decide what he had actually expected. The thought of what, at worst, might meet them in Alfred's apartment had been so repulsive that for the entire drive, he had tried to memorize the lyrics of old pop songs and rivers in Asia.

"Phone for an ambulance, Erik."

Silje strode across the room and poked him hard in the side. He stood, feet astride and hands in the air, fingers slightly fanned out, as if about to pick up a child.

"Summon two," she insisted. "We need two ambulances, Erik."

"I don't know what I had expected," he said.

"Erik! Take out your phone and call an ambulance. Now!"

He did not know why she didn't do this herself. His hands refused to budge. There was a cold prickle of running perspiration in his armpits.

"She wanted to go to the police," Alfred complained from the corner beside the kitchen. "She wanted to go to the police, you see. I couldn't find the photographs! I searched everywhere at Hermine's, but I found . . . You understand I couldn't let her go to the police."

The corpulent man heaved himself up from the corner. Now and again his arms lunged vigorously into the air in a comical parody of karate.

"I haven't done anything wrong, you know," he said loudly and laughed. "Just take her with you. Just take her with you and disappear."

A fresh pounce with stiff fingers struck Silje in the stomach as she tried to approach the man.

"*Call for reinforcements*," she shouted, taking a step back. "*Now!*"

Finally Erik succeeded in lowering his arms. His mouth was unbearably parched. He bit his lip and made the cut worse by digging his front teeth deep into the soft flesh, feeling how painful it was.

In astonishment, he became aware of the taste of his own blood and at last took out his phone.


"As you can appreciate, there's been a lot going on here. Where in the world have you been? You look totally . . . sick. Is something wrong?"

Hanne Wilhelmsen looked really miserable. In her eagerness to tell her about the events of the day, Annmari had failed to notice that her colleague's eyes were bloodshot and swollen. Her mouth had an unfamiliar, discouraged expression—something vulnerable that Annmari could not recollect having seen before. Hanne's entire body seemed shattered.

"Last night I met a ghost," Hanne said with a joyless smile. "Today has somehow been marked by that. But I'll survive. Isn't that what you're supposed to say?"

"Where have you been?"

At first Hanne did not reply. It was now half an hour before midnight, and the pitch darkness was closing in on the cold window-panes. A candle, about to gutter, flickered on the far edge of the desk.

"You should take care with that," Hanne said dully. "Last time you nearly set fire to the whole building."

"I've taken the decoration off. That was what caught on fire. Where have you been? This day has been an absolute merry-go-round. The Stahlberg case is rolling away like an express train, and I would be much happier if my chief investigator saw the value of being accessible in the midst of—"

"I've been working," Hanne interrupted her. "You must realize that much. First of all, I slept late. After that, I was playing my part."

She produced two plastic bags from her voluminous shoulder bag. There was a clunking noise as she placed them on the desk between her and the Police Prosecutor.

"If I'm not entirely mistaken," she said, "these are the guns that were used to kill four people last Thursday. In two or three days we'll know for certain. And this . . ."

She placed a document beside the weapons.

". . . is a special report from me. About how they were found. I've embroidered the story as best I can, so that a promising but fairly naive and overenthusiastic young man won't have his career in the police destroyed before he's begun. I'm asking you to back me in this. He's called Audun Natholmen. Take note of that name."

Annmari did not move a muscle. Her eyes were fixed on Hanne. A faint sound of her breathing, short and wheezy, was the only noise that could be heard.

Hanne crossed her arms, smiling listlessly, and closed her eyes.

The guns—a pistol and a revolver, wrapped in plastic—lay in front of her, but she did not even dare to examine them more closely. The candle flickered and would soon burn down: the wick began to splutter. The fluorescent light on the ceiling flashed on and off with a harsh blue glare. Then the light tube died completely.

"Are you joking?" Annmari finally asked. "Hanne Wilhelmsen, are you pulling my leg?"

Her voice was anxious, almost childish.

"Are you ill?" she suddenly added, her voice trembling. "Hanne! What on earth is this? You look unwell. Where did you get these from?"

Hanne opened her eyes slowly, as if waking from a dream she did not want to lose hold of. "It's so dark in here," she said, reaching forward to the table lamp. "There. That's better. No, I'm not unwell. I'm . . ."

She used her right hand to push the report over to Annmari, who did not want to take it.

"Explain this to me instead. Tell me."

"Read it," Hanne said.

Hesitantly, and still without taking a closer look at the guns, Annmari pulled the report toward her. After a few minutes, she looked up from the final page and laid the document on the far side of her desk, as if the paper reeked of something nauseous.

"This is scandalous, Hanne. They could have ruined everything! These young men most certainly have not thought of securing evidence in the area. How . . . how in hell could he think of doing something so . . . so *completely idiotic*? And why have you written this report that makes you into a scapegoat to such an extent? Write another one, Hanne. This young man is finished anyway. Behaving so impetuously on the basis of a tip he's received while on duty, without technicians, without . . . There's no reason on earth for you to go down the drain along with him. I refuse permission for you to hand this in."

"It has been handed in," Hanne said. "To you. And I'm taking the blame on myself because the blame actually belongs to me. I've tried to think back to what I said to Audun. Reconstructed all of it. As it states in the report, I expressed myself extremely ambiguously. Of course, I meant it only as a joke, but I ought to have realized that he would understand my words as some kind of . . . approval."

"Hanne . . ."

Annmari was more composed now; it was as if the power relationship between them had shifted all at once. She adjusted the desk lamp and took a new candle out of a drawer.

"Maybe I should find something else to do," Hanne broke in, "in any case."

She smiled a genuine, surprised smile.

"My time in the police might well be over. There's so much else I could think of doing. I'm at the right age. I'm forty-two. If I'm going to do something else with my life, then I should grab the chance now."

Annmari inserted the candle into the holder and lit it. Then she got to her feet and crossed over to Hanne. She crouched down. Hanne shrank away. Her arms were still folded over her chest, like a knot.

"You won't survive without this job," Annmari said calmly. "And this job would be unbelievably more boring without you. I just wish . . . that you could be a bit more strategic sometimes. As far as other people are concerned. I've never understood why you have to challenge the system as if your life depended on it. I haven't been here as long as you have, but I've heard stories about what you were like. In the past. Distant, okay, but always according to the book. Always irreproachable. What . . . what happened, Hanne?"

"I got tired. I couldn't stand it anymore."

"Stand what? What is it you couldn't stand?"

Hanne's eyes began to brim.

"I'm not crying," she said. "It's just an infection."

Warily, Annmari tried to take her hand.

"I'm not really crying," Hanne said loudly. "These eyes of mine are just so fucking sore. And I really can't bring myself to talk about my personal business. That evidence there should be more than enough for us to be going on with."

She nodded in the direction of the guns.

"More than enough," she repeated, struggling to change position in her seat without touching Annmari.

"They're really out to get you, Hanne."

"Who?"

"Management. They're pissed off. You've played on so many concessions in this system of ours that their patience is running out. The Superintendent—"

"He's most angry at *you.*"

"I don't know. Anyway, it's not me we're talking about. The Superintendent is really annoyed that you can never work as part of a team, that you never . . . You know what I mean. What *he* means. Puntvold is also fed up to the back teeth. He's been at me no fewer than three times to get rid of you. And that's just in the course of this past week."

"Two-faced bastard!" Hanne said indignantly. "He's been sucking up to me, you know."

"He thinks you should take a vacation. That you're overworked. That this fuss you've made about Sidensvans is a sidetrack. And to be honest, he's not alone in thinking that."

"What about you, then?" Hanne asked, finally looking her in the eye. "Do you agree?"

Annmari stood up and shook her leg.

"To some extent," she said, sitting down in her chair again. "I agree that a vacation would do you good. After all, that was the intention, wasn't it? That you should have two weeks off over Christmas?"

"Is Sidensvans a sidetrack, in your opinion?"

Annmari still would not touch the guns. She simply studied them, through the plastic, as if she could not yet take in that they had turned up.

"Knut Sidensvans is the victim of a brutal crime," she said. "And as such, he's definitely important. But the way this case has exploded now, I can't quite see that there's any great hurry to investigate him in particular. Of course it will have to be done. But we have limited resources. We're overflowing with evidence. It's as if a dam's been opened. We have to hasten slowly. Find some relevance in it all, build it stone by stone, and ensure that the prosecution, when it eventually comes about, is as unassailable as possible. All in good time, Hanne."

"But listen to me!"

Hanne shoved the evidence bags aside with the back of her hand, nonchalant and reckless, before leaning forward to the Police Prosecutor.

"We ought to secure these as soon as possible," Annmari said, pointing. "They can't just lie here and—"

"A crime," Hanne said loudly, and Annmari almost jumped out of her skin, "has its own entirely special character. Sometimes I think that a crime has its own . . . personality. What has helped me over all these years is that I always try to put myself in the perpetrator's shoes. Get under the skin of the crime. I try . . ."

She put her hand behind her ear and gave a fleeting smile.

"I try to listen," she said. "To what it tells me."

"And the Stahlberg crime tells you—"

"Many things. In the first place, that it can't have been planned. Not the way it was carried out, at least. Of course someone may have had plans that evening, to kill one or several of the victims, but the whole crime scene is too chaotic, too . . . loud. Too noisy. The perpetrator—or perpetrators—for instance, had amazing luck not to be seen, not to be heard."

"Silencers," Annmari said, pointing.

"But think of the shrieks. The screams."

"But Hermine was seen. Seen running from the crime scene."

"Maybe." Hanne nodded energetically. "It's certainly possible. Of course, we don't know for sure that it was her, but it's certainly possible that Hermine committed the murders. If this woman gun dealer of Billy T.'s—"

"Woman?"

"Forget it. If the gun dealer can identify this Glock here, then Hermine's well and truly caught out. But listen, Annmari. Listen to the crime. Try to follow the logic of the murders."

Annmari found herself actually listening, holding her breath in an effort perhaps to sense a voice, through the wall, from the guns, inside her own head.

"Can you hear it?"

Hanne's eyes locked on to hers.

"The situation is chaotic," she said softly. "Sidensvans has paid a visit. A welcome guest. He has to be received hospitably, with champagne and open sandwiches. Cake. The father of the house opens the door. Happy, perhaps. Then Sidensvans is shot."

"But we don't know—"

"Sidensvans was shot first, Annmari. Look at it now. Listen. He falls forward. Hermann—"

"Hanne! We haven't yet reconstructed it all. We're working flat out on—"

"Listen to me, for Christ's sake!"

Hanne was stretched out across the desk now and grabbed both of Annmari's hands.

"The perpetrator is standing on the stairs, or at the front door. He or she shoots Sidensvans. After that, the person goes up on the landing and shoots Hermann. Preben must have come rushing through. Then he was attacked as well. That's the only way the placing of the bodies can be explained. Sidensvans with his overcoat on and his feet across the threshold. Hermann just inside from him, and Preben—"

"Okay then!"

Annmari pulled back her hands.

"Of course, that's what we've used as some sort of working hypothesis, but what—"

"The perpetrator then goes farther inside the apartment. We've thought the whole time that it was to get Turid. She had to die too. But what if the perpetrator was not looking for her at all? What if the murderer just wanted to make sure there were no witnesses to it all?"

"But she—"

"Sidensvans was killed *first*, Annmari. If Hermine is the guilty party, then I want to know what she had against Sidensvans. The way this case is speaking to me, it's telling a story of a murder that went wrong."

"Four murders."

"That might not have been intended to happen at all. That we today, eight days later, are sitting with buckets of evidence that might already be sufficient for a conviction, that ought to tell us something. Have you ever . . ."

She smacked herself hard on the forehead, as if the pain would make her thoughts clearer, her words more convincing.

"Have you ever experienced a case in which we've stumbled across so much evidence in such a short time? Have you?"

Hanne was almost screaming. Annmari raised her palms and hushed her.

"No, but—"

"The Stahlbergs were a broken family," Hanne said, suddenly quiet. "A beautiful facade in the process of cracking open badly. But family members hating one another does not mean that they kill one another.

We owe it to the three suspects to think along alternative lines. For a while. If for no other reason than for the sake of appearances. We owe it to ourselves to do that."

She rose stiffly from her chair.

"I have to go," she said. "I've lots of mail to sort through."

"Now? It's half past midnight!"

"It has to be done sometime. And by the way . . ."

With her hand on the door handle, she turned toward Annmari for the last time.

"If Hermine is able to commit murder," she said slowly, "something she might well be—why, then, didn't she kill Alfred? Why on earth didn't she kill a guy like that instead?"

Then, with a shrug, she left Annmari sitting on her own again.

Hanne Wilhelmsen had emptied her pigeonhole, crammed full of mail, in the deserted front office. The in-box in her own office was also stacked high. For more than a week, she had only managed to sort roughly through what had been pressed into her hand. It would take hours on end to sift through all of it. Since she wouldn't get any sleep anyway, she would sit at her desk for as long as she could bear to. She was obviously no longer particularly welcome at headquarters. Fair enough, then, to work through the night, with no others to relate to. Undisturbed, the way she liked best.

She was abnormal and different. Obstinate and lacking in flexibility. Maybe she had always been like that. Kåre might be right: there could be something wrong with her, from birth onward, something genetic perhaps, an inherited defect that made her impossible to love, even as a little child. For so many years she had thought that her differentness was something she had chosen. But maybe it was all an illusion. She had not chosen. She *was* defective.

Gritting her teeth, she unscrewed the lid of a half-empty soda bottle.

It was not only her fault. Not everything was her fault. A four-year-old should not hear that she is a waif who was found on a rubbish heap, she mused, just because she did not read as early as her siblings. Of course, her father had been joking. But she was a child, and she had believed him.

Hanne breathed more easily.

She had a home; she had Nefis. They belonged together, the two of them. And Mary. Alexander had arrived, and they were a complete family now.

She began to place the internal envelopes in one bundle, the official envelopes bearing logos in another, and everything she was not quite sure what to do with she placed in a final pile. When everything had finally been sorted, her chest sank. Three piles of paper towered on her desk.

"My God," she muttered. "Might as well pour water through a sieve."

When she carefully tried to push two of the bundles back, to make room to work on the last pile, everything toppled over. Documents and envelopes, loose sheets and notifications now lay in a haphazard heap on the floor. Her headache suddenly grew more intense.

One letter had sailed all the way over to the door. For a minute or two she sat, nonplussed, wondering whether to leave it all lying there. Go home. Sleep. The cleaner would take it all away. Someone else could take care of the damn mail.

Of course they couldn't.

Starting at the door was possibly not such a bad idea. The law of chance was just as good as any other system, it struck her, feeling discouraged.

The envelope that was lying on its own, just inside the threshold, was from Telenor, the phone company.

Hanne ripped it open and let her fingers run over the close print of the columns that showed which numbers Knut Sidensvans had called during the final period of his life. Five calls on the day of his murder and more than forty in the previous week. Some of them were quite lengthy.

Hanne went back to her seat without taking her eyes off the document. Letters and papers rustled around her feet: they covered almost half the floor area now. She sat down slowly and switched on her computer. The printout gave only the numbers Sidensvans had phoned and been contacted by, no names. She must have forgotten to specify what she wanted. The court order had been easy to obtain. It would take days to order a new printout.

The computer screen flickered blue and eventually settled.

The search program was highly efficient.

The day of Knut Sidensvans's death, he had called the University Library twice. Both calls had lasted less than two minutes. At the crack of dawn he had had a longer conversation with the Meteorological Institute. At 1:32 p.m., he had obviously ordered Chinese takeout. She had no need to look up his very last phone call. The number was very familiar. Sidensvans had spoken to someone at police headquarters, Grønlandsleiret 44.

At 2:29 p.m. on Thursday, December 19, the very last phone conversation Knut Sidensvans had had was with someone in the police department.

That was actually not so strange.

He was working on an article about the police force. Knut Sidensvans was going to write about the police and naturally had sources there.

Not particularly strange.

The very last phone call in the man's life.

Once again, Hanne felt that unfamiliar anxiety. It swamped her, a sadness mixed with anxiety that made her indecisive and long to go home. She struggled to remember when she had last felt like this, whether she had ever before felt that a case terrified her and made her want to let go.

When it dawned on her, she felt hot. As she keyed in telephone information, she noticed that her hands were ice-cold.

"Åshild Meier," she requested. "In Drøbak. Put me through, please."

The publisher's editor picked up after three rings, obviously half-asleep.

"So," she said, taken aback, once Hanne had duly apologized for the lateness of the hour. "This book is quite comprehensive. It will be more of a reference book, a . . . altogether more than thirty articles, in fact, and when we've decided on the order of the articles, instead of a more chronological, uniform—"

"What was Sidensvans to write about?" Hanne interrupted her. "I just want to know what he was to write about."

"He had taken it on himself to describe the development of crime in the major cities," Åshild Meier said. "From 1970 until the present day. With Sidensvans's knowledge of statistics, we thought he would be well suited to draw some pictures of . . . trends, you might say. He was going to compare the development in Oslo and Bergen with three selected smaller cities. An enormous task, of course. Several of the articles could be considered more as dissertations. But then we don't plan to have the book ready for publication until January 2006, either. By then the Police Directorate will have been in existence for five years. But of course you know that."

"How far had he reached?"

Hanne thought the woman at the other end must be able to hear her pulse and tried not to seem breathless.

"Well . . ."

Åshild Meier paused.

"We've had some difficulty obtaining researcher status for him," she said. "You see, he's not attached to any research institution. It was necessary for him to have access to all the archives and that sort of thing. But in the end the Directorate arranged it."

"So how far had he reached?"

"Not very far. He hadn't yet written anything, I believe. But according to what he told me the last time I spoke to him, he had plowed through a considerable amount of material. Why? What's this about, actually?"

Hanne did not answer. Cold sweat was running from her left armpit. She thought she could hear footsteps in the corridor. It was normal to hear footsteps in the corridor, she thought, but these were slow, and when she pricked up her ears, they were gone.

"Hello?"

"I'm still here," she said swiftly. "Had he told you anything about what he had discovered?"

"No—"

"And you're absolutely sure of that?"

"Yes!"

For the first time Åshild Meier seemed impatient.

"Sorry," Hanne said, pinching the bridge of her nose. "I'm really sorry for waking you."

"That's okay," said the tired voice at the other end of the line. "Was there anything else you wanted?"

"No. Thanks. Goodnight. Apologies again."

When she put down the phone, the actual click of the receiver in its cradle was enough to terrify her. She must go home. Her brain needed some rest. Her nerves.

Once before, she had felt like this. Then she had been young and popular, almost worshiped, with her cool control of everything and everyone. When she shut her eyes, she could recall the date. October 11, 1992. A Sunday. Late afternoon. She was in the midst of a case with dramatic consequences reaching all the way into the government. Outside her own office, she had been struck down: suddenly, unexpectedly, and unseen. The blow had left her with a headache that, admittedly, eased off for spells, but at times like this, with fluctuating temperatures and cold, damp air, it made her depressed and often unable to sleep.

However, it wasn't the attack itself she was thinking about.

It was the anxiety of that time that seized her. The terror of the first few seconds, after waking in the hospital, suddenly felt so immediate on this post-Christmas night more than ten years later. Hanne tried to understand her own reactions. With her fingers pressed on her temples, she counted to ten over and over again, like a mantra.

Now she knew what had come over her: it was alarm at being unprotected. Fear that there was no longer a secure bulkhead against them out there.

Now it was the silence outside the door that threatened her.

# SATURDAY, DECEMBER 28

It was ten to nine in the morning, and once again Hanne stood in Knut Sidensvans's apartment. She was alone this time and spent some time sensing the atmosphere in the over-filled living room. The towering piles of books and periodicals spread over the floor created a miniature city: skyscrapers of knowledge with narrow streets in between. She walked slowly from the door to the writing desk—one step to the left, two to the right, and then straight ahead. She peered at the top book in a stack that reached to her thigh. It was about schnauzers and was written in German.

This time she risked switching on the desk lamp. She carefully took out silicone gloves, drew them on, and touched the switch. The light was pointing diagonally; all of a sudden she noticed a passport, partly visible underneath a newspaper on the far edge of the vast work table.

Warily, she jiggled the passport out, moving the small red booklet ever so slightly. She had only seen Sidensvans once, after he had been shot in the head. A dog had eaten parts of his ear and feasted on his brain. She leafed through the pages.

The photograph showed a serious man with a round face, and there was something indecisive about the soft contours of his chin. His nose was small, his forehead broad with a high, receding hairline, and he had a peculiar quiff of combed-back hair, elegantly slicked down at the crown with something that must be hair cream or gel. Sidensvans was neither handsome nor ugly. He looked pretty ordinary, a cliché of a public servant. Hanne held the photograph up to the lamplight.

It was the eyes that made him special.

The passport photograph was in color, but so small that Hanne had to lean in to the beam of light in order to study it. Sidensvans had deep-set eyes, emphasizing the unsympathetic expression given by his sullen mouth, turned down defiantly at the corners.

She put the passport down carefully and set to work.

The first thing she did was to photograph the apartment. It crossed her mind that others should have done this, as she diligently made sure to document the striking difference between the chaos on the floor and the meticulous piles on the massive desk. This was not her job, but she continued all the same. Determined and purposeful: her anxiety of the previous night was changing into a fanatical tension. It seemed as if the camera helped her to see more clearly, as if the restricted segment in the viewfinder made it easier to concentrate. She slowly lowered the device. Her eyes ran again over the table, over the bundles of blank sheets of paper, a book about an old master thief, and an organization chart of the Oslo Police District. She lifted a newspaper and found an offprint of an article about unlawful use of police custody. Underneath a glass paperweight she found a report from the *Aftenposten* newspaper. The author was a well-known criminologist, and the article dealt with the police practice of dropping cases in which the identity of the perpetrator was known. Hanne remembered the piece, even though it was several years old. She carefully put the paperweight back in place.

Something was missing.

She knew something was missing.

Although Knut Sidensvans had not reached very far in his work on the article about the development of crime in major cities, he must have made good progress. Less than two hours ago, Hanne Wilhelmsen had sweet-talked her way into a visit at first light to the long-term archives, where all dropped and closed cases in the Oslo Police District were stored. A grumpy archivist had made an early rise in order to assist. It had taken only minutes to establish that Knut Sidensvans had never set foot in there. His name was not in any of the records. Hanne's disappointment must have been obvious. The yawning archivist ran his hand thoughtfully over his hair and shuffled off on his own initiative to check the folders of mail.

"Here," he said eventually. "So that's where I got the name from. I thought that, you see, when I saw that unusual name of his in the newspaper. I've heard of that fellow, I thought. But then I couldn't think where. Here you are."

He handed her a letter.

It was from the Police Directorate and dated October 23. The text pointed out to Oslo's Police Chief that Knut Sidensvans would require access to all archived cases in the course of the following year. He would be grateful for the greatest possible cooperation.

"Copy to us," the man said, pointing further down on the sheet of paper. "It is addressed to the Chief of Police. And it's to Bergen, you see. You ought to phone the Bergen police. He may have started there, you know. I *knew* I had heard of that guy before!"

He yawned again, and Hanne left him. She wanted to leave Grønlandsleiret, get away from her colleagues' field of vision, away from questions to which she did not yet know the answers. Not until she passed the Munch Museum on her way to Sidensvans's apartment did she stop to call her old friend from work, Severin Heger. He had at last dared to apply for a post in his hometown, after having come out of both the closet and the Security Service with a bang. Now he was Superintendent in the Bergen Police and, impressively enough, it took him only nineteen minutes to return her call.

"He's been here, Hanne. A number of times."

His dialect was stronger now than when he had hidden himself away on the top-secret stories of police headquarters. He continued to talk enthusiastically.

"Odd guy, or so they say here. And, Hanne . . . I don't like to say this, but there's a lot to suggest that he was permitted to take copies of quite a few cases. My friend in our archives section here couldn't entirely see the logic of Sidensvans being allowed to take as many notes as he wanted but not to take copies. So he—"

"Severin," Hanne had interrupted him. "Why the hell has no one from your district told us that Sidensvans has been in contact with you? Here we are, in the middle of the homicide case of the century, and someone over at your place is skulking around, someone who might well have vital information about one of our victims! I get—"

"It's the holidays, Hanne. It's Christmas, for God's sake!"

"Find out which cases he took away with him, Severin. Find that out for me."

"That could take time."

"As fast as possible. And you—"

"You sound really fucking stressed out, Hanne."

"Keep your mouth shut about it. Until after the weekend."

"But you asked me to find out—"

"As discreetly as possible, okay?"

The phone line crackled as he laughed.

"Same old Hanne, I see. Secretive and—"

"After the weekend. Please, Severin. Thanks."

Hanne had severed the connection before he managed to answer. By then she had almost reached the apartment at Ola Narr. A neighbor had greeted her in the stairwell on her way up, as if she belonged there. It didn't feel like that to her. Sidensvans's living room had taken on the character of a graveyard: a dusty mausoleum dedicated to a learned man whom no one would miss.

Hanne Wilhelmsen's knowledge of computers was far more than could be expected of a police officer. Nevertheless, what she now embarked on was totally unacceptable. They had their own people for tasks such as this: competent specialists who knew exactly what they were doing and would not be in danger of damaging anything. Hanne was aware that there were viruses that destroyed the workings as soon as any intruders tried to log on. There were advanced programs that would delete evidence, if it existed, on the hard disk she was starting up. She was aware of all of this when her finger closed in on the On switch. She could wipe everything with one keystroke, and yet she pressed the key.

The computer began to hum.

The image on the screen flickered.

The Microsoft tune suddenly boomed from the loudspeakers; startled, she turned down the volume.

He had not even protected the computer with a password.

Knut Sidensvans can't have been afraid. He had not felt threatened by anything or anyone. The computer was an open book, and there were no codes, secret passwords, or automatic viruses. No sly programs that could protect what he must have discovered and stored. Hanne began her search.

It was hardly credible.

The computer was almost empty.

Her fingers raced over the keyboard, picking up speed.

In the folder for My Documents she found a short text about the rhododendron plant and a scanned article about the pattern of immigrant settlement in Oslo. Nothing else. She opened folder after folder. Some he had created himself. They were empty, with meaningless file names. In the folder for My Photos, she found a photograph of a red luxury car.

The room felt hot. Surprised, Hanne realized that she was still wearing her outdoor jacket. She pulled it off and put it carefully on the floor, where there was only just space for it among all the piles of magazines and books.

She opened Outlook Express, without connecting to the Internet.

The mailbox contained six or seven spam emails and a message from Telenor about cheaper broadband. Apart from that, nothing. She checked Sent Mail. Three uninteresting emails. Drafts. Nothing. Deleted Messages. Empty.

She hesitated, but not for long.

With her eyes nailed to the Inbox image on the screen, she connected the computer to the Internet. Four seconds later, the messages pinged in.

The recipient was sidensvans@online.no.

But it was the sender's email address that took her aback.

knutsiden@online.no.

The man had sent four emails to himself.

The way Nefis sometimes did.

Hanne broke out in a sweat: again that cold sweat, running in fat droplets along the sides of her body. Thirst made her tongue seem too large for her mouth. Slowly, still careful not to topple anything, she picked her way out of the living room and into the kitchen. A sour stench of rotting food assailed her when she opened the door. They should have asked someone to empty the fridge, to remove the half-eaten bread, gone disgustingly moldy, lying in a breadbox of clear plastic. If nothing else, then out of respect for the murder victim: a man who had lived so quietly and had then been slaughtered in the shadow of something so much greater than himself.

Hanne let the water run for a long time. Instead of finding a glass in the wall cabinets, she leaned over the sink and put her mouth to the stream of water.

When she straightened up, wiping her chin with the back of her hand, she recalled why Nefis had two email addresses and often sent documents to herself at the end of the workday. With her eyes closed, Hanne could hear her voice, singsong, with the trace of accent that had almost disappeared now: "An extra safeguard. If the backup fails and the computer goes on fire overnight, then my work is on a server somewhere out there in the ether and can be downloaded tomorrow morning."

Knut Sidensvans was not afraid of a break-in. He was afraid of losing important documents.

Hanne turned off the tap. Then she entered Sidensvans's living room and opened the files he had sent to himself. There were not many. It took her ten minutes to get them printed out and sorted. Half an hour later she had read them all. It took another thirty minutes for her to understand what she had read.

Painstakingly she folded the sheets of paper and logged out of the machine. She tucked the papers down the waistband of her trousers, before pulling on her jacket. The anxiety of the last twenty-four hours, that deep unease that had bothered her in recent days, for which she had not found any explanation, was gone.

She swore instead. She uttered all the oaths she could think of, blaspheming as she locked the door behind her. When she dashed downstairs to catch a taxi as fast as possible, she mumbled in time to the clicking of her heels on the concrete: *Shit. Shit. Shit!*

There was a lot to be done. The first priority was to speak to Henrik Heinz Backe.

It was a different woman this time. She was younger and did not seem so friendly. Carl-Christian Stahlberg wondered whether they used women to make him more cooperative. More truthful. He was eager to be cooperative and truthful, but it was too difficult to arrive at what was not a lie without telling lies.

"So, Hermine bought a gun," the woman insisted. "Do you know anything about that?"

Her voice was light, with a very slight lisp around the "s." She had a name that contained a number of lisping sounds, but he couldn't remember what it was. It felt as if the glue in his brain was used up; he remembered so little, and no names. Not even the lawyer's. He was a well-known personality in the media, that much CC did know. Mabelle must have pulled some strings. Hawk-eyed and vigorous, the lawyer listened attentively throughout the interview, but Carl-Christian could no longer recollect his name.

"What?"

"Have you taken in anything at all of what I've been saying?" the woman asked.

"Yes," he answered.

"Have you any knowledge of your sister Hermine buying a gun on November 16 this year?"

"No."

He wanted to say yes, but it was as if his mouth was choosing its own words, completely independent of his thoughts. Maybe that was fine. His thoughts were so jumbled, and there was nothing but nonsense inside his head. It was just as well that his mouth was running away with itself of its own volition. He smiled.

"This isn't actually very amusing," the woman said.

"No," he replied.

"I want to show you some photographs we have found."

*Photos*, Carl-Christian Stahlberg thought.

The woman has some photos.

But the photographs had been burned. He remembered that. They were lying as ash and nothingness in the fireplace.

"They may seem . . . offensive. I apologize for that. But it's important . . ."

He had burned all the photographs. He was certain of that. It was as if his brain had received a jolt; his thoughts seemed to fall into place, into order, some kind of system descended on it all, and he smiled again. The lawyer appeared annoyed. He snatched up the copies for himself, before the policewoman had managed to display them on the table.

"Is this necessary?" he said, shielding them from Carl-Christian's view. "I can't comprehend how it can be useful to anyone for my client to be forced to respond to these."

Carl-Christian could understand none of this. The photographs in the safe in Kampen were gone. He had destroyed them himself, as Mabelle had requested.

"Photographs," he said, flustered.

"I must ask you to give them back to me," the woman said.

The lawyer reluctantly handed them over. Carl-Christian waited. Now he really must concentrate. This was important. He had most definitely destroyed the photographs of Mabelle. They no longer existed; they could not possibly be here, in a slim bundle on the table in front of him. He did not even dare to check. Instead he glanced up. His gaze stopped at the ceiling light.

His father might have had an extra set. The photographs might have been lying in Eckersbergs gate, inside Hermann's writing desk. The police had found them there.

The woman placed her hand on his arm, making him look down in confusion.

They weren't photographs of Mabelle. They were pictures of Hermine.

When he saw who was standing behind her, and after a few seconds at last realized what his sister and Uncle Alfred were doing, he leaned to one side and threw up.

No one said anything. He vomited over himself and the floor, but no one did anything.

Carl-Christian felt a flash of light inside his head, a silent, white explosion. It was as if everything at once became so clear—all the years in his family, all the quarrels, the discord, his mother's pained looks, and his father's heavy-handed bullying of them all, and Hermine's maneuvering through the difficult mine field of which the Stahlberg family had always consisted. He pictured his uncle in his mind's eye, ingratiating and incomprehensible, deceitful and yet never disowned.

It dawned on Carl-Christian, as in a revelation, why Hermann had given his daughter a fortune on her twentieth birthday. He suddenly appreciated, as he retched yet again, that he should have seen this long ago. Everything would have been different if only he had been willing to see.

When he finally sat upright again, he had to take tight hold of the table to avoid falling off his chair. He felt light-headed and his stomach was empty and hot. There was no room inside him for anything other than this one thing: he hated his father more intensely than ever before. Hated him.

"I killed them," he said. "I was the one who murdered my parents and my brother."

Silje Sørensen's mouth fell open. Of all the contrived lies, of all the untruths this man had served up in the course of a total of more than eleven hours of questioning since his arrest on Christmas Day, this was the most obvious. Silje let her gaze slide from Carl-Christian to his lawyer in an effort to understand. She could not fathom her own certainty and sought the lawyer's help as she stammered: "Why . . . but that can't—"

"I killed them," Carl-Christian repeated angrily; he was on his feet now.

Then, grabbing the top photograph, he tore it into tiny pieces.

"My boy!"

Delighted, the lady in Blindernveien stretched out her arms in an embrace.

"You weren't supposed to arrive until Monday! And you're here already."

Her son knelt down and let his mother hold him tight.

"I thought it was too long," he murmured, half smothered by her thick woolen jacket. "I couldn't let you sit here on your own. Stephanie and the children won't arrive until Monday morning. I thought the two of us could have a couple of days to ourselves. Now that it's all at a bit of a distance."

"You're so kind," his mother said, not wanting to let him go. "What with your work and everything—"

"There's not such a lot to do now, over Christmas," he said, finally extricating himself. "There were just a few things I needed to attend to. Since what happened to Dad came about so suddenly and I had to—"

"All the way from France," his mother said. "You're a good boy, Terje. Coming all that way twice in one week. Things are not so difficult for me now. Such a good boy."

Laughing, Terje Wetterland went out to the kitchen to put on some water for tea.

"It's the least I could do," he shouted, rattling cups. "I had such a guilty conscience for leaving you at all. We shall . . . What's this, by the way?"

"What's what, my boy? The tea's in the jar with the lid beside the—"

"I mean these papers lying on the kitchen table."

"Oh, those . . ."

He had returned to the doorway now.

"It's just a folder your dad had left lying here at home. It was beside his bed. The night he—"

Tears spilled from her eyes, and she closed them.

"Dear Mom," Terje Wetterland said, sitting down beside her. "We'll get used to this. I'll make sure I have a bit more to do here in Norway, and then I'll be able to visit more often. We'll get through this, Mom."

Suddenly she dried her face.

"Of course. I was afraid of forgetting those papers in the bedroom, so I left them out so that you would find them. Would you put them on the shelf in the hallway, please? Then you can take them with you when you clear out his files. Because you said that . . . You'll stay long enough to sort out your father's papers?"

"Yes," he said, heading back to the kitchen. "And to have a nice time with you. The children are really looking forward to seeing you. They're so upset about their grandfather. Where did you say the tea . . . No, I've found the container. Camilla has made a lovely drawing she says she'll put inside the coffin. It was quite touching; she sat for hours on end with it last night."

Terje Wetterland rinsed the glass teapot. Old tea leaves were wedged in the strainer, and he tried to poke out the worst of them. In the end he gave up and called out: "You don't make tea very often!"

"Is it too old? Has it completely lost its aroma?"

"No, not at all. It'll be fine."

The whistling kettle screeched. He placed the kettle on the kitchen table, filled the strainer with tea, and poured the boiling water over it. The strainer was still blocked and the water ran over the edge, all of a sudden; he burned his hand and whispered an oath.

"What is it, dearest?"

"Nothing," he shouted as he held his hand under the running tap.

Slowly, he watched as a blister the size of a krone coin sprouted at the base of his thumb, smarting painfully.

"*Merde*," he whispered again, and turned to find a hand towel.

The tea had spread over the table surface, threatening to soak into the papers that had begun to slide out of their folder. He grabbed the cloth and slapped it down on the table. The golden liquid splashed all over the place. With a loud groan, he whisked the documents off the table and held them above his head, as if worried that the tea stain would damage them.

"What is it? What are you up to out there?"

"Nothing," he muttered, blowing on his burn. "Everything's okay."

The documents were apparently unharmed, apart from a light-brown streak and a couple of spatters on the top sheet. Terje Wetterland was taken aback.

"What is this in fact, Mom?"

"What? Can't you come in here and talk to me? It's so tiresome with all this shouting."

Slowly, without taking his eyes off the documents, he walked back to the living room.

"Do you know what these are about?" he asked, trying not to let his own disquiet color his voice.

"Is something wrong? Is there a problem?"

His mother was not so restrained.

"No, not really. Nothing wrong. But I think I should phone the police."

"The police?"

"Take it easy, Mom. It's just that these . . ."

He leafed carefully through the papers, feeling that he ought not to do so. This was not his business: it was like reading someone else's letter. But he had to. He read, noting names and dates; he struggled to focus; his glasses misted up. He took them off and read through it again.

"Mom," he said finally. "Was the Stahlberg family Dad's client?"

Jenny stood in front of the big puddle on the sidewalk. Concentrating, she put her feet together before she jumped in, making a tremendous splash. Billy T. swore vehemently and grabbed his daughter by the arm. He pulled her away while the youngster screamed and kicked at his legs.

"Daddy's soaking wet," he complained. "You mustn't do that!"

"That hurts!" the child wailed. "Ouch!"

He let her go and hunkered down. Snot had congealed under her nose and, feeling discouraged, Billy T. noticed the constantly recurring infection that formed yellow pus in the corners of her eyes.

"Listen to me, my girl."

He forced a smile as he patted her arm.

"Hurt," Jenny whimpered.

"Sorry. But we got so wet. Now Daddy just has to make one phone call—"

"No."

"Yes. I'm just going to say a few words to Hanne, and then we'll—"

"No!"

Jenny began to shriek. People hurrying past them alongside the stores in Markveien glared skeptically at him as he grabbed the back of her snowsuit and carried her forward like a bag of bones. Only when he was well inside the park at Olav Ryes plass did he deposit her resolutely on the ground.

"Here," he said. "Here's a huge puddle for you. Jump in it. Then Daddy will just make one phone call before we go to McDonald's. But if you get yourself too wet, then we'll have to go home again. Okay?"

Jenny stomped out into the enclosed pond in the middle of the park. The mixture of snow and water, dog excrement and litter sprayed out with every step. She laughed and stood beside the dead fountain in the center, picking her nose.

"Hanne," Billy T. said with relief when, surprisingly enough, someone answered at the other end. "I've tried a hundred times to get in touch with you."

"Eleven," she corrected him. "But I really don't have time. What is it?"

"You're in deep trouble. You were supposed to interview Carl-Christian this morning!"

"I sent text messages to both the Superintendent and Annmari," she barked. "There must be others in that damn building who can conduct an interview from time to time!"

"But, damn it, you have to pick up the phone when we call you!"

"Then I wouldn't get anything else done. I had to switch it off."

"Jenny! *Jenny!*" He smacked his forehead and groaned noisily. "Well, it's your choice, Jenny. Now we have to go straight home."

The little girl had sat down to play with a stray puppy that was licking her face boisterously.

"Tone-Marit is really ill," he moaned into the receiver. "I just have to go home and take care of Jenny for a few hours. My God—"

"Are you phoning to tell me I'm persona non grata at headquarters, or did you have something important to tell me?"

"I . . ."

When, that morning, he had awakened from a sweaty dream and begun to rummage through the pile of old newspapers Tone-Marit had stacked in the hallway, it was as a result of a sudden impulse. When he finally found the copy of *Aftenposten* from Friday, December 20, and tracked down the article he recalled from his visit to Ronny Berntsen, he grew worried. Two hours later, at police headquarters, after having lied more than he could ever remember doing in years, he had reached a state of certainty and deep anxiety.

"That gun," he said, clearing his throat. "The revolver—"

"Yes?"

"You know that the pistol—"

"You were talking about the revolver, Billy T."

"Yes. The pistol came from Sølvi Jotun. It was sold to Hermine. We're pretty sure about that now. Sølvi recognized an indentation on the stock. She's in a cell now and is going to kill me when she finally gets out. I—"

"You had no choice, Billy T. You couldn't protect her any longer. We'll see how we can help her later. But what about this revolver?"

"It's ours."

"Ours."

Hanne repeated the word—not as a question, not in surprise. She was simply confirming it, as if he was telling her something she had known for a long time, an everyday piece of information that, to be honest, was not particularly sensational.

"Yes, well, not exactly ours . . ."

He was almost whispering. The streetcar rumbled down Thorvald Meyers gate, and Jenny had set out on a swim through the dirty water. The puppy squealed in glee and snatched off her hat. The dog owner no longer seemed so cheerful; she looked at Billy T. in reproach and pointed at the child, who was now dripping wet.

"It's a confiscated gun, Hanne. It was seized by us seven months ago and should right now be under lock and key as precisely that: a confiscated gun. I recognized it from a picture taken the day the murders took place. I've checked."

Hanne said nothing. Billy T. gulped. The silence between them was impenetrable, pleasant—verging on the relationship they had once had, at a time when they had hardly needed to ask to know what the other was thinking.

"You're a genius," she said at last, at the other end of the phone. "Do you know that? A bloody genius. Can you get rid of Jenny?"

"No."

"Drive her home to us. Nefis and Mary can—"

"I have to go home for some dry clothes," he broke in.

"To hell with that. Nefis will find something. You must . . ."

It took her only three minutes to explain to him what he had to do. He disconnected the call and tucked his phone into his breast pocket. Then he stepped out into the pond. Carefully he lifted Jenny up and settled her in his arms, like a baby; she leaned her head back and smiled at him, a big smile with pearly white teeth. He put his face against hers, his mouth to hers, a childish mouth full of laughter and spittle and the residue of caramel candies like a trace of sweetness on her lips. He kissed her on the nose, on her cheeks; he smacked his lips and blew raspberries, and Jenny laughed loudly for a long time.

"I love you," he mumbled into her ear as he began to head for the car. "I love you, you little monster."

It took Hanne twenty minutes to gain access to Henrik Heinz Backe. Of course he had not opened the door when she had rung the door-bell. Only after hammering on the door, throwing stones at the win-dows, shouting and screaming, and finally trying to pick the lock with her credit card and a pocket screwdriver was she rewarded by a grouchy face as the door opened a crack. To be on the safe side, she had thrust her foot forward. After considerable persuasion, she was finally allowed inside.

The furniture in the apartment was heavy and old-fashioned, and a faint odor of unwashed male hit her as she followed Backe unbidden into the living room. Nevertheless, the place had an atmosphere of some sort of coziness. The bookshelves were crammed, and there were crocheted cloths and runners on the tables. In the windows sat three geraniums, each in its own Delft pot and shriveling in the heat. The sofa was decorated with embroidered cushions. An enormous chandelier was suspended from the ceiling. Three of the bulbs were gone; the lighting in the room was lopsided. All of a sudden, it struck Hanne that the apartment was like the one belonging to the Stahlbergs, of course, but only a mirror image; it made her dizzy when she tried to calculate where the kitchen was located.

"Flowers are not my forte," Backe said, as he sat down in an arm-chair. "It was my wife who was good at that sort of thing."

Hanne chose the sofa; she had a good view of the entire living room from there, and she tried not to be too obvious when she studied his face. He was not drunk. Even though the smell of liquor had been noticeable when he had finally opened the door, his gait was steady all the same. His slurred speech was more a result of his lack of teeth rather than a high blood-alcohol count. He was dressed in gray pants and some kind of smoking jacket with a white shirt underneath; every-thing was apparently clean.

"I've met you before," he said, scratching the back of his hand in a confused gesture.

"Yes. I drove you home a week ago. Do you remember?"

"Unn really had a talent with flowers," he said, smiling. "You should have seen the garden here. In the spring. The summer. It was so beautiful."

An old striking clock ponderously struck the hour.

"Time flies," Backe said.

"You said that you were a retired insurance consultant," Hanne said.

"This was my wife's childhood home. We moved here in fifty-eight. No . . ."

He swept a faint smile away with his hand, embarrassed at his own forgetfulness.

"Eighty-five, I mean. That's when we moved here. My parents-in-law had passed away by then. Both of them. Time flies."

"And before that you lived in Bergen, didn't you?"

He looked up.

"Bergen? Why, yes. We lived in Bergen for years."

"And you were in the police, I understand?"

The clock struck again; there must have been something wrong with it. Backe stood up and disappeared into the kitchen. When he returned, he was carrying a tumbler filled to the brim with brown liquid. He made no move to offer Hanne anything.

"It's not easy to live alone after all these years," he said, sitting down in another chair. "Insurance consultant. That's what I was. I'm a pensioner now."

The gray-blue veil descended over his eyes. Hanne dried her hands on her pants. She clasped them and supported her elbows on her knees as she craned forward.

"This is extremely important, Backe. I'd really like you to answer my questions."

He stared at her, but she was still doubtful as to whether he actually saw her.

"You had a case," she said tentatively. "You had several—I've come across this here . . ."

She put her right hand under her jacket and flicked through the pages.

"This one," she said softly as she skirted around the table.

Backe fumbled with his glass, sloshing the liquid, and was left rubbing the armrest with his finger in rhythmic circles. Finally he looked up and grabbed the sheets of paper.

"Unn would have been devastated," he said quietly. He was right about that.

"Who?" Hanne said.

"I drank too much. I always drank too much."

As if to underscore his own point, he emptied half the glass in one swallow.

"Unn made allowances for me. She always tried to get me to stop. But it was so . . . She wouldn't have put up with this. You understand . . ."

His face had changed, and a sense of calm had settled over his features.

"Drinking is expensive," he said with a little cough. "I let myself be persuaded to take the money. I regretted it, of course. Regretted it terribly. Wanted to give it back. Wanted to blow the whistle. But he was right. It would have been the death of Unn. Yes, yes, that much is true."

His gaze slid over the pages. Hanne was unsure whether he was really reading. She crouched down to get a better view of him, and he flinched, as if he had only now discovered that she was there.

"But Unn's not here anymore," he said.

"This is so important," Hanne whispered, afraid to frighten him, afraid he might retreat again into his failing memory. "What was it that happened?"

"The boy was only eighteen. A good family, you know. And good families in Bergen . . ."

Now he was laughing. Hanne was struck by how beautiful his voice became, deep and melodious.

". . . are better than any others, you know! Drunk driving. Drove into a lamppost. A trivial affair."

The rest of his drink went down the hatch.

"But the case definitely shouldn't have been dropped. He was new, so first of all, I tried to do the right thing. I sent it back and said there must have been a mistake. But he didn't back down."

Befuddled, he glanced down into the empty glass.

"I just poured some more a minute ago," he said, his slurring more obvious now.

"What happened?" Hanne asked.

"He still wouldn't do anything and said the case should be dropped. Typical rich folk, getting off more easily. Just like those . . ."

He stared fiercely at the wall dividing his apartment from the Stahlbergs'.

". . . fucking snobs in there. Thinking they're better than . . ."

Backe was becoming genuinely agitated. Spittle sprayed as he spoke and he flung out his right arm.

"And my parents-in-law," he roared. "I was never good enough for them. For Unn!"

His spouse's name made him slump back again, exhausted, his breathing labored. He inspected the glass once more, indicating his intention to stand up. Hanne pressed her hand gently on his chest.

"Wait a minute," she said in a friendly tone. "I'll get you a refill afterward. Who told you it would be the death of Unn?"

"It wasn't really so very much money," he said as if he had not heard her. "But when I threatened to go further up the ranks, he began to make threats. When that didn't help either, he burst into tears. Tears! Huh! A grown man—"

"Who?" Hanne asked.

"You can see it for yourself. Our names are there. He had already accepted the money. I got half. I accepted half of it. I accepted . . ."

His tears spilled over.

"A grown man," he mumbled. "A grown man sniveling like a child."

Hanne took his glass. When she returned with more liquor, he had already started talking.

"Of course I understood this wasn't the first time. But he promised it would be the last. I accepted the money. Twenty-five thousand kroner, that's what I got. Then I quit. The shame . . . the shame has never let up. It never ended. An insurance consultant. That's what I am. Do you think they're dying?"

He was looking at her now, straight in the eye, a confused gaze that made her want to smooth his hair with her hand and pat him on the cheek. Instead she asked: "Who?"

"The geraniums. I've tried to water them. Maybe they got too much. Unn was the one who attended to that kind of thing. Well, well."

Slowly he subsided back into the chair. The clock struck five times, a ragged chime, the workings hiccupping violently. The strong smell of spilled liquor stung her nostrils. Cautiously she loosened his grip on the documents, case papers from an obviously unlawfully dropped case from Bergen in 1984. She placed them with the three other case files, cases shelved just as hair-raisingly despite knowledge of the perpetrators and the existence of sufficient evidence. None of them was particularly serious: a couple of cases of drunk driving, a speeding violation, and an attack on a taxi driver. Cases that could be made to disappear, that could easily be stamped and archived. They had lain there in the vast archives, unread and unseen, shielded by Backe's shame, guilt, and love for his wife, until they had surfaced in the course of Knut Sidensvans's research into crime in major Norwegian cities eighteen years later.

"Do you think she'll forgive me?" Backe asked under his breath.

Hanne stuffed the papers in the waistband of her pants and pulled on her jacket. She turned around when she reached the door. The decrepit man seemed so small in that spacious living room, so out of place, as if he had just dropped in accidentally and inappropriately. He raised his glass to his mouth and drank.

"I'm convinced of that," she said, nodding. "She forgave you a long time ago."

"Only if . . ." Hermine whispered, struggling to cough.

Her lungs lacked sufficient strength and her diaphragm muscles let her down. When she continued speaking, Hanne Wilhelmsen could hear the mucus vibrate on her vocal cords.

"Only if you promise me that's why you're here."

"I swear," Hanne said, raising her hand slightly aloft, as if contemplating taking a sacred oath.

The doctor stared doubtfully from the patient to the Chief Inspector.

"I'm still not sure," she said. "And to tell the truth, this is the first time I've ever been called on by a police officer acting alone."

"Chief Inspector," Hanne corrected her, without looking at her. "And now you've examined my police ID so thoroughly that it'll soon disintegrate. Besides, I assume you're not exactly used to being overrun with police officers. With all due respect, of course. I don't mean to be difficult, Dr. Farmen. But this is incredibly important."

"Please," Hermine said, sucking water through a straw. "She's said it won't take very long."

The doctor still hesitated. Stroking her patient's forehead, she studied her eyes and checked the instruments by the headboard with deft, neat hands. She seemed genuinely concerned. Once again she inspected Hanne, who immediately felt nonplussed about the coffee stain on the front of her sweater.

"It's important," Hermine said. "I really must talk to her."

"Half an hour is all you're getting," the doctor declared. "Thirty minutes, and not a second more."

At last they were alone. Hanne glanced at the door. Her bladder was so full that she found it difficult to stand still. Even though the room was equipped with its own bathroom, she did not dare to make use of it. She scarcely dared to pull the chair by the window closer to the bed.

"You're quite sure," she asked softly as she sat down, "that this is okay?"

"You say you believe we're innocent. All of us: CC, Mabelle, and me."

Hermine lifted her hand and moved it halfway toward Hanne's. Then, feebly, she let it fall, as if she no longer possessed the energy to put her trust in anything.

"I'm absolutely certain," Hanne said. "Whether I can manage to convince the others is partly up to you."

"I was so spaced out. You wouldn't believe it."

"When?"

"When it all happened. When I went to . . ."

Once again she struggled to cough.

"Here," Hanne said, offering her water from a glass with a straw. "I think I'll just ask you a few questions. That will save time. The first thing I need to know is whether you were in Eckersbergs gate on Thursday, December 19. Last Thursday."

"Yes. No. I mean, I went there, but something happened. I didn't go in. I mean, I never went into my mother and father's house, I . . ."

Hermine closed her eyes. She seemed so tiny in the massive hospital bed. Her left eye, blue and swollen, was almost glued shut and her lips were cracked, with dried blood in the corners.

"Let's start at the beginning, Hermine. So you had intended to visit your parents."

"Yes."

"Did you have a gun with you?"

Hermine nodded timidly, grimacing as if it were painful to move her neck.

"A pistol," she groaned. "A pistol with a silencer."

"Why didn't you go in, Hermine?"

"It was kept in an apartment that CC and Mabelle have, in Kampen. It was lying there inside a safe."

"I'd like to know what happened when you got there."

"The pistol belonged to CC and Mabelle. I'd bought a gun for them, since—"

Tears spilled from her injured eye. Her frail rib cage heaved underneath the quilt, rapidly, and a silent sob made it difficult for her to speak.

"Relax, Hermine. Try to relax. Everything will be fine now if only you can manage to tell me your story. Do try."

"I was just so livid. So unbelievably livid. Mother phoned me that afternoon and said that Father was going to change everything. That all the agreements we had made, all the promises, all . . . he didn't give a shit about any of it. Mother seemed sorry, as if she didn't really want to . . . That's what Mother was like. Pathetic. She always tried to smooth things over. She let Father decide. Everything. He ruled us. And Mother accepted it. But now she seemed really sad. She . . . Mother most likely took this whole quarrel terribly to heart. Between Father and CC. But did she do anything?"

A fit of coughing ensued. Hanne tried to help her. She took hold around Hermine's back, feeling her shoulder blades, sharp and skinny, against her arm: she lifted her up and moved her forward in the bed.

"It's not the cough itself that's so awful," Hermine said, when Hanne lowered her again onto the pillows. "The problem is that I've such a pain in my gut."

"Why didn't you go inside, Hermine?"

"I think . . . at least now I think in fact that Mother wanted me to come. She didn't say that right out, but why would she actually phone and tell me about this meeting if . . . Even though Father and I have had dreadful arguments in recent months, it's as if I'm the one who . . ."

Her tentative smile made a deep crack on her bottom lip start to bleed.

"I've always been the bridge builder. The little apple of Daddy's eye, in fact. At least that's how it's always looked to the others."

Her smile developed into an ironic grin.

"Maybe Mother thought I could prevent it all. A lawyer was going to come with papers, to complete the transfer of the shipping company to Preben. Father was fed up with the whole argument with CC, Mother said. He would not allow himself to be threatened any longer. He had so much on CC that he no longer believed the court actions would go ahead. He had hired a new lawyer, she told me. Someone who was not linked to the shipping company at all. Father was furious with his regular lawyers and thought they paid too much attention to CC's interests in all of this. He felt they concerned themselves too much with Carl-Christian. They were planning almost to have a party, or at least that's the impression I got. That awful evening. Mother seemed quite scared, in fact. She was so . . ."

Now the tears were flowing from both eyes and her mouth was puckered tight again, as if to hold back the tears.

"I was just so incredibly spaced out and so damn tired of it all. Tired of Father, tired of all his dodges, of him always using money and inheritance to keep all of us down, in our place, where he wanted us. I was sick and tired of Mother always making these sorts of secret phone calls to me, as if I was the one who should take responsibility for preventing him from destroying the family. He wrote a will earlier in the year; it must have been in August. Or September. Mother told me about it. He had written it himself, she said, because he was fed up with these company lawyers who made such a fuss all the time about what was fairest for CC. Mother said that CC was squeezed out entirely. I've never seen the will and didn't want to mention it to CC or Mabelle. It was so awkward; it was so . . . fucking horrendous. Father had disinherited him, no less. That was when I began to devise this plan about the photographs. The kind of pictures that . . . I arranged some quite . . ."

Her grip tightened on the quilt cover and her knuckles whitened. Her whole body seemed tense and Hanne began to worry.

"Relax," she whispered. "There're only the two of us here. Everything will be fine now."

"That no one ever stopped him," Hermine whispered.

"Your father?"

"Alfred. That no one stopped him. I was only ten when it started."

Hanne loosened Hermine's stiff fingers one by one and forced her hand into her own.

"It was as though it didn't matter too much," Hermine said. "In the beginning, I just had to look at him. When he—"

"Don't go into details. We'll do that later. I understand what you mean."

"I got such lovely rewards. Money. Presents. Jewelry. I suppose that's what's bothered me most since then, that it . . ."

Suddenly she seemed to regain her strength. With a jolt, she sat up straight in the bed, pulling her hand back, and hid her face. Her sobs turned into prolonged, howling screams.

"I didn't have very much against it," she sobbed. "That's why it was never possible to stop. I just let it happen. I was so happy with the presents, and it didn't really matter so much, not in the beginning, when he only . . . But then, eventually, as I got bigger—"

"I simply can't go along with this," Dr. Farmen said firmly. Hanne had not heard her approach. "I must ask you to leave this room at once."

"I'll decide that," Hermine said, surprisingly composed. Taking a deep breath, she dried her eyes and continued: "I'm an adult, and I'm not in prison. You don't decide things for me."

"Yes," the doctor insisted. "This isn't doing you any good. You are my medical responsibility for as long as you are here. I heard your screams from the far end of the corridor."

"Dr. Farmen," Hermine said slowly, with a delicate paradoxical authority: all of a sudden, the wealthy man's daughter came to the fore, "I wish to speak to Hanne Wilhelmsen here. It's of crucial importance for my health that I manage to finish what I have to say to her. So in fact *I'm* the one who must ask *you* to leave. Now!"

The physician stared at her patient in astonishment, before breaking into an open, warm smile.

"You're going to be all right, Hermine. I'm pleased about that." However, her smile vanished abruptly when she gazed at Hanne and declared: "You'll have to take responsibility for this conversation. Just so you're aware of that."

Hanne could swear that the doctor tried to slam the door when she left. It was impossible: it slid slowly closed behind her.

"The worst thing is that I never succeeded in extricating myself from it," Hermine said, as if they had never been interrupted. "One thing led to another and then another. In the end it was as if I had, in a way . . . accepted it. But Father and Mother . . ."

Again she slumped weakly on to the pillows.

"Even though I can't claim they knew about it, there was a lot to suggest that the thought wasn't entirely remote. I got . . . Do you know that I received a huge sum of money on my twentieth birthday?"

Hanne nodded.

"I was over the moon of course. Ten million kroner. I had no idea they even *had* so much money. At least, enough to give away just like that. CC was really annoyed. But after all, he was going to take over the shipping company. And Preben was far beyond the seas. So I took the money. I took the money, even though . . . Father said that . . . Father said that I'd been given the money for being a good girl and thinking about the family. The family's reputation. I didn't give a damn about it at that time. Pushed it out of my mind, with the thought that he must have meant I should behave decorously and not fool around too much out on the town. That sort of thing. But later I realized that he knew. He must have understood what was going on between Alfred and me. At least to some degree. Probably no more than a suspicion. A thought that grew too uncomfortable for him to take to its conclusion, for what would happen to the family reputation if . . . Better to ensure that I kept my mouth shut. Actually, I was bought off. Pure and simple. Idiot that I was—*idiot that I am!*" Her fists hit the quilt with a hollow thud. "I just accepted it and let everything slide."

"Right up until now—"

"Right up until now. But when I found out about that will earlier this year, I realized it was time to do something. Take responsibility, in a sense."

She laughed hoarsely.

"So I set up a camera in Alfred's bedroom. I've always had a key. The photographs turned out well. I went to Father. Told him I would circulate them. He got angry. Raging. At me! At *me*, not at Alfred."

It seemed as though the story had become easier to tell in the form of a telegram.

"I stood my ground. Then he begged. And pleaded. In fact, it was wonderful. I got what I wanted. He got the photographs. I got a new will. A fair one." For the first time, her face relaxed into something resembling a real smile. "So something came out of it, after all. I have it at home. I have copies of the photographs as well. Stupid Father, for not getting hold of the film."

Hanne remained silent. She did not reveal that the new will had been found. That it was invalid. Hermine's sacrifice had been for nothing, and sooner or later she would have to find that out. It would have to be later.

"Okay," Hanne said.

"I need some water," Hermine said.

"And I really, really need to go to the bathroom!"

"There's a bathroom in there."

"I'll just be a minute."

Hermine followed her with her eyes. She felt easier now. Slowly she raised her right hand to her face and removed the bandage from the wound she had sustained when she had cut herself on the broken whisky glass. It had started to heal. Underneath the bandage, her skin was chalk-white, pale, and wrinkled with moisture. But the wound had closed, and it was no longer so painful to move her thumb. The beginnings of a scar were still outlined in red, though partially healed, and assumed the shape of a smile when she splayed her fingers.

"It seems so long ago," she said, when Hanne returned and the noise of the flushing tank made her look up.

"What is it?"

"I cut myself. I was drunk. And doped up. A week ago. Before I landed in the hospital. The last time, that is. It seems such a terribly long time ago. That I took the pistol with me . . . I don't understand why I did that. I was completely zonked out. Brought it probably just to frighten them, I think. I've never felt so angry, ever. There was a gun, and I just took it with me. If Father wouldn't be moved by anything else, I could use it to threaten him; then at least he would be scared of me now. Don't know—"

"Did you really think your father would let himself be terrorized by a gun?"

"I was in no fit state to think anything at all. Honestly! I wasn't thinking at all, okay? An impulsive act, isn't that what it's called? I was in the apartment in Kampen when Mother called me on my phone—Mabelle has an apartment there, you see. I've been allowed to use it for . . . different things. CC doesn't bother about it at all. But there's a safe there, something Mabelle organized once, ages ago. Useful to have, I suppose. The pistol was in it."

Her eyes drifted shut again.

"I'm so exhausted," she murmured. "So dreadfully exhausted. And I don't entirely understand—I've never thought about it . . . I arranged a gun because Mabelle wanted to have one. She thought she needed to be able to protect herself from the family. After all the things Father got up to, then . . . But why was it kept there in the apartment in Kampen? I've never thought about—"

"Did Mabelle believe it might be necessary to defend herself with a *gun*? From Hermann Stahlberg?"

For the first time during the conversation, Hanne felt provoked. This family was so crazy that Hermine's account until now had seemed plausible. Logical even, in its own absurd fashion, because it was true. This last part, though, seemed blatantly false.

And Hanne realized that it was.

Admittedly, Hermine was telling the truth, about what she knew and had been told, but the story was not accurate. Not on this point. The gun had never been acquired to protect anyone. That was a lie—a falsehood that only a rundown drug addict with impaired critical faculties would be able to trust.

Mabelle and Carl-Christian had planned to kill Hermann, and maybe also Turid. Now that Hanne was sure of that, for the first time since Billy T. had phoned her one evening eight interminable days ago, it was as if she barely had energy to think any further. She squeezed her hands together, digging her nails into the fleshy part at the base of her thumb, before getting to her feet and heading for the sink on the wall. She let the water run for a long time. Unpacking a mug wrapped in plastic that she found on a little glass shelf, she filled it to the brim.

A few more hours, she thought, as she drank. You can face a few more hours.

Mabelle and Carl-Christian had procured the gun. They had made plans. They had a motive, the best motive in the world. They were almost certainly in the process of creating the opportunity. But they weren't ready. Not yet. The murders in Eckersbergs gate were so brutal, so barbaric, and pointed so convincingly to them that they couldn't possibly have committed them themselves. To be honest, Mabelle and Carl-Christian would have made a better job of them. They wanted to kill Hermann Stahlberg and probably would have succeeded in doing so in the fullness of time, and in a far more sophisticated fashion than turning the family home into a slaughterhouse.

But someone had beaten them to it.

That must be how it had been. Only that allowed everything to assume some meaning, a compelling coherence. All the lies those two had served up—obvious untruths, Carl-Christian's paralysis, his conspicuous anxiety about becoming entangled in a web of fabrications and detours that trapped him in a corner—all of it made sense only if there was an unattractive, dangerous truth to hide. The truth was that they had not killed anyone. The lie beyond the truth was that they had never considered doing it.

Hanne struggled to keep her voice steady: "Did you agree with Mabelle? That Hermann might be . . . dangerous, sort of thing?"

"Agree? I don't know. I was on a real bender. My head hasn't been very clear, to put it mildly. It seemed sensible enough to me. After all, Father had ensured that Mabelle was arrested just for using her own car. He had got his hands on some damn photos of Mabelle that he used to threaten CC. My father is . . ."

It looked as if she might have fallen asleep. Her head slid silently to one side. Her mouth was half open, her breathing slow and even.

"Hermine . . ." Hanne warily clutched Hermine's hand. "What happened when you arrived at Eckersbergs gate? Why didn't you go inside? I *must* know why you never went in."

"What? Oh. I nearly dozed off. Water, please."

Once again Hanne raised the glass to Hermine's mouth. Her lips fumbled with the straw.

"I got so scared," she said, running her hand over her mouth.

"Of what?" Hanne asked quietly, even though she knew the answer.

"An animal. A dog. It was the most ugly, hellish . . . Do you know, for a few seconds afterward, when I was running along the sidewalk to make my escape, I thought it might have been a nightmare. That I was on a really bad trip. It's true I'm frightened of all dogs, but that beast was . . . I dropped the gun. Dropped it right there, just beside the gatepost at Mother and Father's place."

Hanne had begun to take notes. "Did you go back?" she asked, without looking up from her notepad.

"Yes, after a while. I've no idea how long afterward. At first I ran, and then I couldn't do it anymore. I felt bad, sick to my stomach. My head began to clear a little, in a manner of speaking. Out of pure fear, I expect. I felt like an idiot. I was terrified out of my wits. Just think if anyone were to find the pistol! With a silencer and everything. Pretty dramatic, eh? And covered in my fingerprints. Even if it hadn't been used for anything, it wouldn't exactly look very good if something like that were found outside my parents' house, when everyone knew we were in the midst of a terrible family dispute. I pulled myself together and went back. I hoped the animal would be gone, and it was. But—"

"Someone came," Hanne said. "A man came."

"Yes. How do you know that?"

"Tell me."

"In fact, *two* men came. I'd just rounded the corner when I saw a guy who had stopped in front of the garden path. It looked as if he wasn't entirely sure where he was going. I was so terrified that I nearly . . . My God, I think I've never been so afraid. Just as I turned to run off, just as the man began to walk up to the entrance to Mother and Father's apartment, I saw another guy, farther along the street. The first man had obviously not spotted my pistol, because he didn't bend down or . . . He didn't stop when he reached the place where I'd dropped it. All of a sudden that hideous dog appeared. So I hesitated for a moment, then thought I should try all the same—to pick up the gun, I mean—but then I noticed that the other man . . . You believe me, don't you?"

"I believe you."

Hermine squinted nervously at the notepad. "Why are you suddenly taking notes, then? Isn't that the sort of thing you do to expose lies? You draw attention to inconsistencies?"

Hanne folded the notepad and put her pen into her bag. "You haven't come out with any inconsistencies, Hermine. On the contrary. What did the other man do? The man who came from behind?"

"I don't know."

"Don't you remember?"

"I just don't know. Now, as I'm telling you this, I'm not even sure whether he was actually heading into the building. I just . . . I got the impression he was. There was something about . . . the way he was moving. He glanced up at the building somehow, it was . . . I don't know. Anyway, I was completely paralyzed for a few seconds. Then I took off. Again. Didn't dare to search for the pistol. Didn't stop until I got home. After that, I doped myself up. When the pigs—sorry, the police—came that night, I was in the middle of . . ."

The hand she drew over her eyes seemed even skinnier than before.

"I can't face anymore. I need to sleep. Sleep now."

Her eyes slid shut and she gasped softly, almost inaudibly, like an infant before succumbing to sleep. Hanne sat there for a few minutes until she was certain that Hermine was sleeping soundly. Then she grabbed her jacket and left the hospital as quietly as she could.

• • •

Annmari Skar and Håkon Sand sat in the corridor. Each stared at her from the uncomfortable chairs, without making any sign of speaking or any move to stand up.

"Damn it," Hanne hissed. "Have you been telling tales now? Couldn't you stand me taking time off after all? You, the one who almost forced me to take a break!"

"I haven't told any tales," Annmari said, unruffled. "I've spoken to Håkon, who is senior to both of us, in case you've forgotten. Your behavior made it imperative to take action."

"Thanks for not interrupting my interview anyway," Hanne said tartly as she began to stride along the corridor. "I've actually solved this case."

"Hanne!"

Though she did not look back, she did slow down. Håkon's voice had something different about it, an unfamiliar strength and an edge of fury that she had never heard before.

"Hanne," he said again, and this time she wheeled around. "You can't go on like this," he said.

He was standing directly in front of her and grasped her hand. Annmari still sat in silence, twenty feet farther along the corridor.

"At one time it was the three of us," he said softly, almost whispering. "You and me and Billy T. You could get away with causing a bit of havoc then. We all could. It was fun. It was a different time. A completely different time, with different methods. We two are friends, Hanne, and you put up with a lot from your friends. Annmari is not a friend. She is your colleague and your senior officer, at least as far as decisions about the prosecution are concerned."

"At present I haven't asked for anyone to be remanded in custody," Hanne said caustically. "And, to put it mildly, I take exception to you turning up here and . . . Was it that bitch of a doctor who phoned?"

"Hanne! Have you lost your mind altogether?"

Their faces were only inches apart. She felt the warmth of his breath on her lips.

"Sorry," she mumbled as she cast her eyes down. "Sorry, Håkon. I don't know what's up with me."

"You're worn out," he said sadly. "But we must stop always blaming that. We're always worn out, Hanne. Being a police officer is a fucking Sisyphean task. That's just the way it is. You have to accept that. People get sick of us always arguing, Hanne. If you can't stand the heat, then for fuck's sake get out of the kitchen!"

Swaying her hips, Hanne wrinkled her brow and looked him up and down as if she had suddenly, unexpectedly, encountered a stranger.

"Cut it out, Hanne." He was whispering now and dragged her with him a few yards farther away from Annmari.

"Everything seemed to be going so smoothly, you know," he said. "With you, I mean. You and Billy T. had even made friends again and—"

"Keep him out of this."

"Is it your father . . . I mean, is it the death and—"

"Did you hear what I said?"

"What?"

"Didn't you hear me just tell you that this case is solved?"

Now he was laughing. Long-suffering, Håkon scratched his head and laughed even louder.

"Are you in deadly earnest?" he said eventually. "Do you really mean that CC and Mabelle are innocent? And Hermine, too, for that matter? Carl-Christian has confessed, do you realize—"

"Silje knows that's a bare-faced lie. In her opinion, CC is protecting his sister. But Silje is mistaken. Hermine is also innocent. Of the murders, at least. The three Stahlbergs have done a lot that's fucking off-the-wall, but they haven't actually killed anyone. Only a couple of minor issues remain, and then you'll get to know all of it. Just let me get them out of the way and then we can talk later."

"Hanne—"

"You said it yourself, Håkon. We're friends. Let me have this one chance."

Without waiting for a reply, she broke into a run. The last thing she heard before reaching the double glass doors leading into the next corridor was Håkon's puzzled voice suggesting to Annmari: "We'll give her a few more hours, then? A few more hours?"

•  •  •

The cold, damp wind gusted up through the gently sloping valley. The mild weather of the past few days had licked the snow from the trees: their dark, bare outlines stood starkly against the evening sky. The ski trails were hard. The snow had long ago turned to ice on the tracks, with a watery surface that made it difficult to walk. They had driven as far as possible. In the end they reached a barrier where none of the keys they had collected from the forest ranger would fit. Billy T. and Hanne had to start walking for the final stretch. Hanne regretted not having taken the time to put on more appropriate clothes.

"Skates would have been better than boots," Billy T. commented as he narrowly avoided falling over.

"Don't complain. We'll soon be there." She unfolded the piece of paper and checked the sketch map.

"How did you come to think of checking the tapes at the central switchboard?" he asked. "It must have been difficult to get that done without kicking up too much fuss."

"Sidensvans's telephone printout," she replied. "He had phoned the Oslo Police District several times in the course of the last month, something that was pretty natural, if you think of what he was working on. But I found it a touch conspicuous that the very last phone conversation in his life was with us, no less. When I discovered that he had also called the police the previous day, then I wanted to know who it was he had asked to speak to. Both times."

Walking became more difficult. The track curved around a hillside and grew increasingly steep. The forest seemed totally dead and the monotonous whistling of the wind through the naked treetops was the only sound to be heard.

"Do you think he's up there?" Billy T. panted, struggling on the upward slope. "He may have gone away. Abroad, or something like that."

"Jens Puntvold hasn't gone away," Hanne said. "He's waiting for us."

"I don't understand how you can be so sure."

"The motive," Hanne said, stopping.

Perspiration made her sweater cling to her back, but her hands were ice-cold. Slowly she brought them together and raised them to her mouth.

"Think what kind of man he is," she said, blowing. "He's already fallen. His honor has been lost. When he learned that the revolver from the lake in here . . ."

She peered over to the west.

"When he understood this afternoon that the maneuver of switching his own lawful revolver for a confiscated one had been uncovered, then he knew it was only a matter of time. Before we found out the rest of it, I mean. That the gun he had left behind, to make sure that the count would tally after the photo session, was his own."

"The boys said that photographing the confiscated items happened in a rush," Billy T. said. "But then we're used to that, aren't we? Puntvold and all those campaigns of his. But why—"

"He must have been absolutely desperate," Hanne broke in. "The head of CID's own legally registered gun! Which he flashes every time he swaggers about in the Løvenskiold firing range. He almost certainly planned to take it out again. Later. He would probably have found an excuse."

Kicking the ice, she clapped her hands before thrusting them into her pockets.

"This whole saga actually resulted from such a crazy mix-up," Billy T. said.

"Yes. The Stahlbergs were expecting this lawyer. Wetterland. Wasn't that his name? Knut Sidensvans was going to see Henrik Backe. Something must have happened to cause Hermann to open the door. Maybe the same thing that happened to me: Backe refused to answer. Or maybe . . . maybe the Stahlberg family thought it was Wetterland who had arrived. Silje phoned me about the documents an hour ago. Hermann had apparently decided that enough was enough. CC was going to be forced out. Wetterland had prepared papers in which almost everything was transferred to Preben. Merely as an advance on his inheritance. They were intending to have a real celebration. And when Sidensvans turned up . . . they could see the little garden path in front of the building from the living room window. That would explain the open champagne bottle, by the way."

She gave a chuckle before adding: "Even though it's more polite to wait until everyone is present, in actual fact. A bit too eager in my opinion, opening the bottle because you see your guest arriving! When Jens Puntvold opened the entrance door on his way in, he must have thought that Sidensvans and Backe had already started talking. Of course he couldn't see Hermann Stahlberg from the stairway. He just heard the booming voice of an old man and must have been in a total panic."

"Well, he'd probably been pretty shaky for more than a week already."

"Exactly. He must have been scared shitless when Sidensvans wanted to talk to him the first time. Probably Sidensvans himself didn't appreciate what a bombshell he had stumbled on. I think they must have met. Puntvold would most likely have wanted to see this man. Check out the threat he posed, in a manner of speaking. Maybe Sidensvans originally just wanted to talk. Question him a little. And then he would have grown more suspicious."

The forest path finally leveled out. Despite the heavy clouds of mist that drained all their surroundings of color and light, the location was a perfect spot. The small valley opened out just here, at an elevation that extended a half mile or so in the direction of the crest of a hill farther north. The place was more of a small holding than an actual summer cottage. Two houses, one larger than the other, were pleasantly situated beside a stream; they could hear the gurgling of water over ice. The red buildings seemed well maintained, even though both could have used a coat of paint.

Leaving the path, they drew back toward the trunks of the pine trees.

"Dropping the case was a really stupid idea," she said under her breath as she studied the buildings for any sign of life. "Conspicuous in all four cases, but totally illogical as far as the rich man's son accused of drunk driving was concerned. All of them minor affairs. Precisely the kind of case that can easily be dropped without much fuss being made. No one asks about them. If it hadn't been for the tenacious Henrik Heinz Backe."

"Minor affairs," Billy T. repeated. "But letting yourself be corrupted is no minor affair."

Hanne shuffled her feet, teeth chattering, in an attempt to keep warm.

"Definitely not. A policeman is finished as soon as he accepts more than a cup of coffee. Here we're talking about 50,000 kroner. And Sidensvans was on his tail. You see, he'd phoned the head of CID twice more. Last Wednesday afternoon. That matches the timing of that sudden appointment with *Aftenposten* to write a story about confiscated guns. Then Sidensvans called again."

A magpie squawked as it took off from a tree at the edge of the forest to fly past them.

"At half past two on the day of the murders," Hanne said. "Of course for the time being, we can only take a guess at what was said. Anyway, Puntvold realized that everything he had worked for, all he had dreamed of—his entire existence—was at stake. Everything, in a way, that . . . *was* CID Chief Jens Puntvold."

Grinning, Billy T. used his hands to warm his ears. "What a damn situation he was faced with! Maybe the first shot was no more than a reflex action. Pent-up anxiety and fear somehow. After all, he must have been worried all these years."

"He probably kept up with things," Hanne said pensively, trying to watch for movement on the small holding a couple of hundred yards in the distance. "Henrik Backe was the only one who posed a threat. Puntvold has followed his progress, Billy T. Believe you me. He has seen the old sergeant go to the dogs. Noted his alcoholism and the first signs of senility. Gradually felt more secure. Until Unn died. The guarantee of Backe's silence has gone now. But nothing was really dangerous, not yet. Puntvold is familiar with Backe's condition. He must have been. But then Sidensvans pops up. It was not only Puntvold's professional career that was at risk. We're talking about Jens Puntvold's whole life, Billy T. His entire existence. In fact, I don't have any difficulty picturing him firing the first shot at Sidensvans. My God, just look at what it takes for people to commit suicide!"

"It's easier to commit suicide than to kill other people."

"Some people kill their own children," Hanne said, stopping again. "It was when I first thought of men who actually choose to take the lives of their own children . . ."

A strong gust made her stoop into the wind.

"Only then was I able to imagine that it was possible to kill others to avoid falling yourself, to avoid losing your honor. When the first shot has been fired, there's no way back. Everyone in the apartment had to die."

"Do you call that an . . . honor killing?"

"Not really. According to the traditional honor killing—to the extent that such a thing exists—the perpetrator will stand by his actions, at least in his own circle. Honor is achieved, or restored, through the murder. The crime in itself is the point and therefore not really a crime in the perpetrator's eyes. It's more of a . . . duty. In our culture we are . . . more cowardly, perhaps." She shook her head. "No. Not more cowardly. But for us, too, murder can be committed in order to defend honor. Suicide can be committed to stop an investigation, shift the focus, and displace sympathy. Murder can be committed to prevent compromising facts from becoming known. Honor-shattering facts."

"Such as that the probable next police commissioner in Norway allowed himself to be thoroughly corrupted at the start of his career?" Billy T. suggested.

"Such as that sort of thing, yes."

Faintly and at a distance, from behind the hills that rose south of the level elevation, they could hear a rhythmic, pounding drone.

"How many are coming?" she asked.

"Six armed officers."

"Ridiculous to use a helicopter, though. They're just pissed off because I insisted on doing this myself. So much drama! Totally unnecessary. Puntvold is sitting down there, waiting. He knows that the battle is lost. He has no honor left to defend."

She smiled as she gently nudged his shoulder.

"They could have come on foot like us! Now he'll be able to hear them from a long way off."

"Not really," Billy T. said, loath to let her go. "Listen!"

All was silent once again. Only the water in the stream could be heard over the rustling in the treetops. Billy T. put his arm around Hanne's shoulders and she leaned heavily against his body. They stood like this, drawing warmth from each other, as they waited.

"Did you get rid of that betting slip?" she said into the wind, barely audible.

"Yes."

"Good."

"Has he been following you, Hanne?"

"Probably not. He's just been afraid. Hardly slept. Gone through my office. Read my papers. Wanted to know what I was up to. Whether I was closing in. I'm not the one who had reason to be worried, really. It was Jens Puntvold. Scared of me. Terribly scared. Returning the keys to Sidensvans's overcoat, for example, was idiotic. I'm 100 percent certain that I checked the lining. It was the very first thing that made me look inward. Into headquarters. Into the police force. Not convinced perhaps, but that was when I became really troubled."

"Why do you think," Billy T. began, kissing her hair as he pulled her even closer to him, "that he picked up Hermine's pistol? He didn't need it. It only made—"

"Difficult to say," Hanne said. Her eyes followed a narrow gray plume rising from the chimney, almost merging into the sky.

"Reflex. What would you have done if you'd spotted a gun on the street?"

"Picked it up. You're right—he is at home. There's a fire on. Do you know where his lady friend is?"

"She's been taken care of. Come on."

Hanne pulled out of his arms and began to walk. The path sloped down gently before snaking around a clump of trees and broadening out, almost becoming a little road, up to the courtyard.

"Wait!" Billy T. hissed, afraid to shout. "The guys aren't in place yet. Wait!"

"Puntvold isn't dangerous," Hanne said. "How many times do I have to tell you? He killed to retain his honor. He won't kill out of shame." She turned around just as Billy T. lost his footing. He tried desperately to catch hold of a small tree, but missed. His other foot slipped away from underneath him.

"You're falling too often these days," Hanne said. "You'll have to invest in crampons."

"Shh," he said peevishly, struggling to get up. "For fuck's sake, Hanne!

Now you're being insanely unprofessional. Puntvold has a number of guns. Wait . . . we should wait for the others. They're going to land on the small football field, and we have to . . . Hanne! Wait!"

She had broken into a run.

When she reached the door of the larger of the two red buildings, she stopped for a moment. She caught herself thinking of Cecilie. She ought to have visited her parents at Christmas. Visited the grave, maybe with flowers, lanterns, and candles. The garden of remembrance in the corner of the vast graveyard was always so quiet, so well kept. Hanne had finally started to visit it. It brought such peace, she thought; it's peace that I want, and I want to go home to my people.

She grasped the door handle as Billy T. arrived, running along the path, and stepped inside.

Jens Puntvold sat in a chair with his face turned to Hanne. When he raised the gun, she smiled in surprise and it crossed her mind that Nefis had been acting so strangely of late. She sometimes went quiet all of a sudden, without any reason; she no longer drank alcohol and seemed so vulnerable, so sensitive. All the same, everything would be better now, once Hanne had taken a vacation. Perhaps she would resign from the police force. She was so obstinate, so headstrong. Could no longer cooperate, not with anyone. Her brother was right. She was defective. It was time to quit.

The shot pitched her backward.

Her torso twisted and her left shoulder was dislocated by the powerful rotation. In the fall, the bizarre fall that took so much time, she ended up feeling astonishment that she was still able to see. Billy T. was standing in the doorway. She saw his face, distorted, and in the most fleeting second before she hit the floor, she smiled.

"If only she had," Jens Puntvold began to speak, tossing his gun away, "if only she had . . ."

But Hanne Wilhelmsen could not hear him.

And many miles away, along a low wall outside a newly constructed building in Frogner, a mangy dog scurried around. He was old and resembled a hyena. His neck was broad and high, his tail slung low. The creature had lived all his life in an area no larger than fifteen or sixteen blocks. Lots of people had tried to do away with him over the years, but he was an experienced dog, shrewd and strong, and he knew his territory far better than the people who lived there.

The animal was limping badly. Along his left flank, a wound glistened in the light from the street lamp; pus and bacteria had eaten their way deep into the flesh. The dog was shivering from cold and fever. He had not had anything to eat in three days. His strength was ebbing. The aroma of greasy food hovered above all the garbage sheds and backyards, but he lacked the energy to open the lids, to topple the bins. He was only able to drink rainwater and half-melted snow from puddles on the sidewalk.

Slightly farther along the street there was a cellar with a damaged trapdoor. The dog could no longer bear to set his back paw on the ground. He hobbled across the road in the shelter of the shadows of the massive oak trees. A whimper became a rasping growl as he negotiated a tear in the mesh fence. The metal wires dug deep into the cut, and it began to bleed again. He did not pause to lick the wound: he had already licked his haunch so much that he had no fur left. Instead he dragged himself on, around the building, behind a pile of wood, underneath a tarpaulin, and finally: the trapdoor was askew.

Far inside the cellar on a rug someone had thrown out, in the depths of a corner where water was dripping down the ice-cold wall, he lay down.

And so he fell asleep, never to wake again.

# About the Author

Anne Holt has worked as a journalist and a news anchor, and she spent two years working for the Oslo Police Department before founding her own law firm and serving as Norway's minister for justice from 1996 to 1997. Since her first book in 1993, Holt's work has been published in thirty languages and sold more than seven million copies. She is the recipient of several awards, including the Riverton Prize and the Norwegian Booksellers' Prize, and she was short-listed for an Edgar Award in 2012. She was also short-listed for the 2012 Shamus Award and the 2012 Macavity Award. In October 2012, Anne Holt was awarded the Great Calibre Award of Honor in Poland for her entire authorship. She lives in Oslo with her family.

35674050729723